Wish in One Hand

by B.E. Sanderson

Acknowledgements:

I'd like to thank everyone who believed in this book over all those years, but especially my friend and editor, Janet Corcoran – without whom (see Janet, I can use whom) this wouldn't have been half as readable. I'd also like to send a special shout-out to JB Lynn and Silver James – my other go-to gals – who have given me support and encouragement, as well as the occasional ass kicking. As always, I couldn't have done this without Hubs. You'll never know how much this means to me.

ONE

~-~-~-~-~-~-~

No one bothered to ask if I wanted to be a genie. A modern woman living in the Roaring Twenties would never conceive of such a thing. And I was nothing if not a modern woman. To my mother's dismay, I wore my hair and my skirts short. I drank at speakeasies. I danced with gangsters. Hell, I *smoked*, for petesakes. Lord knows, I'd certainly gotten too old for fairy stories anymore.

My father, Reggie, on the other hand? He held the position of dreamer in the family. Always looking for the next big thing. If he could steal it? Even better. Me, I spent years chasing the next big party. In fact, I'd been out celebrating with friends before my mother's idea of a twentieth birthday extravaganza when the package had arrived.

A plain box, wrapped in brown paper tied with twine, waited on the foyer table when I came stumbling home from our liquid lunch. My friends made themselves scarce in the foyer of our building, staggering away with promises to return later and ruin Evangeline's plans for the rest of my birthday. Such good friends I had then.

"Marriageable age," my mother had mumbled at me that morning in lieu of a sentimental greeting. Evangeline made it clear before I graduated high school: she wanted me married and out of the house as soon as possible. Since she gave birth to me at the ripe, old age of seventeen, she figured she should have at least a grandchild or two bouncing on her alcoholic knee.

I didn't care about tying myself to any man. Lucky for me neither did Reggie. As he often told his dear wife, "Josephine Eugenia Mayweather will do as she damned well pleases."

Personally, I planned to join the family business. I was young. I was invincible. And I would tell Reggie he had a new partner as soon as possible. I imagined myself locating him and demanding my place in his life. He could teach me how to relieve the world of its monetary burdens. I'd kiss Evangeline and my old life goodbye as soon as the party guests left. Then, I'd board a tramp steamer headed to the newly created country of Turkey.

But I had a package to open first.

I called out to my mother, but she was either soaking her brain in absinthe or sleeping off an earlier drunk. Servants scurried around the place, preparing for the party. Somewhere deeper in the apartment, duck and pheasant and veal waited to be consumed. My stomach rumbled. Too bad for it, curiosity overwhelmed my appetite.

Grabbing Reggie's gift, I raced up the grand staircase to my room. I kicked off my Mary Janes and flopped onto the impossibly-girly canopy bed my mother thought proper for a female child—whether she was of age or not.

The shipping label said '*Constantinople*', but I wouldn't bet my catburglar father could still be found there. Odds were even he'd moved to the next port of call and his next score. At least he'd bothered to send a gift. Unconcerned with the black smudges the box would leave, I pushed it across the silk bedspread Reggie sent from the Orient the year before and wrestled the twine free. The paper I tore away lay forgotten on a goose-down pillow. Packing material tumbled to the floor along with a beige envelope.

When I leaned over the side of the bed, I saw Reggie's bold strokes: *To my dearest Daughter*. Time enough for birthday wishes later. His note would only contain professions of a father's love, perhaps along with his schedule. I never doubted he loved me. Whether he actually adhered to his schedule was a crapshoot.

My eyes fixed on the package's contents. Peeking between the remaining shreds of paper lay a rosewood box. I didn't have Reggie's knowledge of antiques *yet*, but I recognized a prized piece when I saw it. The intricate carvings showed primitive but exquisite artistry. Ivory had been inlaid to create each delicate flower.

I crouched, visually devouring every nook and cranny of its beauty. My fingers itched to trace the designs, but I savored the visual meal before allowing myself a bite. I held onto the delicious delay as long as I could, teasing my innate impatience until I couldn't stand myself. I reached out, caressing the silky wood the way a loving hand might slip tenderly over its paramour's cheek.

A gentle breeze ruffled my bangs as I lifted the lid. I stifled my disappointment when I realized my only present was the box itself. A really lovely gift, to be sure. I'd simply hoped to find at least a necklace nestled in its velvet interior.

"Expecting baubles perhaps, my young Master?" said a voice from behind me. The second those words hit my ears, the box filled with a rainbow's worth of light and color. I flung the possessed thing away, scattering gems of every size and shape across my bed. A single emerald the size of a walnut teetered on the edge for a moment and then dropped, clattering on the floor below.

For an instant I was torn between lunging for the jewel and seeing who'd entered my bedroom without permission. Self-preservation won out, but only just. When I eased myself around, a gorgeous boy sat on my dressing table.

Not as old as the boys I played at romancing, which meant he couldn't have been my guest. The dusky-skinned Mediterranean never could've made it past my mother's prejudices, so he couldn't have been hers either.

I narrowed my eyes. "Is this some sort of prank?"

A dark lock of hair fell across his forehead. Darker eyes twinkled in amusement. "Not any I would know of," he said. Except for a braided vest, he sat before me unclothed from the waist up, giving lie to my earlier impression. He was nothing if not a man. Ebony hair graced muscles I'd only ever read about in dimestore tawdries.

"What are you doing here if this isn't a joke?"

"I am the surprise you hoped for when you opened your gift." He snapped his fingers. All at once my room turned from Victorian Virgin to Art Deco Dream. "A palace more suited to a woman such as yourself, is it not?"

I scrubbed at my eyes as I considered whether that scoundrel Wally slipped something into my drink at lunch. The chubby-cheeked bastard fancied himself a regular W.C. Fields. Lord knew he had the girth and the nose for it, but he never was very funny.

I opened one eye. Everything appeared unchanged. No hallucination then. "Who... *What* are you?"

A slow smile creased his face, each tooth an ivory example of perfection. "At least you have brains enough under your silly haircut to ask the right questions."

"What's wrong with my hair?" I touched the sleek, brown bob Evangeline hated. "And what do you mean by right questions?" Still he met me with his damn grin. "What's wrong with you?" When he still gave me nothing but a silly face, I stamped my foot against the bed's footboard. "I wish you'd either answer my questions or get out of my room. I have things to do."

"As you wish, so I must answer." I waited for a moment, but he didn't leave. Instead he raised a single finger. "I am here because your father sent me." A second digit went into the air. "As to the 'who', before today the world has known me by a great many names, but my mother graced me with 'Stavros'. And your third question is easy enough to discern if you but think for a moment.

"As for your hair, it is a matter of taste. A woman's hair should be long enough for her lover's hands to twine through. Short hair is such a waste." My mouth fell open. "The right questions to ask means instead of wasting time discerning my identity, you went straight to the heart of the issue. And lastly, nothing is wrong with me, my dear. I am simply djinn."

"You're gin?" A giggle slipped out before I could stop it. "I wonder whose bathtub *you* came out of."

Stavros' aggravated sigh sounded much like Evangeline's when I went racing out for a night on the town. "I believe people of this generation call my people 'genies', but we prefer to be called by our ancestral name: Djinn. D-J-I-N-N." Suddenly he appeared beside me. One finger traced along my jaw line. "And as such, I belong to you."

"You belong to me?"

"Surely that head of yours received some sort of education. Your elders perhaps read you stories." Reaching past me, he lifted the rosewood box. "You rubbed my lamp, so to speak."

As he drew the box to himself, his arm brushed my breast, lingering just long enough to make my pulse race. "You touched the place to which I am bound. My home, if you will. By the Rules, I now belong to you."

I searched my head to remember the one story a much younger me read. "So I make three wishes and you have to grant them?"

He winked at me. "Every Master has three wishes. You are no different."

My first wish popped into my head in an instant. "I wish my father was here." The breeze from nowhere ruffled my hair again.

Stavros snapped his fingers. I didn't have time to blink before Reggie stood between the two of us.

I expected a smile from the man I hadn't seen in nearly a year. I hoped he'd wrap me into a bear hug like he had when I was small. He did neither. Once he finally focused on my face, murderous rage bloomed in his eyes.

"Josephine." His voice rumbled barely above a growl. "What have you done?" His gaze sliced from me to Stavros and back, stopping briefly on the new furnishings. "You were told to wait before you made any wishes!"

"I wasn't..." The forgotten envelope leapt to mind. "I didn't..." And like that, the adulthood I'd been so certain of failed me. I became seven again, scolded for something I hadn't known I'd done. The injustice of it bubbled up.

"Well, you're here now, aren't you?" I shook my finger at him. "And if you think you can come in here and make my last two wishes, you've got another think coming. I ought to—"

"One," Stavros said, halting the rest of my tirade.

"One what?"

"One wish. You have only one left."

I thought Reggie wanted to kill me before. The fury leaching from him told me we'd reached the place where simple homicide would be too kind.

"You wasted a wish on redecorating, didn't you, you silly bitch?"

All my certainty left me in a rush. My father—the man who always doted on me, the man who defended me even to his wife—never spoke to me like that.

"I didn't—"

"She didn't." Stavros chimed in. "All of this beauty? A mere sample of my powers." He ditched the smile to click his tongue in mock sorrow. "She did something so much sillier. She used her first wish to make me answer her."

Reggie's palm collided with my cheek before I knew enough to flinch.

"And *then* she wished for you."

I ducked and feinted toward the door, but my father's hand closed around my upper arm. In all my life, he'd never struck me, but after one slap, my brain started running through all the other things he'd never done and whether he was capable of *them*, too.

"Why couldn't you, for once in your empty little life, stop to think?" He noticed the grooves his fingers were leaving in my flesh and dropped his hand. "This is a mess."

"We still have one wish and then—"

"It isn't enough, Jojo. I'm in too deep. There's too much to fix with just one wish."

"Don't you have any of yours left?" I spoke the question before he jerked me to face him.

"I have one. Only one left. And I need it."

I'd never seen my father so frantic. Evangeline always said the day would come when I'd realize Reggie was no 'shining example of manhood'. I never dreamed seeing him as a regular Joe would be like this.

My brain raced for a way to fix this. I'd gotten out of scrapes before. Hadn't I led a half dozen friends out of a raid on the speakeasy last month? I could do this. If only my father acted like himself again, we'd think of something together. If I had more wishes—

"I wish for more wishes."

As my father shouted "No," I heard Stavros ask how many.

Why limit myself? With all the wishes I want, I can take care of whatever this problem is. Reggie never has to steal again. Evangeline can stop drinking herself into a stupor.

"How about unlimited wishes?"

Reggie's shriek echoed in the background. I didn't focus on him. I knew what I was doing.

"You have to say the words."

I didn't hesitate. "I wish for unlimited wishes."

The breeze turned into a hurricane in my ears. My hair whipped, stinging my cheeks. I shivered as a sweat broke out along my arms. And through my tearing eyes, Stavros stood grinning as the same rush enveloped him, too.

When it all fell away, I felt more alive than ever before.

"See, Daddy," I said. "I can fix everything now." I gazed around for him, but he wasn't immediately visible. Seconds later, I found him, crouched on the floor weeping into his hands. "Reggie?"

"Oh, Jojo."

Behind me came a tap-tap-tapping to outdo Poe's Raven. Whipping around to face the source, I found the Greek boy looking more like a man than before. In his hands, the lid to the rosewood box opened and closed like a strange mouth, waiting to consume me.

"Since neither of us has any use for this anymore." He gave the box one last clack before dropping it and crushing it beneath his heel. "You might want to choose your own sanctuary before I choose one for you."

"Wh... What's he talking about, Daddy?"

Reggie raised his head. Tears streamed down his flushed cheeks. "He owns you now, Josephine. The wish. You've changed places with him. Now you're the genie and he's the Master."

TWO

~-~-~-~-~-~-~-~

"And that's when you think he killed your father?" Mena said from her perch on the arm of my sofa.

I threw a handful of popcorn at her. "I thought I was talking to my best friend, not the resident shrink." She froze the kernels mid-air, grabbing the closest between thumb and forefinger before tossing it into her mouth.

"I'm both. Get over it." She snatched another piece and tossed it at my mouth. "It's your fault, you know. You're the one who wanted to watch the father-issue movie of all time."

"You agreed."

"I can't refuse a chance to ogle Ewan McGregor, even if it's in *Big Fish*. Why do you think I pick the new *Star Wars* when it's my turn?" She shot me a bright smile. Her pearly white teeth glowed against her olive skin.

"That's not the only reason you agreed."

"Of course not. You think I'd pass up a chance to wade around in your misplaced guilt?" She swept the remaining airborne snacks into a nearby trashcan. "Well, now the movie is over and you've sussed out my ulterior motives, I should return to work. The last rescue you brought me? She's in a bad way."

No big surprise there. Not every djinn approached freedom from the healthiest mental standpoint. The Ethiopian I brought back a few days before was not in a sane place. I tried every trick in my bag to coax the poor lady out of her sanctuary. Even though eventually she responded, Mena hadn't been able to convince her to speak.

"Good luck," I called to my friend's retreating back. I don't know who benefitted more from our weekly movie nights. I needed the time to decompress, but Mena had to need more than a few hours of sanity once a week. Making a mental note to add more days off to her calendar, whether she wanted them or not, I pushed myself away from my overstuffed sofa. I grabbed the remaining popcorn as I whistled into the depths of my home.

The click-click-click of claws on stone echoed back to me.

"You missed movie night." A shaggy white head came into view. "Lucky for you, we didn't eat all the popcorn." I threw a single, white morsel and Major deftly caught it without missing a step. He sat in front of me, expectance radiating from his supreme Dogness. Rather than torture him kernel by kernel, I set the bowl down. Any other dog his size would inhale the contents and beg for more. Not mine. He ate slowly, savoring.

"Your time starving on the streets of Copenhagen definitely taught you the value of treats." I ruffled the long, white fur around his neck. "Ready for dinner?" The fluttering of his plumed tail was the only answer I ever got.

Seconds after I set his large bowl of kibbles down, the wall nearby beeped at me. Only my business partner could be buzzing me on movie night.

"What's up, Baz?"

"I'm not interrupting, am I?"

I refrained from pointing out to Basil if he'd come down like I asked, he wouldn't need to wonder. Bless his good British work ethic, but all his efforts were definitely making him a dull boy. Considering our yearly auction would occur in a little over a week, I couldn't fault him, but still, the man needed a break almost more than Mena.

"We finished about an hour ago. And before you ask, Mena's back in the vault charming the princess."

"It's really too bad about the poor bird. Her rescue went a mite smoother than expected, but still—"

"Out with it, Basil." His stalling had to mean this wasn't a social call. "No. Nix that. Do not come out with anything. I have a bed waiting downstairs. Barring that, a dozen boxes in the library need to be unpacked and catalogued. And then there's the auction."

"Don't you worry about the auction. I'll bring you on if I need help. And if you need someone to help you with those boxes—"

"I changed my mind. If we keep this up, we'll be here all night. Spit it out."

"I need you out to New York. Tonight, if at all possible."

"The Big Apple?" I hated rescuing genies in metropolitan areas, but NYC presented a whole different set of issues, especially since 9-11.

"Upstate," he said, and I breathed a sigh of relief. Besides the tactical nightmare New York presents, the city that never sleeps holds too many bad memories. "From what the network says, it's an estate. Hundreds of acres surrounding the place."

"Great, then it'll wait 'til tomorrow."

"Umm… the owner? He's gone and shuffled off his mortal coil. We don't have much time before the inheritors arrive to pick things over."

"Say no more." Once someone touched whatever bling the genie called home, rescuing him would present a whole new pile of problems. Especially since the new Master probably wouldn't be too keen on losing his shiny, new windfall. "When do I leave? And how the hell am I getting there?"

"Still bagged from the last rescue?"

I sent a few feelers to my powers. "I'm probably at about twenty percent. Enough to get me out, but not back, and vice versa."

"Understood. Save it for emergencies." He paused a moment, probably checking his own tank. "I'm good for your trip out, but if there's trouble, you really will have to get yourself back."

"Then we're agreed. I'll be upstairs for a briefing and then off to The Empire State."

~-~-~-~-~-~-~-~

Basil said this would be *easy-peasy*. Hearing a centuries-old, tweed-loving genie use the phrase, in and of itself, should've been a heads-up. But, no. I took him at his word and dropped into upstate New York blind.

Literally.

I closed my eyes in Colorado and, before the breeze of teleportation could ruffle my hair, I stood in what could've been a storeroom at the Louvre. Except I knew better. Some guy with more cash than ethics had whipped out his double-platinum, diamond-encrusted Visa and bought a great many things he should never own.

Judging from what I saw at first glance, this Master was a naughty monkey. No fewer than a dozen works of art reported lost or stolen graced his gallery. In one corner sat a jackal sculpture I knew for a fact went missing from a prestigious Italian museum.

If only his immoral behavior had stopped at owning another person. Not that I have any room to talk, what with the whole set of rapacious genes galloping through me. But I'd never stoop to slavery.

Growing up as the daughter of a cat burglar does have its advantages, though. As my fingers inched toward a priceless Faberge egg, I had to accept that being Reggie's child had its disadvantages, too. One big one in particular—the need to touch things I have no business touching. A fingertip on the egg's cloisonné surface started an alarm-ageddon loud enough to blow out eardrums in Pennsylvania.

I jerked my hand away and threw a quick wish. The alarms stopped, but the damage had been done. Even in this sleepy backwoods, I had ten minutes tops before the authorities arrived.

My senses made short work of locating the genie in question. His sanctuary—his lamp away from home, so to speak—sat nestled on a velvet bed in an ornate showcase. Stifling a cringe over the cliché of a genie living in a lamp—especially one as gaudy and gem-encrusted as this—I smashed the glass and snatched the offensive thing.

And suddenly life became way more interesting than I needed.

The initial appearance of a genie to any new friend usually ends up as 'whoomp, here I am'. Some djinn like a little more pizzazz. This bastard's full pyrotechnic display shot me halfway across the room.

Only quick thinking and energy I couldn't afford to waste stopped me from destroying a couple million dollars worth of masterpieces.

"Sunuvabitch," I shouted as the smoke coalesced into a human shape. Before I knew it, I found myself staring at a stand-in for Omar Sharif, *Lawrence of Arabia* style, but with more flair.

"You are not my Master," he said without looking at me.

"Damn straight I'm not." Throughout time, the whole Master/genie transaction has required more personal contact than latex gloves allow. Unless one of them had been pierced somehow, say by tiny shards of glass from a broken display case. "Shit."

Omar's eyes finally rested on me while I cursed my stupid luck. Luck plus lack of rest between missions, to be more specific. Usually alerts from the network were weeks, sometimes months, apart. This one, only days after purloining the Ethiopian princess from a forgotten antiques store in New Orleans, might wreck me.

As soon as Omar opened his mouth again, I figured I'd met our princess's new playmate in the vault.

"You are not my Master."

"You said that, but this time I can't agree with you." After stripping off my useless gloves, I let the garish lamp dangle from the crook of one finger. "Sorry, bud. But don't worry, I won't be your Master any longer than absolutely necessary. We'll get it—" My brain stopped working when my new friend slid a wicked scimitar from his sash.

"Whoa there, buddy," I said, stepping back before I wound up as the world's largest shish kabob.

Aside from being dangerous as hell—it could probably slice, dice *and* make julienne fries—the blade represented centuries of history and a beautiful culture. Whatever era Omar hailed from could never have made high-quality steel like this. The delicate filigree etched along its surface almost had me weeping. As he shifted the hilt from hand to hand, my dealer's eye tallied the worth of its embedded gems. Any human could retire on the rubies alone.

"Be a good boy and get back into your lamp so we can get the hell out of here before the nice humans show up."

His eyes narrowed as confusion clouded his expression. "No," he said, as if a single word sufficed to refute all the frigging rules.

Outside someone shouted something unintelligible through a megaphone. "Great," I told the maniac with the fancy machete. "The lovely police officers—human police officers, by the way—have arrived and I don't think we really want them to find us in here."

The Bedouin shot a quick glance toward the room's perimeter walkway. Through the high windows, searchlight appeared. It seemed like overkill for one random burglary. The human homeowner must've had a lot of pull in the tiny Catskills town to draw this kind of attention. Omar didn't even blink. Instead, he turned his attention and his sword back to me.

"I hate to pull rank on you, but them's the breaks. I'm your Master; you're my slave. Yada yada yada. Now, get back in your box so we can both get the hell out of here."

All things being equal, I don't usually have to say too much more, and I typically say it in a nicer manner. Too bad things were definitely not equal. Instead of capitulating, the guy ignored me. I don't know what world he thought he lived in, but in mine, no sane Djinn would ever think of blowing off a Master's authority.

Apparently, 'no sane Djinn' said it all. I wasn't dealing with a genie in his right mind. As he waved his curved meat cleaver in my face, I realized he had to be more than a few cards short of a Hallmark store.

"You've got to be kidding me," I said.

"You are not my Master."

I really wanted the guy to give it a rest. Outside, the bullhorn freak had stopped shouting, which only meant things were about to get a whole lot worse, and there I stood, haggling with a whacko who refused to obey my orders. Fine, if he wouldn't come nicely, I was going to have to get tough.

"I command you to return to your sanctuary until your services are required." I said the words and then settled back on my heels waiting for the formality to hit him. It never fails.

Except when it does.

My reward? A hiss of air in front of me, my favorite turtleneck in ruins, and a line of blood welling up millimeters above my breasticles.

"Sharp." And then the burn hit me like the world's largest paper cut. Holding back a gasp, I fought not to hit him with the last of my power. I didn't want to hurt the guy—not that I thought I really could. I also didn't want a spot in a pissing contest I had a snowball's chance in Tahiti of winning.

Pooling my power, I aimed what little energy I had toward the psycho. He didn't even flinch. Before I could open my mouth, he grabbed my wrist and pulled me so hard I thought my arm would rip off. Good thing I'm put together well, or the world would be calling me Lefty now. With my arm attached, though, he had the perfect leverage to swing me hard against the glass case he just exited. Shards flew everywhere. Several more cuts opened on my arms and face even as the slice across my chest closed.

While my new set of wounds healed, my options danced through my head. Let's say the conga line was short. I needed to get the flock away from there. I needed to take *Señor* Slash along, when he obviously didn't enjoy my company. Boiling it all down in my available seconds offered only one real option.

I sucked down the pain and released the wish I'd been building just for him.

"I wish you back into your sanctuary until you are summoned." I don't like forcing people to do things they don't have a choice in. Of course, hating something doesn't mean I won't if I have to. I just don't have a fine appreciation for it.

Apparently, the idea didn't thrill Omar either. I watched as he tried to fight the wish. Genies may not like the wishes we're given, but we have to fulfill them regardless. Sure, we can hold off at first, but after that? Well, at first, the feeling is only uncomfortable. Ants crawling up your arms, maybe. A little longer and the ants start to burrow under your skin. If you can hold out for a little longer, the ants explode into a million tiny bursts of acid. No one can make it past the acid stage.

Looked like my new buddy Omar was giving it the old college try, though. I expected him to give in after a couple minutes. After five, he was barely sweating. If not for the muscles twitching along his jaw line, I'd wonder whether he had it right and I wasn't his Master after all.

"You. Are. Not. My. Master," he ground out.

"Give it up, bud."

I about fell over when he did. A half-smile twitched at the corners of my mouth when he changed to smoke and retreated back into the lamp. As a final insult, though, he turned the damn thing's temperature up to scorch. Despite the blisters, I held on.

Well, for a moment anyway.

"Drop it, lady, and put your hands up."

As soon as the words connected with my brain, my fingers let go. Lucky for everyone concerned, Omar didn't make an encore appearance. As far as luck went, though, I doubted I'd get any more.

I raised my hands. *Just another day in paradise.*

"Where'd he go?" the officer said, gesturing with his gun toward the empty space Omar had occupied. The poor kid looked fresh out of the academy. Hell, I'd be surprised if he was older than I'd been the day I opened the wrong birthday present. The sweat soaking his uniform in the place's glacial air conditioning didn't help. Neither did the shaking hands. Of course, the tremor could've been caused by seeing a grown man evaporate.

"What guy?" I said as I sent a few mental expletives toward the heavens. Bad enough the cops showed up, but now I'd have to tweak this one's memory before I could beat feet back to Colorado. I really hate messing with people's minds.

"Your accomplice. The one with the..." The kid seemed little iffy even before he swallowed what I hoped was chewing gum and not, heaven forbid, chewing tobacco. When he didn't initiate the Technicolor Yawn sequence, I figured he'd be fine, despite the fact he wasn't so much speaking as squeaking. "Was he... Was that a *sword*?"

"What?" As hard as it was to pass up a good zinger, I made myself ignore the fact he'd pronounced the silent W. "Oh. Him. He said something about being with a roving troupe of actors. I think they're doing Shakespeare in the park. Or maybe he's got an Arabian Nights complex." I hoped the babbling could buy me the time I needed to take stock of my reserves and think of a way out of this.

"Regardless, he had an alternate engagement. Sorry he couldn't stay and entertain the troops." The stock report told me I hadn't used as much power as I feared. I let the energy heal my remaining abrasions as I formulated a new wish.

"Speaking of which," I continued, playing to his stunned silence. "I have a doctor's appointment I need to get to."

The officer leveled his gun at me. "You ain't going nowhere, lady."

"Sorry to disappoint." The barrel of his service revolver pointed toward my stomach. If he fired before I could stop him, I'd survive, but being able to survive a gunshot doesn't make them hurt any less.

I released the wish then realized neither the kid nor his weapon came alone. In the span of seconds, I heard his fellow officers ascending the stairs with more caution than the kid showed. If I had any chance of getting away, my exit had to be quick, perfect wording or not. Releasing a bubble of power, I told the officer, "I wish you would take a little nap now and wake up in about fifteen minutes not remembering anything about me or my strange friend."

The officer collapsed against the doorframe and slid to the floor. Within seconds his snore erupted so loud I feared his co-workers would come running. As luck would have it, the kid's deviated septum seemed to stop them momentarily.

Enough time to give the place a quick cleaning.

When the rest of the officers mustered the courage to investigate, they wouldn't find a shred of evidence to show a robbery occurred. And their brother in blue? He'd wake up with a headache and a strange story about selective amnesia. I didn't care how he explained what happened. I'd be long gone.

Hoping I hadn't miscalculated my juice, I closed my eyes and wished myself home.

THREE

~_~_~_~_~_~_~

All the goodies in that mansion made me miss my father's wealth, but not nearly as much as my Colorado storage garage did. Nothing like an unwelcome glimpse into my current reality. I might've chosen this landing point, but four stark metal walls plus my vehicle didn't equal mahogany floors and Persian rugs.

A wolf spider scuttled across the concrete. *Plus, I never had to worry about creepy-crawlies back home. One of these days I'm going to have to fumigate. Or at least deodorize.* The mouse rotting in the corner almost proved more than my djinned-up olfactory nerves could tolerate.

They hadn't quite recovered from the stench minutes later when I pulled up to a low-slung commercial building. Estes Park wasn't much more than a quaint tourist town at the gateway to Rocky Mountain National Park, but it suited our needs. Quiet for the most part, most of the year, Estes stood far enough away from Denver to separate us from the mortals and yet close enough to do business with the rest of the world.

The sign outside my little slice of corrugated steel heaven says *Mayweather Antiquities*. Which is as close to the truth as I can come. Few things are more antique than your average genie. Besides, when I started this racket, I wanted some kind of legitimate enterprise to show mortals. If they had any inkling what my business really did, we'd be screwed blue and tattooed. Villagers coming after us with torches and pitchforks or picketing outside begging for a few freebie wishes don't appeal to me.

I have nightmares about the other possibility: being captured and studied.

Of course, the fact we actually do sell antiques helps us hide. After living a few centuries, genies accumulate a lot of crap. When they want to unload, we're the place. Without antiques from ancient people, I can't imagine how we'd fund everything we do.

We're the first step between the slavery of a Master and running loose around the world. As such, we provide a place to acclimate to freedom. Plus, we give them vocational training, if they choose to become human again. Education isn't cheap, no matter who you are, and it's not like we can wish up the tuition. The Feds would be all over us, thinking we were counterfeiters. And wishing up gold disrupts the world market. Rather than deal with the hassle, we sell old things.

Turns out everyone's got to make a living somehow, even those with phenomenal power.

The billboard out front shook me out of my musings and amped up my tiredness level. *Mayweather Antiquities Annual Auction!* I really didn't have the patience for a crowd of dealers haggling over maple cabinets and the Blue Willow to fill them. Still, the influx of moolah from attendees who'd come from all over the country meant I couldn't avoid it.

Shoving thoughts of the auction aside, I carted my bag of Bedouin inside. Deep in the building's bowels, a fifth of Tanqueray and my cozy home called my name. I simply needed to attend to the pulsing personage I acquired in the Empire State first.

"Mayweather Antiquities. How may I direct your call?" I heard as I pushed through the doors. The strawberry blonde behind the reception desk looked up. "Miss Mayweather...?"

I shook my head. Whoever called could either wait or talk to Basil.

"...hasn't arrived yet. Certainly, ma'am. Mr. Hadresham will take your call. Please hold." She punched a couple buttons and gazed back at me. "Basil's looking for you."

I shot a look over my shoulder. "It's barely light yet. What are you doing here?"

"Basil has us at all hands on deck, what with the auction and all, so I offered to man the lines early. You'd be surprised how often the east coast forgets we're two hours behind."

"I doubt it." I didn't exactly think about the time in other states.

"You're in a mood. Rough night?" Her eyes traveled down my newly tailored turtleneck. "Late night in LoDo or early rave at that new Goth place in Westchester?" She smiled. "You sure didn't get that around Estes."

I started to answer, but thought better of it. If Renee wanted to assume I'd been out partying, I wouldn't disabuse her. I sure as hell couldn't tell her the truth.

"But if you found someplace to thrash here in town, you'd better give details."

Renee was a good kid. Woman, I amended. At twenty-something, she couldn't quite carry off 'kid' anymore. Like at ninety-something I wasn't quite an old lady. Although, with her ponytail and those freckles dusting her nose, she barely looked old enough to drive. My fingers drifted toward my own similar hairstyle. Not for the first time I wondered what would happen if I showed my true self to the world. Hell, I'd look younger than Renee. Instead, I allowed people to think my forties were creeping up and, thanks to a repeating wish, I'd look a year older every year until the day I 'died'.

"Jo?"

Back to reality. "Sorry. I was woolgathering. What's up?"

"Maybe I don't want to know what bar you were at." She looked pointedly at my shirt again, and I thanked the gods black hid bloodstains. "I'm not that hard core."

"Good to know." I didn't want to think about how hard core my employee actually got. In the end, it wasn't any of my business. "So, how's things?" Like Reggie always said, *When in doubt, distract.* Lucky me, Renee was easily distracted.

"Oh, you know the drill, up to my Underoos in alligators." And loving every minute of it judging by the gleam in her eye. "The phones have been crazy ahead of the auction. Basil says this might be the biggest sale yet. Which reminds me..." She handed over a stack of pink papers. "I don't know why I tolerate your voice mail phobia." Giving a little wink, she added, "By the way, someone named Ben Aaron has been trying to reach you. He stopped leaving messages after about the fifth call."

"Ben who?" I said as I realized her mistake. "You mean Ezekiel ben Aron?"

"Oh. Sorry. You know me and accents. Especially ones like his."

I remembered how his caramel and honey tone once flowed over me and immediately understood. It's hard to listen when all that sexy hits your ears. "Do me a favor. If he calls again, send him to voice mail."

"Where he can rot?" Renee smiled and shook her head. "Let me guess, he's an old boyfriend. Or he's selling something you don't want."

"Right on both counts."

"His words will never darken another message slip."

I let a little chuckle slip out. Whatever else anyone could say about our Renee, she kept me in a better mood than I would've been without her. That alone made her worth keeping around. Life would've been much easier if I staffed the whole place with genies and former djinn. When I lost our last receptionist to the real world, and none of the brethren wanted the job, Renee's humanity proved to be exactly what I needed after wrangling genies.

When she held the back of her hand up to her forehead in a perfect Sarah Bernhard pose, I laughed harder. I know she thought I slipped a gear, but trying again to explain silent movies wasn't worth the time or the effort. One of these days, though, I'd have to invite her to movie night and show why she reminded me of the old actress.

Yeah, right after I told her my real species. Then I'd show her what my apartment really looked like. For all she knew, I had a cot in the back, between shelves filled with antique geegaws. And she could never know differently. Telling her would only land me in deep shit with my brethren. Not that I was their favorite child anyway.

You're disturbing the natural order was the nicest thing they'd said about me. If most of the masterless genies had it their way, they'd shut the whole operation down. They got their freedom the old fashioned way, either through their Master dying, like I had, or through some kind of trickery, like the bastard who made me. It only followed other enslaved brethren should do the same. Well, their ideas sounded like bullshit to me, and I wasn't afraid to say it.

Which explained part of the reason Zeke became a 'former' boyfriend.

Shaking off the memories of that shittiest of shitty days, I sorted out the messages from Mr. ben Aron. His pile went straight into the circular file. Why he chose now to call me was a mystery I didn't have the energy to solve. Maybe something happened in the djinn circles I wasn't allowed into. I had enough on my mind without worrying what the *olde guarde* did these days anyway.

I hitched my messenger bag higher across my chest as I made my escape from the reception area. Luckily, the phone rang and Renee became too occupied to do more than wave. If given half a chance, she'd be prying more information from me. As tired as I was, I might give it to her.

Walking toward the back, I marveled again at the two halves of my life. Up front, Mayweather Antiquities looked like any other human venture. We had potted plants some company or other tended once a week. There were couches for visitors. We had a break room with a Bunn and more snacks than our small human staff could ever eat. Through one door lay a conference room where potential buyers could get a better look at individual items. Another opened into a space where we hold our auctions.

The innards of the building, the places no human ever set foot, showed a different perspective altogether. Past the human-friendly areas with their motivational posters, reprinted lithographs, and immaculate rhododendrons, you experienced the mutant child of a *ménage a trois* between a carnival, an eclectic museum, and a ritzy hotel. In short, nothing anyone would expect inside an industrial warehouse and everything uber-powerful beings would expect in their halfway house.

Of course, the juggling act keeps things moving around here. Things have to stay inordinately normal for the sake of humanity. And very not normal for the sake of the djinn.

As I keyed in the code to let me pass from one area to the other, I was reminded how, to the outside world, this foyer had to be a highly secure storage closet at the back of the building. There wasn't room for anything else. Human perception wouldn't allow for it. Good thing genies aren't hampered by the laws of physics. When the light flashed from red to green, I pulled the door open and walked into what shouldn't have been possible—a long hallway straight back into the mountainside.

Gilded doors lined the walls on either side. We only had a dozen or so genies in residence and none of them were permanent guests. Don't get me wrong. I love my brethren, but I don't want any of them staying permanently. Sooner or later every freed djinn has to take his first steps into the world, whether that world accepts his existence or not. And he has to do it knowing the world he used to bend to his will could possibly hurt him, depending on what he's chosen as his future path.

Damn near every one of my rescues has options. He can keep his powers, exactly as he's always had them, or he can opt to relinquish his magic and live out his remaining days as a mortal. If he picks the former, he has to agree to abide by all the laws of mankind, as well as all the rules imposed by the Djinn Council. If he picks the latter, he needs to keep his mouth shut about who and what he used to be. In either case, every genie passing through our doors agrees to provide some kind of support for the cause. A favor here, a wish there. Maybe pass along some information, or give me a place to crash when I'm out of town. As long as the favors don't get too big, no one complains.

The reason it's 'damn near' and not 'every' genie with options is sometimes we encounter a djinn who doesn't want to be free, and sometimes one is too damaged mentally to unleash on the world. My recent Bedouin acquaintance would probably turn out to be one of the latter. Only time would tell. If Mena could coax him back to sanity, he'd get a new life. I wasn't going to put money on his chances, though. So few of the insane ones ever make it back to reason.

If they did, we wouldn't have so many living inside the vault.

The lamp pulsed inside my bag like the Bedouin read my mind. More likely, Omar didn't want to be trapped in his sanctuary any more than I wanted to keep him there. I didn't have a whole lot of choice in the matter. Whatever this guy's major malfunction was, he obviously wasn't planting with a full bag of beans.

So, as much as I've always hated the concept of the vault, the best place for him really was tucked safely inside a drawer where his sanctuary wouldn't ever accidentally be touched. Until we could make sure he wouldn't slice-n-dice anyone else.

FOUR

~-~-~-~-~-~-~

All the way at the back of the guest area stands a plain enough door. If not for the security panel and the 'Restricted Access' sign, it would look like it led to the janitor's office. Behind it lay Mena's office and the area we refer to as 'the vault'.

With one sweep of my hand and a few short syllables, the djinn security measures fell away. Once I removed the danger of breaking my face on the unseen wall, I stepped to the nearby keypad. Some say using human security to back up genie power is overkill, but they aren't as paranoid as I am. In my line of work, where being lax leads to mayhem, you can't be too careful.

And let's face it. Life's got enough mayhem without turning insane genies loose on the world.

Once I disabled the alarms, the door swung open, wafting jasmine incense and Mena's weird clove cigarettes at me. The incense supposedly relaxes her patients. I guess the cigarettes were to relax her. Lord knows with all the crap she faces, she needs relaxation wherever she can find it. I've always been surprised she doesn't smoke something stronger. With djinn metabolism, drugs don't affect us for long anyway.

Mena stubbed out her smoke when I walked in. Rising, she let her fingers trail along the desk she'd had made out of Brazilian cherry the year before. I could appreciate the gesture. Buying nice things is so much more satisfying than conjuring them out of nothing.

"Princess still is incommunicado."

"Not here for her. I have a new guest for you." I held my messenger bag up for a moment and then let it drop to my side.

"Another one? So soon? Damn."

Truer words were never spoken, but I left the comment alone. "Sorry. I know you're swamped, but you need to squeeze one more in."

She shrugged. "One more won't break me." Inclining her head toward the room's only other door, she added, "It's not like we don't have the space."

With a snap of her fingers the door swung open. The sight greeting me hadn't changed. If I didn't know better, I'd swear I stepped into a bank's safety deposit room. Slots covered the walls, with room for more if needed. Since I'd designed the drawers to hold our kind's mentally ill, I hated needing so many already. Still, we couldn't let demented djinn roam the world.

Genies aren't allowed to kill people with our magic, but once a wish is generated, we're not liable anymore. Ever hear of the Chicago fire? Mrs. O'Leary's cow took the rap, but the bovine didn't do it. From what I understand, a freed genie lost his marbles somewhere along the way and decided fire was pretty.

If this Bedouin nutcase had half the power I sensed he did, he could make Chicago look like the candles on a birthday cake.

I stared at the back of Mena's head as she let her hand trail along the wall. Her long fingernails clicked at the spaces between the drawers, echoing in the empty room. The sound annoyed me more than necessary.

"Mena. Please."

With one final click, she turned to stare at me. The lady's cappuccino skin reminded me of one thing to settle both our nerves. Using the last dribble of my power, I wished for a low table, graced with two cups of the finest Columbian ambrosia.

"You're going to hell for calling more Styrofoam into existence, you know." She snapped her fingers and chairs appeared around the table. Regardless of her comment, she picked up a cup and sipped delicately at the contents.

"I'll un-create it when we're finished, if it'll make you happy."

"This. This makes me happy." In the middle of the table, a small clay bowl with an ill-fitting lid appeared. "She," Mena pointed at the Princess' sanctuary, "does not."

"I thought you were making progress." I recognized the object. After all, I'd claimed it less than a week before. Rumor had it she'd been a princess in Ethiopia at some point, but her choice of sanctuaries didn't jibe. Of course, it beat the supposed czar who called a Scooby-Doo lunchbox home. Not by much, but still.

"I am, but she's being a pain in the ass." She put her feet on the table and gave her newest patient a thump with one lambskin boot.

"A whole tribe once worshipped that 'pain in the ass'."

"And I'm betting they were worshipping a babbling child for at least the past few decades. Her mind's shot."

"Is that a technical term?" I inhaled the scent of my morning's first java. *Glorious.* "Have you tried a translation wish on her?"

She nodded. "I've tried every language I could think of. Ishtar's tits, Jo, I threw something at her in Klingon, for petesakes."

"Klingon?"

"Desperation can bring a person to strange lengths." Her long sip of coffee had me wondering how fast her tongue healed to deal with the burn. "I almost had her once, but I don't think she meant 'chicken, chicken, chicken, whirligig bush crying pennies'. Or maybe she did. She's fairly well wrecked."

My diminutive friend shook her black braid over one shoulder. "Sorry. I shouldn't speak about my patients in those terms."

"Frustrating morning?"

"You have no idea." Mena yawned as she arched into a lazy-cat stretch. "I wish it was next week already."

"Lucky for you our wishes don't change time. You don't want the Council after you."

"If the Rules allowed it, I'd be living the high life in sunny Spain circa ten thousand B.C." She set the empty cup down and gave something more akin to a grimace than a smile. "I hear it was quiet back then."

"If you could avoid the dinosaurs," I shot back, trying to coax a real smile. It worked.

"If you believe that, you need to spend more time reading history rather than combing through those damn archives of yours."

"The archives are history. Our history."

"Not my history. Unless you're reading about India before the Brits. Those were the days, my friend. Lice, amoebic dysentery, tigers eating people left and right." She shuddered. She never talked much about her past, but when she did, it never seemed pleasant.

"But enough about me." She snapped her fingers and her chair turned into a damask sofa. A pillow appeared behind her and she leaned into it. "Is it just me or do we seem to be getting more damaged djinn than ever before? If this keeps up, I'm going to need a bigger place."

My eyes fell on the rows of locked drawers again. Too many of the rooms for transitioning genies sat empty and too many of these drawers were full. Whether something happened to cause it or it was purely a coincidence, I couldn't tell. I knew for certain I'd take my spot as the advance team over delving into supernatural psyches any day and twice on Sundays. Mena, on the other hand, lived for the challenges of bringing a mind back from the fetid swamp.

And she had the *bona fide* degree from Stanford to prove it.

"So, what goodie did you bring today?"

I withdrew the tightly wrapped prize from my bag. No way I wanted to touch that damn thing again. As I handed it over, I shook my head. "This one seems batshit crazy. But I could've met him on a bad day."

She arched one eyebrow and stared hard at my freshly aerated shirt. "Claws?"

"I wish. This one came complete with his own Ginsu and a kung fu grip to boot." I flexed my hand, testing my djinn healing powers. Other than a few twinges, everything felt normal.

She shook her head at me. "You need to be more careful."

"I was careful." Her eyebrow arched again and I knew I was caught. "Okay, fine. I thought about being careful. But let's face it, careful or not, the guy's just nuts."

Tucking the packaged Bedouin into the crook of her elbow, she unsealed an empty slot with a few quick motions. With another puff of power, she transferred his sanctuary into its new home.

"I'll deal with him later." She tapped the back of her wrist as though a watch actually resided there. "Not that I don't love the company, but don't you have someplace else to be?"

"Trying to get rid of me?"

She rolled her eyes. "I have to get back to our Princess, and anyway, Baz wants you."

"So Renee said. Any idea what he wants?" I hoped he didn't want to rehash the rescue. Basil never went into the field, and usually I went over every detail so he could live vicariously. Today, the thought dragged on me. With any luck, my partner had some last minute auction issues to cover. Not something I particularly wanted either, but better than a blow-by-blow of Omar's capture. For this one freaking moment, however, I wanted to be left alone.

Mena tilted her head to one side. "No clue."

Without knowing Baz's problem, I couldn't blow him off. I desperately needed a shower and twenty winks, but a trip upstairs had to come first. Damn it.

"Well..." I pushed myself out of the too-comfy chair. "...if he happens to call, tell him I'm on my way. Unless you think I should stay, and, you know, make sure you're not julienned."

"That bad?"

"He ignored the Master/genie rule."

Her eyes grew wide. "You don't mean... Please tell me you didn't have to use a wish." I nodded. "You're slipping."

"Or he's so far gone, the little rules don't matter anymore." I let out a sick laugh. "Let's hope he's not past the big Rules applying anymore."

"Is that even possible?" She gave a little laugh.

"You know what they say."

"Anything's possible with magic?" She shook her head, dislodging a few strands from her slick braid. On me, loose hair looked like bed-head. On her, it looked all sexy and gorgeous. If she wasn't my best friend, I could really learn to hate her. "Now quit stalling and get upstairs before he comes looking for you."

I started for the door but her next words stopped me. "And you might want to wish up a quick shower before you reach his office." She gave an overly dramatic sniff. "Or at least conjure some perfume, along with an outfit Cuisinart didn't design."

"If I have time," I said. *And if I can scare up enough juice.* Generating power would be out of the question for the next few days at least. Being Master-less means never having to do things you don't want to do, but it also means having to wait around for energy to accumulate on its own. The magic I released on the rescue could keep me at brownout levels for days.

Before turning my feet toward our corporate offices, I spared a brief glance for the door at the end of the hall. It sported the same scary warnings and all the same security gadgets as the vault, but its purpose was much more mundane. Behind the doorway, a stairwell led down to my home.

Exhaling hard, I turned away from my creature comforts. Something had Basil in enough of a tizzy to hunt me down, which meant his needs had to be more important than my rest. At least they better be.

When I reached the top floor, though, his office was vacant. Well, vacant of people.

"Hello, Major." The furry white mountain fell on me. Between his happy licks, I told him to behave. Giving one last gleeful slurp, he sat back on his haunches. He looked like his birthday had arrived, with me as the sole present. I didn't blame him for his exuberance. After all, if someone found me starving and brought me to live in luxury, I'd have my birthday every day, too.

"What are you doing upstairs?" I asked, ruffling his ears. Silence came back at me. I considered again trying to wish for him to talk. Fear of disappointment held me back. My heart would break if my favorite fur-person couldn't converse beyond *hungry, happy, outside*.

With the trail my thoughts followed, hearing someone say, "I needed some company this morning" damn near freaked me out.

Good thing for my pulse, I realized the words came from behind me and sounded like Basil. When my heart stopped racing, I eased to one side so my partner could get to his desk. "And I figured he'd agree with me. Isn't that right, mate?"

Major wagged his fluffy tail in agreement before easing to the floor. My dog could go from awake to comatose in six seconds flat.

Once Basil settled into his chair, I took stock of my business partner. Any casual onlooker would think nothing ever bothered him. His demeanor always oozed calm. In fact, if he enjoyed serving other people, he would make the perfect butler. After a couple hundred years as a genie, though, I think the servitude mentality got scrubbed clean out of him. He scoured away the street urchin on his own.

Still, I knew Basil better than any casual person. His perfection was a shell. The haphazard way he'd shoved his handkerchief into his breast pocket alone told me something frazzled him. I smiled. A little frazzle every once in a while did the man good. It kept him from becoming stodgy in his old age—especially since his true form looked barely old enough to drive. Like me, Basil hid his real self. The slim young man from the streets of London could easily pass for forty now. And the slight paunch was a stroke of genius. Too many perfect people in one place would draw attention.

"Rough morning?" he asked as he pushed a cup of coffee my way. When I held up my own, he kept both for himself. I cringed inside. Baz doubling up on the caffeine meant the situation was worse than I imagined.

"You heard about Omar?"

"You know better than anyone how news travels here." He spoke without looking at me. It would've been rude if he hadn't been furiously beating his keyboard at the time. "Mena rang to let me know you arrived. She filled me in as much as she was able." He finished the last syllable, punctuating it with a harsh jab at the Enter key. Seconds later his printer started spitting out paper.

I stepped over Major, careful not to flatten his tail, and beelined for the buttery-soft leather chair Basil kept special for me. No sooner had my buns created their own perfect space than I ended up with a massive dog head in my lap. As I watched white hair cover my black slacks, I waited for Basil to spill his mind.

"So the Bedouin? Worse than usual, I take it?" he said as he slipped the collated sheets into a manila folder. Each movement seemed too slow.

"I had to use a wish on him."

"You must be slipping."

His words came out, and I stifled a laugh. "You and Mena compare notes? No matter what she says, I'm not slipping. This djinn is not only powerful, but he's more than a few grains short of an hourglass." I flexed my arm, and the joint popped, making me feel every one of those years my original birth certificate indicated.

"Anything I should fix for you?"

"Brother Baz makes it all better?" I grinned. Given he's a couple hundred years older, the Englishman could never pass for my brother, and we both knew it. His light coloring alone killed the comparison. Add the fact our features are totally different, and you bury it. He's a young, hot Michael York. I'm Gilda Radner doing Lora Croft in a bad SNL skit.

"If I were your brother," he said, "you'd mind better. Reggie should've spanked you more as a child. If you'd been my sibling, I would've made certain of it."

"As if I don't suffer enough humiliation on a daily basis." Considering my fruitless tries to secure the Bedouin without using a wish, maybe my friends were right. My shoulder picked the moment to send a twinge of pain down my arm, as if to punctuate my thoughts.

"Seriously, Jo, I can have you right as rain in a jiff. You're too tapped to do it yourself. Admit it."

I didn't want to. Admitting it would be admitting my limited battery life. At less than a century old, I maintained a special place on the list genies in the building. I was the weakest. It was embarrassing.

"Thanks, but I'm okay." I stuffed the pain to the back of my consciousness. "I'm almost back to normal anyway. Save your energy for when I show up with my arm hanging by a tendon." Which could happen sooner rather than later if this latest rescue indicated anything.

I stared intently at my partner. He wouldn't look at me. He merely pushed his newly created folder back and forth across his desk.

"Spit it out already, Baz, before you wear a hole in that thing."

"I don't have a great deal of information."

My heart sank as I realized what the damn folder held, and why he was stalling so hard. "Another rescue? Already?"

"It came in while you were in New York."

"Can't I get to it next week?"

He shook his head. "The target's location is scheduled to be demolished tomorrow."

Any other day, I would've teased him about his pronunciation of schedule, but this wasn't the time. "Wrecking ball or explosives?"

"Does it matter?"

In the scheme of things, not really. Sanctuaries have a strange way of surviving damn near anything. One made it through Nagasaki.

"It can wait." It would have to. The skirmish with Omar tapped me out. Basil most likely ran on fumes.

He gave a curt shake of his head. "A cleanup crew will scour the place as soon as the dust clears. Something about hazardous material leakage. If they swoop in—"

"They'll bury it in a deep hole and cover it with concrete. Then it's bye-bye genie." Being trapped inside your sanctuary for years before some human finds it is bad enough. A djinn buried in a hole full of toxic waste would be sentenced to an eternity of solitary confinement. As much as I hated to admit it, Basil was right. R & R had to wait. "If your offer of a little healing still stands, I'll take it."

FIVE

~-~-~-~-~-~-~

Basil's wish dropped me in a soft spot. I counted it as the highlight of my trip. Even before I opened my eyes, north Florida sucked. Vines closed around my ankles like a scene from *Swamp Thing*. The smell of decay wafted from every direction. A child's begging voice bounced against steel before it rang in my ears.

I stood for an instant with my eyes shut tight, absorbing the sensations. Truth be told, I didn't want to see what I'd gotten into. Hell, I wanted to hop the first wish back to Colorado. But what I wanted didn't enter into this equation. I had a job to do. That the job would probably be infinitely harder than I imagined couldn't stop me from doing it.

Pushing a bit of power, I adjusted my sight for the glaring midday sun and then opened my eyes. Sure enough, I stood in the ass end of The Industrial Park Capitalism Forgot. Pretty much as expected. What I didn't expect I found after expanding my senses to pinpoint my target.

The rescue lay straight ahead and, just my luck, the begging voice I heard belonged to him. As if a begging genie didn't tip me off to sheer craptasticness, he had company. And for a bit of extra fun, his guest felt neither brethren nor human.

Tapping my earpiece connected me with home.

"Basil?" I said before he chirped his salutation. "What the hell have you gotten me into?"

"Don't know what you're talking about, love." I explained what little I knew of the situation. "Do you want an extraction," he said, "or should I send reinforcements?"

Back at the building, the whimpering subsided into the low tones of conversation. "I've never needed saving before. Whatever this thing is, it sounds like the worst part's over. Probably only a misunderstanding between species."

The paranormal world commanded a lot of shelf-space at the bookstores, but as a rule we didn't mix and mingle, either with each other or with mortals. I scented the air again. No vampiric taint. No hint of fur, feathers or fins to indicate a lycanth encounter. Only djinn, along with something so foreign it triggered my gag reflex.

Basil had no idea what I faced. Maybe if he stood where I stood, a big ol' whiff might help him place the thing. After all, at a few centuries old, he probably stumbled across this species at some point.

"I'll call you if it gets weirder," I told Basil before hanging up. Realizing this could all be paranoia sticking its ugly proboscis where it didn't belong, I went for the deep breathing, Zen thing. And promptly gagged. I really needed to stop inhaling through my nose, if only so I could introduce myself without barfing on the guy. It wasn't his fault his chosen locale stunk like a summertime garbage scow. As soon as I removed the offense, this whole issue would go away and I could leave the odiferous area.

Yeah, that's the ticket.

Kicking off the kudzu, I slogged toward the dilapidated structure. The thought crossed my mind to proceed with caution, but if that had been my style, I'd be taking a dirt nap from old age instead of sweating like a pig in north Florida. Besides, the few other species I'd encountered in my travels didn't want to mess with me any more than I wanted to mess with them. As long as everyone respects everyone else and minds their own business, we all get along marvelously well. Sort of.

As I drew closer to the building, my confident stride slowed and my little used caution kicked in. The air throbbed with a sticky mix of energy—the unknown being's and my unhappy rescue.

"Complete my wish." The first intelligible words from inside the building sure didn't make *me* happy.

"I can't. It burns."

From the sounds of it, the genie was straining against an unfulfilled wish. Which seemed impossible. We don't make moral judgments. They wish; we grant. Unless the wish is against the Rules. And then, they don't burn. A Master asks for what the gods won't allow, and the wish simply dissipates. No muss, no fuss. The gods made the Rules easy to avoid. No killing, no raising the dead, no unmaking the Universe, etc., and you're good to go.

No, the wish wasn't prohibited. But probably very nasty.

The voices dropped to mumbling again as I pasted myself next to a hole in the rusty wall. I evaluated my current assets. My juice level still sucked. My body still ached from Omar's not-so-gentle treatment. Only my rapier wit and my less-than-keen fashion sense still thrived.

Maybe I should've taken Basil up on his offer. That thought alone coated my spine with a little steel. *No one comes to Josephine Mayweather's rescue. I'm the rescuer, damn it.*

I craned my head around the corner. The entire building had been reduced to one open space. Literally. Most of the roof had rotted away. The windows were shot. Kudzu had pretty much taken over as the dominant species. A tree growing slightly left of center stood covered in the noxious crud, for petesakes. And I still couldn't see the occupants.

Shifting my sight into the infrared spectrum showed why. They'd picked the only spot in the whole damn place with both a roof and the angle to keep the sun away. I adjusted my eyes again to better see into the shadows and got my first glimpse of the creature I'd been so concerned about.

I had to stifle a laugh.

He looked like any other person. He didn't even have horns or a tail or hooves. What he sported was an overinflated ego and an addiction to campy djinn tales. The topknot we're all supposed to wear graced his otherwise bald head. His chin showed off the pointy beard. His only deviation from the myths: legs instead of the tapering fog all good little storybook genies sport. I'd have to bring this sicko back for Mena. She'd be the first psychologist to document a case of djinnis-envy.

The actual djinn wasn't a laughing matter, though. No sane person could find humor in a blond boy curled into the fetal position. To punctuate my point about sanity, the Genie-Wannabe chuckled as he kicked the child.

"Complete my wish or suffer."

"Leave the kid alone." The words shot out of my mouth before my brain kicked in. If I'd thought before I spoke, I would've realized anyone sick enough to look and act like this freak probably didn't play with a full set of Lincoln Logs.

Lucky me. The damn thing ignored me. A step closer brought me within range to hear him whisper.

"I wish for you to not grant my wish." As the kid screamed, the bastard did a slow turn and winked at me. My heart curled in on itself.

Late at night, Mena and I would sit around drinking gin, pondering impossibilities. The little what-ifs no one can solve. She called them Avyakta—whatever the hell that means. I considered them conundrums—like 'can an omnipotent god create a rock he can't lift?' Shit like that. One night we got as drunk as any genie can get and I pondered the possibility of a wish we couldn't grant. She pointed out the Rules, of course, which mean loads of ungrantable wishes. I countered with the quandary of whether one existed *within* the Rules.

I guess this asshole figured out the answer we hadn't, making the poor kid suffer for it.

"Listen, bud," I said as I stepped closer. "I don't know what your problem is, but step away from the djinn, and we'll chat about it."

His reply? He waved a hand at me like he was swatting some kind of gnat. The next thing I knew, I lay beneath another huge dent in the already trashed metal wall. And as easy as one-two-three, I became nothing to him again. He turned back to the kid, kicking him harder.

Why isn't he protecting himself? I didn't have time to think too hard about it. I had to occupy my time thinking of how to pop my shoulder back into joint without screaming.

"If you would simply do as you're told, this experience will be less painful for you both."

Creepy Dude probably had it right. Didn't mean I agreed with him, though. With a stifled yelp, I righted whatever I'd broken or dislocated, then waded into the fray. "Pick on someone your own size." Not my best witty repartee, but hey, we work with what we got, and I had nothing.

The hand waved again. This time, I was ready. Unfortunately, I hadn't prepared for the sheer amount of power he put behind his punch this time. The shield I threw around myself kept me from splattering. Barely. As the ribbons of torn metal flew past me, I cringed. Without my magic, I would've been shredded. Genies heal fast, but the worse the injury, the longer the recovery. Winding up in rusty slices wasn't my idea of a good time.

Neither was laying in the kudzu after my shield collapsed, but at least I stayed in one piece.

Pride left me as my good sense returned. Tapping my headset, I connected with Colorado. "Baz? Get someone out here double quick. I'm getting my ass handed to me."

"It'd be easier to teleport home, love."

"Not if I want to save this kid." Of course, I didn't have the faintest idea how to circumvent the conundrum Pseudo-Djinn created. Cursing my shitty luck, I checked my batteries. Nowhere near as low as expected, but still not enough to stop the bad guy, let alone counter a wish that evil. "I'll try and hold the fort until reinforcements arrive."

I hung up before he could argue. Either help would show or it wouldn't. I could only hope *someone* arrived before my bloody, little bits were scattered over the better part of the Panhandle. And before the kid was past saving, if he could be saved at all. Since I'd never heard of a wish you couldn't grant, I had no idea what would happen.

I whipped together a quick wish from my limited stores and crossed my fingers. Then I did the 'too stupid to live' thing. I walked back into the warehouse loaded for bear and ready to kick evil dude ass.

He couldn't muster the good graces to look concerned. In fact, he seemed bored shitless as he stood over the writhing body. His hands held a simple dreidel. "Arthur Herbert Walton, I am your Master. You will fulfill my wishes or suffer the consequences."

Still picking on the kid after he made an unfathomable wish went beyond unnecessary cruelty. Then again, cruelty might be what turned this guy on.

"He's already suffering enough, numbnuts."

The creep did a slow turn, staring at me with kohl-rimmed eyes. When he winked again, I wanted to blow him to tiny particles. "Are you still here?" He didn't bother to wave this time. The air rushed past me in the same tired trick. What worked before wouldn't work again. I wouldn't let it. As he unleashed more magic in my direction, I countered with my own, grimacing as his power and mine cancelled each other out.

I readied another wish, hoping he needed time to recover. If everything worked like it should, he'd be immobile long enough to snatch the kid's sanctuary and get us both the hell out of there. I let my wish free. Like clockwork, the asshole stiffened and fell to one side. I rushed forward to reassure the kid before snagging the bauble.

My legs went out from under me, dropping me on top of the other genie. Our attacker pushed again, rolling me across the floor until I fetched up against the indoor tree.

"Enough of this," I heard him say. "Mr. Walton? By now the magic should be ripe. Enjoy your everlasting death."

If I could've caught my breath, I would've chuckled. Pain can be unbearable. It might eventually drive a guy nuts. But pain can't kill. *This guy has to be stupider than I—*

"Sunuvabitch." The energy gathering inside young Arthur surged. Before I could think, the wish went supernova. Only my genie molecules saved my retinas from irreparable scorching. When my eyes healed, I found myself chucked up under the one scraggly tree, wondering whether I had the world's worst sunburn.

And wondering where everyone else went.

I pulled myself to my feet, expecting to feel like I'd gone ten rounds with Mike Tyson and then got blasted with a flame-thrower. Instead, I found myself weirdly refreshed. *Must have hit my head harder than I thought.*

"You okay in there, boss?" I heard from beyond the still-standing—*how are they still standing*—walls. I cast a glance at my shredded clothing, expecting to see yellowing bruises and burnt skin. Everything beneath the tatters glowed a healthy pink.

"Peachy," I said. "But stay outside." Stretching my senses, I tried to feel for the sadist. No sign he'd been there, but poor little Arthur Walton's imprint clung to everything. His particles were now part of the scenery, like he'd rubbed himself all over the place.

I sat for a moment. I didn't know whether to be happy none of my associates would freak out, or to be pissed all my evidence had been blown to molecules. I doubted anyone would believe this story. Hell, I didn't quite believe it, and I'd been there. I cast a glance sideways. The hole where I'd punched through remained, but it didn't help. No one had seen what the place looked like before. As far as they'd know, I hallucinated the whole thing.

"Boss?"

"You can head back," I called from my spot on the ground. "Nothing to see here."

Their magic spread through the room as they checked to make sure I wasn't just being brave. When it receded, their questions hummed along my veins even if no one voiced them. *Fine by me. The fewer people I have to talk to about this, the better.*

"What about the genie you came for?" said a man as he stepped into the building. His eyes cast one way and then the other, confirming visually what his magic already told him. He could smell Arthur as well as I could, but he'd never find him.

"He's already gone." I dropped my head. "I couldn't save him."

The big genie who's name escaped me held out a hand. I didn't take it. "Don't beat yourself crosswise, boss. You know what they say about leading a horse to water. Some genies are too daft to want help."

As thankful as I was for his kind words, I ached to tell him the truth. And then I remembered what my mother faced trying to explain the unexplainable. Best to keep my mouth closed until I could figure out what happened.

"Better luck next time, eh?" said another large fellow. Basil must've gone for the big guns, if not in magic then at least in mass.

I faked a chuckle. "Yeah. Next time." I waved my hands at the boys. "Thanks for coming, but I think we're all set here." They nodded as one and, before I could blink, they were gone. If only everything went so easy.

I reached for my headset, searching for the words to explain the incident without freaking Baz out. Luckily, my rescue squad didn't know the truth. Hell, I wasn't sure of the truth. I only knew once word of this got out... I shook my head. I couldn't bear to think about the repercussions yet.

"Baz?" I ignored his chipper greeting. "Get me home."

"What's happened out there? Lyle arrived and—"

"Get me home and I'll tell you everything. But do me a favor and drop the wards. I don't have the stomach to walk the gauntlet today."

"But what about the djinn? What happened to him?"

I swallowed hard. "He's dead, Baz. Now get me the hell out of here."

SIX

~-~-~-~-~-~-~-~

A second later, I stood in Basil's office. One look at me had him turning a sickly shade of gray. "You can hang up now." He dropped into his chair. "And close your mouth." It shut with an audible snap. He reached to set the phone into its cradle but missed. It clattered to the floor, and he still didn't tear his attention away.

"I can't look too bad. The crew you sent out didn't bat an eye."

"They don't know you like I do, love. To them you're the picture of health. To me, it's as if someone shot your dog and made you watch while they ate him." He rubbed one weary hand across his face. "What in blazes happened? You said the subject died? How?"

A large mug of coffee appeared via wish. I kept it hovering in the air a moment before I reached for it. Even then, my hand shook and hot liquid dribbled into the sensitive spot between my thumb and forefinger. I let it burn. If nothing else, the pain reminded me I had survived.

"Jo?"

I dragged my gaze back to Basil.

"I don't know what happened," I began and then shook my head. "Scratch that. I know what happened but not how. Or why." As I told the story, poor Basil's eyes almost bugged right the hell out. I paused in my retelling and wished a cup of Earl Grey onto his desk. When I finished the tale, his tea still sat untouched.

"So tell me. What the hell was that thing, and how could he make a wish like that?"

Silence greeted me but not ignorance. I could sense that much. He just didn't want to say. I nudged him under the desk with my boot. "Well?"

"We need to tell the Council."

"We aren't saying anything to anyone until I know what we've got going on here. They'll think I'm as crazy as old Omar." Basil's eyes dropped. "Tell me you don't think I've lost my marbles."

"You haven't lost anything, Jo. It's just… Crikey." He rose to stand behind me. With one hand, he caressed my hair. "You haven't gone 'round the bend. It's… I mean, it's not… Talk to them. Please."

His hand left my hair, but when I turned to him, he'd gone. If he'd even been there.

So much for not doubting my sanity.

And he wanted *me* to talk to the Council. They got their kicks trying to shut me down. Handing over a story like this, without proof to back it up? Might as well hand them my commitment papers. Already signed.

I didn't want to think about the shitstorm they'd create if they decided to believe me. It would be worse. We needed to keep this to ourselves long enough to figure out what happened. Stay silent and keep a whole race of genies from learning about a creature that not only *could* kill us but would happily do so.

Such a little wish, so silly it bordered on absurd, couldn't possibly kill a genie. And yet it did. Of course, without a body, I had no evidence he actually died. Trust me, though, no genie could spread particles of himself all over a building and still exist.

My dark thoughts scattered at the sharp crack of wood splintering. As I extricated my fist from the wall, I slid a little power through my skin to heal the deeper gashes. I didn't feel them. I wasn't quite sure I'd ever feel anything the same way again. As for the hole, before long, Baz would clean it up.

Before I could create any more destruction, I borrowed a cue from Basil and left. Thank the gods, I made it to my own office without encountering anyone who'd ask why I looked like I'd seen a thousand ghosts. The door slammed with more force than I intended. Its glass rattled, which made me feel better for some reason, but it didn't break. I sent my elbow through the pane to rectify my mistake.

A kid had died. Things needed to be loud. They needed to break. If there hadn't been people inside, I would've imploded the whole damn building.

Pressing my back against the wall kept me off the floor, but barely. I shook like I'd wandered in from a blizzard, which made sense considering how cold my insides felt. If only I'd been able to stop the bastard, to make the wish go away, to save poor little Arthur before his own frustrated power consumed him.

Ultimate cosmic power, my ass. I couldn't stop one twerp from committing the universal sin. A little part of me tried to console the larger part by pointing out that, fully charged, I couldn't have stopped him. It didn't help.

I gave up trying to stand. Standing seemed pointless. Hell, breathing felt pointless. If that creep didn't think twice about killing a kid, he'd kill anyone. Nothing like a conscience or morals would stop him. He'd take more lives whenever he wanted. *Who's next? Another of my rescues? One of my friends? Will he come to finish the job his pounding didn't accomplish?*

In all the years I walked the earth, only one death ripped my heart this much and, as Mena pointed out, I couldn't be sure I'd seen Reggie die.

According to the newspapers at the time, which Stavros bought by the dozens and slapped in front of me, I disappeared after re-decorating my room. The society pages said I'd run off with a European, based on a note I'd left.

I didn't write it. The Greek thought it was a nice touch.

No mention of Evangeline finding my father's body.

After I 'ran away', my mother fell apart. When Reggie didn't come home from his last trip, Evangeline got a divorce on the grounds of abandonment. A year later, she drank herself into the grave. Her death didn't surprise me. Without me around and after Reggie's money dried up, what else could she do? I knew where they buried her, but without a body, Reggie couldn't be buried. Even his grave wouldn't prove his death. I was left with the memory of my silver letter opener sticking out of Reggie's chest. A memory Mena insisted I dreamed.

And Reggie always hoped to die in his sleep at the ripe old age of a hundred and two. Arthur hadn't been allowed the grace of that end. Not that any genie would.

Gazing at my office with its neatly piled paperwork and its softly humming computer, I realized I needed to be somewhere else.

Anywhere else. Sparring with some other genie until one of us collapsed, maybe. Or drinking enough gin to make myself cross-eyed.

The exorcism of my anger would have to wait, though. I needed to get onto another computer, one away from the network and reserved for my eyes alone.

Every step made me wish I hadn't banned teleports inside the building. My feet became lead. My legs were stumps. I paused outside Mena's office, unsure whether I needed my friend or my therapist. In the end, I gave up trying to figure it out. A whispered wish and four punched numbers got me past my security. I have no idea how I got down the stairwell without falling.

Major, to his credit, waited patiently instead of knocking me down and slathering me in doggie-lovin'. I laid a hand on his head as I passed. His whine told me he sensed the unhappy place I had inside me.

Topping off his bowl to overflowing, I left him daintily munching his kibbles. I would've loved to join him for dinner, but after watching Arthur Walton die the last thing I wanted was food. Besides, too many things still needed doing. Too many archives to delve through. Too many old journals to read. If what my library held could make any sense of this, I had to get to work.

Typically, I'd relish the idea of spending uninterrupted hours surrounded by books and ledgers and journals, most written before I ever set foot on the Earth. I simply wasn't sure if my collection could help me. Especially if my sanity was in question. For all I knew, the incident with Arthur had been a hallucination.

But then who sent the alert, and what happened to the rescue before I arrived?

Thinking along those lines helped me regain a little belief in my mental health. If only increased belief in my brain could cure my own impotence. Finding information in the archives wouldn't tell me what was I supposed to do with it. Alert the Council? They'd spend months debating my mental competence, and triple that many months building a consensus of brethren to explore what they should do about this killer thing either way. Every other genie could explode in a flash of light before they'd make a decision on what beverage they should serve.

Well, Mayweather, whatever you're going to do, you'd better get to it.

As I headed toward the back of my cave, Major's toenails clicked on the stone behind me. At my bedroom, his cold nose poked into my palm. He thought I needed sleep. A dog-sized indent graced the middle of my comforter, showing where he'd spent his day. I laughed about how horrified my mother would've been about a dog on the bed linens.

The damn comforter and her cameo brooch were all I had left of her.

"Go ahead," I said aloud. His huge head swung toward the bed and back to me. With a massive shrug, he padded toward the carved mahogany, leaping into the middle.

A little voice told me a few minutes lying against the mound of warmth wouldn't hurt. Every one of my bones hurt. My bewildered mind craved a break. Hell, I'd reached the point where I'd gladly curl up in a gravel pit if rest would erase the image of a dying boy from my head.

Djinn aren't supposed to die, damn it.

Nothing I did would bring the kid back. Still, this demented *thing* knew how to kill brethren, and he wouldn't stop, not unless I stopped him.

Shaking away the remaining cobwebs of exhaustion, I continued deeper into the cave until I reached a chiseled alcove. The mural painted there suited a whorehouse better than a home, but after so many years, its bacchanalia barely registered. Fauns cavorted amongst nymphs; a unicorn nuzzled his regal head deep in the lap of some unwitting virgin; gods lured unsuspecting mortals into acts best left unmentioned in polite company. Not necessarily what I would've chosen as subject matter, but the creator of my security system had a weird sense of humor.

And people wonder why I don't associate with Zeke if I don't have to.

I should've eradicated the damn thing years ago. It no longer offends me, but it's damn distracting. Maybe once I resolved this new wrinkle in my existence, I'd find the gumption. Loathe it or not, one thing remained certain, this last and best defense for my most precious possessions did an awesome job. Any burglar who evaded my outer rings of security would not only have a difficult time discovering this wasn't art, but would find breaking through it nearly impossible. The daughter of a crook shouldn't have it any other way. Then again, feeling secure shouldn't mean enduring a painful memento from a former lover.

With a wave and a few whispered syllables, a gaping hole replaced the ugly mural. I tried to ignore the symbolism. Pushing Zeke out of my life had been necessary. So what if I had a gaping hole where he used to be?

A draft of stale air surrounded me before I stepped inside. Carrying the perfume of old books and older parchment, the breeze comforted me more than anything else could. I inhaled and let a smile play across my lips. This was my fatted calf.

Most of the objects inside had been hoarded by one ancient or another. When they got tired of their belongings, or if they did the unthinkable and wished themselves out of existence, those belongings ended up here. Consider it a bequest from those who don't leave wills or inheritors. Any acquisitions with monetary value I cycle through the auctions. Everything else—journals, clippings, scribbled pictographs on papyrus—I keep. As for the remainder of my collection, I'd spent the better part of thirty years tracking down those pieces of djinn history.

In theory, Basil had organized it into some kind of searchable system. Technically, I would catalog my acquisitions into a database, or at least shelve them into some kind of logical order. In reality, I didn't have time, and any available manpower had better things to do than sift through musty old paper. Thus, pretty much everything got shoved into a condo-complex of boxes stacked into every available space.

Heaving a deep sigh, I turned away from the clutter and walked toward the small desk tucked into one corner. If I was going to do this, eliminating the easy stuff first would take the least amount of time. After wishing up a pot of java juice, I waded in.

SEVEN

~-~-~-~-~-~-~

"Wakey, wakey. Eggs and bakey." The thud of a plate on my desk coincided with the voice grating against my nerves. Good news: it saved me from a creepy dream. Bad news: I slung a wish before I had time to process the reality around me.

"Whoa there, Quicks Draw," Mena said, mimicking the cartoon donkey perfectly. "A lady shouldn't have to defend herself merely for bringing breakfast."

I raised my head and blinked my bleary eyes to see Mena brushing scrambled eggs off her silk tank top. A slice of bacon perched on her once perfectly-coiffed hair. "Don't sneak up on a gal and you won't have to defend yourself."

"Woke up on the wrong side of the blotter again, I take it?" She snapped her fingers and both the food and the broken plate disappeared. A new meal reappeared seconds later neatly positioned next to the drool stain I'd created.

Nudging a stack of papers aside with one hip, she settled her narrow behind on the corner of my desk. Any other day I would've shooed her away. I think she suspected I wasn't up to the work I had to do, which only ticked me off more. With one eye squinting at me, she did an obvious visual inspection of my personage. From her expression, I came up lacking.

"What?" I barked, trying to tuck a loose tendril of hair behind one ear.

"You should've taken some time for yourself before you started." She picked up an old journal I meant to read and waved it in my face. One of the pages slipped loose and floated onto my lap. Before any more damage occurred, I snatched the volume from her and wished the pages together again.

"I suppose that's your way of telling me I look like hell." I ignored her disregard for my treasures. Mena was more about the here and now than the archival information I loved. Once again, I grudgingly reminded myself differences make friendships interesting.

She lifted one shoulder. "Your words, not mine. I happen to think when a person never takes time to rest, they eventually burn out, even when they're made of smoke and mirrors like we are."

"Is that your professional opinion?"

"My professional opinion is all this crap can wait."

"I'll rest when I'm dea—" The image of Arthur's explosion stopped me cold. "None of this can wait. Didn't Basil tell you what happened?"

Her sleek ponytail kept time with my now-throbbing head. "He let me in on the secret. Baz thought I might be able to provide some insight."

"Well?"

"I've got nothing. I'm a doctor not a psychic." It was pure *Star Trek*, but I couldn't manage a grin. Leaning closer, she stared into my sleepy eyes. "How are you holding up?"

"Are you asking as my friend or as my shrink?" I didn't bother waiting for an answer. Most times Mena can't separate the two anyway. "Any thoughts on what happened out there?"

"Holy mother of Ishtar, Jo. Back when we were playing games and you brought it up, the idea scared me shitless."

"You remembered."

"I couldn't forget. It gave me nightmares." Mena shuddered. "It's been a long time since I had a Master, but can you imagine?"

I didn't have to imagine; I'd seen. "But how did he know? I mean, I brought it up as a lark. I didn't really think it could be done. Did you?"

My friend picked up a piece of parchment and set it back without looking at it. Her fingers drifted to another page and did the same thing.

"Mena? Stop before I can't find anything." Before long, she would've subconsciously rearranged my entire desk.

Her eyes traveled from my piles to my shelving to the floor, never once landing on me. "I haven't been around much longer than you."

"What do you even mean?" Up went her shoulder again. "You knew something like this was possible?"

"Rumors and stories. My sources aren't the most reliable, you know, so whether anything they say is true?" She made a seesaw motion. "Besides, you're more the authority than I on general genie strangeness."

I didn't buy it, but from her sour-pickle expression, the subject made her as uncomfortable as it made me.

Out of the corner of my eye I saw Major strolling into the library. He knew better, but the smell of fried pork belly has overturned many a good dog's training. I tossed a piece of bacon his way and watched as he gulped it down. Licking his lips, he sat at my feet and made puppy eyes at me. When no more pork flew his way, he turned off the charm and, after one of his classic shrugs, settled onto a faux-fur rug.

Taking a page from Major's playbook, I gave up trying to coax information out of my friend. If she didn't want to toss me any scraps, she wouldn't. "You wouldn't happen to know what species to call Creepy Dude, would you?"

She nodded toward my computer. "Nothing in the bible of djinn data?"

"Not in the few minutes I worked before I fell apart." I glanced at the stacks of boxes. "My best bet is probably over there anyway. Any chance you'll help dig with me?"

"Not on your life, lady." She flexed her carefully manicured digits. "And scuff these?"

We both knew she wished her nails the way they were and could simply wish them back, but I wasn't pushing it. Besides, Mena could get down and dirty with the rest of us, and frequently did when wrangling our demented brethren. The only difference: Waging battle with an unstable mind, however bloody the skirmish might be, held way more interest for her than a dusty old pile of papers.

"If you're not going to help, did you have some other reason for coming down?" I dropped the subject rather than butt heads with Mena. She was who she was. That wouldn't change.

I wasn't sure I wanted it to.

"You mean other than feeding your slothful ass?" Her grin spread wide at her own joke. She knew how hard I worked better than anyone except Basil. "I have an update on the gal you brought in last week."

"How is she?"

"Worse. She's now clinging to her damn sanctuary like Linus with his blankie." She shrugged. "Sometimes they have to *regress* before they can *progress*. By the way, how'd you get the whole 'I'm a princess' thing out of her."

"I didn't. I did a little of the research you hate and traced her to her tribe. The verbal history there matched the gal we have here. Only it seemed there might've been two of her."

"Weird. Well, anyway, this one will take a while, if she'll ever open up to me." Mena shook her head, dislodging several tendrils of hair. On me, if that much escaped, I'd look like I crawled out of bed after a week of hard partying.

"Any luck with any of the others?"

A snap of her fingers brought her look back to flawless. "I wish. But I can't leave them to rot in their sanctuaries. That's how some of them got in their mental mess to begin with." Her shoulders sagged for a moment before she pushed herself stick straight again. "Sometimes I wonder if I'm ever doing any good."

"You worked wonders with Michael. He'd still be sitting in a corner, trying to pickle his brains, if you hadn't pulled him out of it. Now he's working on his law degree. You did a good thing."

"But he chose to go human again."

"You make mortality sound worse than hiding in a lamp somewhere playing tiddlywinks with yourself."

"Isn't it?" She shook her head and dropped off my desk. "Anyway, I'm still making the rounds. The princess showed promise, but like I said, we're backpedaling."

"Any chance she'll end up better than Abby-Normal?" My joke fell flat. Despite my best efforts at infusing humor into a humorless situation, both humor and hope were in short supply. Reggie always taught me, *In any given situation comedy works better than tearing out your hair. Smile lines are always more attractive than mange.* My father the philosopher.

Mena ignored my lame attempt at jocularity. "There's always a chance. About the same chance as the sun going supernova during tonight's dinner, but stranger things have happened."

"The unofficial catch phrase for all djinn-kind." In our world, stranger things were par for the course. With the brethren, normal and strange are relative.

Speaking of which, I needed to get my head into the game. Or maybe my back into it. Several backs would work better. "I really could use some help with those boxes."

"Love to, but I'm swamped. Get Baz down here. Better yet, recruit one of the guests. I know one newly returned human who'd love to put cataloguing skills on his resume."

"Bite me." The djinn-turned mortal she had in mind had better things to do than play warehouse employee, and she knew it. "Or do you want to be the one interrupting Michael while he's studying for the bar?"

She actually paled beneath her olive skin. If I had to guess, she'd already been chewed out for coming between the man and his books. "Don't look at me. He threw something big and bound at me last time." Her eyes narrowed and acquired a wicked gleam. "I bet if you asked him, though, he'd definitely drop everything. One word and he'd follow you to the Dark Ages. Hell, he might even rejoin the—"

"Don't finish the thought." I stuffed a triangle of toast in my mouth and tried not to think about the ex-surfer, former genie, would-be lawyer. I didn't need another rescue with a case of gratitude turned infatuation. I certainly didn't want to string Michael along. As soon as he passed the bar, he'd be gone, leading the rest of his mortal life. If he lucked out, he'd find a nice WASP and they'd produce two point five children.

"I suggest you leave all the bookworm stuff alone for now. Rejoin the living. Everything in those boxes also lives inside someone's head somewhere." Her eyes brightened as a smile creased her face. "In fact, I know the perfect—"

I almost sprayed her with my coffee. "Not Zeke."

"Honey, I'm not that cruel, am I?" She shook her head. "Which reminds me. The reprobate's been calling for you." I nodded and, thankfully, she let it drop. I wasn't in the mood to rehash my failed relationship, especially not with my therapist, even if she was my best friend. "Although, Ezekiel could be the answer. Plus he's easier on the eyes."

I shot her a glare alongside a piece of bacon.

"Besides," she continued, dodging the flying pork, "I meant someone you actually think highly of. The best source of information djinn have?" I raised an eyebrow. "Oh come on. If anyone knows what's going on, it's the pirate."

EIGHT

~-~-~-~-~-~-~-~

Mena's suggestion sent waves of discomfort through me. I'd rather have a long vacation complete with cabana boys and fruity drinks. Scantily clad men bearing beverages instead of the trip I faced would've worked out so much better.

Don't get me wrong. I love the pirate. After all, she presents an unending source of information for our kind. If she doesn't know about it, it never happened. Or shouldn't have happened in the first place. She's a wonder.

If only her fees weren't so damn high.

My problem with visiting the pirate doesn't have to do with her rates, though. I can afford to give her whatever she asks, and she's worth every gold doubloon she gouges from me. It isn't the fact she's a bitch either, which she can be. Part of what I love about her is no female born in the 1500s could compare to her attitude and outlook on life.

The problem is she reminds me of what would happen if I ever rejoined the slowly dying. And it scares the crap out of me. Every. Fucking. Time.

After centuries of being one of the Many, Mary Killigrew chose humanity over spending another minute as a djinn. Ever since, she's been growing steadily older. Of course, she hadn't been in first blooms of life to begin with. From what I gathered, she lived forty-some human years before her turning. True, she'd been a hot forty-something at the time, but once time begins marching again, it leaves boot prints all over you. Which meant thirty-some years later, the buxom brigand was more granny than wench.

But that was my hang-up. Not hers.

Being one of the world's only female pirates ever, Mary doesn't do things according to anyone else's whims or notions. Instead of accepting her role as a middle-aged, middle-income gal, and maybe finding a nice banker or lawyer to settle down with, she slipped into the groove best suited to a displaced buccaneer. She opened Golden Wishes Pawn. Sure, it wasn't the same as looting and pillaging, but the lifestyle suited her.

First off, she had the opportunity to surround herself with all the pretties and baubles any self-respecting pirate lady loved. Second, her new life provided the thrill of doing battle by haggling with customers instead of running some poor schmuck through with a cutlass. Most significant, though, her new job gave her all the excitement her heart craved without actually breaking any significant laws.

Lucky for the djinn world, Mary wasn't only a pawnbroker. The store fed her inner brigand, but it didn't feed her gorgeously greedy heart. What she couldn't pile into her coffers by selling and pawning and bartering, she made providing information. For the right price, of course.

Seconds after closing my eyes at home, Mena's wish landed me in the alley behind Golden Wishes. The sweltering heat of southern Nevada enfolded me like a sandpaper blanket. If possible, I would've dropped inside, but she'd paid some crafty djinn a small fortune for the wards surrounding her establishment. Mary wasn't the most trusting of souls. With more security than most banks, she protected her fragile existence like Swarovski crystal.

At a snail's pace, I followed two blue-haired ladies into the retail extravaganza. The biddies stepped to the counter like old pros, providing an earful of quibbling to anyone they passed. The skinny one complained about Mary's AC being up too high. Her squat gal-pal couldn't seem to focus on anything beyond whether they remembered to take something called 'Muffin' for walkies before they left.

Good thing for all concerned, the ladies didn't have to wait for service. Some tattooed girl whose nametag said 'Eloise' sidled up. She gazed at one old lady and then the other like she'd never seen anything like them in her life. The feeling appeared to be mutual. A stalemate of generational proportions ensued until the Complainer set her shocking, purple bag on the Plexiglas counter.

Drawing her words out in practiced boredom, Eloise asked, "Buying, selling or pawning?"

"Selling." One gnarled hand felt around inside her hefty purse.

I leaned against the jewelry case to watch the real life *Pawn Stars* play out. Just as well. Pushing ahead of customers wouldn't win me any points with Killigrew. From the age of the ladies in front of me, my wait wouldn't be a short one. I expected them to dither for the better part of an hour, at least. I didn't expect the Complainer to pull a 9mm Beretta out of her bag. Suddenly I had other ideas about business and patience. I gathered my power around me, prepared to throw a shield around the crazy old bat before she hurt herself or someone else.

The gun waving in Eloise's face didn't seem to faze her.

"You have to wait for the boss. She's the only one who buys firearms." As she turned away from the armed granny, she adopted an expression so bored it surprised me and, after years of dealing with people whose lifespans were measured in centuries, I knew bored. "Ma-ry!"

Gun-toting Granny's friend put down the fake statuette she'd been admiring and winked at me. "We don't mind waiting. As long as it's not too long. We have a wager to make."

I bet they did. A bauble pawned to pay for one more game of Keno, another sold to place a bet on the Super Bowl. I could see these gals slowly frittering away every possession as they lived out their final years in Sin City. Hell, if I had any inkling my final years would ever come, I might take the same approach.

Mortality means never taking it with you.

After a couple minutes, a heavyset woman trundled up from the back of the shop. Mary Killigrew, the kickass pirate of the 16th century, appeared to be more grandmotherly than her blue-haired customers. At some point she could've been a grandma, but since her only son died sometime in the fifteen hundreds, I was pretty sure no grandbabies would ever bounce on those aged knees.

Mary had been a striking woman. Now her long braid sported more pewter strands than copper. For some reason, her hair going gray made me cringe worse than any other aspect of her slow descent into old age. It reminded me if I'd never become a genie, I'd be dead by now. Or if not dead, pretty damn close to it.

For all the things wrong with becoming a genie, at least I'd never have to see that future come to pass.

Mary never had children during her second chance at mortality. She always said she loved the one she had, but she never wanted more. Still, her appearance was more suited to baking cookies for the grandbabies than shooting canons and trimming sails. An image of the pirate bent over platters of pastries while a dozen kiddies played at her feet leapt to mind. My stifled chuckle brought Mary's bright eyes to bear.

"Be with you in a minute, love." A few minutes with the blue-hairs had them counting their cash. In no time, the ladies were off to place a bet on Cheeky Charlie in the fifth at Santa Anita. Their happy cackles tickled my ear as the door closed.

With pressing pawn business handled, Mary whispered something to her tattooed assistant and nodded to me. Eloise pasted on a fresh disaffected look and began attending to the shop. If I knew Mary, we wouldn't be disturbed.

"It's been too long," the old gal said by way of greeting.

"It's been too busy."

"Ye ain't kiddin'. Come then and rest yer weary self." She let out a lilting laugh better suited to her previous self. "Though when I was still one of the Many, nothing wearied me."

"You had it easier back then."

The smile fell away from her face. "If only ye knew what the past held, ye wouldn't be making such statements, not even in jest."

I closed my mouth and slouched against the doorjamb. Thinking about the life she must've withstood before the industrial age made me feel like a heel. I couldn't imagine how hard her human life had been, let alone life as a genie during mankind's witch hunting years. Maybe someday when I could retire, I'd pick her brains about those dark years. If a someday existed for her. Before too long, Mary would succumb to the humanity she chose to embrace. The thought tunneled into my chest with a pointy stick.

"How have you been?" I asked as Mary lowered herself into her own oversized chair.

"Other than the pains of age, I feel right ducky." She gave a wide smile. The best dentures money could buy gleamed at me. "Although I'd bet me last shiny penny ye haven't come to ask after me health, or have ye? Not going to try and lure me back to the Many, are ye? 'Cause I been too long away to live in yer world again."

"If it'd work, I'd drag you back kicking and screaming."

"Ye'd have to drag me, dearie. As much as this body is achin' and expandin', I'd still need a damn good reason to go back." Mary shifted her weight. The chair groaned in protest. "'Tis a good thing we didn't have so many wondrous flavors of ice cream in my day. I'd never have kept a ship afloat." The old gal laughed and winked at me. "Get it? Ice cream? A float?" When her prodding didn't elicit so much as a twitched lip from me, she shook her head. "Must be awfully dicey out there if ye won't appreciate a good pun."

"Pretty obvious, huh?" The full weight of the past few days settled onto my shoulders. What could've been a happy couple hours reacquainting ourselves turned to shit in an instant.

The smile slid off her face and her mood mirrored my own. "Well, now. What exactly can I do for ye today?"

I pushed away from the doorjamb and settled into a chair opposite my friend. "You've got some really interesting knick-knacks." Suddenly, I was unwilling to discuss my reason for visiting. Instead, I picked up the tiny figure of a mermaid. The little girl winked at me before wiggling her tail and doing a perfect dive into the nearby fish tank. "Is she real?"

"As real as ye and I." Mary shook a finger at me. "But ye're stalling. Out with it."

I swallowed hard. There wasn't any easy way to broach this subject, so I dove in. "I lost a genie today."

Reaching over the desk, she patted my hand. "I expect it's not yer first. No worries. Ye'll catch up to the djinn sooner or later. After all, unless he finds a way to free himself, sooner or later he has to meet with ye, doesn't he?"

My mouth hung open as she spoke. Maybe my direct way hadn't been direct enough. "No, Mary. I don't mean he left before I got there. I didn't misplace him. He didn't walk away." With each word, my voice rose until I almost shrieked the last. "He's dead. His Master killed him."

Mary's hand stilled on my own, then slowly began to clench. If she'd still been one of the Many, she would've snapped every single, little bone in my fingers.

"Mary?" I shifted gears from rising hysteria to concern in a second. I never had much schooling—hell, I didn't even play a doctor on TV—but the color she turned couldn't mean anything good. Pushing loose a little magic, I wished for her health.

A sharp gasp filled my ears as her grip loosened. I wasn't sure which of us made the sound, but she looked more normal, so I didn't really care.

"Better?"

"Ye ever use magic on me without permission again, and it'll be the last time ye're allowed to see me."

"You're welcome." I sat back and she did, too. With one hand, Mary reached toward a shelf above her head. She pulled an ancient fifth of some questionable brown potable down. After uncorking it with her dentures, she took a healthy swig. From her grimace, the stuff had to burn all the way down. Didn't stop her from taking another jolt, though.

"I suppose that's yer smartass way of teachin' me manners?" She pointed one crooked digit at me. "Because I was a lady long before yer damn ancestors set foot on this forsaken continent."

"Simply explaining why you're still breathing. Your heart stopped, you old bitch."

"Freebie wishes don't mean freebie information, ye know."

"Got it." With death's visitation on hold for the foreseeable future, I went after what I came for. "Know what's one good thing about you almost dying? It proved you have information worth paying for. So what'll it be?" Whatever she knew, bad or not, the old pirate wouldn't pass up adding to her booty.

"I didn't say I knew anything."

"I'm a little hurt, Mary. You've never taken me for stupid before. I mention a dead djinn, and you keel over. To me, it means you know something." I reached toward her, but she pulled back like I'd killed Arthur myself. "To use your words, 'out with it'."

Her eyes narrowed. "It'll cost ye."

"I wouldn't expect anything else. How much?" Whatever she wanted, I could afford it, but that wasn't how Mary played the game. If we didn't haggle, the transaction lost its appeal.

"Not money."

"And you always said you didn't want any of my filthy magic." Guilt about throwing her words back in her face hammered at me. But her nearly dying scared me shitless. After years of trying to convince her to let me make her old age easier, I had enough of those words to throw.

"Not to heal me, ye fool. I'm human. I'll take my chances the natural way like any other mortal. But I'm not daft. Genies have more uses than simple wishing, darlin'." A greedy gleam lit her eyes. "Of course, wishes could be what I'll be wanting."

"Easy enough. How about one wish up front and another when you pony up with the information?"

Her head shook slowly. "Only need one." Her grin scared me. "Call it a boon, for now. Might be a wish. Might not. We'll settle the details later."

I hid my cringe. One open-ended bargain from this brigand might get me in deep shit with the Council. Still, I needed her knowledge to stop this from happening again.

"You tell me everything I want to know, and I will give you one boon of your choice at the time of your choosing. Deal?" She spit in her hand and held it out to me. After we shook on it, I wished my hand dry. I understood the concept, but spit is just gross.

"First off," she said, "tell me what happened."

"Long story short, I went on a rescue, got the shit kicked out of me by some creepy dude, and..." I paused to let my next words take on weight. "After this psycho Master made an ungrantable wish, the poor djinn went all thermonuclear on me."

"It's not possible," she said on a hiss of breath.

"I thought you'd say that. But it's true. Poor Arthur Walton's bits are scattered all over a warehouse in Florida."

She made a nasty noise and gulped another hit of liquor. Wiping her mouth with the back of one hand, she slammed the bottle down. Her teeth gritted so hard I would've sworn her expensive dental work would explode. "Not what I meant."

"Then what did you mean?"

She narrowed her rheumy eyes. "Ye're too damn young and yet too damn old to be so damn daft."

"Young? I don't think Ninety—"

"Unless ye been walkin' this earth more than a few centuries, yer young. Get over yerself." Her fingertips tapped on the bottle. "I'd've thought your limited years would've made ye a mite smarter, though."

The slow shake of her head combined with the violent gleam in her eye scared me silent. "Ungrantable wishes certainly can be made and djinn can certainly be killed by them. Mind ye, it ain't the easiest thing to do, but it can be done."

"Then what did you mean when you said it wasn't possible?"

She swallowed another long draught and then offered me some. When I refused, she shook the bottle at me. "Ye sure? Gonna need some liquid spine if I'm to tell ye what I know."

"Tell me. Whatever it is I can take it." Then remembering the old gal's usual policy, I added, "Is this going to cost extra?"

"Not one red cent, love."

Every one of my muscles clenched. Mary haggled for fun. Her giving something for nothing was like me stripping naked and skipping through Times Square. Still, it's never wise to look a gift pirate in the dentures. "Thank you. I guess."

"Don't thank me for the bargain 'til ye've heard me out. Ye might not appreciate what ye'll have to pay in the long run."

"Whatever it is, I'll do it." I didn't care. If Mary's boon was unlimited free wishes? Well, I'd have to deal with breaking the Council's rules if the time came. "This asshole needs to pay for what he did."

"What are ye goin' to do? Kill him?" Mary let out a harsh laugh. "Hell, child, ye'll be the unluckiest genie on the face of this good planet if ye ever cross paths with the bugger again. If he's like the rest of his kind, he's a slippery one, he is."

"The rest of his kind? Come on, Mary. If more of these are running around, wouldn't I know about it by now?"

Her head moved slowly from side to side. "It ain't something the brethren talk about. God's blood, Josephine, they ain't somethin' we dare to *think* about. Might be they're somethin' we have nightmares about. Them what were there the last time." She shuddered and patted one hand at her fermented courage. Light from her desk lamp barely made it through the dirty glass, but I caught enough glimmer to see she'd downed more than half.

I snatched the bottle before she could take another drink. Getting a genie drunk is next to impossible, even when we're trying really, really hard. Our metabolism works too fast to maintain a good buzz. Unfortunately, Mary's humanity meant she would get shitfaced faster than I could drag information out of her.

"Mine. Give 'er back before I turn ye into a newt." She chortled over her lame humor and swiped her hand toward the bottle. I jerked it farther from her grasp.

"When you tell me what you're talking about, then you can have it back." Her lips drew into a pout that would've made any man crumble when she was in her prime. On her aging lips, the expression came across as pathetic. "Sorry, but I need you sober. You can drink yourself into a stupor after I leave."

"Promises, promises."

"Do I need to start pouring coffee down your throat or can we do this the easy way?"

She shuddered at the thought of the dark brew I lived on. "Wish me up some tea and we'll give it a go." Before she could draw another breath, a cup of chamomile steamed in front of her. After a short sip, she let out a long sigh.

"Ye want to know what yer up against, do ye?"

"We'd be sharing a better bottle of liquor than that rotgut if I didn't, so yeah."

Threading her hands over her ample waist, she stared into my eyes. "I think ye've run afoul of an Efreet."

A passage from some old mythology book jumped into my head. "You mean evil genies?"

"Yes. And no. Efreet, well, they was once part of the Many, but now they ain't." She reached toward the booze, but let her hand drop into her lap. "It's compli... compli..."

"Complicated?"

"Ye got that right."

"What about this life isn't complicated?" Though my djinn existence had been short, it didn't seem possible I still labored under a boatload of ignorance. Talk about complicating things.

Another sip of tea had her staring longingly at the liquor. "Gone cold already. Be a love and tweak the heat up a little."

I let a small wish fly and steam rose from her cup again. "Last freebie until you tell me what the hell Efreet are. They aren't djinn, but they used to be?" She gave a curt nod before burying her lips in the cup. "What does that even mean?"

She shrugged without looking up.

"Well, if they're like this guy, then they're evil, right?"

"Got it in one." Her eyes focused behind me like the killer lurked there. I had to steel myself to keep from glancing back. "If ye ask me, Efreet are the foulest things ever created. Others? Some of the brethren don't agree, mind ye, but they didn't live through what I did." Her face paled again and this time her thick shoulders trembled. "They wasn't there, I tell ye."

"Who wasn't where?"

"Them knows-it-all folks who think we did wrong. They wasn't the ones fightin' in the last war." Her eyes fell on the liquor with such longing I gave in.

"Just a sip." I pushed the bottle toward her. "Then you tell me what you know minus the hemming and hawing." Mary's nip lasted a whole lot longer than I wanted. Still, after she wiped her lips, she relented.

"Century before last," she began, "them Efreet was runnin' amok. Sure, we done a fair job bearding the blasted things. Had to keep their kind from bleedin' takin' over, doncha know. Those beasties don't breed so much as *appear*. Ye can't keep up with 'em. I remember when—"

"Mary. Focus."

"Right." Her next slug of booze left me cringing. At this rate, she'd be blotto before she fulfilled her side of the bargain. "Most djinn, they was contented to hide in their bottles and lamps and bits of jewelry, hoping the Efreet'd leave 'em alone." More liquor disappeared down her throat and I doubted my decision to give the bottle back. For the moment, though, the booze lubricated her tongue.

"Back in the day, when the dark ones picked off our brothers like some damn bunch of dodos, we put together a council of sorts. Probably the pre... the pre... the start of the Council you hate so much. We meant to put an end to their havoc. The war lasted damn near a decade, but we got every last one of the bastards." She sat back and folded her hands over her belly. "Peace at last. Or so we was thinkin'."

How anyone could've overlooked Mr. Creepy-Goatee baffled me. In fact, I couldn't fathom why I'd never *heard* of anyone else seeing him before I had the misfortune.

"Where's he been hiding all these years?" I pondered out loud. "He sticks out like a Dayglo Mennonite."

Mary's huff of breath ended in a hacking cough. I marshaled all my willpower to keep from turning her back into a genie. Instead, I pushed another wish her way. *Simply to ease her breathing.*

"Cut it out." Her first good breath was wasted on bitching at me. "If it ain't asked for, it don't count toward yer bill, ye know."

"You already said that, you scheming old bat, but I can't get information if you can't talk. Now that you can talk, spill. And Mary," I said, "no more stalling."

"How'd he stay hidden since the last sortie?" The way she repeated my questions made me doubt her interest in answering.

"You heard me. Start talking or I'll buy my information elsewhere."

From the gleam in her greedy little eyes, she recognized my bluff. I didn't have other options. And I would give this old brigand everything I owned before I bent over to Zeke again. To my surprise, her pirate heart must not have been into seeing me either humiliated or destitute. At least not yet.

"The answer is..." Another long swig of brown liquor passed her lips. "He weren't hidin'. He didn't exist at the time. Leastwise not as an Efreet."

She had to be jerking my chain.

"I told you. Them things just appear. One day yer best mate is a genie. The next he's gone an' turned into one of them blasted beasties."

"But how?"

One heavy shoulder lifted as she hiccupped. "No one quite knows. As many of them ye do away with, they come springin' back out of the best djinn. And whether he was yer bestie or not don't matter. Ye just... Well, ye does what ye has to do." A fat tear escaped from between her clenched eyelids.

I understood. Pirate loyalty ran deep. She'd fight her enemies to the end of death itself to protect her friends. Her fighting her friends, even after they'd turned into something she hated, had to have been inconceivable.

"Please tell me you didn't—"

She waved a hand. "The Rules, love. They ain't changed, have they? No, I didn't kill no one. None of us did. How could we with the First Rule tying our bleedin' hands? But sometimes... Sometimes I think we did them blokes a turn so much worse." Letting out a sob, she wrapped her hands around the bottle and drained the remains.

"I can't do this again, Jo. I'm too old." Tossing the empty in one corner where it burst into a thousand shards, she began softly sobbing. "All them scurvy dogs be damned," she mumbled before passing out.

I checked her pulse. The beat felt a lot stronger than I assumed. *Must've put more oomph into the healing wish than I meant.* Once I made sure tattooed Eloise could handle the shop without Mary, I used the last of my batteries to wish myself home. Or at least I assumed I was headed home. When I opened my eyes, I got another of the many shocks I'd received recently.

I wasn't in my garage back home. Not even close. Judging from the mountains rising behind the opulent gardens, I'd arrived *somewhere* in Colorado. How far I landed from my actual destination exceeded my mapping skills.

Which is what I get for flying off half-charged.

"Fancy meeting you here," said a voice I would rather have forgotten. And when I turned toward it, I remembered his voice wasn't the only part of the package I wanted to forget. Zeke's smug grin alone reminded me why I'd spent the better part of three decades wiping him out of my life.

Pressed against the molding of an open patio door, he adopted the appearance of someone who hadn't had a care in the world since before the pyramids rose. Of course, I knew better. On the outside, he was all long lines and bedroom smiles, but behind his promise of pleasure lay snares of steel wire.

Snares I swore I'd escaped long ago.

Those tales of demon women who entrance men and drag them to their doom? Zeke is my djinn equivalent. One look in those smoldering eyes and every one of my female molecules turned to marshmallow fluff. Hell, despite knowing what I know about him, I wanted to dive off the jagged ledge of our shared past into the welcoming future those depths promised.

Sunuvabitch. After all the hurtful things we'd said to each other, he still had me thinking like a bad romance novel. The bastard.

Steeling myself against the onslaught of what could only be leftover lust, I clenched my jaws until my back teeth ached. "What's the big idea?"

"Hello to you, too, Babydoll. Long time, no see."

"Not long enough." I pulled together as much power as I could muster. I couldn't deliver more than the djinn equivalent of a left hook, but if the best I had amounted to a sock to the jaw, I'd live with it. I hoped. Letting the wish fly free, I watched as his head rocked back before adding, "And I told you never to call me Babydoll."

NINE

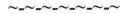

Blood trickled from the corner of Zeke's mouth as he moved one measured step forward. I had nothing left to defend myself, but I stood my ground. As powerful as he was, he could grind me into a fine film and spread me on a cracker any time he wanted. But hell, if he wanted to mess me up, he could've shifted my teleport into a volcano instead of a garden spot.

"Not the brightest thing you've ever done, Ba-by-doll." The extra emphasis on the hated nickname had to be because he knew damn well I couldn't do anything about it. For now. He'd get his later. "For all you know, I could be the killer."

I swallowed hard. For the briefest moment, I considered whether what he intimated was possible, and then I inhaled. The smell wafting through the garden was all Zeke, from the strong odor of Egyptian coffee to the whiff of a baby-soft leather jacket I used to cuddle against. I could even smell a hint of ozone after a summer storm. Exactly like the last night we'd spent together. The night we spent making love, and then fighting. Right before we went our separate ways.

A wicked grin crossed his face like he knew the path my thoughts had taken. The bastard.

"You're still taking life way too seriously, Josie." A snifter of brandy appeared. He held it out to me. When I refused, he lifted the glass to his mouth. "I don't blame you for refusing anything I offer, but why shouldn't you have a drink? You've had one hell of a week, from what I gather."

Since I could count the people who knew about my week on one hand, my suspicions went into overdrive. Not much of a push needed there. On the verge of a full-blown outburst, I hogtied my emotions. Zeke always pushed my buttons. In more ways than one.

"What do you think you know about any of this?"

He shook his head, giving the sunlight a chance to play across tight, black curls the right size for threading around my fingers. "If you ever returned my calls, you'd already know what I know."

"Which is?" I shook off my envy that the sun could touch him and I couldn't.

Zeke clicked his tongue. "Patience, Josie. You haven't taken the time to apologize for blowing me off." His double entendre made me want to slap the smug right off him.

Same ol', same ol'. Once upon a time, his veiled innuendo amused me. I attributed it to part of his charm. Then I grew up.

"You haven't changed. Your mind's still in the gutter."

"Ah, but that's where you're wrong. Well, at least on one point." He shot me an exaggerated wink. "But then again, you've spent too many years gazing at me through sludge-colored glasses." He swept his hand to encompass our surroundings. "If I was still the same man, the one you once referred to as 'shiftless', I wouldn't have all this."

Before I could blink, we stood in a cozy study, complete with crackling logs in the hearth. As his hand passed over the fire, the outside view of a glass and steel palace in the mountains appeared.

Not a huge stretch of the imagination to know it was his home. After all, it looked exactly like the daydreams we'd shared about the home we'd someday build. It didn't matter anymore now than all those years ago. Our shared past was long gone and we were better off.

"Don't give me that shit." I demolished his happy-home illusion with a puff of power. "What you gain by wishing doesn't count. It never did." I remembered the cedar lodge we lived in during our last year together. Back then I still enjoyed the fruits our wishes created and believed work belonged to fools and mortals. Until one day I realized nothing about my life was real. We were living a fairy-story for grownups. The minute we stopped believing in it, and in each other, reality hit like a bag of wet dirt. Our gorgeous home turned back into the fallow farm he'd usurped for our pleasure.

And Zeke went from the doting lover to a gadabout even my mother would've been ashamed of.

"True," he said. "But I'm a changed man. These are the fruits of my actual labor."

"You? Labor?" I stifled a chuckle as I remembered I didn't have the juice to piss this bad boy off. Whatever Zeke thought of himself now, he always had more power than I did. Goading a being who can turn you into a mosquito and then break out the DDT is never a good idea.

"Ever heard of B.A. Security?" he asked, looking smug.

I inclined my head. Of course I'd heard of the largest private personal security company west of the Mississippi. Who hadn't?

Antiques dealers and their clients brought B.A. bodyguards to protect them while they attended our auctions. Still, I didn't see—

"Think, Josie. B? A?"

My jaw dropped. What I'd read about the firm never mentioned the owner's name. If I remembered correctly, the articles painted the CEO as some kind recluse. *Zeke? Reclusive?* He had to be pulling my chain.

"Despite the rumors, B.A. doesn't stand for 'bad ass'," he said, like butter wouldn't dare to soften in his mouth. "Regardless of my letting people assume so."

"Ri-ight." If he owned a Fortune 500 company, I'd get a job as a burro's behind. "Very convenient. Easy enough to borrow a company whose initials match your own."

Zeke didn't blink at my thick sarcasm. Then again, in the old days, he called sarcasm my favorite defense mechanism. From the tilt of his eyebrow, he remembered those heated exchanges, too.

"Feel free to look at the prospectus. We filed with the SEC when we went public last year. From what my herd of accountants tell me, our stock's starting to rival Google."

"I bet." As soon as I got back to the office, I planned to sic Basil on the task. If Zeke was telling the truth, he really had changed. Except he couldn't have. Seeing Ezekiel ben Aron as a stable, productive member of society would throw the reasons I denied myself of his presence *for years* into ruin.

"How's Mayweather Antiquities doing these days?" he said.

"Not in the same league as B.A. Security, if that's what you're asking. Of course, 'genie rescue services' isn't in the yellow pages." He may be making the bigger bucks, but my work was important. The thought may have been petty, but I couldn't let him win.

"People don't use a phonebook anymore, Babydoll."

His smile had my righteous indignation struggling to survive. The way his grins extended to every facial muscle got me every time. This guy had me spitting mad one moment and turning into bodice-ripper heroine the next.

Of course, celibacy does strange things to even the best gal. Before the memory of my last night in Zeke's arms could push into my head, I snipped that line of thinking. I so did not need all my positive memories to creep out of the box I'd stuffed them into.

"Cut the crap, Zeke." My best 'superbitch' tone didn't appear to faze him. "Tell me what possessed you to hijack my teleport."

I half-expected him to laugh. Instead his features darkened. "You refuse to meet with me otherwise."

"Make an appointment."

"I have. You never keep them."

He had me there. Whenever I saw him on my calendar, I tried to fake a quick case of the flu. Of course, he recognized my lame excuses, since djinn anatomy kicks germy ass.

"You limited my choices to a brief kidnapping or storming the walls of your fortress. I've never been crazy about full frontal assaults. I'm a lover not a warrior." He let his words linger in the air as he swirled the thick liquid in its snifter. "Sure you don't want a nip? It's the best Napoleon money can buy."

"Now I know you're pulling my leg. You seriously paid for something?" One of our relationship sticking points—one of several dozen, if memory served—hinged on his need to wish for everything. It reminded me of Reggie's urge to steal even when he had money. Neither man cared to earn a goddamn thing. Both did what they wanted and consequences were too damn bad. I joyfully coveted the idea when I was young, but I'd matured past it.

"How's the weather in your fantasy world, Ezekiel?"

"Excellent. How's it in yours?"

I'd had about enough. "Tell me what you want so I can leave. In case you haven't thought about anyone but yourself, I have work to do."

"Your work is exactly why you're here. I have information about your killer."

Against my better judgment, hope bubbled in my chest. "What do you know about the Efreet?"

He lowered his head. "Let me guess, Mary decided bartering gained her more than keeping her trap shut."

My ex and the pirate never shared a fondness for each other. Good thing Mary sat well protected in her store. Otherwise, Zeke could reduce her to a few cells floating in a Petri-dish somewhere. To my surprise, the anger I expected to boil over never bothered to simmer. Maybe he had changed. A little.

He shook himself, as if dislodging any lingering irritation. When he spoke again, he'd become a more tepid version of himself. "And I wanted to impress you with my insider information skills."

"A modern knight charging to the rescue with data instead of a pig-sticker?" I asked, unable stop goading him. Too bad my zing turned on me, leaving the image of him on a white charger firmly entrenched in my head. Damn Evangeline and all those fairytales she read to my impressionable young self.

When Zeke answered, all emotion had been stripped from his voice. "Something to that effect. I shouldn't be surprised Mary would out-do me. How much did she charge?"

"I don't know yet." My face heated. Making an open-ended bargain with Mary epitomized dim-witted, but saying it out loud made me want to smack myself upside the head with a brick.

To his credit, Zeke only inclined his head at me. "Just how much information did she give for this future golden prize?"

"Not nearly enough." I adopted Mary's accent for a moment. "*The Efreet are abominations!* Which seems likely since the mere thought of them had Mary drinking herself blind."

He actually had the nerve to scoff at me. "Human or no, the pirate can still out-drink most men."

"You didn't see her pounding down some old bottle." Zeke's laughter shut me up quick. I felt stupid enough. I didn't need him laughing at me on top of it.

"The brown one?" He arched an eyebrow. "Did you try it?"

"Oh hell no."

"It's an old concoction from near the beginning of this country. It's distilled from the bark of some tree. It's for her arthritis." He scratched his chin. "I'm pretty sure we call it *aspirin* now."

"Sunuvabitch. She tricked me." I could compete for world's biggest dunce. "Why? Why would she fake being drunk? I only needed a little information. I was more than willing to pay for it."

"Ah, but you asked for information that encroached on a forbidden subject."

"You mean the Efreet? She seemed willing enough at first, although her explanation wasn't too clear."

""First off, talking about the Efreet is akin to discussing sex and religion in proper human society. It's simply not done." He let out a wry chuckle. "You asked questions we aren't allowed to ask. You're lucky she told you anything. Tell me what you asked right before she faked her inebriation?"

"I wondered how this Efreet showed up if the brethren supposedly wiped them out. Or maybe she went limp after I asked how you got rid of them. You know, since the Rules forbid killing."

"Ah."

That's all I got. He just sat there looking wise—probably to force me to figure this out myself. I've always hated when he did that. "So she faked me out. She had me thinking she'd freaked out enough to pickle her brain."

"She probably did freak out. Most likely she feigned unconsciousness to make you bugger off without losing a customer. I'm sure if she could've gotten drunk off her ass, she would've, but the old bat's tolerance is too high. You could've badgered her all day before it kicked in for real."

"The sneaky bit—"

"Cut her some slack, Babydoll," he said, giving my anger a new person to latch onto. "Isn't there a part of your life you'd rather not discuss? I don't blame her for bailing on you. I would've done the same." He raised his damn eyebrow again. "If memory serves, so would you. Avoidance was your M.O. of choice."

Asshole. Referring to the night we parted was a low blow. Thank the gods, I hadn't told him all the other disappointing scenes from my life, like the night I fucked up and Reggie died. No way had I ever mentioned the depths to which Stavros' not-so-gentle tutelage sunk me, or the number of lost human lives I chalked up to my ignorance. I know I never told a soul about my husband. Not even Mena. Benny's death bought me my freedom, but I would carry his sacrifice to my own grave. Along with my guilt. Which in terms of genie longevity basically meant eternity.

Or, with a killer running around, next week.

All of this talk of Mary and mistakes sidetracked me. A fact Zeke counted on, I was certain. Shoving my memories back where they belonged, I focused on the information I needed from my ex.

"So. This war? Was she using it to avoid the truth again or was it real?"

His eyes never left my face, though he wasn't really seeing me anymore. "Oh, it was very real."

"Were you part of it?"

"Let's say I was around then, but otherwise occupied."

"You mean you played the part of Switzerland, right?" *Typical Zeke. Wait until you know who'll win before offering your loyalty.*

"Believe what you choose. If it's easier for you to believe the worst of me, I can live with that." He shook his head. "I've lived with it for this long."

I didn't know what game my old boyfriend was playing, but it knocked me sideways. I always expected when I finally ran into him again, he'd be exactly the same. But the old Zeke never gave in so easily. Somehow this newer, calmer, more centered Ezekiel scared me.

But I couldn't waste time figuring him out.

No matter how sociable he tried to make this, I had to remember I wasn't paying a social call. Knowing Zeke currently had both the AC cranked and the fire stoked should've reminded me of his true nature. In short, the same egocentric ass as always.

"How about we stop dancing around what we think of each other? Tell me why I'm here."

He impaled me with a glance. "I wanted to keep you from walking into a steaming pile of something you don't understand. Direct enough for you?"

Considering how many so-called certainties were unraveling like a cheap sweater around me, I couldn't imagine what else I'd uncover before turning into a big puddle of moron.

Reggie believed in two kinds of marks: the ignorant and the truly stupid. The ignorant can't help themselves, some things they just don't know. The stupid don't care and act like they know everything.

"So explain it to me," I said. "And use small words."

"How long do you have?"

As if on cue, my cell phone turned the TicTacs in my pocket into a mariachi band. *Echo & the Bunnymen* meant only one thing. "It's Baz. Hang on."

I flipped the phone open. "I'm in the middle of something."

"Duarte's on the rampage. He says if you don't..." Basil cleared his throat, adopting the tone we used to mock the senior Council member. "...contact him forthwith, there will be... How shall I put it? Hell to pay."

"I don't have time for his crap, Baz. Tell him I'll call him..." I acquired the same tone. "...post haste. Or as soon as I return to my domicile."

"That won't put him off, love. Something wound his watch extra tight today. I wouldn't brush the bloke off if I were you." I could hear Basil tapping an appointment into my calendar. We both knew I'd ignore it, but now he'd have plausible deniability.

"I don't suppose you could tell—"

"I've told him all he'll accept from *your servant*. Of course, we know how Iago Duarte feels about *the lower classes*."

"Fine. I'll wrap this up. Hold the fort until I get back."

"Not a problem."

With a quick thanks, I ended the call.

"Everything okay?"

I raised an eyebrow. "You almost sound like you care. You must have gotten better at faking it." Even to my own ears, I sounded like a bitch, but playing nice would take too much effort. "Anyway, it's nothing major, but I do need to get back to the office."

We weren't done. Not by a long shot. He'd give me the information I wanted. If not now, then as soon as I fixed Duarte's super-snug tightie-whities.

"This isn't finished," he said, echoing my thoughts.

"You could always tag along." Apparently, my self-preservation wasn't connected to my mouth yet. Still, with the offer out there, I couldn't suck the words back. No matter how much I wanted to. Zeke's jaw hanging open only goaded my stubborn streak.

"Wouldn't you be more comfortable finishing later? I'll supply the gin." The firelight glinted off a slight chip in his front tooth. Sudden memories of the flaw nicking along my throat sent blood rushing to places I was pretty certain had shriveled up. "I could fix a cozy dinner. We can chat afterwards."

Right. Food, wine, cuddling. Just like old times. Like I need those.

"Either come with me now," I said, crushing the imagery, "or be interrogated later. No dinner. Talk only. Take it or leave it, Ezekiel."

His wink told me I'd fallen right into his plans. "Whatever you say, Josephine."

TEN

~-~-~-~-~-~-~

I expected Zeke to wish us both to the warehouse. I guess it wasn't my day for having expectations met. Before I recovered, Zeke hurried me down several shadowed hallways and through a door. I had no clue what he was up to, but as the lights came on, my certainty took another blow.

Somewhere along the way, Zeke became a car buff. The garage I found myself in had to be bigger than my whole cave. Hell, if I had to guess, I'd say it occupied more square footage than Coors Field.

"Jesus," I said as we passed row after row of automobiles. "A Deusenberg? My father had one exactly like it." Zeke didn't bother checking it out. He probably had so many cars he didn't remember the individual models. "Let me guess. They're either not exactly yours, or they're not exactly real."

"Oh, they're real." He thumped the hood of some sporty, Italian thing. "And they're very much mine. Who else would store their belongings in my home?"

I didn't want to think about who Zeke might allow in his home, let alone which of them would keep their things there. Could be Zeke supported an entire harem somewhere in this mammoth building—both djinn and human. I kept my mouth closed for a change. Ezekiel ben Aron might look like a typical guy but he was a powerful being with the libido to match. How he quenched it these days wasn't any of my business. In the end, his love life didn't matter to me one whit.

And if I kept telling myself I didn't care, I might make it true.

As he stopped beside a brand new Hummer, I pushed his sex life out of my head. "This is your idea of transportation in the human world?"

"The president and CEO of a major company must live up to certain expectations, but if you prefer, we could take the Jag." He jerked a thumb toward a line of German autos. "Chose whatever you'd prefer to ride in. Trust me, this is infinitely more comfortable."

All those cars made my Taurus look like a rolling junk pile. "No. That's okay. This'll be fine." I walked to the passenger door. "I guess when you throw this much money around, you get whatever you want. Right?"

He shrugged. "Why have money if you don't spend it on what you love?"

His words sent a shiver down my legs. He spent years showering me with gifts he never paid for. Maybe if he'd bought a few things instead of wishing them into existence. But no. If I was honest with myself, we'd been headed for trouble, power or not. Sure, part of our break-up had to do with a gorgeous, diamond necklace he pulled out of nothingness to honor what he called our 'pressed coal' anniversary. Since we hadn't been together anywhere near seventy-five years, that got the ball rolling. The rest of the fight focused on my need to do something productive with my eternity and his need to *not*. He knew this mission of mine floated around my head for years, yet when I finally wanted to make it a reality, he laughed at me.

Three hours of yelling later, I walked away.

"If you'd like, turn on the radio." His words broke into the head of steam I was rebuilding after all those years. The part of me that wanted to resume the fight where we left it was thoroughly cheesed-off. "I believe one of those satellite providers comes standard with this model. We can test it out."

"You never listen to the radio?"

"I've never driven this car before."

Figures.

"Actually, since we have some time on the drive, why wait to start talking?" I said.

His nod coincided with the engine roaring to life. "My thoughts exactly, but it'll take longer than this drive."

"It would be a start."

His breath came out in one resigned huff. "You have to remember. Once opened, some doors won't shut again."

"I can take it."

"As long as you don't blame the messenger."

Cheap shot. Even if he was right. I hadn't wanted to hear some of the things we yelled at each other all those years ago. And I blamed the messenger to a certain extent.

"I promise to reserve blame until all the facts are in," I said. "And since you're driving, I'll hold any sucker punches."

Silence stretched while the Hummer gathered miles. The stillness accumulated like snow, lying so thick that when he finally spoke, I jumped.

"I believe you inquired about the steaming pile of—"

"Yeah, yeah. Steaming pile of Efreet. They can't all be as bad as the asshole I stumbled across. Can they?"

"Further proof you don't understand what you're poking your nose into." His fingers gripped the steering wheel tight, turning his knuckles white. For the first time, he lost his razor-edged focus on his driving. The bellowing of a tractor trailer pulled him back.

"Maybe we better wait until later." I didn't need to waste the next few days' worth of accumulated power healing multiple fractures.

"Might've been a good idea," he said, "but this conversation is best held where your guests can't eavesdrop. So it's either now or so much later—

"It'll be too late to do any good." I cast a glance his way. His knuckles weren't white anymore, which was good, but he still looked too tense. In the old days, I would've rubbed his shoulders, which often led to things best left to those old days. "I can't believe these Efreet thingies scare the crap out of genies like you. Me, I get. I'm a sparkler by comparison. Aren't you like the top of the supernatural food chain?"

"If you really think so, we need a longer talk."

"I'm kidding." I lied, but he didn't need to know that. "So they're pretty bad ass?"

"Our fear of them has less to do with how bad-ass they are than what they potentially represent." I opened my mouth, but he thundered on. "The brethren last spotted an Efreet in the nineteenth century. At least as far as any of us knows. If this new sighting is any indication, Babydoll, they could've been here all along."

"So, whoever saw them, what? Kept quiet?" I considered the idea and added, "Or preceded Arthur Walton into the dark?"

"One can hope any witnesses aren't, in fact, dead but..." Zeke gave a one shoulder shrug. "...we have no way of knowing. Too many djinn have disappeared over the course of the centuries. These Efreet? Unfortunately, no one knows exactly where they come from, so we can't exactly look out for them."

"Mary's theory is they're djinn who'd turned evil somehow. Is that possible?"

"Almost anything is possible with magic, Josie. You know as well as any of us." He waved a hand to encompass Denver in the distance. "None of them has any idea what we are or what we do, unless it's because of an old myth."

"Or some damn kiddy movie."

"Exactly. Our history with them isn't comparable to some jovial blue guy versus a deranged red guy. It's... The closest analogy is The Civil War."

"Brother fighting brother? Mary intimated as much. Still, I can't see anyone claiming Super-Psycho as a sibling."

Zeke changed lanes before he answered. Once the Hummer headed straight again, he said, "He could've been anyone's brother at one time. Hell, he could've been someone's father before he became what he is now. What we were as mortals isn't necessarily who we are now. Look at you."

"What's that supposed to mean?" I shot him a sidelong glance. "Except for a few improvements and a little aging to keep the humans guessing, I'm who I always was."

A short laugh burst from him as he navigated around a delivery van. "You can't believe you're the same empty-headed flapper you were in 1924."

"I was never—" The truth wouldn't let me finish my protest. "What would you know about it? You weren't there."

"All our pillow talk, Jo? I listened. Did you?"

His words brought back memories I'd stuffed deep in my subconscious. Sweat-slick sheen glistening on his olive skin as we dozed after hours of passion. Words spoken in short gasps until our bodies relaxed into drowsy companionship. The lazy chats afterwards, drifting from one topic to the next.

"I was listening, but it's all in the past." *And I'd appreciate it if you never brought it up again.*

"All of this is in the past. Your past and my past and the past of us all. It's there in history and it's here in the now."

I let his words tumble over me. I didn't want them to be true, but they were. Reggie always taught me to believe the past was something best left behind. *Always move forward, Josephine. There's nothing new to see back there.* But he never told me how much the past could shape me.

"Tell me about the war." My statement echoed into the silence. Zeke didn't answer until he pulled the Hummer onto northbound I-25 and merged with the downtown traffic.

"Truth be told, there isn't much I can tell. Djinn-kind discarded millennia of solitude to band together against the Efreet menace."

"The Efreet menace? You're kidding me. It's like the lead-in for a bad B-movie."

"The phrase worked for us until the culture created a list of clichés to avoid," he said. "Every day, more brethren flowed into their ranks, and we had no clue how to stop the hemorrhage. The only answer was to cut out the disease and cauterize the wound."

"But Mary said the First Rule stopped you from killing them."

He goosed the accelerator. "Exactly. No harm to others," he said, citing one of the First Rule's many interpretations. "With their hands tied, the djinn dealt with the Efreet the only way we... *they* could with their combined power. A hundred brethren tracked down a score or so of Efreet. Then the djinn wished them into a form where they couldn't do any real harm."

"So, transformation instead of death." Made perfect sense to me. I don't know if I could kill someone unless they tried to kill me first, and even then, I'd still have to wonder. "But what were they transformed into? Rocks?"

Zeke shook his head. "Organic material transforms into organic material.

"Trees?"

"I wish. No." Spearing me with a sidelong glance, he said, "Maybe if you'd been around to suggest it, this whole thing would've gone better."

"So? What happened?"

"In retrospect, it sounds foolish, but..." His answer hung so long I could've screamed.

After the Hummer gobbled miles like I eat peanuts, I finally had enough. "Damn it, Zeke."

"Dogs," he spat out louder than I expected. "Okay? The Efreet transformed into dogs."

He didn't twitch a muscle. Every one of them was clenched anyway, whether in anger or embarrassment, I couldn't quite figure. "Between the Efreet's hatred for the canine species and the slur of being called a cur, we thought spending eternity on four paws was poetic justice." He shook his head. "Or irony. Like I said, looking back it sounds foolish."

I tried to hide my disbelief, but Zeke's withering gaze meant I failed miserably.

"Cut your elders some slack, Babydoll."

"You'd have a better shot at getting slack if you stopped calling me 'Babydoll', you know." As I tried to get past the nickname he would *not* quit using, the pieces fell into place. "Elders, hell. If someone else made the decision, you'd join me in teasing them. The dog thing? Your idea. Right?"

I swear Zeke never blushed before, but he turned pink right down to his collar.

"Seriously, Ezekiel? Turning them into dogs was your best idea?"

Before he could answer, a little German aluminum can whipped across three lanes to cut us off. Jerking the wheel and slamming on the brakes saved us, but Zeke's *Fast and Furious* moves didn't save his blood pressure. One whisper under his breath turned the maniac sports car from a wonder of automotive engineering to a roadside car-be-que. The human occupants scrambled out as we flew past.

"What if someone saw?" I didn't want to think about what the Council might do if they caught him using his magic so blatantly.

"No one saw anything." He nodded at the traffic. "They're all too focused on the little dramas in their short lives."

I looked. Not one head turned. Even the occupants weren't fazed by their sudden change in reality. They paced the roadside like nothing had happened, typing furiously into their Blackberries and kicking their too-expensive tires.

As Zeke slowed toward a pending traffic jam, he winked at me. One instant we were on the freeway, the next we were on Highway 36 headed into the mountains.

"Same old, Zeke. When the Council catches you—"

"*If* they catch me. *If.* And they won't. The Council won't act if they never find out, and humanity is too blind to the wonders around them to notice."

"Not all of them."

"Ah, but you assume they're individuals. Take those people back on the freeway. Those weren't individuals. That, my darling, was a herd. If one individual sees me, he'll notice my tricks every time. Putting the same man into a herd makes him oblivious." He gave me another wink. "Try it, Josie. It's both fun and depressing at the same time."

I shook my head. Whether because of his antics or to clear away the massive headache building behind my eyes, I didn't know. "I'll take your word for it. Now, if you're done stalling. Or were you misdirecting there? I can never tell. Either way, answer my question."

"You had a question?"

My breath escaped in a frustrated rush. "You known damn well I did. You suggested the 'let's turn our enemies into pooches' thing, didn't you?" As the words tumbled from my lips, I knew. It represented the kind of twisted logic Zeke found amusing.

"The brethren needed a solution," he said, "and I provided one. The best solution possible under the circumstances, I think. Especially when you consider the amount of power required to capture and transform one Efreet." His fingers tapped along the leather armrest. "You see, power of that magnitude weakened three of us for every one transformation. Genies became easy prey for any Efreet still on two legs, and they used every advantage. A lot of good people died during those years."

"Years?"

"Well, you didn't think hunting the Efreet was easy, did you?"

I pondered the things Zeke said, but I still couldn't explain why no one ever bothered to mention the Efreet before. And it sure didn't tell me why Zeke acted so cagey about the subject.

"Think about it, Josie," he said as though he'd read my thoughts. "I said we cut the wound and then—"

"Cauterized." All at once, I understood his meaning. During those times, knowledge wasn't power. It scared people. They feared knowledge actually caused bad things to happen. In this case, the Many must've assumed too much information about the Efreet might cause a genie to become one.

"I get why they kept it a secret then," I said, "but this is now. You know, the age of 'knowledge is power'? We could've built a database on these things decades ago."

"Old habits are hard to break."

"And djinn habits are some of the oldest."

From that standpoint, Zeke's theory sounded plausible.

"We're here," Zeke said before I could continue my questioning. I shot him a look telling him the conversation wasn't over. To my relief, he nodded. Apparently, the secrecy train finally decided to grind to a halt.

I didn't know how the rest of the brethren would feel about it, but I was getting off here.

ELEVEN

~_~_~_~_~_~_~

From the meat-market expression on Renee's face, Zeke's long and lean frame was just her type. Not that I blamed her. When I first glimpsed him, I must've had the same look on my face.

Wandering down a Soho street in 1972, I caught Zeke studying a splatter of color on a bright yellow canvas. The damn thing hurt my brain, but the man standing next to it made staring worth the headache. He glanced one way and then the next before the abstract painting turned into a pastoral scene worthy of Vermeer. In an instant, I sensed his djinn-ness and fell in love.

Now Renee gazed into those dark eyes with the same adoration I'm sure once graced my own face. And from the twinkle in Zeke's eyes, he wouldn't mind a quickie with my pleasantly padded receptionist.

"Renee?"

Her eyes never left him. "Hi, Jo."

I edged past my unwanted companion, throwing an elbow at his ribs. "Anything come for me?" Her hand fluttered toward the edge of her desk. "Earth to Renee. Messages?"

The woman shook her strawberry blonde curls, finally recognizing Zeke had company. "I'm so sorry. I don't know what..." She stammered like a school kid reading a book report aloud. "I mean—"

"I know exactly what you mean." After years of tolerating many such limp-eyed gazes at my then-boyfriend, her reaction didn't surprise me. Irritated me, maybe, but not surprised. Zeke's not Hollywood hot. He's too angular. And he's too wiry to meet the new pretty-boy molds. Still, he's just, I don't know. *Smokin'*. Add in the confidence he wears like a second skin and most women can't help but be enthralled. Or maybe the pheromones Mediterranean men seem to leak from their pores causes this reaction. His easy smile and those bedroom eyes never failed to make him a Pied Piper for the female set. One thing's certain, at one time, I would've followed him anywhere.

"Renee?" I tried again to chisel past my receptionist's wall of lust. "Where's Basil?"

She sighed. "Basil's looking for you again."

Oh gods, she drank the Kool-Aid.

"I know. He's the reason I'm back. Where is he currently located?"

"Not in his office. Umm, Jo?" She inclined her head toward Zeke. "Are you going to introduce us?"

"Not really." I tried to nudge Zeke away, but he wasn't having any of it. He held out a hand toward my employee. When she mimicked the gesture, he grasped her fingers like he held the most delicate rose, and placed a soft kiss on her wrist. I could've slapped him and fired her.

"Just call him 'Ben'." The venom leaking past my self-control shocked me a little, but I hid it well enough.

"Ben?" His voice was honey dipped in ecstasy. The bastard.

Renee slid her hand away from his. "*This* is the guy you told me about?"

"Don't let the rumors cloud your judgment, Sweet. What's past has passed." He held out his hand once more and, like a damn robot, she put her fingers daintily into his. "Ezekiel ben Aron, at your most humble service. But please, call me Zeke."

Renee giggled. *She actually giggled.* I could've smacked her in the back of the head if it would get her brain back on track. Instead, I tapped the arm now touching my former lover.

"Umm, hate to break this up, but *Basil?*"

"Oh. Yeah." She waved her free hand toward the back. "He said something about cataloguing a special collection with Mena. If he's not there, let me know and I'll page him for you."

Whatever Basil had going on, I now knew it had nothing to do with Duarte's pissy attitude. Our code meant the problem resided in the vault. I shot Zeke a glare and tugged him away from Renee's soft hands.

"Thanks," I said. "I'll find him." Gripping his gray silk sleeve, I pulled my ex from the reception area. Barely in time, from the looks of it. Any longer and our front desk would be covered in adoring gal drool. I love Renee like a second cousin, and there's no way I'd let her follow the twisted road I'd already traveled. Talk about sloppy seconds.

As I led Zeke through the façade of Mayweather Antiquities, I couldn't help but notice his smirk, as if he found our hasty departure amusing. He assumed jealousy was the reason. I couldn't wait to show him the error of assuming. Sure, he used to read me like a cheap, dime-store mystery, but character reading ran both ways. If he knew me, he had to remember how well I knew him, too.

"You don't know me nearly as well as you think you do," he said like he was inside my head. "Besides, you can't begrudge me a few words with a pretty mortal, can you?"

As far as I was concerned, I could begrudge him anything I damned well pleased. "Leave my employees alone." The words were more growl than true speech. Maybe if I growled, he'd listen for a change.

"Or what, Babydoll?" he said. He never did take me seriously during our relationship. I shouldn't have imagined, after decades apart, he'd behave any different. "What will you do? Send me away? I know you too well."

"Don't be an ass." I stopped long enough to open the door from our human offices to our guest quarters. "This is serious. As soon as we take care of—" A crash echoed, derailing my train of thought.

One shout followed. Silence. Then the beginning of Armageddon deafened us.

"What in blazes?"

I didn't bother answering. I darted off in the direction of the noise. Judging from the bits of—*What was that? A lamp? And a Chippendale cabinet? Damn it!*—whizzing toward us, Duarte would absolutely wait longer than he'd like. Again.

As I got closer, I saw my new friend Omar surrounded by a half-dozen genies, all trying to play one-on-one with the djinn Cuisinart. From where I stood, it seemed like a scene from a bad kung-fu movie.

"What in the name of all hells is going on?"

"You are not my Master!" Omar replied.

Oh holy shit, not this crap again. "Don't you know any other tunes?"

Off to one side, Mena shifted on her feet like a boxer. Deep purple bruises darkened along one cheek and the eye above had swelled shut. "He won't say anything else, so I'm guessing not."

I surveyed the situation. Each of my allies had some type of injury. Omar wasn't even winded. The only good thing I noticed: the pretty blood of my friends didn't seem to be painting his scimitar yet.

"Somebody wish him back into the lamp."

"Tried to," Basil called out as I stalked toward the group. "The rotter won't acknowledge The Master's Right."

Behind me, Zeke snorted. "Can't say I blame the guy."

I shot him a nasty look as I continued forward. "Then forget using his wishes against him. Use your own." Several voices spoke at once, all of them saying pretty much the same thing: They already tried.

I nodded toward Mena. "Get his sanctuary. He already obeyed me once. He might again." The lamp appeared and she lofted the object at me. I reached into the air only to find Zeke's hand closing around the handle first.

"Hey, buddy," he said in the tone reserved for convincing me to see things his way. "Why don't we talk things out like good genies?"

The Bedouin growled his well-worn phrase again.

"Right. I am not your Master." The words no sooner left Zeke's mouth then Omar swiped at Michael. Thank the gods, the Bedouin hadn't used his sword hand. Still, my relief quickly melted as

Michael's human frame flew through the air, cracking into the drywall.

I discarded my slow approach, instead running to the crumpled, damaged body of my future lawyer. Blood dribbled from one side of his mouth, staining the travertine tiles. His eyes acquired a scary glaze. Reaching for a whisper of power, I tried healing the damage, but my trip to Vegas still had me tapped out.

"Someone? Anyone. Forget the nutjob and get over here." A djinn I didn't recognize peeled away to take my place at Michael's side. "Heal him quick before we lose him."

Off to one side, a roar blasted my ears as a hot rush of wind ruffled my hair. The next thing I knew I went flying down the hall. As I crashed into one of my guests' quarters, I pondered how many other men would throw me across a building. Because, frankly, I was damn sick of it.

As I regained my feet, Zeke began glowing like a friggin' blast furnace. Before I could think, my ex fast-pitched a sphere of light like I'd never seen. One minute, the Bedouin acting like a maniac, the next, he dropped to the floor like a tipped-over statue.

Omar tried to rise. The unharmed genies jumped him. So many different wishes whipped around him, he became like a giant magic burrito. Too early to feel relief, I turned back to Michael. He remained bleeding and on the verge of death. The genie I ordered to heal him sat against the wall, watching him die.

"What the hell do you think you're doing?" I barked. The djinn shrugged. I'd never seen this guy before, but then again, sometimes we got strays who needed help acclimating to the changing mortal world. I also knew he couldn't have been around long if he hadn't bothered to save one of his fellow brethren.

"Mena!" I called, pushing the moron away. Her head lifted from her place by the Bedouin burrito. Thank the gods she didn't have to ask what I wanted. Without moving an inch, she sent her energy from across the hall. As Michael inhaled sharply and went from nearly dead to simply sleeping, I exhaled the breath I didn't know I held.

"He'll hurt like Hell tomorrow," she said, "but we'll deal with it then."

I turned to give the uncaring djinn a piece of my mind, and maybe a slap upside the head, but he'd wandered off. "Who the hell was he?"

No one had a clue. I'd worry about the sorry asshole later. Anyone who can't feign humanity has to leave Mayweather. It's not a Rule, and definitely not one the Council would enforce, but I make the rules at Mayweather and I enforce them.

"How's your patient?" I tucked my anger into a place where I could access it later.

"Mad as hell, but he'll get over it."

Either he'd get over it or he'd spend the rest of eternity in our version of a rest home, eating tiddlywinks with his fellow inmates. I didn't want another resident locked in the vault, but to keep my friends and the rest of the world safe, I'd do it.

"Take him back inside. Which reminds me. How in blazes did he get out in the first place?"

Mena's olive skin turned ruddy. "I had him out for a bit of therapy. I only turned my back for a minute."

"I didn't know she had the bastard out of his sanctuary," Basil completed. "When I opened the door, he jumped through."

"And you've been playing monkey in the middle since—?"

"Shortly after I spoke with you. What took you so long?"

I glared at the reason for my delay.

"Don't look at me, Babydoll. You said everything could wait."

"From what I knew it *could* wait."

"I didn't want to interrupt your meeting with— " Basil's eyes darted from Zeke to me. "Why aren't you with Mary?"

"Long story." My partner started to ask for details, but I shook my head. "Maybe another time when we aren't more bruised than a bushel of over-ripe peaches. Get cleaned up and get some rest. Later, we'll discuss how to stop this from ever happening again." I shot them all a look that would brook no arguments. "What if he'd gotten outside?"

They all looked properly chastened. "Right. What's done is done. And we've all got stuff to do, so let's do it. Live and learn, right?"

I hooked a finger at Zeke. "You. Follow me." Once out of sight of the others, I turned on the man. "You better tell me what's going on. Especially if what just happened is part of the whole scheme of things."

"Umm, Jo?" Basil's voice drifted from behind us. I hadn't realized he followed along, but I hadn't said anything I couldn't share. Yet.

"What now?" My voice had more snap in it than I liked, but I'd apologize later.

"There's one more thing I didn't tell you."

"You mean other than fun with Sheik Insanity?"

"If I could've foreseen his reaction, I would've stopped it before it began." He acted like I'd insulted his mother, if he'd ever known her identity. "No. I received another alert. A few hours ago, but since you were due shortly, I figured it could wait."

"Can't it?" These recent ones zipped at me too fast to think about, let alone get proper reconnaissance. Another rush job did not make me thrilled with the turn my occupation had taken.

"Not too much longer, no. From what can discern, the sanctuary is boxed up, waiting at a shipping warehouse to be delivered in the morning."

"And I didn't hear about it immediately because?"

His pale skin pinkened. "I wanted more time to research this. It appears to have come from the same source as *Arthur*. I had hoped perhaps your desert friend might know something. His alert was similar, and…" If his eyes went any further downcast, he'd be looking at his own ass. "I had a theory he could be mixed up in this somehow."

Too bad Omar would be useless until his right mind came back. *If it ever did.* "Fine. It is what it is. Tell me where I stop next and then rally the troops to repair whatever damage the Bedouin did." Basil nodded. "And please don't tell me I'm headed to the southeast again. I've had enough humidity and kudzu to last a—" It would've been interesting to watch him try to swallow his own tongue if I hadn't guessed the reason. "No. Don't say it."

"I'd love to send you anywhere else, Jo."

"But you can't."

"No, I can't. It's in Tallahassee."

North Florida, again? I should've known. "When?"

"Tonight," he said, cringing as if I would strike him. Truth be told, I almost did. "If I can get together the juice to teleport you."

I stifled a yawn. No way would I be in any shape to rescue anyone. I needed down time. Even without the Efreet's interference, if the new djinn behaved half as badly as my Bedouin buddy, I'd be screwed. I had to have a few hours to recharge my body, if not my batteries.

"Forget the juice, Baz," I said before the yawn broke free. "Book me a flight out. I'm getting some shut eye."

TWELVE

~-~-~-~-~-~-~

Basil, bless his heart, snagged me a private jet. Traveling in style was hours longer than a teleport, but at least I didn't have to close my eyes or face the nausea zipping through space brought. Ten seconds of Technicolor tornado ought to make anyone want to hurl, but no, it's only me. Lucky, lucky me.

Actual luck kept pace as we landed without incident. I got through the airport with minimal headache and, wonder of wonders, the early morning traffic proved light. I reached my target's location within minutes. Furthermore, the gods of capitalism smiled here instead of spitting on it like the last locale. Every lot had a shiny, new building. Every building was occupied by a healthy-looking business.

So far, so good.

Well, almost good. The number of cars screamed shift change. First shift workers arrived as I eased the rental into the parking lot. Soon, the third shift would be crawling all over the place to go home. Sneaking in unnoticed would've been hard enough. Getting out again with one of their precious packages under my arm would be damn near impossible.

I tested the limits of my power. After hours of plane travel, I'd stored enough energy for maybe a bit of glamour. Not that I would manage anything more elaborate than a cheap cosmetic change. With my luck, I'd accidentally turn my hair green and not be able to change it back. If I had more time between rescues, I could've pulled off a total body transformation, like the one I use to keep my appearance aging in step with the march of time. Of course, with extra time, I would've teleported in and out with no one being the wiser.

Wish in one hand, Reggie always said. I tried not to think of the rest of his phrase. I was in deep enough shit without it.

Shrugging off the piss-poor timing and my drained batteries, I tried to seek the best course of action. Any way I examined the situation, I was screwed blue. Shortly, they'd load the package onto some truck. Soon thereafter, if Basil had correct data, some little girl would receive a gift no child could handle. Hell, I'd been an adult and I couldn't handle a genie.

Voices near my borrowed car shook me from my angsting. I stared at the dashboard and tried to blend in. They didn't pay any attention to me.

"I told that man I wanted a trip to Destin for our anniversary, and you know what he got me?" The shrill voice came from within a gaggle of green uniforms. "A new washing machine, that's what." The other ladies parted, giving me a glimpse of the speaker. To me, she looked like the result of a strange mating between a bulldog and Shirley Temple.

"Like I don't work hard enough all day," she continued while the other hens clucked. "I got to home come and clean his damn clothes. I swear, some days I wish that man would pay more attention to me."

A tingle crept across my fingertips. Blondie wasn't a Master, but when you're short on power, any wish goes. Of course, Duarte and his cronies would shit a Hereford if they caught me granting wishes higgledy-piggledy. Still, desperate times ought to call for a little leeway. Thank goodness Shirley Bulldog's wording was too vague to cause any real ripples in the fabric of the universe. With any luck, the Council would never find out.

I felt dry enough inside to grow tumbleweeds on my spleen as I the wish soaked into me. I held the energy as long as I could, filling my reserves with as much power as such a small source allowed. Then I released only enough to send the stranger's whim gliding away. Somewhere in Leon County, her husband would be overcome with the urge to hang on his wife's every word.

Good thing granting wishes takes less energy than they generate. After I granted it, I still hummed with power. Not enough leftover to teleport, but enough to accomplish the rescue without attracting attention.

I considered the wish recipient. She presented as good a persona to imitate as any. Besides, she owed me. It's not every day someone gets a free wish.

Holding her image in my mind, a small ripple of energy flowed over me. A quick glance in the rearview confirmed I now looked like a forty-something, Southern gal slash union steward. Patting a tight curl into place, I savored the rush of granting a wish. Nothing felt so good. Too bad, small wishes make for small thrills. Letting the buzz go, I followed the throng of employees inside.

The foremost worker swiped his security card to get us all inside. Nice of him, especially considering I would've been screwed otherwise. With my first hurdle out of the way, I gave the guy a huge grin for his efforts. He scowled at me in return. *Not a morning person, I guess.* On any other day, I wouldn't be either.

Shrugging off the ill-tempered dude, I headed into the expanse of package delivery nirvana. The entry opened into one huge room dotted with workstations and forklifts. Multitudinous boxes stood everywhere, stacked in orderly disarray.

Thanks to a sign pointing the way, I located a quiet place to work in seconds. I only needed a quiet moment to zero in on the genie I needed to rescue. With every other green-clad person gathered at the time clock, chances were I'd have the alone time I needed. Once I closed the door, though, I regretted my choice of quiet places to work.

The warehouse must've employed a couple hundred people and, from what I could tell, only had one ladies' room. The tiny space with its cinder block walls amplified every odor and kicked my gag reflex into hyper drive. Once I had my digestive system under control, I filtered the tidal wave of scents to find the one I sought.

Along with another. The Efreet skulked somewhere in the building, too.

Something told me I only sensed the Efreet because he wanted me to. If I were him, stealth would be part of my plan. I figured this 'allowing me to sense him' thing represented flexing his magical muscles. Every bully needs to show his superior strength somehow or the bullying doesn't work.

And if I could sense him, he sensed me, too. Sneaking up on the bastard got crossed off my list of options. I contemplated hiding in the lavatory for a moment, but I couldn't avoid the encounter ahead.

Steeling myself against a flood of mounting unease, I stepped onto the warehouse floor.

"You're late again, Lucille." A pasty-faced woman in coveralls sideswiped me with her bony shoulder. "And breaks come in the middle of shift, not the beginning."

I fought the urge to throw an elbow in return as I hurried away. First the grumpy dude and now this. My rotten luck to mimic someone her co-workers hated. Not a damn thing I could do about it. Not with an Efreet to hunt and a genie to save.

No more than a minute later the two currents of scent converged in my nose. The subject genie remained stationary in back and off to the right. The killer smelled closer to my position, but he was moving away. I'd never cover the distance before the Efreet. Not without tapping my remaining energy.

I needed an idea of where to teleport to, if only to prevent the freaking out of a group of humans. Sharpening my sight, I gazed down the length of the warehouse.

"Got it," I whispered and with a blink of my eyes, I landed nearer to my goal. The killer stayed out of sight, but his presence clung to everything like sticky, hot breath. The djinn sat a few yards to my left, inside one of the many stacked boxes, no doubt.

"Lucille!" A firm grip landed on my shoulder as a squeaky voice damn near shredded my eardrums. As tense as I was, the gal should've considered herself lucky she didn't lose a hand. Turning, I found myself face to overly-large bosom with someone named Ruby, according to the embroidery over her left boob. "I tol' you," she said on a breath smelling of fried fish, "if I ever caught yo' lazy ass back here again, I would mess you up bad. You got a death wish?"

I've got to find a better class of people to imitate. If I could've, I would've taken Lucille's boon away. No one this annoying deserved an attentive husband. Even for a day. "I don't have time for this," I muttered under my breath.

"I don't give a flyin' rat's bee-hind what you have time for," Ruby replied, flipping a mass of beaded braids over one shoulder while flexing her free hand into a fist. "You had time enough to be layin' around last week when we was bustin' our asses. You ain't hidin' back here again. Now get yo' lazy ass back where it belongs or you gonna wish you called in sick again today." The grip on my shoulder tightened to vice-like proportions.

If I'd been human, I would've cried. Good thing I hadn't been human for longer than this lady-wrestler's lifespan. I didn't want to hurt her. She had every right to be pissed at someone like Lucille. But she stood between me and the genie I needed to save. Grabbing her thick wrist, I applied only enough pressure to tell her she'd messed with the wrong bitch. With a yelp, she let go.

"If you want a fight," I growled, "meet me in the parking lot after shift change. Right now, I've got better things to do."

Ruby cradled her arm, shooting hate from her onyx-dark eyes. "I'm gonna mess you up."

"Can't wait." I meant each syllable. Lucille would get whatever Ruby thought she had coming, and then she'd go home to a doting husband. "But not here and not now." I glanced upwards for effect. "Unless you want to lose your job."

With a warning hiss, the hapless Ruby turned toward her work while I slipped behind a rack of shelves. Flexing my senses again, I got a new fix on my two quarries. From what I could tell, the pair were now together. Sending a sarcastic thanks to the gods, I hurried along worker-free rows. The scents grew stronger as I went, but the path grew more maze-like with every step.

"Grant my wish and I will release you from your bonds." The whispered words hit my tweaked hearing like a thunderclap. One more turn and I'd have the duo in sight.

Of course, what I'd do then I couldn't guess. If humans hadn't been crawling all over the place, I could've called in reinforcements. If Evil Dude hadn't been ready to kill another djinn, I'd have beat feet out of there. Life is so much better with a plan. Too bad time and plans were out of the equation. I usually don't mind winging it, but then again, situations where genies explode into a million points of light aren't usual.

With the exception of fluorescent lights bringing glaring clarity to the scene, the sight reminded me of when little Arthur died. Goatee Guy was bent over a cringing child—this time a girl looking no more than a dozen years old.

"I cannot," the girl said, her sweet Germanic accent tinged with agony.

"Wouldn't you like for the pain to stop, sweetling?" he said, with a soft tone and a hard expression.

Cornflower-blue eyes widened. "This agony will cease?"

"Certainly. Simply grant my wish."

A single tear rolled down the girl's alabaster cheek. "You know I cannot. Please."

Unable to stop myself, I stepped from behind the rack. "Get out of here," I told the girl, keeping my eyes on the Efreet. Since last I saw him, he'd changed into a deep, indigo, silk shirt and tight, black pants. Demented lothario meets *Dance Fever*.

"You again. I should not be surprised." Kicking an empty cardboard container, he stepped toward me. On his outstretched hand lay a porcelain box no bigger than a ring case. "He who holds the sanctuary wields control," he said. A guy like him quoting Rules seriously pissed me off. "She goes nowhere without my permission."

His singsong voice sent my anger soaring. From the glint in his eye, he'd been aiming for my exact reaction. "Of course," he continued, "if you brought me your sanctuary, you could take her place. I might rescind her wish after you've granted yours."

Drawing in enough air to float a Zeppelin, I tried to calm myself. His words strived for maximum effect on my frayed nerves. Get me to make the first move. Force me to make mistakes. Given my waning power, I couldn't take him in a fight, even if I played dirty. Besides, I could take a good taunting. After years with Stavros, I learned to shrug off crap like this. Still, controlling myself took more effort than it should have.

"Walk away from here," I said, "and I might let you—"

"Live?"

This asshole finishing my sentences didn't improve my mood at all.

"A shame for you, the Rules still bind you. And if they did not."
His tongue stuck out, scenting the air like a damn snake. "As I
suspected. You have barely enough power to give me a nasty case of
rickets." He waved one hand dismissively. Of course, I flinched. Which
only pissed me off more. "Leave before I do something you'll regret."

Like pushing me through a wall? I managed to pull together
enough backbone to shake my head. He wasn't any better than an evil
child pulling the wings off flies.

I held my hand out to the girl. "Come with me."

She shook her head, unable to force words past her
overwhelming pain.

"You may take her if you dare, Miss Mayweather, but you'll
never save her." His grin showed all those gleaming teeth. "Wherever
you go, all I need do is…" He caressed the box. The girl shuddered.
"And then…" Despite his words, I grabbed the girl's arm and pulled
her close.

"It's extraordinarily simple. Sing along if you remember the
words." He raised a hand toward the child. "Greta Ann Frey, I wish for
you to never ever complete my wishes." As the wish's power coursed
through the girl, it crackled along my arms—a moment of electro-
shock therapy for my very own. When it stopped, a line of blood
flowed from the corner of Greta's eye.

"Why are you doing this?" The words came grinding through
gritted teeth.

"Because I can," came the bastard's flippant answer. "And
because it hurts you so." Power surged again and he disappeared.

I cradled the little genie in my arms, fighting an urge to cry for the first time in years. I barely had time to acknowledge the novelty of my own grief, though. Judging from the heat pouring out of the girl, all hell would break loose any second.

Turns out I didn't have that long.

"Oh my God!" My chesty acquaintance, Ruby, stood at the edge of one rack, her eyes lit with terror. "What did you do to that child?"

My bad luck peaked with the end of my glamour. The sudden disappearance of Lucille's face had Ruby clutching her ample bosom. Her eyes rolled white and she dropped to the floor.

"Crap." A quick check showed the woman's heart hadn't exploded in her chest. Whichever sick deity was laughing at me from its lofty perch missed a prime opportunity to screw me. Getting caught holding a sick kid would be bad enough without a corpse at my feet, too. I nudged Ruby into a more comfortable position and evaluated my surroundings. I needed to teleport elsewhere before my little Germanic time bomb went off. And I needed an empty space to do so.

Sure enough, the gods were still having fun at my expense. A dozen or more footsteps headed toward us. Scooping Greta against my chest, I tried to figure a way out of this mess.

I had to shift her body over one shoulder, but I managed to get my hands on my cell. A press of one button connected me. Basil's voice thrummed into the room. Damn speakerphone.

"No time to talk," I told him. "Get me out of here. Someplace secluded."

"We're all fairly tapped after yesterday's brush with—"

"Now!" The time for debate had scampered off.

"Just a minute."

I don't even have a second. I hefted Greta's limp weight over my other shoulder. Knowing I had crap for options, I headed toward the back hoping I'd find some kind of loading dock. If I snuck out that way, maybe I'd buy enough time for Baz to pull a miracle.

As my life would have it, I located several loading bays, all occupied with people either emptying or loading trucks. If possible, more people occupied this space than the whole rest of the damn building. The best I could do now was find a good hiding spot until Basil came through. Better if everyone forgot I'd been there altogether. *Maybe if Ruby stays unconscious.*

A shout from behind me proved the levels to which my luck had sunk.

"Any time now." I kept my voice low. Staying hidden meant staying safe. I no longer worried whether the humans thought they'd caught a pedophile stealing some little blonde kid. If memory served, Arthur's power reached critical mass not too long after the Efreet's second wish. Time was almost up.

Which meant I wouldn't be the only one who got screwed.

"I saw her!" shouted the now-familiar voice. "Lucille murdered that child!" The words no sooner reached me than the little girl Ruby thought I killed actually went nuclear.

~-~-~-~-~-~-~

"Jo?" Basil's voice echoed from the phone like a horn in the fog. Too bad the ship had already wrecked. "Zeke's on it. You should be—"

"It's too late," I whispered into the darkness. Near the front of the building, people were screaming. Nearby a man whimpered. A woman kept shrieking the words 'I'm blind' over and over until I wanted to knock her out in order to rest my ears.

"Jesus, Jo, what the hell?"

"Forget reinforcements, Baz. We need a full-scale clean-up, and someone to put a spin on this. The human media is gonna have a field day." I rubbed my eyes, making tiny purple stars erupt behind my eyelids. Didn't help me see any better, but they were pretty.

"Anything else?"

"Get me home. If some mortal recovers his eyesight before I do, this whole shitstorm will get a whole lot..."

"...worse," I said as my feet touched carpet. I couldn't decide whether to be happy or to cry like a baby. Sure, I made it out of the warehouse, but I'd left a PR disaster behind. Not to mention the scattered molecules of a cute, little, German girl who never deserved to die.

"The same as last time?"

I didn't bother answering. My rage-filled brain wouldn't allow me to speak. And since Basil didn't deserve the full brunt, my mouth stayed closed.

To his credit, Basil didn't ask any more questions. He didn't need to. Instead, he said something about sending reinforcements to assess the damage. Then he left. As my associate moved away, I stayed in the exact spot where his power dropped me. There wasn't any point in moving. I no longer cared about my research downstairs.

I didn't give two hoots in hell about the bed calling my name. Other matters compressed my gray matter into road pizza.

By the time Baz came back, I wasn't any closer to finding the answer, but his presence snapped me back to the present.

"Everything set for our unexpected cleanup?"

He nodded and reached out a hand to comfort me. I shook my head. *Neither of those dead kids got comfort when they needed it. Why should I?*

THIRTEEN

~-~-~-~-~-~-~-~

The trip from Basil's office to my own barely registered. Renee said something about a doctor's appointment, I think. Someone else might've called my name. Before I knew it, I sat behind my ebony desk, staring at the screensaver with unseeing eyes. Some number of hours must've slipped by because I found myself sitting in the dark when a knock sounded on my door. It opened before I could tell whoever bothered me to go the hell away.

"Jo?" Basil said as he flipped on my kitschy, green banker's lamp. I mumbled my gratitude. The overhead lights would've killed me, I think. As the emerald glow spread across the room, he stepped inside, pulling the door closed behind him. "I hate to bother you, but—"

"But you have to." I didn't blame him. The place pretty much ran itself, but two of us did this job for a reason. "What's up?" I tried to inject a lightness into my tone I didn't feel, but Basil didn't call me on it. His head must've been elsewhere. I know mine had scattered into ions with those children.

"The auction?" he said, pausing as if to make sure I didn't bite his head off. I must've been a huge bitch lately. Although once his question made it through my fog, I did want to smack him. At a time like this, thinking about the business seemed crude.

"Yes?" I pushed my anger to a place where I wouldn't say something I'd regret. Basil couldn't help but think about the business. I didn't really want him to stop. He kept the commercial side of Mayweather running. He knew the biz must go on even while genies died around us.

"I really do hate to bring it up."

"Spit it out, Baz."

"I feel I should cancel, all things considered, but…" I'd never seen Basil look so ill. "Frankly, Jo, at this point, I'm not sure I *can* cancel the blasted thing. Not without flushing ourselves down the loo. Half of the attendees are already in town. The other half are probably enjoying Denver before driving up."

I had to look utterly stupid at that point. His words wouldn't dovetail with the morbidity in my head. "Enjoying Denver?"

"Before the auction weekend. Most of our regular customers have planned this trip for weeks. They're already seeing the sights there before they come here. You've had your head elsewhere, and necessarily so, but day after tomorrow, we'll be jammed to the collars. The catering's already in place. The additional employees are expecting to work. People count on this."

My eyes rolled of their own accord. Without the damn auction, we'd have to run at half budget for the next year. Despite that, part of me wanted to slap a sign on the door telling everyone to bugger off. Sure, we could fund our genie-saving another way, but this works for us. At least, it works as long as we stay consistent. It's hard to put on the show of being a respectable business when you screw your customers.

Heaving a sigh, I shook my head. "Don't cancel."

"But between our Arab friend and the killings..." He let the rest of his thoughts hang in the air. Basil knew as well as I did if our problems and the human world kept connecting, the Council would have our guts for garters.

"Then we'll have to make sure everything stays quiet until after the shindig." I wasn't sure we'd pull it off, but Mayweather Antiquities wouldn't survive otherwise. "Is Omar still wrapped up tight?"

"Like bangers in mash."

"There's that at least." I moved to a more comfortable position, curled on the couch with my knees against my chest. The Efreet couldn't bother me at home, especially since he was living the happy, serial-killer life in north Florida. Still, you never can trust the deranged to be consistent.

Speaking of inconsistencies. "Where's Zeke?"

"Waiting downstairs." I must've shot daggers at my poor partner because he swallowed hard before continuing. "I told the bloke to go home. He said the two of you had business to finish. He spent the night in one of the empty guest rooms."

Life really can't get any more complicated. Really. It can't. An image of Zeke making himself at home on my turf curdled my stomach. I did not want his presence in my life, but I didn't have much choice.

"Fine." I ground the word to dust between my teeth. "I do still have to talk to him, now more than ever."

Basil raised an eyebrow. "I hate to add to your load, love, but..."

"But?"

"Are you planning on broadcasting to the network any time soon? If we tell the guests—"

"What they don't know..." I couldn't make myself complete that statement. The implications were too maudlin. "Keep them in the dark. When the Council finds out, if they haven't already, they'll be breathing down my neck. I don't need our guests joining in."

"The incident has been contained," Basil said. His words almost didn't make it past the ball of stress in my head.

"What?"

"Zeke went out, turned on a little charm, pushed a little magic and spun a wish wiping up the details. Now the shippers think some kind of power surge caused the lights to flare briefly. Then he tweaked their heads a little so they didn't remember it being nearly as bright as it was."

"And, let me guess, he made it so no one remembers seeing me or the kid?"

"Exactly."

As much as I hated twisting brains, I had to admit it was the best course of action. I'd have to thank Zeke the next time I saw him. I hoped I wouldn't choke on the words.

"Now, about keeping this mum?"

A few more days' ignorance couldn't possibly hurt. After the auction I'd have time to get solid information. Plus, I might have the opportunity to prepare for their reactions. One wrong word could have the genie population readying for war.

"Hell," I said. "How am I supposed to tell genies about something they've never been allowed to discuss? 'Hey, guys?

Remember those Efreet things? Oh, you don't? Well, they're nasty and one's wandering around killing djinn.' Yeah, that'll go over great. For all I know, they'll come after me instead."

"They'll understand."

Bless Basil's generous heart, trying to make me feel better when he knew they'd do no such thing. I didn't have the heart to contradict him. Only this whole mess going away—including the part where my ex-lover awaited me downstairs—would make me feel better.

I closed my eyes and tried to think of how to make Zeke go home. I didn't have time to deal with him, no matter what information he held. Of course, I didn't have time for auctions and insane guests and murderous Efreet either, but that's life. If I could, I'd hold off talking to him. If I could, I'd wish for a year to think it all over, but wishes never work like that.

'No killing' might be the First Rule, but messing with time ties for second. It's up there with bringing back the dead and tinkering with the universe. Still, once in a while, the ability to bend a Rule or two might be handy. For instance, at that moment, I would've loved to have Reggie back. I could use his stellar advice. Barring paternal wisdom, a nice black hole to swallow me up would be useful.

With no universal disaster pending, I asked for Zeke's whereabouts.

Baz tapped a few keys on his Blackberry. "According to the security grid, he's in the recreation area with Michael and Mena. Looks like the gents are having a game of billiards while Mena cheers them on."

Without another word, I pushed myself off the couch to locate my wandering djinn encyclopedia. I couldn't think of Zeke any other way without wanting to either kiss him or kill him. One of the options broke my personal rules and the other broke the big Rules, so I was stuck.

I descended the stairs slowly. As crappy as my attitude was, I needed the extra time. Too bad the scant minutes didn't calm me like I hoped. One look at Zeke bent over Mena, who was bent over the pool table, made my already hot temper reach boiling levels. They didn't even *like* each other, for petesakes.

"Just what do you think you're doing?"

Zeke raised his dark-chocolate eyes and grinned. I could've done without the smoldering gaze, but the toothy smile pissed me off worse. I would've slapped him, but the current audience would've made therapy time way too interesting.

"I'm teaching your lovely associate how to bank the 8-ball into the corner pocket without scratching." As he released the last syllable, his arms and hers completed the motion. The white sphere cracked against the black one, easing it past the stripy-red one to drop neatly into the hole.

Mena began to laugh in the lilting way she had. Until then, I never realized I loathed her. One look at my face wiped all traces of amusement from hers. "Sorry." Her words came out mumbled. Which made me feel like a shit.

"Good shot." I tried to squelch the green monster in my head. Mena was *not* trying to steal my man. If stealing an EX-boyfriend could even be possible. Especially at our age. Especially since I knew she hated Zeke with the fire of a thousand marshmallow roasts.

"Feeling better, Michael?" If I kept the interactions light, maybe no one would remember I stormed into the room like a PMS-crazed Medusa sans Midol.

"Almost back to normal, thanks to Mena. She thinks I need to visit the clinic in town, just to be sure, though."

"Whatever you need to do, do it. If only to make sure you're ready for the bar exam. It's soon, isn't it?" He nodded.

With the niceties handled and my blood pressure approaching normal, I focused on the man I didn't want to need. "Can we have a moment alone?"

"Anything you need, I got, Babydoll."

Think calm thoughts. Think calm thoughts. I chanted the mantra in my head, for all the good it did. I used every bit of willpower I could find to let the nickname slide. He had always used it to piss me off. He never understood that I got more pissed because I fell for it every single time. Nodding toward the source of irritation, I walked from the room. In my wake, I heard Mena mumble something about getting back to work. Michael sounded mortified about forgetting his studies and left, too.

As I strode toward the conference room, I felt like a shit. Both Mena and Michael needed whatever downtime they could eke out. Taking their fun away because of Zeke wasn't fair. Of course, dealing with his laughter didn't have anything to do with fairness either.

"We were merely playing a little pool and having fun. You do remember fun, don't you, Josie?" He ambled past me into the conference room, dropping into the chair at the head of the table. My chair.

"You had your fun. Now it's over." I paced along one side of the big oval. I had easily twenty other seats to choose from, none of which I wanted. "After what happened, I think we're done playing games."

"Really, Jo, there's nothing to get upset about. Mena was just—"

"I wasn't talking about your display with my best friend." As the words came out, I admitted his actions were partly why I got so angry. "I was talking about my latest Efreet encounter."

For a moment he stared at me with his hands tented over his nose. "He's taken another life?"

If he wanted to play like he didn't already know, I didn't have the energy to stop him. As much as I didn't want to acknowledge the truth, his question forced the issue.

How one 'yes' could sound so fragile and pathetic, I'll never know.

He shook his head as a low whistle escaped him. "He didn't take nearly as long as I'd hoped. The murders before the last war. They weren't spaced so closely together—"

"And now?"

"This isn't then. At least then, we—I mean, *they* knew who they were up against."

"Cut the crap, Zeke." Opposite him at the table, I placed my hands palms down on the oak surface. "I know you were in the war. You're the one who suggested the punishment, after all. I'll bet you helped carry it out. Didn't you? You lying sack of—" I cut him off before he could protest. "Lying by omission still counts. And before you try to think it, we're not leaving this room until you spill the truth about everything."

"You can't handle—" he began in a really bad Jack Nicholson impression.

I raised a hand. I didn't have the juice to blow-dry his hair and he knew it, but he also knew I might try something more painful than magical. "Out with it. Now."

He stopped being so damned relaxed for once. Eyes I'd seen twinkling in humor more times than I could count grew cold. "It's war, Jo. It's hard. It's ugly. We lost friends, amongst both the allies and the enemy."

"But you turned *them* into dogs."

He pierced me with a hard glare. "Djinn turned Efreet into dogs. The Efreet didn't return the favor. They don't adhere to our Rules, Jo. They want to kill someone, they kill him. Sometimes their own kind, if one stands in the way. And depending on the Efreet's mood, people died in inventively cruel ways." He snorted. "What happened to Arthur horrified you? Well, Babydoll, he did those kids a kindness compared to what I've seen."

He walked to a nearby window where the Rockies rose dark against a moonlit sky, but the scenery didn't appear to interest him. "When I told you I wasn't in the last war with Mary, I meant it. I couldn't be."

"Then how do you know so much about it?" My hands ached to sooth the muscles bunched along his shoulders. Before I lost myself in touching him, I said, "And don't give me any bull about hearing the tale from someone else. I know you as well as you know me."

"The truth, Jo? I know so much about Mary's war because I served in a war exactly like it. Four hundred years earlier." He paced around the table toward me. "And the one before that." Another step in my direction put me on the retreat. "And the one before that." We stopped when my back hit the wall, his face inches from mine. The rage in his eyes made me cringe.

"Hell, Babydoll, I watched Atlantis sink under the waves of the Mediterranean during one such war." Pain etched his features until he barely resembled the man I once loved.

"The last conflict? Let's say I'd had my fill. I couldn't watch another djinn slaughter." His hand cupped my cheek. I'd never seen so much emotion in those eyes without an orgasm nearby. Seeing this side of him scared me shitless. "When you wonder why I became the man who once disgusted you, there's your answer."

As he stepped back, I let his words settle into me. Tucking away the insight I wasn't ready to deal with yet, I tried focusing on the war that might be ahead. Basically, to stop the Efreet we'd need a massive, all-out, group effort. Such an undertaking by beings who didn't really get together for much of anything was unheard of. Creating genie brotherhood of any magnitude isn't easy and it's sure as hell not quick.

When I first realized every djinn deserved to be free, I didn't have a clue how to go about it. Hell, back then I didn't have clue one whether other masterless genies existed, let alone how to locate them. I was only one woman suddenly freed by circumstance, with boatloads of power and no idea how to do anything useful with it. Well, anything beyond granting wishes to whoever got his clammy hands on the brooch I called home.

One thing I did know? I didn't want anyone to have to grant another thoughtless wish simply because their Master said so.

After fighting with Zeke, I spent a lot of time wandering the streets of whatever city looked promising. I scoured newspapers for stories about lottery winners and meteoric rises to fame. Each lead I followed could be a potential genie handing out impossible goodies. Still, my first dozen rescues amounted to nothing more than good luck.

I think the turning point came after scanning a snippet in some tabloid. It wasn't that much of a lead, but I'd reached the point where I'd either chase one more wisp of hope or give up altogether.

Needless to say, the rescue went totally spastic. Even with Reggie's genes working on one side and my djinn curse working on the other, I still floundered my way into that 'lucky' human's home like an elephant on crack. I took a bullet, but the pain never mattered. It only mattered to locate and free the genie. That day I rescued the man who became the first of my network: Basil. Years later, with his help, my self-appointed mission really rocketed.

Now the very idea of a Djinn/Efreet war might tear apart everything I'd worked for, unless I could stop the killer and prove he acted alone. Because if the Efreet made a comeback, the future of djinn-kind made a rough patch of road seem like glass. Hell, we'd be lucky if we had a future after this.

FOURTEEN

~_~_~_~_~_~_~_~

If I could've wished for one whole day to ignore the road ahead, I would've spent it on a tropical island with a stack of books. Instead, I got the auction. When I awoke in the wee hours of morning, I found myself looking down the barrel of a bad day filled with the promise of worse yet to come. Hours of rubbing elbows with humanity lay in my path like a forest of poison ivy and burrs.

Our annual shindig. Dealers from all over the world would be in attendance, along with buyers for a slew of private collectors and some of the more adventurous antiques hunters.

In past years, I enjoyed schmoozing, meeting new people, and selling them things they would cherish for years to come. Too bad, my brain wouldn't let me enjoy the event. It scurried between what I learned from Zeke and what I needed to do with the knowledge. Add in the image of tortured djinn kids plastered in my head and schmoozing seemed vulgar.

And wouldn't you know it, Basil had the place packed. This would probably be our biggest sale yet. We had artifacts from a gaggle of ancient genies, plus a few key pieces of celebrity bling. I just couldn't get into the spirit of it.

In my first few minutes on the floor, representatives from Christie's and Sotheby's introduced themselves before wandering toward the buffet. I should've followed, chatting up some of the more interesting items. A little PR for the company couldn't hurt, but I didn't care.

More proof I wasn't myself, I sure as hell had no interest in eating.

Wonderful aromas filled the room. Baz's caterer must've outdone herself. Mini-quiches filled several platters. Tiny *duck a l'orange* bites lay farther down the table, next to *pate de fois gras* on little crackers shipped in from France for the occasion. All of it wasted on me when I should've been all over the food. Make something into an appetizer, and I'm so there. This time, the thought of future casualties made the idea of gourmet goodies as repulsive as licking the inside of a PortaPotty.

"Penny for your thoughts," Zeke said as he brushed against my arm. He held two crystal flutes filled with mimosas.

I kept my hands folded over my chest. Evangeline would've wept at the thought of perfectly good booze mixed with anything so crass as orange juice. Despite my upbringing, I usually loved the beverage. Considering the recent circumstances, champagne mixed with orange juice sent my innards swirling.

"A whole penny? Trust me, they aren't worth that much."

"Dwelling on *them* again, I take it."

Gazing at the sea of human faces, I couldn't help but wonder what those children might've accomplished if they'd been allowed to live out their human lives instead of becoming djinn.

"They were so young."

"Don't fool yourself, Josie. They both lived plenty of years."

"As slaves maybe."

"They made their own choices."

Considering my change from human to djinn, I was willing to bet neither youngster had been given the choice I ignored having. "You know how it probably went down as well as I do. They got their hands on something shiny and, when faced with a three-wish limit, they thought they'd be smart. The little voice said 'wish for more wishes'. Hell." I fought to keep my voice steady against the pressure building inside me. "Why wish for a few more when you can have them all?"

Zeke set one glass down on the tray of a passing waiter and then squeezed my arm. My story didn't differ too much from anyone else's. Irrational greed swamped me, and then rewarded me by exchanging my humanity for a prison. Sure, I received a shitpot of power as a lovely parting gift, but when you can't escape your circumstances, a prison's a prison however sparkly.

"Maybe you're smart to skip the liquor today," he said as he blinked his own drink away and gave the humans a gentle nudge to look elsewhere.

"Don't wish in here."

"No one saw anything they'd admit to seeing," he said. "You need to hold it together, Josie."

"I'm fine. Just pissed."

"And everyone can tell. Your business needs this, and we all need you in business."

I aimed for his mid-section, but I stopped myself. He was right, damn him.

"Excuse me, Miss Mayweather," one of the temporary help said. "Mr. Hadresham asked me to inform you the auction is beginning."

My mouth closed with a snap over the words I still had for Zeke.

He'd probably been an elder in his human society when he'd been invited to become a genie. He couldn't know how shitty it felt to make a monumental, life-changing decision without either the knowledge or the maturity to back it up.

Like I had.

Nodding at the worker, I waved my hand toward the front of the room. They could start without me on stage, but decorum dictated I should at least fake interest in the festivities.

"Thank you for joining us at the annual Mayweather Antiquities auction," Basil began, his calm, soothing accent reaching into my bones. I should've sat down and talked this out with my partner. We might not have reached any conclusions, but my nerves would've been less jangled. "I trust you've all had ample opportunity to peruse the objects included in today's sale."

Baz continued whipping the customers into a buying frenzy but I stopped listening. When the first strains of the auctioneer hit me, my brain tuned out the garble. I didn't need to know what the items were. I sure as hell didn't care what they sold for. Though I usually found those specifics interesting, my mood was shot. Besides, Basil could handle everything. He always did. One glance at the stage told me the old Cockney bloke was in his element. And he deserved to be proud. He put so much effort into making these things go off without a hitch.

Personally, I would've been happier escaping the whole damn event and crawling back to my library. A few decades down there should be plenty. *This whole thing with the Efreet should be decided by then. Right?*

Movement registered on the edge of my attention. Zeke wandering off in search of more interesting companionship. *Good for him.* Hell, good for both of us. Not only did I make lousy company at the moment, but I also didn't want his particular brand of companionship. Of course, I couldn't help but be unhappy when he cozied up to Renee, offering her the mimosa meant for me.

She shook her head, holding up a tumbler full of bright red liquid. If I expanded my hearing, I would've caught my receptionist saying she didn't drink. Judging from the way she pointed to her glass, she was expounding on the wonders of cranberry juice and tonic. Watching the inestimable Mr. ben Aron trip over his own chivalry would've been funny if he didn't take the rebuff so damn well. In seconds, a waiter appeared with the very cocktail mixture she'd been excitedly explaining.

I really had to hand it to Zeke. He makes the world spin around his little finger without expending more than a little wish power.

Sometimes I really hate the guy.

"Miss Mayweather?" A hand gripped my elbow. Lost in thought, I whirled to face my attacker with a wish on my lips. Good thing I didn't start off on the offensive, since my 'foe' turned out to be a man old enough to be my father. Literally. The guy could've served in the First World War. In fact, he seemed so familiar, he might've actually served alongside Reggie before my father realized there was no profit in fighting the Kaiser and went AWOL.

"I am so sorry to have startled you," he said with a wheezy flourish.

Before I could stop myself, my gaze searched for his oxygen tank, in case he started turning blue. I didn't find one. He was so close to taking the big dirt nap I could almost hear his arteries saying a final prayer. His grip on my arm was surprisingly strong for someone so close to death.

"I'm perfectly fine," I told him.

"I couldn't miss the opportunity to tell you how very much like your aunt you look."

"My aunt?" I began and then I realized why the old guy looked familiar. I'd met him in New York shortly after WWII.

He'd been in antiques himself back when I'd been playing housewife in the Bronx. After my Master and husband became listed amongst the missing in Europe, I had to hock what little we owned to pay the bills. Someone had to keep the lights on until Benny came home.

Maybe if I'd known he'd never come back from Germany, I would've held onto the pieces of our life together, if only to remind me of the man I loved. Unfortunately, I didn't find out Benny was gone until after I'd sold most everything. I was a free djinn with nothing to show for it—no husband and no mementos of our life together. Too bad for Benny he didn't use his last wish to save himself. Holding onto it so he wouldn't lose *me* didn't do him any damn good in the end.

"Are you alright, Miss?" the old man said. His touch on my wrist shook me away from memories I knew better than to wallow in. What's gone is gone, and no amount of wishing would ever bring it back.

"Yes. Yes, of course. I'm fine. My aunt, you said?" The antiques dealer must've thought I was having an aneurysm, but it couldn't be helped. Memories of Benny plus the shock of running into someone from my old existence made me dumber than a box of rocks. If I opened my mouth, my stupidity would come dribbling out. Once I gathered myself, I smiled and said, "Oh. You mean my great aunt, Josephine."

"You're the spitting image of her."

I let out a polite laugh. "My parents must've been psychic. I'm named after her." I never thought using my real name with my real face after so long would bite me in the ass. With all the name and face changes I've undergone, I assumed anyone who knew the real me died a long, frickin' time ago.

"Such a pretty young thing. Pity about her husband. I never met the man, but she must've really loved him to sell so many heirlooms to keep possession of their home." He shook his head. "No one so young should bear such a burden."

My burden had been easy. Benny had endured months of torture at the hands of the Nazis. He never deserved to die the way he did. Hell, no one deserved to die at the hands of those butchers.

"Yes. Yes, it was awful for her." I tried to pluck myself from his grip. I would've done almost anything to get away from the conversation, but he wouldn't let loose. As he continued to ramble about my 'great aunt' and her misfortunes, I could only try and keep the memories at bay. The dam holding my misery didn't seem strong enough to withstand the battering it received.

"I do believe," he finally said, "your associates have arrived at the piece I traveled all this way for. If you'll excuse me."

Holding back my sigh of relief, I accepted his gnarled fingers in a handshake, and he trundled off on his ancient legs. I'd never been happier to see the back of anyone. I turned away from whatever piece held the old man's interest. Likely it would bring more memories boiling to the surface.

With all eyes toward the auctioneer, I slipped away. What I really needed was some air. The way people packed the room, though, it would've been easier getting into a Broadway show on New Year's Eve.

A patch of clear space appeared. I made for it like a drowning rat paddling toward a chunk of driftwood. Within a few ragged breaths, I stepped out onto the side patio. Some smokers and a well-dressed couple arguing about bidding strategies had beaten me outside. As long as none of them touched me, talked to me, or otherwise socialized with me, I didn't care who else shared the space. I let peace settle around me while I inhaled the mountain air.

My peace lasted all of ten seconds.

As the door drifted shut behind me, a ripple of power surged through the gap. My tiny squeak attracted attention. The smokers stepped away when I shrugged and mumbled something about a spider. They probably thought I'd gone nuts. I wish I had. The power I sensed had that sickening 'someone's about to die' feeling to it.

The Efreet had crashed the auction. With him in a room full of mortals, our previous encounters would seem like a pillow fight next to the shitload of trouble he'd bring this time.

Before the idea could morph into a giant pile of angst, I pulled every ion of power I could find, holding it tight until I located my target. As I stepped inside, I realized finding the Efreet would be a bitch and a half. He wanted me to sense him before. Now, I couldn't tell he'd been there. He had to be hiding or transformed somehow. If he looked as creepy as he had before, surely someone would be freaking out.

A quick glance toward the bar found Zeke, propped against the counter, chatting up a skinny brunette. Baz still occupied the dais, overseeing sales. Even Mena appeared unfazed.

They can't sense the killer. Then again, neither can I. Not anymore.

Standing there slack-jawed and doubting my own sanity, I scanned the room. Nothing jumped out at me. I expanded my senses, prying into every nook and cranny for the Efreet bastard. Nothing. The only thing that smelled off was a plate of pâté closer to salmonella on a cracker than a true appetizer. I made a quick mental note to change caterers as the auctioneer announced the next item up for sale.

"Next: Lot 124A. An ancient clay bowl dating to the first century B.C. with rudimentary script that our experts have identified as early Ge'ez. Let's start the bidding at—"

I searched the room again. The item drew my attention away from the edge of total frustration. On the stage, one of the workers held it above his head to give the bidders a better view. Around the room, the object appeared on strategically placed screens. Something about the brown, earthen bowl niggled at my overtaxed wits.

Mena caught my eye with a wave of one hand, unraveling my concentration. Her raised eyebrow made me realize I'd stopped in the middle of the floor like a total loon. I shook my head and walked to where I'd draw less notice. The Efreet had to be in here somewhere. Why I had sensed him and my friends hadn't I couldn't guess. It didn't take a brain surgeon to figure out why I didn't sense him anymore. He was toying with me.

"Lot 124A?" Basil said in a low voice only a djinn could hear. Louder, he addressed the auctioneer. "Terribly sorry, but my list doesn't include any such item." He tapped his clipboard.

In an instant, I reasoned out what had bothered me and irritated my partner. The clay pot didn't appear on the list because it shouldn't have been part of the auction. Inside the dingy, little piece sat our silent Ethiopian princess.

I stepped toward the stage. "There's a mistake," I said. "It isn't meant for—"

As the words dried up in my throat, bands of power encircled me. I couldn't speak. I couldn't move. I sure as hell couldn't use the energy I held. With my luck, I'd been turned into the next statue for my customers to bid on.

"Right," said Basil as if I'd never spoken. "Well, mistakes do happen from time to time. I'm certain everything's quite ducky. We'll simply carry on and sort out the clerical error later."

What the hell? The man who followed protocol to the nth degree wanted to 'simply carry on'? The concept was so foreign to Basil, the Efreet had to be responsible. Not only did the bastard hold me inert, but he'd messed with my partner's brain.

I tried to turn my head. If I could catch Mena's eye—hell, I'd settle for Zeke's—I might be able to warn someone. But I was stiffer than the Venus de Milo. At least the asshole let me keep my arms; I just couldn't use them.

"What's up, Josie?"

Think of the devil and he shall arrive.

"You look like you saw a ghost."

I never thought I'd be glad to have Zeke's breath warming my earlobes again. He chuckled into my ear, which I'd bet he meant to tick me off as much as arouse me. Which it would've done if the paralyzing wish hadn't killed the stimulation.

"Josie? Not still mad about my flirting with Renee, are you?"

On the stage, bidding began. Seasoned attendees clamored to make the piece their own. More offers were being tendered for the worthless piece of junk than anything we'd sold in the past. I didn't know what the Efreet had up his sleeve, but his magic worked the crowd better than my best auctioneer. Only I couldn't understand why no other djinn felt this happening.

"Come on, Babydoll." Zeke blew soft tendrils of hair against my cheek. His teasing tone adopted a harsher edge when I didn't react. "You're taking this jealousy a mite too far."

As his fingers closed around my wrist, Zeke uttered a curse in some ancient language and went still. My heart would've leapt into my throat if I hadn't been frozen. If he'd been caught in the same wish, we were all very screwed.

Near the center aisle, no more than a dozen paces in front of me, the old antiques dealer rose. His cane clattered to the floor beside him. "Ten thousand," he shouted with more life than I assumed a man his age had left.

All around us silence fell. A bid doubling the last offer would've dropped my mouth open, too. I mean, if I wasn't already stone stiff. Basil recovered first, his face widening with a Cheshire-cat grin. Once the customers saw him accepting this unusual behavior, their voices rose in a roar. All the while, the auctioneer waited for the right moment to continue.

"If there are no other bids," he said after a few moments.

Zeke leaned toward me. If I could've exhaled in relief, I would've. "What's going on, Josie?" His power swelled beside me and suddenly my heart began to beat again.

"I don't know." The statement came out as a whisper. "But we can't let anyone else touch the object up for bid."

Crushing the urge to leap on stage and snatch the clay pot away, I bided my time. As long as the Efreet thought he'd handled me, he would ignore me. I hoped. Slowly, I let my eyes wander the crowd. Not one of them glanced my way. They were all glued to the old man. Hell, if I wasn't otherwise occupied, I'd want to know what possessed a man to gamble his money on one dirty bowl. When I met him in New York, he'd been into European antiquities. After all the time that had passed, he still didn't strike me as a 'cradle of civilization' buff. He liked pretty things with flowery flourishes.

Still, stranger things have happened. In fact, all of this could probably be stacked neatly inside the *stranger things* category.

"Going once—"

"Twenty thousand," Zeke shouted. I turned my head slightly to find he'd stepped away from my side. A good thing considering all heads snapped toward my old boyfriend. His eyes remained on the old antiques dealer who did a slow roll of his shoulders before facing Zeke.

And as he did, my heart plummeted into my stomach.

Though he still pretty much looked like the guy who knew me once upon a time, his eyes had changed. They had shifted from watery-blue to dark and cold. I still couldn't feel power radiating off him, but I'd bet my dog I found the Efreet.

"Thirty thousand," he said as a sneer tugged at his thin lips. The fingers on his right hand moved like they had no bones in them and a wash of sickly power swept toward my old boyfriend.

I reached toward him, despite knowing anything I tried would be too late. My 'help' proved less than pointless as Zeke shrugged off the malevolent wish like he was sending an overcooked t-bone back to the kitchen.

The humans milling around felt nothing more than a sudden, inexplicable breeze. Several faces wore expectant smiles as they waited for the next bid to come. In their eyes, this was nothing more than a show, and they drank it in. If they really knew the truth, they'd run and scream instead of smile and clap.

Off to my left, Mena started toward me and stopped. Her expression solidified into a look of confusion. I knew the feeling. The

Efreet had her. How he could be holding her and fighting Zeke at the same time boggled my mind. Talk about some serious wishy mojo going on there. I had to hope my ex had enough power of his own to hold the bastard off.

"We have thirty. Do I hear forty?"

I wanted the auctioneer to shut the hell up, but cutting off the spectacle mid-stream might alert the humans to our little magical drama. With a glance in Zeke's direction, I headed for the podium. He had the Efreet occupied. If I could reach the stage, I might be able to stop this before it got really ugly.

"Fifty," Zeke said. As cool as he must've appeared to the mortals, I could tell the massive defensive wish had taken its toll.

"One hundred thousand." The old man's words were soft but they echoed through the crowd.

This couldn't continue much longer. Sure, both guys could shout ridiculous numbers as long as they wanted. Hell, either of them could probably pay off the national debt without blinking. Sooner or later, though, the Efreet would tire of the game. And that's all it was to him—a game. If he really wanted the princess, he could've taken her without setting up this sick little teleplay.

After Greta and Arthur, I couldn't let him take another one. Not again.

Just as I made my decision, Zeke said, "I think we're about through here, don't you?"

"The current bid is one hundred thousand dollars, sir. Are you prepared to go higher?"

"I'm prepared to end this charade." Zeke sent an extra burst of power toward the Efreet.

Oh gods. Not here. Not now. I wanted to wish myself on stage and deal with the fallout later, but the djinn-world wouldn't recover from a full-blown battle in the midst of a hundred mortals. Too bad I didn't see any other way for this to end. I held my breath and hoped Zeke knew what he was doing.

Except Zeke's wish hadn't been aimed at the Efreet after all. Instead, the entire room fell silent. Against all odds—and against the Rules—time had stopped, at least for the humans. Or maybe my ex only bent the Rules and sped the rest of us up. Either way, the only people who knew what had happened were the brethren who weren't frozen and our enemy. I glanced toward a horrified Basil. A quick sideward glimpse showed me Mena had rejoined the mobile.

Zeke himself fairly glowed with the power he exerted.

And the old man? Well, he was neither old nor a man anymore. The glamour he'd wrapped around himself dissolved in the face of Zeke's wish. There stood the friggin' killer, in all his creepy glory. Every inch of greasy beard, flowing topknot and pearly white teeth on display.

"Well played, Ezekiel," the Efreet said. "But not nearly well enough." He didn't bother moving as his power flowed in several directions at once. The clay bowl went from its pedestal on stage to the Efreet's delicate hand. A wall of perfect energy slammed down around him.

Zeke released a barrage of power I didn't think he still had in him. Nothing got past the damn shield. I added my own energy. Still nothing. Mena recovered and added her power to the mix. Basil stood on stage, staring. He couldn't have been frozen by the same wish cast at me and Mena, so I assumed he'd freaked out so bad he couldn't act. I didn't blame him. I fully planned on freaking out after we handled this.

Maybe if Baz's power had joined the mix, we could've stopped the Efreet. As it stood, our combined power couldn't breach the shield. Instead, we battered ourselves against its power and watched.

Long fingers caressed the filthy object, calling forth a mist. When it coalesced, a young woman appeared. Her skin was as dark as the velvet on a cheap Elvis painting. Somewhere along the way, her eyes had lost their confused haze. Now the startling blue pierced through everything, seeing more than anyone could ever want her to see. She turned those eyes toward me, and I had to look away.

Those scary orbs fell upon the Efreet and she sighed at him like a lover. "Master."

At more than six feet, the Ethiopian princess towered over the Efreet. Too bad height never equates to power among the brethren. The gal knew exactly who held her. As she bowed low enough to put herself beneath his eye level, she continued, "What would you wish of me?"

I couldn't get over the change in her. The pitiful mess I rescued melted back into the goddess she must've once been. The lunacy dissipated. Suddenly, she could've been the sanest person there. With the Efreet as her Master, though, she would've been better off out of her head.

The Efreet flashed a movie-star grin while the rest of us held our breath. I expected the killer to sic his new pet on us. I didn't want to have to hurt the girl. Hell, as tapped as I was, I doubted I could. More likely, she would kick my ass.

Once again, my expectations didn't do me a damn bit of good. He didn't have her attack us while he beat feet in the opposite direction. He didn't even bother to taunt us. He simply whispered a wish to the young woman. Those scary-beautiful eyes rolled back in her head. No power build up. No flash of light. Just dead.

Before her body hit the ground, the Efreet was gone.

FIFTEEN

~-~-~-~-~-~-~

As if watching another murder wasn't bad enough, Zeke's wish dissipated the same instant the Efreet poofed away and his shield went with him. The world righted itself in one fell swoop, leaving the genies in the room more than a little stunned. The humans, on the other hand, didn't notice a damn thing. At first. Then, a dozen eyes sought out the old man who'd been standing *right there* only a moment before. A few startled others looked for Zeke and found him nowhere near his previous location. Most waited for the spectacle to continue with another outlandish bid. Yep, everything was hunky-dory in the mortal world.

And then some gal noticed the body at her feet.

The scream she let loose broke through the crowd's confusion, not to mention shattered an eardrum or two. A man with curly eyebrows rushed forward and crouched over the princess. I was too far away to do anything about his hand reaching for her pulse points. He couldn't possibly miss her lack of a heartbeat. All I could do was keep him from noticing her lack of humanity and hope for the best.

Before any of us could throw a wish to silence him, he shouted for someone to call nine-one-one. The sound finally shook Basil out of his daze. One minute he stood frozen to the stage, the next he became the concerned businessman. I didn't have the luxury. This crowd of humans needed an explanation pretty damn quick or they would freak out. Plus, I had to find the killer. I didn't really think either task was possible.

The Efreet was gone. A glance toward Zeke confirmed he didn't have the faintest idea where the bastard went. On the bright side, if there was one, a pressing problem had removed itself. Another, the human factor, was doing its best to make my day worse. The throng followed human nature and headed for the nearest exit. I couldn't blame them. When faced with a scene they can't wrap their brains around, smart people run. If I hadn't been a genie, I'd have beat feet myself. Lucky me, I had to stay. Gathering what little wits I had left, I pooled my power and shut the place down before any mortals escaped into the world.

Most who weren't trying to flee or to help the victim had their cell phones out. Judging from the concentration on Mena's face, I had her to thank for cleaning up that mess. As if in a trance, scores of fingers pressed 'send' over and over without any success, while others tried to snap pictures and came up with overexposed images.

As I scanned the crowd, I tried to think of how to convince my best customers everything was perfectly normal without scrambling their brains. *Fat chance.*

By the time one of us reached the princess, I had the crowd as controlled as they could be. Mena moved concerned humans away from the body. Concocting something believable for new memories is always easier if there are fewer memories to erase.

"But I'm a doctor," said a thin faced woman as she tried to push past my best friend. I recognized the doc as an auction regular, who was always up for an unusual item to add to her private collection. Bet she didn't plan on this level of unusual when she woke up.

"Poor bird merely needs a lie down," Basil told the doctor as Mena eased her away. "We'll take her to a soft cot and let her rest a bit." He motioned a few of our temp workers over. "Come along, gents. Help me with the young lady." He crooked a finger toward Renee. "Be a love and get some water."

"She doesn't need water," said the man who'd reached the body first. "She's dead." I sent a little wish toward him. As much as I hated doing it, I made the guy doubt his initial assessment.

"Not at all." Basil adopted a perfectly mortified air, as if, simply by the mere suggestion of death at a Mayweather Auction, the man had committed some huge social gaff. "She's a little overcome by the excitement. She'll be fine once she's somewhere quiet."

As familiar as I am with what wishing can accomplish, I jumped when the body moved. It wasn't a grand gesture. Her eyelids fluttered. The soft moan escaping her sounded suspiciously like Mena. A tendril of energy told me she targeted the body with a small bit of wish. The Rules make bringing stuff back from the dead impossible, but they don't prevent faking life every now and then.

"See?" Basil patted the girl's hand as the guys lifted her. "A bit of rest will make her right."

"She could be injured," the doctor said. "She shouldn't be moved until I've examined her."

I usually have a lot of respect for the medical profession. After all, doctors generally try to help. At that point, though, I would've wished this one to Abu Dhabi to get her out of the way. If not for the chance her sudden disappearance could cause a panic, I would've settled for shooting her to a different time zone. I've heard Dubuque is lovely. Lucky for the doc, I didn't need any other supernatural surprises. Instead, I pushed her brain a little and distracted her with something sparkly. Not an easy thing to do with such a sharp mind, but I only needed it to work long enough to move the body.

A quartet of men hefted the corpse. Judging from their bland faces, none of them suspected they held death in their hands. In no time, our unfortunate friend was carried off to 'rest'. The crowd didn't stop milling around lamely until the auctioneer cleared his throat. Then all eyes shifted toward him as the next item came up for bid. Thank the gods, someone wheeled out a gaudy settee. If its ugliness didn't distract our customers, I didn't know what would. With their attention elsewhere, I wished for them to forget about anything untoward at the Mayweather auction.

Simple as that, the drama ended. At least for the mortals. We djinn weren't so lucky. We still had a mess to deal with, even if the danger of being exposed had passed.

With a nod to Zeke, I slipped from the room. Mena tried to follow, but the crowd retarded her progress. Poor Basil took one for the team and remained behind. Most of the event still lay ahead and, while no one would miss my shining presence, Basil represented the face of Mayweather Antiquities to the human world. As long as he acted perfectly normal, the humans would follow his lead. I would fill him in later. At the moment, we needed to circle the wagons and figure out what the hell happened.

And how to make sure it never happens again.

My ass had just begun to enjoy my soft, leather desk chair when the door to my office closed. A ripple of power locked it tight. Tension seized me until I sensed a familiar power.

"So, you want a private party now, Ezekiel?" I snapped my fingers, and he appeared out of nothing with his back against the door. "Didn't we stop having those decades ago?"

"Private for now." Neither of us bothered to mention the invisibility shtick. By all rights, I should've nailed him for skulking around my building unseen. But I didn't have time.

"Mena's right behind me, you know."

"Not anymore." His smile was grim. "Some friendly people did me a favor without knowing they would. I need talk to you alone."

"Why?"

"A few things need to be said without her little ears around." Every inch of him screamed exhaustion, but he didn't move toward a chair. He simply leaned against the damn door.

"Sit. You're making me nervous." When he shook his head, I let it go. If he wanted to collapse into a big puddle, he could go for it. It wasn't as if his presence could keep me from leaving if I wanted to.

"Exactly what do you want to say that Mena shouldn't hear?" I could think of a few things, none of which I wanted to hear either. "Confessing your part in this?" His eyes narrowed. "Or is this where you profess your undying love and apologize for being an ass thirty years ago?"

Neither offhand and wild suggestion thrilled him. From the set of his shoulders, he boiled with more anger now than he ever threw at me during our hours-long arguments. *So what if he's pissed? Why should he be so relaxed?* I wanted him as livid as I was. I couldn't fathom what held him back.

"I have my reasons for keeping your friend out of this discussion," he said. "You'd learn them, if you ever shut the hell up."

Ah, there's the anger. I reveled in it like a mink coat left in storage too long. We always did have the best fights. And the best sex afterwards. But I didn't want to go there. In fact, my next thought was *What the hell am I doing?* Shoving all my weird-ass angst into a place where I could ignore it, I tried to compose myself.

"Whatever you tell me now, I'll tell her later. I trust Mena with my life."

He shrugged. "I'm not as trusting as you. For all I know, your friend allowed all of this to happen. *Someone* had to invite the Efreet inside."

Crossing my hands over the desk pad, I tried to look like the idea didn't faze me. "From what I saw, he popped in. No invite needed."

"He couldn't have 'popped in', Babydoll." He hit me with the nickname as he made air quotes around my own words. "For one thing, Efreet are like vampires. They can't enter someone's home without being welcomed inside. Since you live here and you didn't invite him, someone you trust did." I raised an eyebrow, but didn't interrupt. "For another thing, Mayweather Antiquities, LLC paid me to secure the site. I scattered enough defensive wishes around this place to drop a giant."

"That doesn't mean—"

"It does mean. He's walking around like he owns the damn place. In fact, I'm betting he's been inside for a while. At least long enough to plant a genie in your auction. Hell, Josie, he's probably had enough play time to know everything you know. I'm not the first genie to travel unseen, you know."

I couldn't be sure what pissed Zeke off more, a spy in my midst or someone getting past his wishes, but some twisted part of me felt the need to add the last wrinkle. "Umm, Zeke? The dead gal? He didn't plant her. He stole her out of the vault."

Explosive expletives filled the room. At that point, though, I got what my masochism wanted. He was as pissed as I was now. Only I didn't have the luxury of wallowing in my anger. "She's a recent rescue," I continued once Hurricane Zeke started to blow itself out. "In fact, she came in a few days before Omar. Of course the gal I brought in was more catatonic than violent, but the Efreet fixed that."

"And Mena attended to her?"

"Of course."

"And that doesn't tell you anything? Are you daft?" His question coincided with a knock at the door. "Speak of the devil," he said without moving.

"You better let her in."

"I don't think so."

"She'll keep knocking."

"Let her."

"She'll wonder what's going on."

"She'll survive. Curiosity only kills cats." He crossed his arms behind his neck and rested his head against them. "You still haven't answered my question."

I glared at my old boyfriend. Despite his more relaxed demeanor, he wasn't playing around. He really didn't trust Mena. Talk about a cliché when the boyfriend and the best friend hate each other. I knew why she didn't like him. She hadn't been around when my pieces needed picking up, but I'd told her enough about my past with the Israelite for her to take my side. Why he had a problem with her, though, I couldn't guess.

"You want an answer? Fine. It's a coincidence. Besides, she's not the only one allowed into the vault." I sat up straighter and tried to stare him down. Needless to say, I didn't win. "Who will you accuse next? Baz? If so, then you might as well point a finger at me. I'm in and out of the vault all the time."

"I'm not accusing anyone, Josie. I'm trying to figure out how something that should never happen actually did. There's a flaw in your security, and it's happened since I installed those wishes. I'm trying to see how deep the breach goes. And right now, I think your biggest breach is beating down your office door."

I shook my head. "You're a little more paranoid than usual."

"For gods' sakes, Josie, you're not paranoid enough. It's obvious this is some kind of personal vendetta. Why can't you see the Efreet has a man on the inside?" A strange look passed over his features. "What I can't figure is why an Efreet would have a gripe against you in the first place."

"What can I say?" I batted my eyelashes. "I have an adverse affect on men."

He ignored my lame jab. "Search your memory. Could you be acquainted with the Efreet in some way?"

"I don't know anything about him other than he's killed two... no, *three* people in front of me. If I had to venture a guess, I'd say he's some asshole trying to make serial killer of the year."

"His name is Amun," Zeke said like the name should ring a bell. It didn't. "The last time I saw him, he wasn't nearly as decked out for a masquerade ball, but then again, the last time I saw him, he was a genie. And a friend of mine."

"Was he sane then?"

"Funny." His head tilted to one side, like Major listening to a cheese wrapper crinkle. The imagery would've been hilarious if not for the glare Zeke shot me. "Believe it or not, Babydoll, I have plenty of friends."

Realizing how my question must've sounded, I said, "As much as I enjoy zinging you, I only meant since he's clearly off his rocker now, was he deranged then?"

"Let's say he was a few bars short of a cantata, but he remained one of the Many." He shook his head. "I never expected him to cross over to the Efreet. He was too attached to the Rules. Christ on a cracker, Josie, he dropped out of the world because he couldn't take how easily others bent the Rules. He'd rant about it for weeks on end."

"Dropped out?"

Zeke gave one short nod. "Dropped out. Last I knew he claimed to be headed to Atlantis until the world righted itself. A few decades maybe. I never could've imagined he'd spend centuries there." His gaze fell to the floor. "I honestly never dreamed he'd come back like this."

"Can we even do that?"

"Do what? Turn into an Efreet?" He swallowed hard and shook his head. I had a feeling his answer had less to do with the question than trying to clear an unpleasant image from his head.

"Actually, I meant hide in Atlantis. But now I want the answer to your question instead. I know Mary hinted how the Efreet came from a djinn gone bad, but she 'passed out' before she would elaborate."

One shoulder raised meant to make me think he didn't know. But I'd seen the move before. He knew a lot more than he wanted to admit. "You'd have to ask someone who was there."

"Like Mary? I think not." This pulling information out of unwilling people thing had gotten old. If I didn't get real answers soon, I'd start pulling other parts. Maybe I'd start with the tonsils and work my way down.

His laugh didn't hold a stitch of mirth. "I'm fairly sure Mary only knows how to catch them. She'd sooner swim in an active volcano than learn how to become an Efreet." Releasing a breath too deep for human lungs, he said, "I suggest something along the lines of skipping the middle man and asking one directly."

"You're kidding, right?" The suggestion seemed bizarre, even for Zeke. "I can't stop this guy from killing people, and you want I should chat him up? Maybe do lunch?"

"Not him. One of the others."

"Wait a goddamn dirty second." His dark eyes bored into me and I wanted to smack him. "There's more than one?"

"In a manner of speaking."

"*In a manner of speaking?* You prick. Quit talking in riddles and spit it out." I rose from the desk and stalked toward him. "Are more Efreet running around or not?"

"Well, it's complicated."

"Give it a whirl. Either you got them all during the last war or you didn't."

"*They* got them all. Which is why you'll need one of the punished ones."

I stopped an inch short of poking him in the eye. "Dogs? Wouldn't they all be dead by now? I mean, a dog's lifespan is what? Fifteen years?" And then the truth dawned on me. "I see now. You left them with a djinn's lifespan but not the power. Wow, what a shitty thing to do."

He didn't even look ashamed.

"Holy shit, Zeke. You're serious."

"Deadly. And it's part of the reason we're locked in here. No one else can know." He threaded his fingers through his tight curls. "As much as you hate to hear this, Josie, you still don't know a lot about being a genie. Stavros should've taught you better. You should've pushed harder to find out what you really are." His eyes shifted to stare at his shoes. With a half-assed shrug, he said, "And I should've been more open once I realized how ignorant you really were. My bad."

"Your bad?" The idea of hitting him sounded awesome. Not productive, but awesome. *To hell with productive.* I punched him in the face. When my hand stopped throbbing, and he stopped laughing at me, I sat back down. "Okay, so I didn't know about the Efreet. I'm over it. Tell me something else you think I don't know."

"You don't know the rules, Josie."

"I know the damn Rules."

"I don't mean the big Rules." He rubbed his cheek. "The little ones. The ones you keep tripping over. The ones you piss the Council off with. We genies have spent years living under them because we understand the necessity."

I cocked my head. "I don't see how—"

"Simple. Breaking the big Rules is like a human breaking the laws of physics. Impossible. The little rules are more social constructs meant to keep order, like the speed limit or shoplifting. Things you can do but shouldn't. And if you get caught—"

"What? You get a stint in genie jail?" I didn't see why Zeke looked so concerned. "So what?"

"Consorting with the Efreet carries a stiff penalty."

I stared at him open-mouthed. "Consorting? Seriously? Do genies talk like that anymore? Don't worry, Zeke, I'm not sleeping with... Oh, you can*not* be serious. I'm not allowed to *talk* to one?"

"Not unless you want to become a walking fur coat."

"Great Godfrey Daniels. Is the djinn answer to everything poochification?"

The lazy shrug appeared, making me want to knock him upside the head again. "What can I say, Babydoll. It works for us."

"This isn't funny."

"None of it ever was."

The knocking resumed, only more jackhammer than fist this time. Zeke shrugged one last time and rose from the floor. "Remember: If you want to find out the truth, let me know. It'll be easier than you think in some ways. Not so easy in others."

"How's that differ from the rest of my life?"

Zeke didn't bother answering. He knew the score better than I did. With a simple wish, he released the door. It burst open behind him.

"What the?" Mena said, too out of breath for a girl who didn't need to breathe. "Sorry, Jo. It's only that we have a bit of a problem."

Whatever problem she came up with couldn't compare to the idea of being turned into a dog because I wanted a few answers. All of this seemed too ludicrous. Sure, being a genie had its problems, but I never envisioned this level of crap.

"Another one?" I waved toward my desk. "Put it on the stack. The more the merrier."

A large, Moorish man in an Armani suit pushed into my office. "I believe I am the problem to which your secretary referred."

"Well, ain't that freakin' peachy. Iago Duarte." I tried to ignore Mena sputtering over the clerical help crack. "What brings you to my little domicile? Slumming?"

He peered down his aquiline nose like I was some sort of serf in his kingdom. Well, everyone's got a right to their attitude, but he forgot one thing. He wasn't in his kingdom anymore. He was in mine. And I was already too pissed to care.

SIXTEEN

~_~_~_~_~_~_~

"I've come about the disturbance," Duarte said, probably storing my 'slumming' comment away for ammunition against me later. I resisted asking if his disturbance felt like a million souls crying out. He didn't seem like a *Star Wars* fan. And his sense of humor sucked.

"Disturbance?" He couldn't know about the auction debacle so soon, which meant he'd heard about the shipping warehouse. Not a huge stretch, given his huge estate stood in the same general area. The rumors about him monitoring everything djinn weren't far-fetched after all. In fact, given his presence here, they were entirely likely.

Damn him.

Every sensible cell I had told me to refrain from pissing this guy off. I did manage to keep from slapping his face, so I counted it as a win. After all, Duarte supposedly had enough power to turn me into a drooling puddle every day for a year without a recharge. Plus, he controlled the Council. Never a good idea to tick off the guy who holds the reins of government, no matter how loosely-based it is.

"We're concerned about reports of several..." He tapped his gloves against the palm of his hand. Strange enough given I hadn't met anyone who wore driving gloves since the 1920s. Stranger still since Duarte didn't drive. "How should I put it? Untoward things occurring at your establishment as of late."

"Nothing we can't handle." If he meant inside Mayweather, maybe he hadn't heard about Greta after all. Maybe luck decided to hang out on my side for a change.

I glanced toward Zeke. He simply shrugged before lowering his shapely ass onto my suede sofa. This was my battle, but it still hurt that he didn't have my back. I understood him backing off with the Moor. After all, Duarte fancied himself as 'the authorities' when it came to brethren conduct, supernatural peacekeeper, whether we wanted one or not. I considered him more as an immortal Torquemada sans the personality and flashy clothes. He certainly hailed from Spain, albeit a few shades darker than your average Inquisitor.

"I beg to differ," he said, not moving from his spot by the door. Unlike Zeke, though, he stood ramrod straight. I hoped it meant he didn't plan on staying. More likely, he couldn't pry the stick out of his ass long enough to relax. Definitely, he'd come to be judge and jury for whatever crimes he thought I committed. Why waste time on a trial when you can show up, pass sentence, and carry it out?

"You allowed one of the Many to appear amongst the beings in your care."

"Stop calling them 'beings in my care' like they're my pets. They're *humans*." I glared into his surprisingly light eyes. "We don't own them, but if you remember correctly, they frequently own us." The Moor flinched, probably remembering the Master he once had.

"Furthermore, they weren't in my care. They came to conduct business."

"Business?"

"You haven't been paying attention, Duarte. I run a business here. This is the day of our annual auction—"

"You're selling humans? Another transgression." For a second, I assumed he was being deliberately obtuse. Too bad his incredulous attitude couldn't be faked.

"I don't sell living things. Those were customers for my *antiques* business. They buy the old things our brethren no longer want."

"And yet, this day's sales included one of your brethren," he said. *Son of a bitch set me up.* He never thought I sold 'people', plural. "Care to explain?"

I gave myself two seconds to steady my nerves. Not nearly enough by a long shot, but all the time I had. "The sanctuary in question wasn't included in the sale. The Ef—" He held up a hand, effectively cutting me off.

Just as well. I didn't really want Duarte to know about the Efreet anyway.

"The events leading to a Djinn sanctuary on the auction block," he said, "are neither here nor there. Suffice it to say, with so many humans present for the event, their world was exposed to ours. You know the rules, Miss Mayweather."

Little 'r' rules again. Except this time I couldn't claim ignorance. Even Stavros hadn't been so cruel as to leave me ignorant about keeping our existence hidden.

"The exposure was accidental and I dealt with it." *With the help of a few friends.* I kept that to myself. They didn't need to be dragged into this. "None of the humans know anything supernatural happened. They all think they got treated to an interesting little sideshow."

"I'm heartened to know you feel secure in your safety measures. Unfortunately for you, I do not share your optimism." His left eyebrow rose and hung there, twitching above his eye. "And neither do my associates."

My heart dropped into my stomach. For the most part, what passed for a djinn governing body listened to Duarte, but only as long as it benefitted their interests. Which meant infractions like this shouldn't have bothered any of the other members. Except from the sounds of it, he had the support of the Council as a whole.

"So you say," Zeke said from his spot on the couch.

He lay stretched with his feet up on one arm and his head nestled on his hands at the other end. *About time you spoke up*, I thought in his general direction. Whether he believed it or not, he had as much as stake as I did.

"I speak the truth," Duarte said, "but you need not take my word for it. I can summon any one of a dozen brethren to verify my claim." He stabbed a finger at my ex. "And you would do well to distance yourself from this situation, Ezekiel. You are not far from our notice yourself. You and your constant business dealings with mortals. It won't be long before the Council brings you to heel."

Zeke, bless his heart, let out a snort. "Save your shallow threats for the kids, Jim."

I could imagine smoke filtering out of Duarte's ears. "You shall address me as—"

"Iago. James. Jim. Whatever. The point is you shouldn't come into another djinn's house uninvited and then threaten them. It's bad etiquette. What's more, it might backfire on you."

A slow grin spread across Duarte's full lips. "I would never dream of entering anyone's domicile uninvited."

Before I could stop myself, a single name escaped me. "Basil."

"Of course. He lives within these walls as well, does he not?" I hated to agree with anything issuing from his mouth, but he was right. Damn it. "And so, your servant, I mean, business partner invited me inside. Presumably because he believes, much as I do, you have lost control of this mission of yours." He held a hand up against my pending protest. "You have taken upon yourself a task that, while admirable, exceeds your abilities. As such, the Council is suspending your operations, both mortal and otherwise, until you pose no threat to the anonymity of our species."

And so he finally comes out with his real purpose.

"But..." I began and then degenerated to sputtering. Thank goodness Zeke was there or I might've made a fool of myself. Well, more of one.

"Your authority doesn't extend as far as you assume," my old lover said. Duarte seemed too busy preening to notice, but Zeke had quietly gathered his power. If this confrontation became a genuine skirmish, my ex could wipe the Moor off the continent. *Yay.*

"In fact," he continued, "if I were you..." He flexed his energy for show, but the moron was still too occupied to notice. "...I'd rephrase your words into a helpful suggestion rather than an order. Understand, Jimbo?"

Zeke's deliberate misuse of Duarte's name broke through the egotistical shell. "I will do no such thing. This is not a request. She will suspend her activities or—"

"What?" A glance toward Zeke revealed him at the most comfortable I'd ever seen. The sight scared the crap out of me. Poor Duarte didn't know who he was messing with, or he'd know the Israelite was his most dangerous when he looked the most laid back. "Listen to me, Jimmy boy. You are going to leave. You will not come back and bother this nice lady. You won't ruffle a single hair out of place. Do you understand me?"

For good measure, Zeke flooded the room with his essence so the Moor couldn't help but notice. Duarte sputtered all over himself for a few seconds. The show would've been satisfying if I hadn't been so pissed.

"Why... Why would I do any such thing?" he asked when he recovered his voice.

"Because you know I could break you in an instant." Zeke let the threat hang in the air. "And because you have better ways to occupy your time than rousting Jo's business."

"Nothing is more important than stopping this..." Iago appeared to search for a word, and I prepared to slap him if the wrong one came out. "...*woman*. She could expose us to human scrutiny. She may already have. You should be well aware of the danger this poses for all djinn-kind."

"We've weathered worse. In fact, we may be facing a danger far more deadly than some auction hunters talking to the tabloids."

"What could be worse than—"

"An Efreet outbreak." Zeke dropped the E-bomb before I could stop him. I shot him my best 'shut the hell up' look. He ignored me. I did not want the Council aware of this. Not yet. Now it would leak to the general genie populous. Which might put us in the middle of some kind of phenomenal panic.

Or worse, the war I had been trying to avoid.

Duarte's dark skin acquired a sickly pallor. "You lie. You will not distract me by speaking of things better left to silence. The Council will hear of this."

"Go for it, Bud. By the time you and your buddies decide how to punish me, half our brethren could be turned. Do you want an Efreet outbreak on your head?"

"Nothing will 'be on my head', as you put it, because those *abominations* have not returned."

Zeke gave a little shrug. "At least one is running around while you waste time rousting Jo. And every passing minute, he's as free as a drachma on the sidewalk and as crazy as the merchant who lost it." He sat forward and placed his hands on his thighs. As calm as he seemed, I could tell he wanted to blast Duarte into the next life. Or maybe I was wishful thinking. "The magic tricks in front of those humans you pretend to give a shit about? They sure as hell weren't committed by Josie. She actually cares about the people you can't be bothered to look down your nose at."

"I'm sure I don't know to what you are referring."

"The enslaved. I know your life as a free djinn means you don't have to think about them, but they're out there, and like always, the Efreet preys on them."

"An Efreet? After all these years?" The Moor's tone came out haughty then reduced to a whisper. "It's impossible."

"Oh, it's possible." I threw extra steel into my voice. No clue where it came from, but Reggie taught me *when you can't be brave, fake it.* "Ask the djinn who were there. Since Basil's already been so helpful, why not start with him?"

Duarte scowled at the both of us before he backed away. "Don't think I won't investigate your allegations. Neither should you think this information excuses your behavior. If you persist in associating with mortals, and the Many suffer in the slightest, you will answer for the crime."

I tried not to let it show on my face, but I wasn't aware anything djinn did qualified as an actual crime. Breaking the Rules wasn't possible, and despite Zeke's earlier hints, I refused to believe the Council's rules amounted to more than guidelines for behavior. Since keeping our existence secret was in the best interest of all djinn, I couldn't imagine a need to criminalize it.

Of course, until a few days ago, I couldn't imagine a djinn could be killed and I'd already seen three murders.

"Do I make myself clear?" Duarte said, like some annoyed schoolmaster.

Zeke ignored him, but I nodded. I didn't understand a damn thing about the Moor, but my capitulation could get him out of my hair quicker. No sooner did the guy have my assent and he teleported away, leaving a slightly musty odor behind. He made me wish I'd added 'no teleporting out by unauthorized personnel' to my security protocols.

"Jimmy didn't used to stink up the place with his magic. Must be a new affectation," Zeke said. Suddenly, the scent of toasted marshmallows filled the room. My favorite. Whether he did it to prove a point or to make me happy, I didn't know. All I knew was my stomach rumbled.

"Bastard," I hissed.

"Duarte's always been one," he said, mistaking my meaning.

I couldn't care less about our recent visitor's parentage. Zeke knew I hadn't eaten. Hell, I wouldn't be surprised if he did the food trick to distract me.

"Something to do with a Moorish Lord," he continued, talking over my rumbling belly, "and a Spanish serving girl. I could ask, if you'd like, but he's touchy about his family tree."

I shot Zeke a look that would've killed if the Rules didn't forbid it. "We've got other things to worry about than the genealogy of a huge pain in my ass. Like this jacked-up branch of brethren politics trying to shut me down." A dozen or so older members of Council scattered throughout the world did not a Supreme Court make. "Maybe they'll be too distracted by the Efreet."

"You were never so lucky, Babydoll."

I debated telling him where he could shove his sense of humor, along with his nickname, when a familiar face poked back into my office. In the decades I've known Mena, nothing has ruffled her, but from her frizzled hair to her twitching toes, she was about as ruffled as a gal could get.

"What's wrong now?"

"Omar." Admittedly, with everything else going on, a lot of things slipped into the back of my head, but I had no clue why she was looking at me funny until she continued. "You know... your Bedouin buddy?"

Right about then, I realized she must've thought I'd slipped a gear. "Of course." I shook myself back to business at hand. "The perfect end to a perfect day."

"He should still be a glorified mummy." Zeke pre-empted my own dumb questions.

"We-ell." Mena blushed beneath her olive skin. "I didn't think he should stay paralyzed forever. I loosened the bonds a little so he'd be more comfortable."

"Damn social workers," Zeke muttered under his breath.

"He's loose? Again?" I shot Zeke a dirty look. An image of another round of 'lunatic in the halls' leapt into my head. "I do *not* need this right now. Seriously, Mena. Couldn't you have waited until tomorrow to play with Omar? Or is that asking too much?"

"I'm sorry. After what happened, I hoped he'd be more amenable to questioning. I'm sorry."

I felt like an ass for making Mena feel like shit. What can I say, it's a vicious circle. "Where is he this time?"

"He's still in the vault, but he's doing his damndest to tear the place apart."

"And the other residents?" I didn't want to think about Omar releasing the other loonies. We'd not only be facing a long night, but a long series of years.

"They're safe. As soon as he started freaking out, I engaged the security protocols." She ran a shaking hand through her hair. "But if he breaks out, I can't imagine any of our security magic would keep him from releasing the others."

Or from breaking out into the world.

SEVENTEEN

~-~-~-~-~-~-~

After Mena's second unwelcome surprise, my third of the day, I cursed our security measures. If not for them, Zeke could've zapped all of us to the vault in an instant. As it stood, we lost the element of surprise anyway. Once the locks clicked open, dear sweet Omar would slice us into ticker tape suitable for the Macy's parade.

"You hang back," I told Zeke. "So far, you're the only one who could stop him. We absolutely cannot let Omar leave this building."

He gave a grudging nod as Mena and I removed the locks. From what I heard, she mumbled 'open sesame', but I didn't have time to ponder the wisdom of using the world's oldest password. As soon as the magical security fell away, my fingers flew over the keypad. With any luck, the Bedouin would be too wrapped up in his own insanity to notice us.

And damned if luck hadn't decided to hang out with us. As the door swung open, we saw Omar trying to punch a hole through the opposite wall. From the rubble scattered at his feet, he'd made some headway, too. If he got past the concrete, though, he'd be disappointed. The whole mountainside waited beyond those cinder blocks.

While our resident whackjob beat holy hell out of the wall, we slipped in behind him. The door whooshing shut nearly killed my confidence; the lock snicking into place almost sent me running out the way we came. Sure, we'd trapped the nutcase inside, but we trapped ourselves with him.

"Yo, Omar," I called, swallowing my unease. If you think dogs excel at smelling fear, you ain't seen nothing. Stuffing every iota of dread as deep as I could, I edged toward the guy.

Fortune smiled on us a little more. The crazed desert dweller didn't turn. For a second I regretted calling him out. If he kept his focus off us, maybe we could jump him.

"You are not my Master."

Denial's not just a river in Egypt, bud. I couldn't help rolling my eyes. I suspected, if he'd caught the motion, he wouldn't give a rat's tiny hiney whether I made faces or not. He wanted out. And I'd bet he'd be perfectly willing to come through us if he had to. Knocking two gals around had to be preferable to chiseling a hole through a mountain.

"The Master is here," he said before I could throw a wish or verbal barb. With one slow movement, he turned to face me. "I must unite with my Master. I must be free."

With Omar's eyes focused my way, Mena used the opportunity to flank him. She made it about two steps before he threw a wish in her direction and slammed her against the door. I figured she'd be okay. I mean, once she got her arm to stop making such a gross right angle. Looking at it made me want to toss my cookies. Instead, I choked down my feelings and adopted my best custodial tone.

"Easy there, big guy. We're here to help."

"The only help I require is my release. Why can I not blink away from this evil place?"

Calling my place 'evil' didn't improve my mood, but at least the guy spoke in complete sentences without the word 'Master' for a change. It showed some small progress and I'd take whatever I could get.

"You don't have a Master anymore. I can help you."

"I require no assistance from one such as you. I only require the Master, and you are not my Master." His hands spanned a foot apart, almost like a guy in those sandwich commercials. Except he wouldn't be presenting me with a cheap, semi-tasty sub. Energy crackled between his palms, lifting the hair off my scalp.

My very own Van de Graff generator. Whee.

I opened my mouth, but I couldn't think of what anyone could possibly say to stop this nut from turning me into deep-fried genie. Mena had the Psych degrees. I was merely the offspring of a burglar and an addict. At the moment, I didn't think Reggie's skill set would get me anywhere. Stealing Omar got me into this mess in the first place.

On the other hand, Evangeline's penchant for all things addictive might be an asset for once. If I could figure out what fix this guy needed, I'd have him.

"I hear you saying you need your Master." Channeling my inner Dr. Phil, I said, "Is that really what you want? Wouldn't you rather be free?" I hadn't met a genie yet who didn't yearn for freedom, despite how deep some buried the yearning. Stockholm's got nothing on our syndromes.

"My Master promised me freedom. His last wish will set me free."

I swallowed a heavy sigh. If I had a pot of coffee for every Master who promised to use his last wish for a djinn's freedom, I'd never be tired again. And hell, my caffeine consumption might stop the drug trade in Columbia. Everyone would be growing java for my consumption instead of cocaine. On the other hand, if I had to rely on Masters to actually keep their promises, I'd have better luck getting my caffeine fix inside the Mormon Tabernacle.

Once upon a time, I had counted on that promise, too. Whether Benny actually intended to use his last wish for my freedom was moot. The Nazis murdered him, and his death set me free. My freedom qualified more as blind luck than a promise kept, even if the luck felt more bad than good. My heart got torn out, but hey, I was free.

"I need the Master. I need to be free again."

And the addiction I'd been hoping for reared its ugly head. The poor guy was twisting inside his skin to get a taste of freedom. Simple really. No one wants to belong to someone else, and when you add in centuries of being unable to live life on your own terms, freedom itself becomes the jones you can never find a fix for.

"I can free you." The words crooned toward him like he was a child. "All you have to do is accept me as your new Master."

"No," he shouted, making the reinforced walls rattle. "You are not my Master."

"You sound like a broken record." Behind me, Mena gasped. I had no clue whether she'd set the wicked break in her arm or I'd said the totally wrong thing. If it was the former, great. I could use her backup. If not, tough. I didn't have time for the soft-n-fluffy bunny approach.

"If you're so anxious to get to your Master, maybe it would be better if you started out telling us who the hell he is." The genie moved his mouth, but no sound came out. "I wish I was better at lip-reading," I mumbled. Suddenly, his motions made perfect sense.

"Sunuvabitch," I said. "Amun." Omar nodded solemnly and, if I read it right, with a bit of pride. *Well, screw that. Time for some tough love—genie style.*

"You'll never be free when you're waiting on some Efreet, ya know." Omar's eyes widened, and the power he tossed from hand to hand lessened an amp or two. "He's been in the building for a while now, right? His presence is why you're so jazzed.

"Funny how your Efreet Master dropped by earlier and didn't bother to reclaim you. Nope. He had better things to do, like killing a pretty genie gal." I tapped one finger on my chin. Corny, I know, but I was winging it. "You're less important to him as a possession than she was as a corpse. And you'd don't even belong to the guy anymore. He doesn't *own* you."

"He did not come because I failed him. I will not fail again."

"Failed? What, because you didn't go to him when he didn't bother trying to get in here to you?"

The Bedouin's head hung a fraction lower. "I failed because I have not completed his second wish. I need to explain. He must understand why I cannot, so he can set me free."

I swallowed hard. Here lay a wrinkle I hadn't anticipated. Regardless of whether I'd touched his sanctuary, he couldn't truly serve a new Master until all the wishes issued from his previous one were completed. Unless I could find a loophole.

"What did he wish for?"

Omar's lips parted but no sound came out. After seconds of fruitless mouth motion, he let out an audible sigh. "I cannot repeat the wish; I am only to carry it out. You must allow me to reach my Master. I must complete the wish."

I shook my head. The only explanation for this dude not already exploding into a million sparkles? At least his wish *could be* completed. Maybe the Efreet included a timeframe or some other nonsense. Still, the fact this guy managed to hold on so long without granting the wish explained a lot. I'd be freaking out, too.

"If you accept me as your Master..." I hoped against hope I could bypass the stupid-ass Rules for once. "...and renounce the Efreet, the wish will dissipate. You can let the pain go." I didn't know for certain if I spoke the truth, but it sounded good. Hell, I'd tell this guy a million bald-faced lies to settle him down.

Omar's nose crinkled. "You cannot speak the truth."

"Listen, bud," I said as my frustration carried me past caution and right into some kind of warped indignation. "You want to be free, right? You want it more than fulfilling some stupid wish from some damned Efreet, don't you? I mean, for petesakes, he's an..." I groped for the right words and Mary's proclamation fell from my lips. "...an abomination." I could only hope this genie belonged to the Efreet Hate Club.

"The entire race is an abomination, but—"

"But nothing. You know what your Master is. You don't want to help an abomination, do you? Well, I'm your way out." At least I hoped I was.

Mena's hand touched my shoulder. I glanced back to let her take over. She nodded at me to continue. I didn't know what I was doing, but I must've gotten something semi-right.

"You know what I think?" I continued. "I think it's time to let the bastard stew in his own bodily fluids for a while. Let a brethren help you."

"You are brethren?" Man, was Omar ever confused.

"I might be a girl, but I'm as much a brethren as you are. Take a sniff."

Finally a glimmer of sanity passed over the Bedouin's face. "You are djinn."

Thank the gods for *eau de genie*—one whiff separates your friends from your enemies. "Every square inch. Now, let's release the power you're holding onto. Then we'll have a nice long talk about what you can do with your freedom."

I was sure my ploy wouldn't work. After all, the guy had been raging like a frigging baboon on crack since I rescued him. And I had to face facts, even if I talked the guy down, I wasn't sure I could free him from the damn Efreet.

Thank the gods, luck stayed with me. Omar lowered his hands, letting his magic melt into the air. All at once, my image of the guy became more 'lost puppy' than 'killer Doberman'. I motioned to Mena. Her trepidation as she crossed to him radiated around her. For his part, Omar didn't even blink aggressively. Once her hand rested on his arm, all his tension drained away.

"What it is you wish of me, oh kindest of Masters?" he said, his eyes trained on the ground instead of my face. I appreciated him better as a whackjob. At least then, he didn't seem deflated and a little pathetic.

"Right now? Renounce the Efreet."

His solemn oath flew out so fast I barely heard him speak. With them, a huge weight appeared to float off him.

"Thanks," I said. "Now I need some peace. Later, we'll talk. Okay?"

Mena nodded. I must've done something right, but I found no victory in the win. Instead, I felt like a heel

She mouthed at me. *Give him time.* If I had to guess, I'd say she assumed the cause of my angst lay in the fact submissive genies rubbed me the wrong way. But my self-loathing took precedence over old annoyances.

"He has all the time he needs. On the other hand, I don't. Let me know when I can fulfill my promise." Mena's eyebrows raised along with Omar's eyes. Judging from the glimmer of doubt in those deep brown pools, the Bedouin assumed I would welch on our deal.

"Prove to Mena you're no longer a menace," I told him, "and you'll be free, okay?"

He had such renewed hope on his face I couldn't bear to look anymore. As I turned away, I didn't want to consider whether he would make it back to sanity. I didn't want to be forced to become the dishonest bitch he expected.

Once I reached the doorway out of the madhouse, I spoke over my shoulder. "When you think he's ready to answer some questions, call me."

"I am ready now, my most-perfect Master."

A cringe seeped up my spine. No matter how many rescued brethren call me 'Master', I'm never going to like it. I didn't start this mission to create a cadre of my own slaves. I did this so the slavery would stop.

"Maybe," I told him, "but I'm not buying it yet. I'll be back when you've had time to rest and recuperate." *And time to do the same myself.* Too many days like this one and I'd be booking a vacation in Atlantis myself. "And please, for gods' sakes, stop calling me Master."

When the door swung open, my soft bed and my softer dog called to me. After the day I'd had, I cursed the fact that human pharmaceuticals and inebriants only have a passing effect on djinn metabolism. *What the hell, it doesn't hurt to give it the old college try.*

"How'd it go?" Zeke said from beside me. I damn near jumped out of my skin.

"Don't do that!" I punctuated the statement by punching his bicep.

"Went well, huh?" He looked me over. "Since you're not broken into a million tiny pieces, I'm guessing your nomadic friend is playing nice. Or did you have to use a wish again?"

I really didn't like people harping on my past errors. "I talked him down."

"Great. How'd you manage it?"

"The usual way." I really didn't want to talk to Zeke about this. Anyone else would've taken my answer and left it at that. Not him.

"Which was?" Laying a finger alongside my chin, he urged me to look him in the eyes. If I did, all my shame would come pouring out. Still, I needed something to drown in. What better place than Zeke's eyes?

"I got him to accept me as a Master." I had to hope he wouldn't ask the obvious question.

But he asked it anyway. "What did you promise to get him to agree? He didn't seem so amenable before. I hope it wasn't a night of unbridled—"

"I promised his freedom. Okay?"

"Not too imaginative, Josie. So why act like your dog just died?"

I shook away from his touch. "I don't like making promises I can't keep."

"So keep it. I mean, you planned on freeing him anyway. He's not really any worse off than before. Unless you're dying to have a slave now."

"You know better. If I believed in slavery, I wouldn't have started this damn mission." And though I left it unsaid, we were both thinking my obsession with freeing my brethren caused the fight that broke us up.

Zeke held his hands up in mock surrender. "Easy, Josie. I didn't really imagine you'd want a slave. I'm merely trying to figure out your major maladjustment. You promised him freedom. And he'll get it. Right? So why are you all twisted up?"

"His previous Master was the Efreet." After pushing Zeke's mouth closed, I said, "Because of that, he may never be right enough to be freed." The frustration seeped into my voice unbidden and I gave in to it. "When I gave my word, I suspected I couldn't keep it, and I gave it anyway. It's a shitty thing to do."

"Maybe his acceptance of you as his Master is the first step toward sanity." I tried to deny it, but he wouldn't let me. "Think about it, Josie. It's hard enough being slave to some crackpot human. Imagine how hard he had it strapped to a lunatic like Amun." He draped his arm around my shoulders, pulling me close. "Go easy on yourself. You did the right thing. I know you'll do the right thing once he returns to normal, no matter how long it takes. One thing I could always count on was you doing the right thing."

"Oh yeah? Then why's Duarte gunning for my ass?" I let Zeke guide me down the hallway. I didn't know where we were headed. I didn't care. As long as we ended up somewhere I wouldn't have to think about the Council or Omar or dead kids or the Efreet.

"Forget the Moor. Chances are, he'll be so busy drumming up troops for a new war with 'the Efreet menace', he won't have time to bother with you." A small chuckle bubbled in my chest at his exaggerated air quotes. Lame or not, his attempt at humor worked. "I know if Jimmy Duarte mentions the Efreet to his buddies, they'll either laugh him off the planet, or they'll be too wrapped up in their own panic to care about you. Your narrow behind won't be on a platter any time soon."

I nudged him with my shoulder, but I couldn't fight the smile on my face. Even when things had been on the ugly side of 'horribly wrong' between us, he could still lighten my mood.

"So what now?" I asked. He smiled and my current mental state almost made me suggest a 'what now' where both of us ended up panting and sweaty.

"A night on the town, of course."

Not what I expected, but not a bad idea either. Lord knows, Basil's told me often enough to step away from the place. I never had the time, of course. In fact, now didn't seem optimum either, but my breaking point wasn't too far off. A couple hours away from the asylum wouldn't hurt, even if I spent those hours with a man I swore I'd never be alone with again.

"Okay." I crushed my qualms into lint and brushed them aside. "What town do we unleash ourselves upon?"

EIGHTEEN

~-~-~-~-~-~-~-~

Zeke mentioning Venice didn't surprise me. After all, we'd wined and dined in some of the world's finest restaurants. The minute the city's name left his mouth, an image of gondola rides and soft lights relaxed me. It sounded like the perfect locale for some R and R. Plus, Italy happened to be a place we never visited during our romance. With everything else going on, I couldn't handle a bittersweet trip down Reminiscing Road, too.

The *idea* of Venice had been pleasant. When we teleported into a hotel room overlooking the Vegas Strip? Not so much.

"You said..." As I gazed at the view, a realization hit me. He hadn't lied. Not exactly. We *were* in Venice, but the casino, not the city of love. I should've been grateful. Instead, a little disappointment crept into my veins. Shrugging, I resigned myself to the fact Italy or Nevada still wasn't Colorado. I wouldn't allow a little thing like locale ruin my mini-vacation.

"I calculated a night in Vegas would circumvent the wasted time translating menus or wishing up better language skills." He nudged me with his shoulder. "Think positive, Babydoll. Here we can dine in restaurants boasting well-known chefs and never venture too far."

Excellent food is always a big plus, but in Sin City, only one person pops into my head. And pirates aren't known for their cooking skills. "I don't suppose we can avoid Mary since we're in her neighborhood."

He shook his head. "She'll find out one way or another. But we'll leave that worry for later. We've got tonight."

I almost thought he was going to break into an old '70s song. Memories of slow dancing in front of the fire merged with reminiscing about what came afterwards. If my thoughts drifted there, I'd forget my resolve and want to recreate the scene.

"This is a bad idea." The chance of waking up against Zeke's lean frame was almost more than my shaky nerves could handle. "I am not staying here with you. I can guess your plans, but the answer is no."

He ignored me and strolled to the en suite phone. "Legasse or Puck? Although, I've heard Kellor is a fairly good chef, too. I mean, if you're looking for something less commercial television."

I stood my ground. Two could play the ignoring game. "I mean it, Zeke. I'm not spending the night with you."

"Or, if you're not hungry, we could stroll down the strip and see how much trouble we can cause. Maybe spend the evening pretending to be human tourists. Remember Toronto?"

"Ze-ke," I said through gritted teeth.

"Face it, Josie," he said. "I'm not going to discuss anything with you until you relax. Choose where you want to eat or I'm ordering room service." His hand hovered over the receiver. "You have ten seconds before I call down to the kitchens."

Images of our last night in a hotel together swam through my head, reminding me I wasn't exactly hungry. Well, not for food. Which meant if I didn't make a dining choice, we'd spend the next hour alone anyway. Eating or not, depending on my willpower.

I pointed my senses inward and tallied my available energy. I probably had enough juice to get outside the door, but my batteries still needed to recharge. If I couldn't catch a cab and make it to McCarran before Zeke caught up with me, I'd be trapped with him for the duration. Besides, running away from the man only worked for so long. Our current proximity was proof enough. After decades apart, he could still catch me.

"Puck." I considered the other options. "I don't feel like any 'Bam' tonight and I'm not in the mood for Italian."

"Keller it is then." I raised my eyebrows and he winked. "I've been in the mood for French all day." His gaze drifted over me in its slow, lazy way stopping at my lower lip. Damned if I hadn't walked face first into his innuendo. Leave it to Zeke to slip sex into a gourmet meal. "You aren't exactly dressed for it, though."

For a moment, I didn't know if he meant dinner or a night of passion. Power rippling toward me answered the question. As parts of me experienced a sudden chill, I almost slapped him. One downward glance showed me not quite as naked as the breeze would indicate but only just. The dress he wished me into didn't amount to much more than a couple handkerchiefs and some dental floss.

"Ze-eke."

"What? You look incredible."

"Fix it."

A devilish grin slid across his mouth. "If I've traumatized your sensibilities, fix it yourself. I happen to like how you look."

What a waste of power. Before my energy hoarding tendencies overwhelmed my modesty, I slipped a wish over myself. Zeke's frustrated groan told me I'd chosen my outfit well.

"You are a cruel, cruel woman, Babydoll."

"Live with it. At least now I'm presentable."

"You're more than presentable." His gaze was so intense I could feel it slide from my shoulders to my feet and back again. "Who knew the old idea of leaving something to the imagination could be so wicked?"

I glanced down. Soft, chocolate-brown velvet, gathered in gentle folds, fell to below my knees. Each ripple accentuated my curves without showing them. All in all, the dress looked tastefully demure. Frankly, I didn't see why Zeke made so much fuss, but I stopped trying to figure out what scuttled through the Hebrew's head ages ago. Analyzing him led only to madness.

Or, at the very least, irritation.

"I'm not going to forget myself and sleep with you, Zeke," I said as he hooked my hand over his arm, "so you might as well cancel the room."

He tipped his head toward me. "If you don't mind, I'll keep it. We'll still need a safe place to teleport. Besides, after you hear my reason for choosing Sin City for your mini-vacation, you'll agree to the overnight stay." Giving a theatrical wink, he eased me out the door. "And maybe all of tomorrow, too."

"Dream on."

"I have a lot of dreams, Josie, and the best of them still involve you."

His statement shut me up for the entire trip to the restaurant. I had to admit, just a little, he might not be the man I once knew, but falling back in love with him was out of the question. Too much time had passed and too much blood had gone under the bridge. I didn't want to know his dreams. I sure as hell didn't need to wonder whether they included me. Lord knows, I never had dreams about him.

Well, not more than once or twice. A night.

The restaurant Zeke chose was probably amazing. I didn't notice. The food they served probably tasted exquisite. It floated over my tongue, but I don't remember tasting any of it. As if I didn't have enough occupying my mental real estate, this night sent my emotions into a tailspin. The bastard probably planned the whole evening, right down to my internal imbalance.

Zeke played the consummate dinner companion. He steered clear of every subject but the most banal. He talked about the weather in Denver. He expounded on the latest Hugh Jackman movie. He speculated about the upcoming football season. He also explained an off-Broadway play he'd seen the month before, in detail so exact it was like I'd seen the damn thing with him.

To any passerby, I must've looked like any other piece of arm-candy—all fluff and no substance. I answered him politely, nodded a lot, but added little to the conversation. I hadn't seen a play in decades. I hadn't followed football since before the Colts left Baltimore and Lombardi was a coach, not a trophy. Hell, the newest cinematic spectaculars passed me by. I spent too much time working.

How Zeke managed to get any real work done with all his jet-setting shocked the shit out of me.

"And that, Josie, is how I got on the set of Grey's Anatomy. When the season finale comes out, watch the gallery above the operating room. I'm sitting just left of center. No lines, of course, but then again, if Duarte watches television, it'll be better if I didn't open my mouth on camera."

The instant our overly anal pal's name slipped out, Zeke realized his error. In a nanosecond, our night of empty fun ended.

"He can't really do anything, can he?"

"You know my thoughts on the subject," he said, developing a sudden interest in the decadent dessert he'd insisted I order. I didn't think anyone could squeeze so much chocolate into such a small helping, but one bite satisfied my cravings.

"He'll attempt to whip the brethren into some kind of fireworks display," Zeke continued, "but the thought of one loose Efreet will freak them out so much, he won't muster so much as a sparkler worth out of them. And once you eradicate the Efreet yourself, they can't say much of anything against you. In fact, I'd be willing to bet they'll remain silent even if you don't stop the Efreet."

"Ever the optimist? This is new." I pointed at him with my fork. "When did you change?"

"Around 1776." He scooped a large bite of gooey goodness into his mouth. After swallowing, though, his features became melancholy.

"Not good?"

"This? It's amazing." He shook his head. "No. I never noticed something before. Back then, you never really bothered to discover anything about me. Now? For all you know, I could've changed entirely since you walked away from us. You would know, if you hadn't cut me out of your life."

"I didn't—"

"And stopped returning my calls."

"I've been—"

"And blocked me from teleporting anywhere near the building." He tapped the edge of the plate with his fork. "And created a wish so every time I walked toward the building it turned me in the other direction."

"It's for security rea—"

"For every djinn or special for me?"

Well, he had me there. Other djinn could get onto the property without permission. Most could come as far as the lobby without needing an escort. "Fine. I admit it. I didn't want to know anything about you or your current life." *Or to find out you were thriving without me.* "Is that what you want to hear?"

"It's a start."

I gathered my clutch and wrap. "It's all you'll get right now. We don't have time to sit chatting anymore. Other things are—"

"Far more pressing. I know." He lifted a hand toward our waiter. "Check please."

"Back to Colorado?" I asked. As much as I didn't want a romantic evening with Zeke, I really didn't want to end the night either. I told myself my urge to stay had to do with avoiding the mess back home. My heart knew part of me wanted more time with my old lover.

I could've kicked that part.

"In a while." He glanced at the Rolex I hadn't noticed. "You need to chat with someone before we leave Vegas."

"Then pay the bill and let's go. I don't want to hang around this town any longer than we have to." *I don't have that much willpower.* Too much more time in his company, and I might forget why I left him in the first place. In fact, the longer the night went on, the less I could remember why leaving him had been so damn important.

Oh yeah, because I didn't want to fritter away my eternity with the rest of djinn-kind enslaved.

Zeke sipped at his wine. "We can't leave yet." He indicated the understated wealth on his wrist. "She's probably in bed by now, and you know how much humans need their rest."

"Please tell me you didn't drag me back to talk to Mary again." I could've slapped him. "She still won't tell me anything." Plus, as much as I hated to admit it, Mary's fake inebriation hurt my feelings.

The waiter arrived and Zeke laid a platinum card on the little silver tray. "Mary has the information you need. You need to ask the right questions."

"And wave the right amount of cash in her face?"

"I wouldn't have it any other way. I know the pirate's price, and I'm always willing to pay it." He downed the last of his Cabernet and signed the receipt. "The question is, how much are you willing to pay?"

I narrowed my eyes at my dinner companion. "Mary asked the same thing." Somehow I didn't think either of them meant finances. They sure weren't talking about our friendly barter system. Still, whatever the cost, I'd still pay less than those dead genies.

"This night wasn't supposed to be about angst, Babydoll." His too-chipper voice broke through my gathering gloom.

"Huh?"

"You look like you swallowed a black hole, and it sucked the light right out of you." Standing, he interlaced his fingers with my own. "And I know exactly how to revive it."

I tried to pull my fingers free, but the bastard wouldn't let go. "I am *not* sleeping with you," Maybe my tone held enough oomph to get him to back off.

"You have a dirty mind." His stunned look wasn't fooling anyone. The man never had a shocked moment in his life. "I don't know whether to be happy or amazed your mind reached the gutter level since we parted. I'm definitely put out I didn't go there first." He flashed a cheesy grin. "I merely thought we should scatter some major fundage along The Strip while we wait for the old gal to wake up."

"And whose 'fundage' did you plan on scattering?" I learned a long time ago spreading djinn-created wealth around was never a good idea. Flooding the human monetary system with money leads to chaos. Magical money is worse, especially when the serial numbers lead humanity to think we're counterfeiters.

"My own," he said. "I make a tidy sum every year. And I don't mean I create it out of thin air. I earn it."

I cocked my head. Part of me understood I had work to do back in Colorado. We could always teleport back in the morning to interrogate the pirate. Still, the thought of dealing with the mess back home made my stomach squirm. I couldn't escape the fact it would all have to be handled sooner or later. I wanted to opt for later.

"You're thinking too much. Let go a little bit," he said, like he read my thoughts. "The kiddies will be fine for one night." I arched an eyebrow. "There's nothing to do about the Efreet until he shows himself again or we track him down ourselves. If he makes an appearance tonight, we'll be the first teleport to wherever he is. Otherwise, we need do some digging. And who better to dig into than Mary Killigrew? Trust me."

"What about Duarte?" I couldn't stop digging in my heels.

"Only the gods know what Duarte's about. All the more reason to push him out of your mind for the night, too. For the love of all things holy, Josie, when did you last take a night off?"

"I took a whole week off last month."

"You mean the week between alerts when Baz did inventory? From what I heard, when you weren't ensconced in your library, you holed up in the cave, petting the damned dog and scouring the internet for other djinn. Some vacation." He steered me toward the casino floor before my feet could head for the elevators. "How's your mural working out for you, by the way?"

I glared at him. "It's lewd."

"And hence the reason it works so well. Thieves drooling over porn are too busy to actually wonder whether anything's behind it. Brilliant idea, if you ask me."

"I didn't." I dug my heels into the casino's weirdly patterned carpet. "Where do you think you're taking me now?"

"To have a little fun, if only for one night." He pulled me firmly against his side and curled my arm around his. Whispering in my ear, he said, "Let go, Josie-girl. You know you want to."

"What I want and what I get—"

"Never end up being the same thing." He really needed to stop finishing my sentences. Especially since he was so damn right all the time. "Do something you want for once." He snorted into my ear. "You used to let loose all the time. What happened to that carefree gal? All work and no play makes my Babydoll too damn dull for immortality. Let go. A little. It won't hurt. I promise."

I didn't want to admit it, but he was right. Maybe if I'd taken some time off before this shit storm hit, I'd be weathering it better now. As dragged out as I felt, I was damn near ready to throw in the towel and let the Efreet do whatever he pleased.

"Fine. One night." He flashed his imperfect smile at me. "But no sex, Ezekiel."

A mock groan slipped from him. "Who knew you had such a one track mind, Josephine? I only planned a little harmless fun, like drinking and gambling."

I don't know whether he meant it for my ears, but I could've sworn I heard him add, "The real fun's for later."

I would've been more relaxed for our night out if I'd known how much later Zeke meant. We strolled from one casino to the next, up the strip and back down again until my magically enhanced body sported sore feet and drooping eyelids. When I wanted nothing more than to drop into the suite's luxurious bed, he cajoled me into visiting a little place in Henderson for breakfast. After all those years, Zeke still knew how to wake me up—a good cup of joe and a plate of Belgian waffles.

As I used the last bite of feather-light pastry to wipe the sticky, sweet, strawberry sauce from the plate, he tapped my mug. I glanced over at him, more than a little embarrassment coloring my cheeks. If this had been a real date, my eating habits would've scared any other man into the hills.

"Mary should be up by now. Have you finished or should I have the kitchen staff roll out another cartload?"

"Not nice," I said as I refilled my java. "You've seen me eat. This shouldn't be a shock." As a human, I ate like any other girl. Well, any girl who watched her figure. Once I became djinn, I let all thoughts of tiny waists go to hell. Since calories don't mean squat to djinn metabolisms, I enjoyed every plate of food I could stuff into my face. Besides, with all the power I burn, I'm constantly hungry.

At least that's what I tell myself, especially when waffles are involved.

Zeke let out a soft laugh. "I'd forgotten about you and breakfast. Remember when you got us thrown out of the restaurant in Macon?"

"The Waffle Cottage." As much as I started out avoiding reminiscences with the old boyfriend, we actually spent the night remembering fun times. By tacit agreement, we stuck to the happy and the silly instead of wallowing in the dour and mirthless. Needless to say, we had a lot of material. "They shouldn't refer to themselves as an abode of breakfast goodness," I said, adopting the haughtiest tone I could, "if they don't expect patrons to consume a great deal of their wares."

"You cleaned them out, Josie," he said when he stopped laughing. "They're supposed to be open around the clock. They had to close because they ran out of food."

I lifted one shoulder. "I still maintain they should've known better." A lilting sound filled the diner and several heads turned my way.

"You should laugh more often," he said. "It suits you."

All at once, memories of two dead children fell on me like a sack of leftover oatmeal. "If I had more to laugh about, I would."

He reached toward me, but the moment had poofed away. I wasted an entire night enjoying myself but, with the sunrise, came the guilt. Those djinn would never enjoy themselves again. How could I and still live with myself?

"Let's get out of here." I grabbed my clutch and slid out of the vinyl booth. As I stood, I noticed the regular customers staring. No big surprise since both Zeke and I were dressed to the nines, but every glance felt like an accusation. I'd spent the night acting like a party-girl when I really should've jumped back into the fray. Besides, Mary would die laughing if we showed up like this.

"We should change before we visit the pirate," Zeke said.

"Stop that."

"Stop what?" He grabbed my hand and led me toward the back of the parking lot.

"E.S.P. or whatever you're doing."

"Djinn aren't telepathic. I merely read your face. You always were very expressive."

As he guided me past a pair of early birds in search of a breakfast special, I whispered, "I used to think djinn couldn't be murdered either, so telepathy isn't a stretch."

"Apples and oranges. I'm telling you, I haven't been reading your mind. You simply hate admitting I know you well enough to anticipate your thoughts." He tugged me alongside the building, behind a rancid dumpster. "So live with it."

Before I could stop myself, I stuck my tongue out. When we wished ourselves away, his deep-throated chuckle hung in the space we left behind.

NINETEEN

~-~-~-~-~-~-~-~

My case of the giggles subsided when we dropped in front of an old tract house. The paint around the windows peeled in the hot Nevada sun. Despite the early hour, the city was on the verge of parboiling. Desiccated plants littered the unintentionally xeriscaped yard. All in all, too dry a place for a pirate and too ugly for an English lady.

"This can't be where Mary lives." She raked in plenty of money from both the pawnshop and her informant work. Why she would live in such a shitty locale, I couldn't begin to fathom.

"This is where her presence is strongest, so I'm going with 'she lives here'." He lifted one eyebrow. "Or this could be her love nest. You never know with Mary."

Thirty years earlier, I would've believed my old friend had a love nest somewhere. Once every nook and cranny of her life probably had a lover stowed in it. Hell, if you found a dictionary from Mary's heyday, her picture would be the illustration for 'bawdy'. Now, though, I couldn't imagine her as a cougar, with some young hottie in any kind of love nest, even a trashed-out version like this.

"Are ye going to stand on the sidewalk all day, chattering like a couple of wrens, or are ye coming in?" Mary's voice rang through the clear, desert air so loud I half-expected her neighbors to shout at us. No one poked their heads out. In fact, the whole area seemed strangely still. "Most of these folks work for a living, usually third shift, so they're either still workin' or they're still abed. Don't ye worry. No one saw ye arrive."

"How did you know we were here?" I blurted.

"A special barter from a friend of mine. Owns a top-notch security company, if I heard right. He called it Genie-B-Gone, or some such nonsense. A little somethin' so no magical blokes'll sneak up on me in my own place. Ain't I right, love?" She nodded toward my companion.

"Quite right, Mrs. Killigrew," he said, returning her nod.

"Such a polite boy ye can be when ye want something. Why don't ye come inside and tell me what? Excepting a little of the hair of the dog, which ye both appear to need." Her gaze traveled over our attire, which I realized we'd been too distracted to change. "A night on the town afore ye bothered to visit ol' Mary Killigrew, eh?"

"Something like that," I said as I pushed the gate open. If she could feign drunkenness, I could pretend to have been drinking. Damn near tripping over my own feet certainly helped reinforce the idea. A gecko skittered along the edge of her paver path, reminding me to watch where I stepped. I didn't need a murdered lizard on my conscience, too. I also didn't need to break an ankle in my ridiculously high heels.

As soon as I stepped across the threshold, I found myself back in the t-shirt and shorts I'd worn the day before, with my shit-kickers firmly in place. "Thanks."

"Not my doing. I liked you better the other way. Most likely the awesome security *someone* installed for Mrs. Killigrew."

Mary winked. "Removes all transformation wishes before allowing entry into my gracious home. Wasn't that how ye put it, love?"

"Exactly."

I elbowed him. "At least having me back to my old self will help you focus."

"I wouldn't bet on it," he said, waggling his eyebrows at me. His antics damn near set me giggling again, but I tamped it down. Now was not the time.

Mary poked him in the ribs. "What exactly is it you need to focus on other than Jo's fine frame, you old Arab devil?"

"I'm embarrassed you'd bring up such a thing, you gorgeous limey tart." Her face split into a wide smile as he scooped her into a rib-crushing hug.

"I'll skip the love fest, guys. I'm too tired and too 'melting pot' to play along."

As they continued their jokes without me, I wandered farther into Mary's tiny home. Her entire living space could fit inside my library with room to spare. Down one hall, I spotted the only bedroom. So much for a love nest. From appearances, Mary hadn't slept much the night before either. The bed was a mess, blankets tossed on the floor and sheets in a sweaty ridge down the middle, but sans lover.

With a glance backward, I continued into the kitchen and began opening cupboards. Pilfering around a djinn's house could be an ass-kicking offense, but the need for caffeine overruled my social graces.

"Cups are to port of the stove," Mary said as she followed. "And your devil's brew is under the sink, with the rest of the poisons." With too much effort, she lowered herself onto an orange vinyl chair. Judging from that and the avocado appliances, she hadn't remodeled since she bought the place. It didn't look like she'd dusted in a while either. Although she swore being human again made her happy, the place didn't reflect a contented woman.

Or she didn't really live there. I gave a little mental shrug. If she didn't want genies locating her actual residence, I couldn't blame her.

After finding the jar of ancient instant crystals and whipping up a pot of hot water, I settled myself at the table. As my eyes shifted from one awkward countenance to the other, I found myself at a loss for words. The visit had been Zeke's idea, but he wasn't saying a damn thing to get the ball rolling. I tried shooting him an encouraging look, but his eyes remained on our host.

"Mary," he blurted when I figured he'd gone mute. "What happened to you?"

"Got old, love. It happens to the best of humans, ye know."

He shook his head. I could see the same frustration I experienced every time I saw her. Mary didn't have to age. Hell, she didn't *have to* return to the Many. I'd give her any amount of vitality she wanted. Any of her friends would.

Except every time I suggested it, she threatened to run me through. Damn her.

"Let's not spend the morning wallowing in fears of my impending death. Ye have exactly one hour before I got to open the store, so I suggest ye get to talking."

I stared at Zeke. Nothing. Finally, I jabbed him in the ribs.

"What? Oh. Yeah." He cleared his throat.

"Ye come about them damned Efreet again, didn't ye?" She reached across the table and patted my hand. "I'm sorry about what I done before. Shameful thing for a gal like me to get pissed off her arse, but ever since I took back my humanity, the hard stuff sneaks up on me."

I couldn't tell if by 'hard stuff' she meant the booze or the topic. "Zeke seems to think you have information for us." Her eyes narrowed in his direction. "Whatever payment you want is yours."

"No worries, love, yer original bargain still holds." She rubbed her gnarled hands over her face. "Although, I've no idea why ben Aron here thinks I know more than him. Then again, I've forgotten more about the whole messy business than most of our ilk ever knew. Excepting yer man here."

She leveled a hard look his way. "Which makes me wonder why ye dragged her to me instead of spilling what ye know. Ye've been at it longer than the rest of us." Her face reddened. "Or didn't ye want yer young mate to know yer age?"

"He told me," I said, not giving any hint I'd gotten the information recently.

"Well, whatever yer reasons, time's a wastin'. Ask yer questions. " She lifted her mug and toasted us with her alcohol-free Earl Grey. "The worst you can expect is me becoming a hyper old boiler," she added with a wink.

I let go of my frustration with her and grinned. "I'd pay cash to see it."

"Ye may end up paying more than cash before we're through."
With those words, my smile fell away. "Zeke said something to the effect before we came. What the hell do you mean? I get there's more to this than I could've imagined. I mean, if genies can be killed with an ungrantable wish, any of us could be next. I'm willing to chance my life, if I have to, in order to stop this bastard."

"It's not only *your* life you're risking. A lot more brethren could be lost if this becomes an outbreak."

"Sure, there are risks. The more Efreet there are, the more djinn are in danger. But I don't understand how asking questions would make it worse."

"Could be yer curiosity is what causes the outbreak this time 'round," the pirate said.

"It's happened before, Babydoll," Zeke inserted, answering my next question. "Think about it. It always begins with 'where do Efreet come from?' Right?"

"It's the obvious beginning, yeah." I stared at him and his eyes dropped toward a crack in the Formica tabletop. "You can't honestly believe knowing where Efreet come from turns a genie into one."

Mary shrugged. "It's been known to happen." The possibility was too surreal to wrap my brain around. "Ye ain't been around long enough to see it happen... to yer friends and others ye know. To the ones ye love. After centuries of life, some genies can't take the living of it anymore. Once they have the key to becoming Efreet, they jump at the chance."

"There's got to be more to it. If knowing how to change makes it happen, then stopping the information would've stopped the transformations." My pointed stare hit each of them. "Since we have a new Efreet running around, you're obviously mistaken somehow. Their existence has been kept secret since the last war, right? So where did this freak come from?"

They both shrugged, almost in unison.

"Okay. Well, neither of you are Efreet, so I assume you're clueless about what causes the change. Because if you knew, you wouldn't try to sell me this bullshit."

"Truth be told, love, none of the living djinn, them what didn't turn, know the changing wish. But we've all known brethren who've turned. We know what they were thinking last we saw of them. To a man, they were depressed or bored or feelin' like caged animals."

"If these people were your friends, why not just ask?"

"They weren't exactly stickin' around to share the details. Djinn and Efreet have never been real chatty." She cracked her knuckles. "They come showin' their faces around, and we turn them into the dogs they are."

A derisive snort pushed through me. "So, you don't exactly know anything to help me stop this." I glared at Zeke. "Remind me why you brought me here again. This is a colossal waste of time. But I'm guessing you already knew it would be."

For the first time, Zeke didn't feign the hurt in his eyes. "You needed—"

"I needed to buckle down and work this problem. Christ, Zeke, the bastard killed someone at my auction. Steps from my home. He murdered two children and then offed a poor deranged woman. In front of me. You couldn't possibly think frittering away my time would make me happy." I stood up and clenched my fists until my nails bit into my palms.

"You of all people should know I'm not playing around," I said. "And I'm sure as hell not trying to stir up trouble, despite what Duarte thinks. People are dying." I released my grip long enough to point a finger from him to her. My broken skin dripped spots on Mary's worn linoleum in the moments before my hands healed. "Whatever this silence did for djinn-kind, it never prevented the possibility of an Efreet outbreak.

"As a matter of fact, if this dumb sunuvabitch stumbled across the way to transform himself without any hints, what's to stop him from sharing his info with anyone else? Who's going to stop him from urging others to join him?" I turned toward Mary. "Are *you*?"

Neither said a word. At that point, I wasn't sure I wanted them to. I had myself halfway convinced I needed to teleport to Longs' Peak. Wait this thing out or at the very least give myself time to think. Both looked ashamed. Well, they had every reason to be. And not only for dragging me away from my work. In the past, promoting ignorance might've meant keeping people safe, but we were in the twenty-fucking-first century for godsakes.

"So." My jaw clenched so hard I could hear my teeth whimper under the strain. "If you don't have the answer, and you're two of the oldest djinn I know, then where the hell am I supposed to get answers?"

Mary's eyes fell and Zeke suddenly found interest in a cockroach crawling up the wall.

"Enough is e-goddamn-nuff. I'll find the answer, whether you help me or not." They kept avoiding my eyes. "I mean, it's not like I'll switch over to the other team after I—"

"Won't ye?" Mary's voice wasn't much above a whisper, but it came at me like a shout.

"How could you think...? I'm not a dissatisfied customer here. Crappy as my days can be, I still like being a genie. I'm not tired. I'm not bored. Gods, sometimes I wish boredom came with all of this. I'd *love* to be bored." I ruffled my hands through my hair. "And I'm sure as hell not confused about my role in this dysfunctional family."

They both sat watching me and all at once, the fire inside me banked. This wasn't some stupid cast-off concern. Behind their eyes lay full-blown, irrational fear.

"Whatever you might've believed before, believe me when I tell you this: I'm not the kind to succumb to something just because I learned about it. I spent decades studying the Nazis to figure out why they did what they did." *Why they took my Benny from me.* "I didn't become one of them, did I?"

Mary glanced up, a question brewing behind her eyes. "It happened a long time ago," I told her, "and it no longer matters." Whatever spawned people like the Nazis, knowing how they got as messed up as they did wouldn't resurrect my first love.

I lowered myself into the chair, trying not to knock the wobbly seat over. "The point I'm trying to make," I said, sliding my hands across the tabletop, "is knowing won't make a person follow others into the hell of it. Each individual makes his own decisions about right and wrong."

My having to explain any of this to Zeke killed me. Still, no matter how urbane the man had become, he hailed from a scary and ignorant point in mankind's history. So did Mary. Stupid misconceptions develop over a long time. Changing those ideas? Even longer. If they worked at it. Which they didn't.

Until now, I hoped.

I hadn't convinced the old pirate. My one hope lay in neither one trying to refute my words. My hopes multiplied when Zeke finally opened his mouth.

"Fine. You are your own person," he said, almost like the fact left a bad taste in his mouth. "But the truth is, we really don't have any answers. For that, you need to talk to an Efreet. They're the only ones who really know what happened."

Great. The only Efreet I know is a lunatic.

"It's not like I can cuddle up with Amun and say 'pretty please'. I think he'd just as soon kill me as spit at me." Mary and Zeke exchanged one of those 'frustrated as hell' looks, like I should be able to figure this out on my own.

"I believe I already hinted at another way," he said. "You weren't thrilled then. You're not going to be any more thrilled now."

"Like any of this crap blows my skirt up, so what's the diff... Oh please. Not the dog thing again. You can't seriously expect me to converse with some random pooch."

"It's the only way." Mary didn't look happy about the suggestion. "If ye can find one that'll talk and not bite. The ungrateful bastards."

"You made them into pets, Mary. They have every reason to be ungrateful."

"Not my idea. If I'd been in charge of punishment, they'd be in the ground. With the Rules in the way, they turned 'em to something harmless."

"So I'm supposed to what? Visit local dog parks asking if anyone happens to be an Efreet?"

"Not necessary," Zeke said, suddenly unable to meet my eyes again.

"Spill it. How much worse could it be?"

"What yer man here is sayin' is ye won't need to track one down." She narrowed her eyes and stared at him. "He knows where one's at. Ain't I right?"

"And where would that be?" I swore to myself if he dodged the question one more fricking time, I would go ballistic on his ass.

He mumbled and I shook my head. I couldn't have heard him right. "What?"

"Your cave," he said with more force than necessary. "One's been with you for the past few years."

A great, *and ironic*, bark of laughter escaped me. "Major's an Efreet? Ri-ight. Pull the other leg, it's shorter." One look at his face, though, told me this was no joke. "You can't be serious. You mean one of those things lives in my *home* and no one bothered to warn me?"

"I didn't know," Mary said. "I swear."

"And I didn't know until saw him the day before the auction." Zeke had the good sense to look sheepish, but I still wanted to throttle him. "It's not like I could've met the beast before now. Maybe if you hadn't been avoiding me—"

"Oh no, you don't. Don't you dare try to put this back on me." I contemplated the soft, white fur I buried my face in every night. "You have to be wrong. I could sense the other Efreet."

"He hasn't been an Efreet for a long time, Josie. He's a dog. An immortal dog, sure, but a dog all the same. I'm not precisely sure the transformed know what they once were. For all intents and purposes, he's merely a pet." Zeke reached for my hand. He's lucky he didn't pull back a stump. "If I hadn't been present when the turning happened, I would've never known Major's true nature."

"You did this? You changed a man into my dog?"

Mary swallowed hard enough to ingest a softball. "No, love. That would be my doing."

TWENTY

~-~-~-~-~-~-~

Life had already lined the old pirate's face with enough wrinkles
to make a roadmap of pain. In the space of minutes, those creases
became more pronounced. Admitting to her participation in the
Efreet's punishment seemed to sap her energy as much as the act
itself probably had.

Before I learned of the Efreet, being shackled to my sanctuary
and kowtowing to some human was my concept of the worst a genie
could face. The thought of being trapped inside a form with no way to
communicate made my skin crawl. My only hope for this guy was that
his mind had been reduced to canine levels. Otherwise, the
transformation would be a more cruel and unusual punishment than
any human judge could envision making a law against.

"Why didn't you just kill them all?"

Mary shook her head. "The Rules. No killin'. Even them what
deserves it."

"So, he was a murderer?"

Zeke walked to the window. Minutes passed before he spoke.
"As far as we know, they all were."

"Which means you don't know about him for sure."

"Don't be giving them blaggards the benefit of the doubt." The
pirate no sooner rasped out the admonishment then she fell into a
coughing fit. When I reached out, she shook her head and righted

herself. "Them Efreet are a murderous bunch, if I ever seen one." One shaky hand waved toward Zeke. "And he knows it. He saw damn near as much as I. Can ye still doubt, or is yer memory slippin' after all these years?"

Before he could answer, Mary sat forward with an unpleasant tilt to her lips. "Ye doubted afore the last war, didn't ye? That's why ye stayed away."

His reflection in the smudgy glass showed eyes wet with unshed tears. "What we did—"

When a shudder wracked his detached façade, the sudden urge to wrap my arms around him swept through me. No matter what I did now, I couldn't make this all better. Some memories are painful for a reason. And they can't be wiped away like tearstains on a child's cheek.

"It doesn't matter," he continued. "We did what we thought was right at the time. I simply found didn't have the stomach for it anymore."

"Right at the time?" Mary asked, her voice rising toward a shriek. "We done what always needed to be done. Ye won't convince me—not ever—them beasties didn't deserve what they got."

The verbal barbs and volleys went on for several more minutes while I sat in silence. I wasn't sure who was winning, but I didn't care. I had moved beyond it all, thinking about my furry pal waiting back home. This was no minor infraction worthy of a tap on the muzzle with a rolled up newspaper. And even if I could, I wasn't sure I would. If you asked me, he'd suffered enough for the crimes of the past.

When the bickering died down to nothing, the quiet made me jump. My eyes scanned the room, seeking out whatever danger would interrupt their tirades. Nothing seemed out of order. From what I could tell, Zeke had said all he was going to say. Without anyone fighting back, Mary's angry words hit a bottleneck inside her.

"You acted as judge and jury for what you assumed were a bunch of murderers." My words sank into the heavy stillness. Mary nodded, but Zeke remained silent as a statue. Neither one had come any closer to ponying-up the information I needed. Well, I'd had enough mental masturbation for one day. "Guilty until proven otherwise? Remind me not to ask you for legal advice. Sans evidence, you found the Efreet guilty and poochified them." I let the words hit whatever tender flesh they might. "What really pisses me off is you didn't care who got punished."

The old pirate gasped and I feared her old ticker finally decided to explode. Instead, her temper blew. "Ye sound like a blasted human." Her lips drew back so tightly against her teeth the color bled from them. "Ye're talkin' the laws of today. Back when they was killin' our own, we knew what to do. We didn't need no evidence. We knew enough to stop them."

"And you didn't care how. You sentenced them to an eternity of incarceration. All of it in solitary confinement, by the way. It would've been more humane to kill them outright." All at once the fight went out of me. If one of my closest friends couldn't see why I'd find all this so utterly wrong, I didn't know what else to say. "And I've held one of your convicts in my arms like some damn teddy-bear, so I could sleep easier at night. I treated him like a brainless animal, when he used to be one of the Many."

"The blighter gave up being of the Many when he turned Efreet." Mary's sneer would've been unattractive on anyone, but it morphed the pirate into a crone from the worst of Grimm's fairytales. "Ye need to throw that scurvy dog in the pound the minute ye get back to yer cave." The cackle she let out didn't help her looks or my nerves.

"Enough." I held my voice steady and low. If I hadn't, I would've started screaming. Once I started, I doubted I'd be able to stop. "This isn't getting us anywhere. I need to talk to an Efreet, and one is waiting at home." I rose from the table, unable to meet Mary's eyes. "One of you, I don't care who, is going to tell me how to wish him back to his true form."

Mary's lips locked shut. Zeke remained lost in memories of his own. Without another word to either of them, I left the little house on the edge of Sin City, wondering if the pirate's choice of homes hadn't been appropriate after all.

I didn't appreciate how badly the whole meeting affected me until I realized I didn't close my eyes for the teleport. The trip to Estes Park from Las Vegas lasted only a few seconds, but in that time, the world's colors swirling by so fast made me sicker than a dog. No pun intended. Not to mention, in my haste, I neglected to walk home from a human-free area. Instead I dropped into the fricking lobby. My brain paused long enough to wonder why security allowed a teleport into the building. And then I vomited all over the marble floor.

"Miss? Excuse me, Miss? Are you okay?" I heard Renee, but I didn't really care. All I wanted was to get rid of breakfast as quickly as possible.

A hand landed on my back as another held my hair.

"Can I get you some water?"

"Water?" The croak barely sounded like me. I turned in time to see Renee headed for the water cooler.

"Jo?" Basil's voice hit me like a cool breeze. His hand wrapped around my upper arm and he gently drew me to my feet. "What the hell happened?"

"Teleport. Forgot." I swallowed the bile rising in my throat. "Vertigo."

"That's not what I'm talking about. Your face. You look like a teen again."

Crap. Mary. "The pirate's security wipes out transformation wishes." A rush of energy flowed over me. "Did Renee notice?"

He glanced in her direction. "She might have, but she won't remember for long." I shot him a look. "A younger version of you dropped from nowhere in front of her. Shall I let her remember the experience enough to contact the media?"

"Damn. Sorry. Wasn't thinking." I fought another wave of nausea. "Take care of her, will you? I have something I have to do."

"Bloody right you do." He gripped my arm harder. "Duarte's been a royal pain in my arse. The Bedouin's driving Mena up a wall. The guests want to know what's going on."

"Nothing I can do about it right now. And if I have to talk to the Moor now, I'm going to ralph all over his Italian loafers."

"Next time close your damn eyes."

Right. I'll get right on it.

My partner was definitely pissed. I didn't blame him. I needed to kick Zeke's ass for dragging me to Vegas, right after I kicked my own for letting him. "I promise I'll call Duarte later. Tell Mena I'll deal with Omar the second I'm done with one other thing."

"What other thing?"

"Something more important."

"More important than keeping that bloke from ruining our lives?" He clicked his tongue at me. I wasn't the naughty girl here, but I didn't have the patience to argue about the newest blunder. "I'm telling you right now, Jo, things don't look good. Rumor has it Duarte called an assembly of the Many. I haven't heard of anyone calling an assembly in—"

"One hundred and fifty years, give or take a decade?"

Basil shivered like I walked over his grave. "That's neither here nor there. You need to stop this Efreet before our lives get any more out of hand. An assembly could shut us down for real. And they wouldn't stop there. Duarte is sure to mete out some type of punishment."

I pushed away his steadying hand and leveled a hard look his way. I could handle being scolded like a child, but I'd be damned if I'd take being threatened.

"You mean 'turning me into a dog' type punishment?" His gasp pissed me off more than I believed possible. "You *knew*? You knew all along what they did, and you didn't tell me?"

Basil's silence spoke for him. And silence, as annoying as it could be, was better than whatever fibs he cooked up trying to save his own ass. Maybe if he'd bothered to share this informational tidbit three years ago when I found the damn dog, I would've felt more charitable. As it stood, charity had taken the afternoon off. An urge to knock a few Cockney teeth down his limey throat became paramount. He'd look stupid toothless, but the satisfaction would be cathartic.

As much as hurting Basil sounded fun, though, if I knocked him into next week, it wouldn't solve anything. My fist remained clenched at my side. Which was amazing considering my next thought.

If he knew Major's true nature, his confusion when I dropped into his office had been an act. I assumed he might know something, but everything? After all we'd been through and all the years working side by side. If I hadn't still needed him as a person, Basil would've ended up as a gnat.

"So, I guess this means I'm the only one who didn't know about Major."

"Major? What about him? Last I knew he was in the cave." He looked genuinely concerned, but if he worried about protecting the precious djinn secret, he'd learn pretty damn quick how little I cared about the djinn's unspoken rule. "I fed him yesterday," he continued like his ass wasn't on the line. "I expect he'll be making a racket since he hasn't been walked yet, and you weren't here for breakfast. Wait a minute. What's Major got to do with anything?"

All at once, I couldn't tell whether Basil had become a consummate liar or I really had him stymied. I didn't know what to think, beyond the realization both my composure and my breakfast were having a breakdown. "I need to go downstairs. Now. Don't let anything interrupt me."

"But Duarte."

"I said *anything*, Baz, and I meant it." For an instant, I let myself enjoy the righteous indignation. Then the guilt hit me. Basil had kept things from me, but we'd been friends for longer than most humans stay married. "You'll have to trust me." I tried to throttle back the anger. "There's something I need to do."

"Puttering around in the library?" he said, complete with a dash of snark.

I didn't bother acknowledging either his statement or his tone. Although, now that he mentioned it, the library might be a place to figure out how to change Major back. After I weaseled some secrets out of him first, of course.

"I'm sorry, Jo. I know those archives are important to you." The tinge of concern crept back into his voice. If he hadn't ticked me off in a major way seconds earlier, I would've made nice. Baz would get over it. Or he wouldn't. Maybe I'd get over it, too. Eventually. "Perhaps if you tell me what's going on, I can help."

"I don't know yet." I glanced at my watch for effect. I didn't need to know the time, but I needed him to understand I didn't have any. "I'll meet you later. And Baz? If I'm not upstairs in an hour, call out the troops. I'll set my security so only you and Mena can come in. No one else. Got it?"

"I don't get any of this, but I understand. If we don't see you, we storm the beaches, so to speak. Anything we might need to know coming through the door?"

"As corny as it sounds, trust no one." After my cryptic remark, I tried for the 'mighty leader' exit, head held high, back straight. Since my legs still wobbled and my stomach felt like it'd spent football season as a practice dummy, I didn't actually pull it off.

A couple of doors in, I saw Renee sitting against the conference table, looking a little weirded out. I blamed the memory shift, but resetting her memories was easier than convincing her the barfing stranger was a hallucination. When she glanced my way, I gave her an encouraging smile.

I expanded my senses before I reached my front door. Everything appeared as I'd left it. Then again, I hadn't felt the Efreet at the auction. Not until he wanted me to. As far as I knew, Amun lurked inside my home, waiting to end this game. Whispering wishes at me wouldn't work, since I wasn't his slave, but who knew what else he had up his puffy sleeves? No time like the present to discover whether I only had a naughty dog to deal with or whether some lunatic waited to kill me.

When the door swung open, the answer became clear. No creepy guy with perfect teeth and a pointy beard jumped out. Instead, a fluffy white monster knocked me down. Before I could reflect on the monster he really was, Major had me laughing with his doggie version of 'oh my god I'm so happy where have you been?'—complete with tail-thumping and copious licks.

"Enough, boy," I said with an injection of 'stern master'. "Down."

He laid one last defiant slurp across my cheek before he settled onto his haunches. Cocking his head to one side, he looked at me like I was the one in trouble.

"Drop the act, bud. I'm not the one who's hiding my true self."
Logic would say he wasn't the one who'd hid it in the first place, but
logic hadn't been invited to this party. Whether he understood me
remained to be seen. Right then, though, I was fed up with the dumb
animal act.

"Seriously, dude. The jig's up." He turned his most insidious
weapon against me: puppy eyes. I focused on the end of his big, wet
nose so I wouldn't drown in those brown pools of doggie hurt. Hell, I
could feel my fingers itching to ruffle his ears.

His head tilted to the other side as if he could hear the
partridges outside whistling to him. I ignored his cuteness and held
firm. All at once, those hurt eyes filled with acceptance. In the space
of a heartbeat, he went from big, loveable furball to the most
insightful canine in the world. In the same instant, I could've kicked
myself for not seeing what he really was.

"Let's talk inside." He nodded before leading the way down my
darkened stairwell. Making sure all the locks were reset, I whispered
a special new wish to keep out everyone but Basil and Mena. If this
confrontation turned ugly and Major went all Cujo on my ass, I didn't
want friend or foe walking in.

I hated to think it, but Amun could be waltzing around my
building. I sure couldn't handle the Efreet. My power dipstick read
empty. Physically, I was toast. Cursing Zeke's *necessary* night-out, I
dragged my exhausted self toward the living room where my
dog/Efreet waited.

Major sat in front of the fireplace, his head held high like a
Westminster show pup. His eyes focused on some point beyond the

rock walls of our... my home. I wasn't sure he even noticed when I entered the room until his tail betrayed us both with a tentative wag.

"We need to talk. Wait. Can you talk?" His head moved slowly from side to side. "But you understand me, right?" After he nodded, I continued. "And you always have?" Another nod raised my blood pressure. "Damn it. You've been eavesdropping on me for years. How am I supposed to trust you?"

He gave me the same furry shrug I spent years believing meant I adopted a truly special beast. Finding out the truth turned out to be more disappointing than I would've thought.

"Are you the Efreet Mary Killigrew transformed in the last war?" At first he nodded, but then shook his head. "She didn't change you or you weren't an Efreet?" His answer came in the form of looking at me like I was stupid.

"How the hell am I supposed to talk to you like *this*?"

He lifted one paw toward his muzzle and then drew it over his right ear. If I didn't know better, I would've thought he was being cute again. And then the magnitude of my stupidity clobbered me. He'd made the same gesture when I met him on the streets. At the time, I assumed he was making himself too adorable to leave behind. He'd been trying to tell me something all along.

"I should either wish for you to speak human or wish for myself to understand dog?" As tired as I was, figuring out that much surprised me. Changing his physical structure to allow for speech would take more power than I had, but shifting my own ears was simple enough.

The wish didn't really work the way I envisioned. His speech came out less like speech than a whoosh of breath and some subtle movement.

"I apologize," were his first words.

"I don't accept." His ears drooped so low, I felt lower than scum. "Yet."

This whole experience hit me harder than I assumed it would. I mean, this creature represented the only living thing that made me 100% happy. He was the fuzzy person I played fetch with. He warmed my feet by the fireplace every winter. He chased rabbits until he tired himself out, and I'd nearly died laughing. Every single snowman I built, he knocked down. I would never have children. He was the closest I'd ever get. And now—

"Acceptance and forgiveness, or lack thereof, are your prerogative, Miss Mayweather."

My eyebrows tightened across my forehead. "After three years of sleeping together, we can ditch the formalities, don't you think?"

"I guess, but you'll pardon me if I'm not entirely comfortable with being casual. You are my Mistress after all. It's engrained in the species."

"That I can forgive. The rest? Time will tell." I stooped until I was at his eye level. "Answer me one question."

"Anything."

"Are you still an Efreet in there?"

To my surprise, Major's whole body shook. For an instant, I was afraid he was having convulsions as the Efreet in him tried to come out. And then my wish translated the noise. He was laughing at me.

"Seriously? You think this is funny?"

"I'm sorry. You said 'in there' like this is something I threw on for one of your Halloween parties." He licked his nose. Probably his way of trying to regain his composure. Or to take care of loose drool. "Your bluntness. It's what first drew me to you in Copenhagen. Plus, you smell like a genie. You were my first and best hope for redemption. I suppose I could say you're partly responsible for the fact I am no longer an Efreet *in here*."

"You're not serious. You've only been with me for a few years."

"Well, I did say 'partly'. I understood a long time ago the impossibility of being both dog and Efreet at the same time. The two are diametrically opposed."

Look at my pup-pup using big words. Of all the pets in the world, I had to adopt one who's smarter than me.

"So if I find a way to change you back, you won't be an Efreet again?"

"That is about the long and the short of it. As I said, one cannot be both." He used that moment to scratch at the back of his ear with one big paw, which, I guessed, came as close as a dog could to looking thoughtful. "I suspect over a century in a form without innate hatred or evil affects anyone."

As I opened my mouth, he cut me off. "Before you ask if every changed Efreet is reformed, I'd say probably not. Assuming all Efreet react the same way in any given situation would be detrimental to your health. Of course, I could be wrong. I only know what I experienced. If, by some quirk of fate, I transformed to my old form, I will become only what I was before I chose life as an Efreet."

Words like his seemed easy enough to say. He could be trying to trick me, but I didn't think so. Then again, like he said, those assumptions would kill me quicker than gift-wrapping myself for Amun with a note: 'Happy Murdering, Mr. Efreet, sir.'

"But right now, Mistress?" he said. "I'd rather you wouldn't."

I needed a moment to reclaim the thread of our conversation. "Wouldn't what?"

"Reverse the transformation." His body shook and the fur rippled across him in big, white waves. "The form I take now is in your hands, of course. For now, though, I'm content to be as I am."

I shook my head. I couldn't imagine being turned into an animal, but more so, I couldn't grasp Major's desire to remain one. "Why?"

"I have my reasons." I suspected I wouldn't get more out of him on the subject, at least not then. "Should I assume the others know my real identity now?"

"Mary Killigrew and Zeke. You remember them?" Major nodded. "Well, Zeke's known since he ran into you a few days ago. He spread the word to Mary."

"I expect she wants to make a coat and a pair of fur-lined gloves out of me." He said without a trace of humor. "I don't blame her. Our last meeting wasn't a happy one."

"I'd imagine not."

He placed a paw on my thigh. "I know I have no right to ask, but I would appreciate if none of the others knew my secret. In my old life, I did *things*, things I'm not proud of, things I feel should still carry repercussions." Once again, he stopped me. "If you can trust me on no other point, trust when I tell you decades of punishment can't cleanse away the acts I committed."

I couldn't imagine anyone holding a forever grudge, but djinn have long memories. Part of the joy of having such long lives, I guess. "Fine. I don't like it, but I'll try not to tell anyone else. Now, you need to do something for me."

"Anything I can do, I will."

"Tell me what turned you into an Efreet."

His eyes slowly closed. As his head rocked from side to side, he whined softly. "I'm sorry, Mistress. I cannot."

"Why?"

"It is forbidden." The words felt like he said all he needed to say to make me understand. Needless to say, they didn't work.

"Well." I infused a little patience into my frustration. "If I needed proof you're djinn again, there it is."

"Pardon me, Mistress?"

"Your answer. The same damn answer I've gotten before." My voice notched up a range. "*We can't tell. It's forbidden.* Blah blah blah. An Efreet wouldn't give a shit about the damn conspiracy of silence."

"It is in place by necessity."

If I had one more person tell me how necessary this whole stupid thing was, I would scream. "First off, stop calling me 'Mistress'. It pisses me off. Second, surrounding the Efreet in mystery is only necessary if you believe knowing about something makes it more attractive. Great Godfrey Daniels, you sound like every nutcase who tried to ban sex ed."

The dog tilted his head at an odd angle and stared at me. "Yeah," I said, "I guess the reference doesn't work for someone who never attended public school. Believe me when I tell you maintaining ignorance didn't work for people trying to keep teens from having sex. And it won't keep any djinn from becoming an Efreet if he really wants to."

Major's shoulders lifted and he let out a big doggie sigh. "You don't understand."

"Don't give me that. I understand. I understand how back in the Ignorant Age, the brethren transformed the Efreet into members of the canine persuasion." All those wished-up dogs roaming the world for decades, centuries even, and all the brethren keeping their existence a secret. Both ideas made me want to hurl. "The infinite wisdom of staying silent didn't stop Amun from turning into an Efreet. Hell, he might not even know how he became one. Do you see where I'm going with this? "

"As you say, Mistr... Miss Mayweather, those willing to turn away from the Many will find a way."

"Not necessarily," I said. "Any djinn educated about the Efreet might not fall into the same trap you did."

He stood on all fours and shivered, which my wish translated into a scoff. "We can debate the logic of a djinn's choice all day. It solves nothing. I cannot tell you how I became an Efreet. Aside from my belief this particular piece of knowledge isn't safe for any genie to hold, the particular point of djinn rules prohibit the spreading of this knowledge."

"They aren't big R rules, damn it."

Major started choking, but he was only laughing harder at me. "The big R rules, as you call them, are beyond our power to enforce. But when the djinn come together in council, as they infrequently do, they can and do enforce the little rules. So much so, you'd wish they were the big R rules one can never break."

His pause coincided with a ridge of fur rising along his back. When his lips curled away from his teeth and a growl rolled out, it scared the shit out of me. Something bad was about to go down. And I didn't mean naughty-dog bad.

"Someone is coming," he said on a low snarl.

"Mena or Basil, maybe? I told them if they didn't see me in an hour to come looking."

His eyes never left the hallway leading upstairs, despite his whole head shaking. "Their scents are familiar to me. This... It's not them. Neither is it Efreet. It's djinn. Old, angry djinn."

For the first time since I chiseled my home from the mountainside, I regretted the lack of a back door. "Are they already inside?"

"Not yet. But your security wishes have collapsed." Doggie lips twisted into a strange smile. "I believe they are having issues with your passcode. Still, their ignorance has its limits. If you don't mind, Mistress, I think dropping your anti-teleport wish would be wise."

"What do you smell?"

"Fear like I haven't scented since they burned witches in Roermond." He shuddered as he took another whiff. "And Iago Duarte."

TWENTY-ONE

~-~-~-~-~-~-~-~

Major no sooner finished saying the name when the door at the top of the stairs burst inward. Gathering every last bit of power I could squeeze out of myself, I released the building's security along with a wish to drop me and my dog outside.

Nothing happened.

"They put up a shield of their own," said Major.

Sunuvabitch, was my first passing thought. On its heels came a rapid scramble for a way out of this mess. If Duarte could break down my door and waltz into my domain uninvited, he had more clout than I assumed. Aside from the rules about trespassing, hadn't Zeke hinted there was some kind of Rule about invites and abodes, too?

"Miss Mayweather." The Moor's oily voice echoed off the stone walls I'd carved as protection. Fat lot of good they did me.

"You weren't invited." Of course, even if Zeke had been right, Duarte could have found a loophole. Either way, I hoped to use his transgression against him. "Turn around and I won't get the Council involved." My voice contained a hell of a lot more bravado than I felt, but Reggie taught me if I couldn't impress people with courage, I should baffle them with bullshit. *Fake it 'til you make it, Josephine.*

It didn't always work, but I had to take a shot.

"You're in no position to make demands," Duarte said from near the bottom of the stairs. "Turn over the beast or I will take him by force."

You, I thought in the dog's general direction. *Stay.*

"I don't hand over my possessions to *anyone* without a fight." I had no idea why he hadn't wished Major to him in the first place. Then my own words echoed in my head. For the first time in as long as I could remember, the Rules would actually help me. "And no djinn may take from another what isn't freely offered."

Duarte walked from the darkened hall. "True. If he were a possession. However, I believe the infamous Josephine Mayweather would die rather than own another being."

I almost laughed in the guy's face. His position couldn't be anywhere near as stable as he pretended, not if he started throwing my own philosophy in my face. Reigning in my humor, I adopted a façade of confident boredom. I had the bored down pat. If only I felt half as confident. "My beliefs don't matter. Only the gods who created the Rules matter. And they believe one being can own another. Therefore," I said, "you need to run along."

The Moor's overinflated ego wilted like a birthday balloon left in the sun. "Hand the Efreet over at once. He must be dealt with properly."

"He's not uranium. He's a dog."

"He is Efreet."

"Was. He was an Efreet. And as such, he already got sentenced and punished. Unless, of course, you don't have any respect for your cronies' kangaroo court. Lord knows I don't agree with a damn thing they did, but you always have. Haven't you?"

"Their punishment has been deemed insufficient."

I shrugged. "By who? You? As far as I'm concerned, he's still doing time for crimes committed a century and a half ago." I swept my hand down Major's back. "And, in case you haven't noticed, he's done hard time. Any rational being would consider this solitary confinement enough of a sentence." Duarte's sour face didn't agree, but then again, I never considered him rational.

"Besides." I pressed the advantage. "Who appointed you judge, jury and executioner?"

"The Council will be convened."

"Call a war crimes tribunal for all I care." *Perfect for a goose-stepper like you.* "Whatever you're going to do, though, do it somewhere else. You're trespassing. And I'm too busy to entertain your sorry ass." I wasn't sure where my bluster came from, but I'd hold onto it with both hands. "Now leave before I call someone to assist in your departure."

Maybe I pushed it too far. Instead of being intimidated, Duarte's mouth spread into a wide grin, showing horsey teeth and too much gums. "Once word of this transgression spreads, you will find your friends are few and far between."

"I think," said a voice from behind the Moor, "you'll find Josie has more friends than you anticipated."

Duarte became as pale as his dark skin allowed. "Ezekiel. I remember you as a man who picked his battles. Are you certain this one is worth your time? This is no more your fight than the last war."

"Very certain." Zeke stepped into the room. The glow from my cave wall lit his face, turning him into Puck and Pan and Hermes rolled into one. "You mess with the Babydoll, you mess with me."

Mena's voice floated from the darkness. "And he's not the only one." For some reason, she came off as way more potent than I gave her credit for. The air around her hiding spot crackled so loud, it almost sounded like bacon frying back there. I don't know who staged this melodrama, but if Duarte's reactions were any indication, the show had been timed for maximum effect.

"Basil would've joined us," she said, "but he became very busy all of a sudden. Something about a cavalry. He said scores of severely peeved genies would arrive shortly."

Basil wouldn't dare. He knew those freed djinn didn't owe me a damn thing. Still, what a brilliant bluff. Duarte swallowed so hard he should've choked on his own tongue. His hand waved above his head and several unknown faces melted out of the shadows.

The bastard brought backup. The fact I hadn't sensed the other genies scared the bejeezus out of me. I must really be slipping.

"This isn't over," Duarte said in true Snidely Whiplash fashion. Too bad for him I was no Dudley Do-Right.

"Come into my home without permission again and you'll see how over this all is." The words came out of my mouth, but I doubted whether my brain had actually engaged. "Now, my friends and I have an Efreet to stop." I waved my hand in true Evangeline fashion. My mother could communicate more with one gesture than a one-armed deaf man in a political debate.

"I'd say it's been a pleasure, but we both know how much I hate to lie."

Instantly, the Moor and his thugs teleported away. As air rushed into the space they'd left, my ears popped. Leave it to him to take a happy event like his departure and turn it into an uncomfortable experience. *Asshole.*

Not bothering to check for a seat beneath my ass, I let my buckling knees have their way and dropped like a sack of wet dirt. Thank goodness calmer heads created a chair under me before I fell too far.

"What are you doing here?" My words were meant for no one in particular.

But Zeke answered with "I followed you home."

At the same time, Mena let loose "There was a disturbance in the force. A great evil headed in your direction."

"I had it under control."

"Sure you did." Zeke didn't believe a word I said, but that was nothing new. I could've slapped him as he dropped onto my couch.

Mena looked from him, to me and back again. "If you don't need me," she said, "I'll find Baz and fill him in on the deets. You know, in case Duarte corners him. Besides, someone's got to figure out how the reprobate bypassed security."

"I thought Basil let him in. Wait." Mena's face pinkened beneath her olive skin. Her bluff must've been bigger than I originally thought. "He's not in the building, is he?"

"I don't know." Her slim shoulder lifted. "He could be. Although, exactly where is anyone's guess. He might've said something about visiting a sick friend."

I let out a laugh. "You're supposed to be the honest one."

"If your secrets are as big as I think they are, I'm still the honest one." She cast a sidelong glance at the furry person now occupying the entire rug in front of the fireplace.

"She knows," Major said in a drawn-out whimper. He placed his head on his paws. "How many more are witness to my shame?"

"Secrets?" I tried to seem as innocent as possible with a dog's voice in my head. "I don't know what you're talking about."

"I'm talking about the fluffy, white Efreet." She hooked a thumb toward my mortified pooch. "Zeke thought I ought to know. I live here, too. Besides, after hearing Duarte's demands, I could've put the rest together myself." A low growl rumbled in Major's chest. "Don't sweat it, puptart. I make my living by not spilling other people's beans. Ishtar's tits, you must think I'm either stupid or a horrible therapist."

The fur on Major's hackles lowered slightly. Until Zeke spoke.

"So, Babydoll, you learn anything from the hairball?" Another growl reverberated through my cave. "Easy fella. Believe it or not, I'm on your side, too." Zeke turned his gaze toward me. "I assume since he's still on all fours, you didn't manage to turn him back on your own."

"I didn't try."

"Probably for the best. In the past, it's taken three djinn to make the wish, so you'll probably need three to reverse it."

"Let me guess: The Rules."

"Bingo. Something about the decision being left to multiple consciences. Keeps a genie honest." He glanced from Mena to me again. "We've got a quorum now. Let's get it over with."

Major bared his teeth and padded toward Zeke.

"Sit." Doggie-butt hit the rug. Those obedience classes really paid off, considering he was a former Efreet. Maybe Amun should attend a few.

"Come on." Zeke paid little attention to the angry canine. "We should be able to contain one Efreet."

"He's not an Efreet anymore," I said, "and he doesn't want to change back." Mena let out a little squeak. Zeke simply raised an eyebrow. "Consider it his own personal hair shirt. No pun intended."

"So he won't change back, and he won't talk to you," Mena said. "Where does that leave us?"

"At a dead end."

"Another pun?" Zeke asked.

"I'd like to hope when this is over, it'll still seem punny. But hope's running pretty short right now." I turned toward Mena. "Any luck with the Bedouin?"

"I'm not his Master." The sarcasm was unmistakable and totally understandable. "I think the only one he'll talk to now is you. Or possibly the Efreet, but I doubt it would be in anyone's best interest to open that door again."

"Crap," I whispered as something occurred to me.

"What?" The two of them speaking in unison made for a weird surround-sound effect. Major echoed the sentiment, but to the others, he only whimpered a little.

"Open doors," I said, almost to myself. "In all the kerfluffle, I forgot. I dropped my security wishes for a quick escape and I forgot to reset everything after he left. For all we know, the Efreet has already reclaimed his slave."

TWENTY-TWO

~-~-~-~-~-~-~

Expanding my senses throughout the building didn't indicate anything out of place. A faint trace of something nasty lingered like scum on the surface of a pond, but I didn't get an inkling whatever left it was still there. Unless the killer had hidden himself again, he'd beat feet.

Upstairs, I sensed a little uneasiness from Renee as she filed her nails. Michael studied in his room, fully healed and blissfully ignorant of anything but his books. Our other guests went about their lives. All seemed right with my world, except for Basil's curious absence.

"Where did you say Baz went?"

Mena shrugged. "He might've said something about checking on a sick friend, but I can't be sure. He muttered something as he passed me in the hall, about an hour before Duarte showed up. For all I know, he's back by now."

I knew different, and so would she if she bothered to check. Sometimes Mena's compulsion to help her fellow djinn only went so far. She could spend days wrestling with someone's deep psychological scars. Checking on Basil? Too much effort for her.

"Wherever he is, he's on his own." Another genie in the building would be handy. The guests weren't under any obligation to help, and I didn't want to start begging favors now. Risking themselves had never been part of the agreement. If worse came to worst, many of them would step up. I just didn't want it to come to that.

As my friends headed toward my home's only exit and entrance, I asked, "Give me a sec to secure this place again." Zeke offered to do the honors, security being his gig and all, but I refused. No use handing my ex more keys to the palace, so to speak. I had enough problems in my life already. "Okay. Time to see what kind of trouble the Bedouin might've gotten into."

"If he's still here," Zeke said under his breath.

I shot him a look. So what if my senses couldn't penetrate the vault? I was trying to think positive for once, damn him. Pointedly ignoring Negative Nellie, I snapped my fingers at the dog/djinn.

"You might as well join us. Since I now know you aren't merely a pooch, you can come earn your kibbles." From the way Zeke and Mena shot me looks, they thought I'd slipped a gear.

"I will assist in any way possible," Major said. My companions probably heard a couple yips and a hooting yowl.

"If you want to listen in…" I pointed to one ear. "… wish for the ability to understand dog. We're not having top-secret conversations about the fate of the djinn world." A small bit of power surged over my associates. Major woofed a translated welcome. "Sorry to cut this short," I said, essentially killing question and answer period, "but we've work to do."

Reaching the outer hall, Mena begged off as 'useless with Omar'—her words, not mine—and headed for our offices. "Maybe Basil left a note or something."

I shook my head. I got that she didn't want to be present when I witnessed her failure. His ignoring her probably pinched in all the wrong places. Too often, she came down too hard on herself. Many of the tetched djinn I rescued owed their sanity to Mena. The ones she couldn't help, Freud himself couldn't have fixed. Still, I suspected my best friend wore the unsalvageable ones around her neck every day. And she thought I needed to chill out?

When I reached the vault, my security still stood. But not for lack of trying on the part of the Efreet. The skanky slime was dissipating, but it was there. Nothing like a reminder of how close we came to losing the Bedouin.

I don't know what Zeke expected once we got inside, but I know I sure as hell didn't expect Omar in full *Lawrence of Arabia* gear standing in the middle of the room. He'd drawn his scimitar. His eyes pulsed with hate. And, he didn't move a hair. He simply stared at the doorway as we came through.

"The Efreet has been here," Omar growled.

"Inside?"

"He did not enter. No. The abomination ventured no further than the hallway, but I sensed him there. He came to reclaim me." The scimitar swished through the air and my heart dropped.

Back to square one, then.

"It's just you and me, bud." The man glanced Zeke's way and dismissed him. "Amun's gone. You okay with that?"

"He is gone?"

I wasn't one hundred percent sure, but I wouldn't share my uncertainties with the man holding a ginormous Ginsu. "Sure he is." I spoke to him as if he were a child, but if Omar got his undies in a wad, I'd have to deal. "You can put the cutlery down now."

His gaze lowered but his weapon didn't. "The abomination will return."

"Do you want him to?"

And my one, little question snapped Omar out of his trance. His sword arm faltered. The glazed look left him. "What? You would ask such a thing of me?"

"Well…" I glanced toward his super-sharp blade. One hand rubbed over my ribcage. The slice was long gone, but the memory remained.

He waved his sword again. "I did not draw my blade for you, my precious Master. This is for him. I will remove his head from his shoulders and present it to you if he ever approaches me again. I swear to you."

I exhaled a deeply held breath. Zeke relaxed his stance beside me. Major realized the danger had passed and lowered to the floor. I wasn't quite so forgiving, but then again, I'm not a dog. Knowing the Bedouin recognized his Rule-bound connection to me was a step in the right direction. Unfortunately, the fact he now appeared to be playing with a full set of Monopoly pieces didn't reassure me. If the Efreet managed to reclaim him, he'd be back to whacko in seconds flat.

"Good to know you're watching out for yourself this time." No enslaved genie had a choice about his Master. If we could pick and choose, maybe the servitude wouldn't be so bad. I mean, other than not being allowed to think and act for yourself.

The Bedouin still held his sword, but he didn't seem as ready to cleave anyone's head from their shoulders. I glanced back and closed the door with a silent wish. "Better?"

He sheathed his weapon. "Much. Thank you, my Master."

"First off, I told you to drop the Master thing. Call me Jo. And this is—"

"Ezekiel," Omar said with a nod. "It is good to see you have not succumbed."

I arched an eyebrow toward my companion. *Is there anyone he doesn't know?*

"How about—?" I said, waving toward my dog.

"Trygvyr." The Bedouin's hand strayed toward his hilt.

"Your real name, I assume?"

His furry head shook. "Once upon a time. But he doesn't exist anymore."

Curiouser and curiouser. This whole damn thing had turned into an educational chat, and we hadn't even started yet. "You know these people?"

"We were acquainted once, when I still walked free," the Bedouin answered. "During the first war, I fought beside Ezekiel. And the last, I fought against..." He inclined his head toward the former Efreet.

"But you're not a free djinn," I blurted without thinking. "I mean, I assumed only masterless genies fought in the wars."

Omar's head lowered until his chin touched his chest. "Circumstances change, even for those who see how much they remain the same."

"Wait just a cotton-picking minute. What?"

Zeke lifted one shoulder. He had a lot of explaining to do when this was over. "Freedom isn't a permanent state," he said, pinning this squarely on my own ignorance. "Someone should have told you a long time before you met me."

Ah, so he thought he could blame my ignorance and my creator. *Freaking peachy. Who else is he going to shift this onto?* And then I realized the blame never belonged to Stavros. Zeke sure as hell didn't own it, no matter how much I wanted him to. Hell, today's standby of blaming my parents wouldn't work either. Sure, Evangeline made the ice cubes in her drinks warm by comparison. And Reggie had been a big kid who thought only other people needed boundaries. Still, as crappy an example as he'd been, he did tell me *you can't know what you don't know.* Too bad only so much of this problem could be foisted off on someone else. In the end, I owned my own fucking ignorance.

Sooner or later, Reggie also said, *you need to try and figure out what you don't know and learn it yourself.*

I broke away from my thoughts to find Omar with pity in his eyes. Zeke, to his credit, found something more interesting along the edge of one wall. If I didn't know better, I'd think he found another bug to inspect. As pissed as I was, I almost wished up a hairy, eight-legged present for him.

"Fine. I need some... Okay, I need *a lot* of extra education." I stuffed my anger into a tight ball and shoved it into the back of my head. "When this is over, you can enroll me in Brethren U. Right now, pointing out the sum-total of my djinn ignorance isn't helping. Tell me as much as you can about this Efreet so we can stop him. Are you in, Omar?"

His eyes narrowed as he glanced around the room. "To whom are you speaking?"

Damn. I'd referred to the poor guy by the pet name I'd chosen out of the air.

"When she gets flustered, her manners fly out the window," Zeke told the Bedouin. "Allow me to introduce you. Josephine Mayweather, may I present Sheik Kha—"

Omar, or whoever he was, cut Zeke off. "As your acquaintance said, the man no longer exists."

"Well, we have to call you something."

"Omar will suffice, my Mast... Josephine. I believe you asked about my former... The Efreet?" He rubbed his hand over his beard. "Amun, I believe his name once was."

Zeke nodded. "I remembered him. Rumor had it he'd left for Atlantis."

Omar shook his head as if dislodging a bad memory. "He is not what he once was. The Amun we knew, he held a gentle soul. His departure from djinn society, such as it ever was, occurred because he refused to accept changes to the world. He wanted everything to remain as always." A sadness swept over the Bedouin's features. "If he could've wished to stop time, he would've. He never understood everything changes sooner or later. The world moves onward. I was a man, then I was a djinn. I was a slave and then I was free only to become a slave again."

"Did Amun enslave you?"

His head moved slowly from side to side. "My own folly enslaved me. Amun merely seized the advantage my foolhardy behavior provided. If not Amun, someone else easily would've claimed me."

A glance toward Zeke told me this interview sat on my shoulders. Damn him. I was spoiling for a fight already and I'd never found a better man to fight with. Good thing for him, now wasn't the time.

"How did you lose your freedom?" A small part of me hoped he'd outline some huge, protracted ritual held by the light of the blue moon. Of course, life's never simple, but a gal can hope.

"I made the mistake of longing for the time when someone else made my decisions. I wished for a Master." Omar appeared so forlorn I gently scooted the scimitar away from him. "Amun overheard my imprudent musing. He must've known what I intended before I gave voice to my feelings. I no more than uttered the words and he appeared to accept my forfeiture."

"It's not possible." I didn't need Zeke to tell me how stupid I sounded, but he said it anyway. Omar echoed the sentiment, albeit more nicely.

"With magic anything is possible. Words have very definite meaning, and used the wrong way, the power all brethren enjoy can twist itself into something we never intended."

Whichever gods made these damn Rules are sick bastards. In my opinion, they all needed to be bitch-slapped.

"It doesn't matter," I said. "What's done is done." Big words for someone who suddenly felt so small. Learning how a few words would cost me my freedom hit my confidence like Derek Jeter's bat. "What we need to worry about now is stopping Amun." Although how we would accomplish that when I couldn't stop tripping over my own ignorance was anyone's guess. "Do you know where he is?"

Omar shook his head. "He enslaved me and kept me inside the lamp until he required my services. I last saw him in the place where you found me."

"Does he have any more wishes left?" Zeke asked

"One. His second wish set my course and bound me to him."

Amun must've given the wording a lot of thought if he accomplished both goals with one wish. Most people spit out a wish with so many loopholes, they're lucky to keep their genie long enough to enjoy the benefits. Some think before they wish, unlike myself, but it's rare for anyone to piggyback several gifts on one wish.

"Your Egyptian friend is smarter than I hoped."

"He's been at it a long time, Josie. Plus he's had a lot of alone time to consider his options. A couple hundred years, at least."

"Atlantis time. Got ya. So the place really exists?"

"Consider it a water park of monumental proportions," Zeke said. "Very quiet unless you like conversing with the fishes, though."

"Or the merfolk find you," added Major.

I remembered the tiny thing in Mary's office. If I'd actually seen a real live mermaid, I didn't want to think about it and further destabilize my rock-solid knowledge of the world. Merfolk floating around wouldn't do me any good. Later, though, I needed some serious classroom time.

"Atlantis is a place for solitude," my ex said. "Last anyone knew, Amun wanted to be alone."

"Then what brought him to the surface?"

"Only he can answer your question." Omar dragged a hand over his face and added, "As much as I am loathe to suggest it."

"What?" Talking to these guys felt like pulling fishhooks out of my eyeballs. If one of them didn't pony up with some answers, and quick, I might transform someone into a toad. If I could get away with it.

"Perhaps some other *being* suggested Amun rejoin the world."

"Like these merfolk you mentioned?" As I asked, I hoped the answer wouldn't lead to a whole new species of problems.

"No. They care little for our goings-on."

"So, you're saying he might've been approached by, what, another Efreet? Down in Atlantis?"

"I'd rather not think another Efreet awaits us, but anything is possible."

Major barked his agreement as we felt a hiss of incoming air. The Bedouin pulled his sword before the rest of us could react.

"You are not my Master!"

I turned to see Mena's face drain to pasty-pale. "It's okay, Omar. She's a friend."

"Not her, Josephine. The Other. Amun."

As he spoke the name, I realized Mena's grimace didn't have a damn thing to do with Omar's pig-sticker. At that point, the dagger protruding from her back seemed more important.

TWENTY-THREE

~-~-~-~-~-~-~-~

As my best friend slid to the floor, I culled every ounce of energy I could. The sad little sparkle would barely light a firecracker. I had two choices: bitch about my weak batteries or do whatever damage I could. Cramming every available ion into a ball, I hunted for a place to aim. The Bedouin stepped beside me, his eyes no longer focused on a single point. Across the narrow room, Zeke crackled like a live wire with no place to direct the flow.

As quickly as he'd come, Amun was gone.

"He expected to find one half-sane djinn, not a welcoming party." I heard Zeke's words as I dropped to my knees beside Mena. I didn't care why Amun left as long as he was gone. Slipping a bit of my sparse energy toward her, I let out a sigh of relief. She still lived. Whatever the Efreet did, though, weakened her with each passing second. In one careful motion, I pulled the blade free, using the last of my power to wish for her health. The wound closed. Her eyelids flickered. She fell into a deeper unconsciousness. But nothing else.

"I don't have enough," came a raspy voice I identified as my own. Zeke was busy strengthening the vault's security, and every protective measure he dropped made us a little safer. Still, I hated him a little for not being able to help. I needed him. Mena needed him. Motioning toward a tear-blurred Omar, I shifted the body in my arms. "Help her."

"Only if you wish it, my Master."

Like I needed the reminder. *Damn Rules.* Of course, if he wanted, he could help without a wish. Ally or not, Omar had played the game too long to forget the basic genie *modus operandi. 'Never give it away for free.'* What a bunch of supernatural whores.

"Fine. It's a wish. Now heal her, damn it."

"You must say the words."

I could've slapped him, but I knew the way the game was played. "I wish for you to bring Mena back to full health."

I couldn't see the wish, but its power made the hair on my arms stand on end. It started as a flicker. Before it dissipated, a surge massive enough to easily electrocute any human hammered Mena and myself. By the time the wish was complete, my friend breathed easier and Omar slumped against the wall. Me? My muscles twitched uncontrollably, but I could live with feeling like I'd licked a transformer if it meant my best friend would live.

Once I caught my breath, I asked the first question on my mind. "What the hell happened here?" When no answer came, I nudged the Bedouin with the toe of my boot. "Seriously, dude, what was that?"

"A poisonous wish. On the knife." His words came out hissed between rapid breaths. "Efreet. They can kill quick. Or they can kill slow"

Well, it explained why I couldn't heal her on my own. Healing never takes too much energy. "Why would he care how she died?"

"Amun's upping the stakes," Zeke said, after creating a layer of wishes so thick the gods themselves would've had a tough time. "Go ahead, asshole. Get through those." His words tumbled out right before he crumpled to the floor.

I let my gaze travel from one genie to the next. "Who is this guy? Super-djinn?"

"Efreet," Omar corrected. "The djinn are not to blame for this."

I wasn't so sure. Being a genie had driven Amun and others like him to become Efreet. Hell, the djinn life had driven Omar to wish for someone to order him around again. Personally, I didn't get the reasoning, but then again, I hadn't lived nearly as long as most brethren. Maybe after a few centuries, I'd be off my rocker, too.

"The djinn as a whole are not to blame." Major's voice echoed in my head, giving me an instant headache. "It's a matter of how each djinn deals with the power he possesses and the Rules he must strain against. A being cannot be given both a wealth of power and a leash."

"Ironic coming from a dog." Zeke's muffled zinger came from where he cradled his head on his arms. "So, you're finally barking out a few pearls of wisdom for us. How convenient."

"Knock it off. If he's willing to talk, let him talk."

"Thank you, Josephine." The dog sat back on his haunches. "I see now nothing worse can happen than already has. Still, you must to keep this knowledge to yourselves until we understand its ramifications. If for no other reason than your safety."

"My lips are sealed," Zeke said. When he raised his tired face, he'd sealed his mouth into one solid space.

"Knock it off," I told him after a few seconds. "You're creeping me out."

In a blink, he returned to normal. "Too bad I can't carry on a conversation like that."

"Too bad you couldn't stop talking instead of going all horror movie," I told him. "Then at least Major... err, Trygvyr might have a chance to finish." Turning toward my furry companion, I said, "I don't really know what to call you anymore."

"I am both Trygvyr and Major, and neither. Call me what you will."

I tried not to roll my eyes. Breaking the subservience was hard enough in a newly freed djinn, I couldn't imagine changing the behavior of a djinn who'd been a dog for fifteen decades.

"For now, let's stick with Major. At least while you're in dog form. I'm having a tough enough time wrapping my brain around this."

"As you wish." He lowered to the floor, laying his huge head on his paws. Omar called forth a chair and sat. Zeke went back to burying his face in his arms. We were as ready as any group of people for what had to be bad news.

"The djinn," he began, "we are powerful beings, but not without limits."

"Tell us something we don't already know, mutt."

"Have you never felt the need to break free from those limits, Ezekiel?" the dog asked. "I realize you've been without the constraints of a Master for longer than any of us, but don't you still feel bound?"

Zeke raised his head. "I don't know what you think you know, but I'm not bound to anything."

"If you believe you're totally free, you are more trapped than you know." Major lifted his own head, curling his lips until his ivory daggers showed. "Unless you think living under the Rules makes one free."

At those words, Zeke's exhaustion seemed to melt away. "An old friend once told me 'wise people, even though all laws were abolished, would still lead the same life.' Rules don't stop me from doing anything I would want to do anyway." Knowing Zeke had been friends with Aristophanes impressed me. No wonder our pillow talk frequently turned into deep philosophical conversations.

"You've never wished for a lost loved one to be returned?" Major said. The pain in his voice seeped into my bones. I mourned with him, especially when an agonized whine underscored his words. "Or wished for a wicked Master to meet his own demise? You are a better man than I if you didn't. From the day I became djinn, I cursed the chains placed on my powers. I realized only when I removed my bonds would I receive the justice I craved."

"So you became an Efreet to get around the Rules?" I could almost understand the reasoning. Hell, I couldn't count the number of times I cursed working within Rules I never had a hand in creating and didn't always believe were right. But then again, as much as I bitched, I would never dream of avoiding them altogether.

His huge head shook. "You have it backwards. I dismissed the Rules. And then became an Efreet."

Almost as one, we held our breath. Hear a *pin* drop? A deaf man could've heard a feather float by.

"It can't be so simple," I said into the stillness, "or there'd be more Efreet."

"Renouncing the very structure by which you exist is not as simple a thing as you think. Becoming Efreet takes a saturation of belief. When you can no longer live within the Rules, when you believe they have caused every hurtful thing you've ever endured or will ever endure again, only then you can truly renounce the Rules. Once a djinn does so, the transformation is instantaneous. All he needs say are the words, like any Master's wish. Except this Master is within yourself."

I sat stunned. When Major spoke again, I almost jumped out of my skin.

"Perhaps I should've waited," he said, nodding toward the Bedouin, "until we were alone."

Omar drew himself up. "Your information is of no value to me. I'm not such a fool. Our kind cannot exist without Rules to govern us."

"But you can," Major insisted. "And the experience is exhilarating. At first. The killing becomes an opiate after a time. Then, like any drug, you need more to feel anything. Until one day, you wake up, strung out, hung over, and hating yourself."

"Wait a second. You? You're a killer like Amun?" I suddenly wanted to hurl up every meal I'd eaten since birth. All the trust I placed in him gave me a case of the creeping willies. Every time he could've torn out my throat instead of licking my cheek. The instances he could've bitten the hand that fed him, and torn it clean off.

"No! I swear on my soul, I never harmed the innocent, as I would never harm you. I never took a life than didn't deserve taking. But the price became too high. Soon I wanted to kill for the slightest infraction." He shook his head. "When the djinn came in the last war, I could've destroyed them all, but suddenly, centuries of my life became clear. I left myself open to their punishment. I didn't fight them. I couldn't."

I reached a hand toward him without thinking. One look at it and he sighed.

"Your sympathy gives me hope, Mistress. But I don't deserve it. I deserved the penalty they handed down and more. I've known this truth since the day they sentenced me to this beastly form."

"Which is why you won't let me change you back."

"I deserve no less than the full extent of my punishment."

I contemplated the years Trygvyr already spent as a dog. I'd only had him since Copenhagen, when he followed me from one street to the next until I couldn't help but bring him home. And I spent three years thinking I had the luckiest dog in the world. Too bad I didn't know what an unlucky genie he'd been. His need to take his punishment only made me want to transform him more. He'd learned his lesson.

"So," Zeke said, saving me from my own fruitless thoughts, "where does that leave us? We know perhaps how Amun got the way he was but knowing doesn't help us stop him."

"It's a step in the right direction," said Mena. She was still stretched across the floor, and her eyes still didn't seem to be focusing right, but she was alive. Alive and apparently feisty enough to join in the conversation.

"How so?"

"We could stop other djinn from following him," I said.

"I'll worry about keeping more genies from getting dead. You worry about saving the lost," Zeke told me.

"And about keeping any others from turning into slaves again." I couldn't imagine the pain Omar endured losing his freedom. I could only pray no more genies would suffer the same fate.

"That, too."

I stared into Major's dark eyes, finally understanding what the soulfulness behind his expressive eyes really meant. Trygvyr was only a man who'd once made bad choices—choices any of us were capable of making. Maybe he made his decisions for the right reasons, but whatever pain he suffered didn't excuse his crimes afterwards. And he knew it.

If a rehabilitated criminal ever existed, it was him.

"Thank you for your help," I said. "I won't pretend I wouldn't feel better with your power on our side, but the information you've provided, it's more than we knew about the Efreet before."

"For whatever that's worth." Petulant didn't look good on Zeke. After knowing what he'd experienced with the Efreet, though, I couldn't bring myself to harass him.

"Information is never worthless." The Bedouin's seriousness was a palpable thing. "Men must simply ask the right questions and use the answers they receive to the best of their abilities."

"Major? I don't know if you'd feel like you were betraying your former species, but can you tell us about any Efreet weaknesses?"

He shook himself. "I owe them no allegiance, but I can't think of anything, unless their pervasive hubris counts as a weapon."

"Our secret weapon is unjustified pride?" Zeke asked. "Great."

"Pride goeth before destruction," said Omar. All eyes turned toward the Bedouin. "Not being Christian does not mean I ignore their occasional wisdom."

A half-ass, long shot of a plan began forming in the back of my head. Part one was putting itself together. I had to hope the rest would fall into place. There still remained the niggling question of—

"How does Amun keep getting into the building?" Zeke said. He *had* to stop doing that.

"I hate to think it, but could Basil be inviting him in like he did with Duarte?" Mena rose to a sitting position. She'd seen better days, but she'd recover.

After her question, though, I couldn't be sure I would. Mena had been my best friend for years, but Baz was my oldest friend. He couldn't be the traitor. We'd been through too much together to believe he'd betray me. On the other hand, I couldn't put it outside the realm of possibility.

"He said he went to visit a sick friend?" Convincing myself of his innocence was an uphill battle. It got worse when Mena nodded.

"Hard to visit a sick friend when djinn don't get sick." Leave it to Zeke to point out the obvious when I couldn't bring myself to. "Of course, he associates with a lot of mortals in your business. Maybe he stopped over to see one of them."

Even grasping at straws, I couldn't latch onto the idea. I couldn't envision how a sick friend would keep Basil away in the face of the shitstorm we were enduring.

TWENTY-FOUR

~-~-~-~-~-~-~-~

I left Omar in Mena's capable, if unsteady, hands. The Bedouin seemed sane enough. Besides, we'd be a short shout away if his psychological bedrock started crumbling again. What he needed was more acclimation to our world, not a fight. Sticking close to Mena would be his best bet.

Zeke and I headed toward the company's offices with Major trailing behind. I worried a little about the dog's mental status. He seemed depressed, but I didn't have time to coax him toward emotional well-being. To borrow a phrase from Reggie: *Sometimes a man has to pull himself up by his own bootstraps, especially when the world is kicking him in the teeth.*

Major didn't wear boots, but he'd still have to pull himself up. If this boiled into a war, we would need every available wish. Hell, Trygvyr could be the keystone to stopping this conflict ahead of time. The sooner he understood that, the better off we'd be. No one else had to die.

And I hoped no one would.

"Baz?" I spoke from outside his open office door, trying to keep my voice suspicion-free. Better if my visit appeared innocuous. Hell, he could assume I wanted to discuss the company picnic for all I cared. As long as he didn't think this was a staged intervention, it was all good.

The whir of his computer came from his otherwise quiet office. It didn't get my hopes up. No keys tapping on a workday? Strange even on a good day, and this wasn't a good day.

"Hello?" Still nothing.

"He's not here," Mr. Obvious ben Aron said as he stepped past me. "But someone was."

Any retort I had died in my throat as I surveyed the office. A small cyclone had blown through. Or maybe some giant toddler had thrown a temper tantrum. Baz's desk chair lay on one side. All the drawers in both filing cabinets hung open, their contents chucked all over the floor. Someone had ripped the 18th century divan he adored to shreds. His poor, prized ficus lay on one side, a mass of torn leaves and scattered dirt.

One thing was certain. He didn't do this. The right proper Basil Hadresham couldn't stand unorganized papers on his desk. A mess of this proportion would give the poor guy seizures.

"Odin's hairy ba—" Major stopped in the doorway. After a few tentative steps inside, he began snorfling through the mess. When he lifted his nose, he said, "He didn't leave too long ago and, from the smell, something scared him half out of his mind." He pressed his nose against the carpet, inhaling deeply. "Mister Hadresham. And the Efreet. No one else. Not your scent from a few days ago. I don't even detect my own odor."

"Amun didn't hide his presence?" I said, remembering the day of the auction. "Why mask the others?"

"He's messing with you." Zeke retrieved a shattered vase, setting the pieces on the desk.

The dog gave a canine shrug. "Sounds reasonable."

Pieces of Basil's favorite Manchester United mug crunched beneath my heels as I strode across the room. I brushed the litter from the top of the farthest cabinet and removed the dictionary. The book itself seemed intact. Opening its cover unveiled a story no dictionary should ever tell.

"Either he moved his sanctuary without telling me, or we've got bigger problems than we thought." I turned the volume so the others could see the book's hollow interior. "And I have a feeling Baz wouldn't move it of his own choice."

My companions fell silent as the implications set in. In all likelihood, their thoughts weren't too far from my own.

"If Amun has Basil's pocket watch—" I shot Major a look. No one should know what his sanctuary looked like. "Look. People do things around dogs they wouldn't do around other people. He didn't notice me over there on the rug when he disappeared into his watch last year. He came out holding an old photo, then sat at his desk crying."

How many private and personal moments we'd unintentionally stored in the djinn/dog's head for all eternity, I didn't know. All the things I'd done and said when I was alone with him creeped me out.

No time to worry about that now.

What Major left unsaid worried me enough. Basil's sanctuary had disappeared, which meant he probably landed in the same boat as Omar—enslaved again. With the Efreet in control. As if that worst case scenario weren't bad enough, the killer could possibly have access to all of Mayweather, including the private residences.

"Think about the situation for a moment, Mistress." If a good dog is judged by its ability to sense its owner's emotions, I had the best one ever. "If Amun controls Basil, he would have no need of Mena to access the vault."

"Maybe he didn't, Muttly. He could've used her as a distraction." Zeke brushed off the ruined furniture and plopped down like he hadn't crushed my burgeoning hopes. "Let's look at the bigger picture. Why would he need Omar back? He already used the guy to get to Josie, and it worked. The Bedouin got himself 'rescued' …" He actually paused for his damn air quotes. "…then she brought him inside the building. From there, the Efreet merely piggybacked his genie connection to gain all the access he needed. Afterward, Omar became expendable, which explains why Amun never broke him out of the vault."

I tried speaking but couldn't get a word out before Zeke railroaded over me.

"Once Amun had an in, he used someone else, most likely Basil, to get Josie out to Florida so he could kill someone in front of her. The victims were never the point. His point was always to get to her."

"You can stop talking about me like I'm not in the room." I shook my head. "We're back to the same damn question. Why would Amun arrange all this on my account? I'm no one. What on Earth would the creep accomplish?

"Could this…" I swept my hand to encompass the mess we found ourselves standing in. "…be a trick? We come up here to question Baz—"

"And when we get here," Zeke said, kicking an overturned table, "our bloody-good Brit is gone." He turned toward me, his face colored with barely restrained anger. "I'm not inclined to believe he would betray you, but I could be wrong."

"So we're back to whether this might be—"

"A trick? Damn straight it could."

I mentally scrolled through my years with Basil, trying to examine the past objectively. As squirreled up as my head was, though, I couldn't be certain anything rational still existed in my world. With all the crap a supernatural powerhouse can pull, I couldn't rule out the possibility he'd hid something this massive.

I sniffed the air. The dog would know best, but I didn't detect anything about Basil than what I'd known for years. If he really turned into an Efreet-lover, wouldn't I smell something different about him?

"Whether he asked for it or got taken by surprise, I suspect Baz has returned to the slave life by now." Zeke pointed to one of the few things in the place not trashed—the computer. "How much work did he do on that thing?"

"Everything. The antiques business. The rescue work. All networked to his personal machine. He has a whole setup in his apartment for the really sensitive stuff." I moved several scattered objects off the desk. As soon as I touched the mouse, the screen blossomed to life. "He must've had it in sleep mode."

I half-expected the hard drive to be wiped clean. It's what I'd do if I played for the villain team. Destroy evidence and fuck the opposition along the way. *Guilty until proven innocent?* I cursed my mistrust. When a splash screen came up with the words 'Enter user name and password', I could've kicked myself.

"This is definitely Basil's doing. My computer is on the network, but I've never seen this before."

Zeke placed his hands on my shoulders. Damn, the man could move quietly when he wanted. "Do you have any idea how to get past this?"

"Depends on whether the terminal expects me to access it using Basil's info or my own. If I enter my information, chances are I'll get nothing except my own directory."

"Basil's info then?"

"I don't have the faintest."

"Try BazMan1742," Major said. I stared pointedly until his tail started its guilty wag. "What? I can't be blamed for their indiscretions when I'm sitting next to them. Oh, by the way, the genie in room 187 is conducting sexual liaisons with—"

"Yeah, yeah. Great. What consenting djinn do in their own time is no one's business. Do you have the password to this thing, too?"

"I can't always see the keyboard from down here," he said. My chest clenched. I'd never figure it out on my own. "But Basil has a bad habit of saying it every time he types it."

The thought of a dog who could access all of our secure data didn't help. Hell, the killer could've turned into a mosquito and gained access to every inch of our human security.

"Remind me to change all my passwords when you're not around." Major gave a resigned huff and provided the information. In seconds, the computer rewarded me with Basil's desktop, complete with Tower of London wallpaper. "I'm in. I think."

Before I had a chance to access anything, Basil's voice echoed around me. "Since you used a password only the dog would know, I'll assume I'm talking to you, love," he said with a slight tremor in his voice. "I do hope the whole bloody process didn't take too long."

"What the hell?"

Major shook his coat and stared. "Sound file, streaming through the speakers."

"I know that. How the hell do you?"

"I'm a canine, not an idiot. When you're away, I keep Basil company. He talks while he works." I narrowed my eyes. "Don't look so surprised. You do it all the time, too."

I ignored his dig. "You said this was streaming?" I leaned closer to the microphone. "Baz? Can you hear me?"

"I meant the voice is coming through the speakers. I didn't realize streaming meant something else."

"That's okay," Zeke said, nudging the dog's shoulder. "You're nothing but a mutt."

"And you're nothing but an ass," the dog said before he stuck his big, pink tongue out.

"Okay, boys. Enough." I shot Major a look. "So you're saying this is pre-recorded?"

"I expect so. From the tenor of his voice, he was terrified."

Basil cleared his throat. "Stop wondering how I accomplished this. We don't have time. Amun is coming. The blighter may already be here. I can't escape him, but I hope you find this in time to stop him from doing to me what he did to those kids."

I wanted to throw up. Bad enough the bastard made Basil a slave again. If he killed my friend, I might renounce the Rules in order to wish his nasty ass dead.

"That answers one question." Zeke's words didn't make it through my thoughts as anything but a burble. As I stared with my mouth hanging open, he said, "The question of whether Basil went by choice?" I nodded as the recording drew my attention.

"I didn't mean for this to happen. If this is the last bit you hear from me, I have to explain." He sucked in a choked breath. "I never intended the wish behind all this. I wanted a wee bit of peace is all. You understand, don't you, love? What with the constant alerts, and the auction debacle, along with those deaths. When I considered my life as a lad doing as I pleased, I wanted an escape back to... I don't know... freedom from all the duty and the rules."

Whether he meant big or little 'r' rules wasn't evident in his voice. Either way, he wanted to shirk the responsibility of making his own decisions, if only for a moment of peace.

"Amun appeared seconds after I wished for a Master's rule again. I made a silly, stupid wish. I didn't really mean it, Jo, but..." His voice fell away for more heartbeats than I wanted to count.

"The Efreet arrived, ensnared me, then left to do something he said was important. He told me to wait for 'im. Forbade me from calling you. The bloke didn't include computers, or you wouldn't be 'earing this either. Oh, Jo. I'm so sorry I let 'im in. I didn't 'ave any idea the 'avoc I'd cause. I didn't. Protect y'self, love. Amun is—"

A pop echoed in the office, silencing Basil's voice. I checked to make sure the computer wasn't smoking. Since it hadn't fried, I assumed the noise occurred when Amun sucked his new slave away.

I tried to find the sound file, but Baz buried it deep, probably to keep Amun from accessing it. Why he left it for me and set Major up with a password ahead of time, I didn't know. I had a sinking feeling I couldn't ask my resident geek any time soon.

Zeke leaned past me, quickly locating the file. I didn't bother asking how. With his security background, he probably knew more about computers than I'd ever want to learn.

"The time stamp shows about fifteen minutes before Mena got the surprise of *her* life."

"Bastard works quick," I said. "He jumped on Basil's ignorance, then went after Mena." A sick thought slid into my consciousness. Picking up the phone, I punched an extension and ignored how much my hands shook. When the therapist's voice filled the office, I let my stomach settle back out of my throat.

"What's wrong?" she asked.

"Your sanctuary. Do you have it with you?"

Her long pause made my lunch rise. "It's *safe*."

"You don't sound sure."

"Would you tell me if I asked about yours?"

"Right now? In a heartbeat." My thoughts turned to my own sanctuary—a brooch from my mother's estate. If the insides of a wish-laden jewelry box in a safe at the back of my hidden library weren't safe, nowhere would be. After I regained my freedom, I would be damned if another person touched it again. If Amun managed his way past the illusions and the wards, he couldn't handle my sanctuary without getting his ass magically kicked until he cursed ever coming back from Atlantis.

Satisfied with my own freedom, I gave Mena the Cliff Notes version of why I needed to know. "I guess my sanctuary is as safe as it can be, considering the circumstances."

I had to take her word for it. Without knowing Amun's location, or who he could have watching us, we couldn't exactly move the damn things around.

"We need to hide the sanctuaries still inside the building," Major said, echoing my thoughts. Mine and Mena's were safe. Zeke's had to be somewhere outside the building. Leaving Omar's and—

"The guests." The world twirled around me like an eyes-wide-open teleport. "We have to get them and their sanctuaries the hell out of here."

Zeke cleared his throat. He didn't act like he wanted to make whatever he had on his mind public, but as I watched, he discarded his misgivings. "Fine," he said. "Teleport everyone to my place. If Amun wants them, he'll have to come through the best security money can build, and the one genie who can still kick his ass."

"You sound pretty sure of yourself."

"You want references?"

He had a point. If the djinn CEO of a major security firm couldn't keep the brethren safe, no one could. "Fine by me. You get your place ready for a bunch of refugees, and I'll expedite the process on this end. Well, plus change every code and wish in the—" Before I continued through my list, Zeke zapped himself away, leaving me talking to a trashed room while the dog stared at me.

"Well, Ollie, this is a fine mess we've gotten ourselves into."

"Laurel and Hardy? Really?"

"Television keeps me company while I'm trapped in the cave. Be glad I didn't quote *The Three Stooges*." He scratched at one ear. "What is your plan?"

I shook my head. I spent too many years and too much effort building Mayweather Antiquities to let some whackjob drive me away. Still, with the information we had, I couldn't afford to stay behind while everyone else headed for safety.

I didn't want to admit it, but running was the only way.

"We lock her down, then beat feet." As soon as I made the decision, my list of tasks got longer.

"First things first," Major said, rising to all four feet. "Your human employees and guests need to leave. If Duarte, et al are angry now, let a human get harmed, especially a former genie."

I hadn't considered that annoying jackboot's reaction, but the dog had it right. The Moorish bastard would party on my freshly transformed ass if any mortal under my protection got so much as ruffled.

"Call Renee. All the employees need to go home. Tell her we're fumigating the building or something. Maybe taking an extended vacation," I said before my brain engaged.

"You want I should bark at them until they leave?" Major's voice split through my thoughts. I could've kicked myself for not considering that little wrinkle.

"Sorry." My face went sunburn hot. "I'll go down there and... Shit, too much to do and too little of me. It'd help if we weren't down to the three of us—"

"Plus guests."

"No. They need to get out of here. No more cheap labor for Amun." I didn't know a dog could feel regret until I saw it on Major. "Don't sweat it. I know you'd help if you could, but you're not exactly in the position. I'm cool with it. I'll pull Mena and... No, not Omar."

"If you used them both, they still won't be enough assistance to get everyone out quickly." He shook his head like the saddest pooch ever. "I don't want to suggest this but..."

Great. Now what?

For a moment, Major appeared to be trying to use his powers. Poor thing looked constipated with unspent energy. After a hundred and fifty years of not using his powers, I half expected wishes to shoot out his ears. When nothing happened, he sat a little straighter, like a man about to request his last cigarette and a blindfold.

"It's no use," he said. "It never has been."

"What?" I wrinkled my nose. "You've tried using your powers before?"

"Only every single day for the first century or so. After a while, I gave up. With everything you need right now, I had to try."

"That's okay, buddy." I patted him on the head. In return, I got bared teeth and a low growl. "Sorry. Force of habit."

"Go ahead. Do it."

I raised an eyebrow. I'd never been one to smack him on the nose for growling, but then again, he never growled at me before.

"I mean, go ahead. Return me to the Many. Whatever the consequences. I made my bed. Now is as good a time as any to lie in it."

TWENTY-FIVE

~-~-~-~-~-~-~

"Love to," I told the dog who would be djinn again, "but a transformation on any scale takes a helluva lot more energy than I have. Hell, from what I've heard, you need three fully-charged genies." Major's request would've gone over a whole lot better before Zeke left. We were running a little short of available brethren to tap.

"Omar and Mena," I said aloud.

His furry head nodded. "They are the best chance for success. If you don't wish to involve your guests, that is."

Suddenly, something I hadn't thought of struck me upside the head. Only hours before the pooch had been dead set against returning to the Many. Now, with the biggest power source out of the picture, he decided to drive the bandwagon? Sure, he could've *right that moment* realized how useful he would be, assuming his motivation was providing *me* assistance. But my situation hadn't changed much. Whether dog or djinn, it still smelled like Shit Creek, and my boat still floated a helluva a long ways up it.

Call it paranoia, but I could only figure out one reason he'd get all gung-ho about transforming.

"One question, Trygvyr." His true name set the dog back on his dewclaws. I wanted to believe he stood against the Efreet, but maybe his rational mind hadn't driven his change of heart. "Whose side are

~ 293 ~

you really on?" I didn't believe I'd get an honest answer, but I had to ask.

When he recovered from my unexpected sideswipe, he shook his head slowly. "I am on the side of right, Mistress. Thank the gods, right happens to be with you."

"Spoken like a true djinn. Or maybe a true Efreet." I speared him with a glance. "Where's your sanctuary?"

And all at once, he didn't need to say a word to make me feel like a complete shit. His puppy eyes took care of that. If I'd spilled Mountain Dew and spanked him for whizzing inside, he wouldn't have been this hurt.

"Probably where I hid it before Mary Killigrew turned me." He dropped his words carefully. "I haven't touched it since. Fairly difficult trick without thumbs, you know. I'll happily take you there, once you take care of this mess." With the downtrodden tail thump he always gave after a scolding, he dropped my self-worth into the dumper. "What I can say with perfect certainty is Amun does not control me, not only because he couldn't have located my sanctuary, but also because I am no longer one of the Many. He could wave my sacred home around from sunup to sundown. I still wouldn't follow him."

His great, furry head shook causing loose fur to create a halo around us. "I understand your distrust. I do. But isn't warranted." He placed one big paw on my thigh and hit me with those soft, brown eyes, so filled with misery he damn near broke my heart. "I would gladly die before I helped the Efreet. It is their fault, and my own, I spent so much time in this form. If I must relinquish my well-deserved punishment to aid in Amun's defeat, I do so willingly."

My feeling of total shitness intensified. I could've blamed my distrust on Basil's disappearance, but that would only get me so far. I had no excuses for doubting Major.

"Sorry." The one word squeezed out of me wrapped in a thorny blanket. It wasn't anywhere near enough. You said 'sorry' when you wigged out over something stupid, like a chewed shoe. This felt more like bitch-slapping a friend you didn't meet until you were twenty because you had a shitty eighteenth birthday.

"As I said, I understand."

He might've, but I sure didn't. Chalk it up to never having a pet. Or maybe chalk it up to having nothing but a pet for years.

"I have no way to prove my loyalty," he continued, "except by my actions."

With his paw on my leg and those beautiful eyes staring into me, any lingering doubts melted away. If evil lurked under his mound of fur, the cute-puppy trick worked. He laid his head on my lap, going for the hat trick of the canine world. My heartstrings pulled harder than a tugboat moving a freighter. The damn dog wielded his wiles like every other pooch, but with the brains of a genie. Damn him.

In the end, though, however he tugged at my emotions didn't matter. In my heart, I needed him as a genie more than he deserved to remain a dog. Presented with his submission, dragging my feet just seemed stupid. Plus, it was a chicken-shit move on my part. To be totally honest, the excuses I created were because I didn't want to get hurt. A betrayal from Major would cut me worse than anything Zeke had ever done.

Fear never accomplishes anything. Reggie's voice floated up from my memory. As much as I dreaded the worst, I couldn't move forward without Major's help. If he deceived me, I'd regret trusting him. But he'd regret it more. We'd turn him into something way worse than a dog. Like a fire hydrant.

"Fine." I shouted—more at myself than anyone in particular. "Let's get you back on two feet and get this damn evacuation under way."

The walk downstairs didn't take as long as my muddled head wanted. I needed time. I fought the urge to zap myself onto a beach for a couple hours. Time was something I didn't have in abundance. If only the Rules allowed messing with the clock. I could start this day over with a fresh mind. I could go back and save Arthur Walton. Hell, with enough time, I might figure out what I did to piss the Efreet off in the first place. For that matter, zipping back to 1924 meant I could stop myself from opening Reggie's damn package.

But second-guessing that bonehead play gives me a headache. I should know. I've retraced the what-ifs so many times I've worn a rut in my brain. All the years of wanting the past to be different taught me you can't go back, no matter how much you might wish it. The only thing is move forward and do the best you can along the way.

I could only hope my best ended up good enough to stop Amun.

We found the vault as secure as we left it. After undoing the wishes we'd laid on the place, I punched in my security code, and the door whooshed open.

"I didn't know if the extra security..." Mena's uncertain voice hit me. In our relationship, I'd always been the less certain one. Having the tables flip didn't comfort me, especially with a lunatic running around. Not that she hadn't earned a little uncertainty, but I needed her to snap out of it quick.

"From what I sensed, you were perfectly safe."

"It's just Amun. He didn't have any trouble releasing the magic locks before." She twisted a strand of hair around one finger, only to release it into a curling loop and twist it again. "The numerical code hung him up." Another first happened when Mena let out a high-pitched giggle. "All those years under the sea left him with a technological handicap."

I narrowed my eyes at this strange incarnation of my friend. She looked like Mena. I mean, except for the dark rings under her eyes and the sallow complexion. The psychologist bordered on hysteria. Part of me wanted to give her a Valium and make her lie down. Whatever extra oomph the Efreet put into stabbing my friend did more damage than Omar's wish could fix. Hell, the more I watched her, the more I wondered if damage like hers *could* be fixed.

"Listen," I said, laying a hand on her arm, "I'm sorry Amun went through you to get to me."

Her mouth closed with a snap, and she shrugged. "I'm just glad he picked me and not a human like Michael." A shudder went through her small frame. "I can't imagine. I mean, Amun's knife against—"

"Which brings me around to why I'm here." I couldn't be sure heaping added stress on her sketchy mental state was a good idea, but I didn't have any choice. As I gave her the details, I watched for signs of further crumbling. Luckily, the more I talked, the more stable she grew. "So, you see why I need help clearing the building."

The thought of leaving the vault's secure walls turned Mena a little green, but she nodded. I checked Omar's reaction. A muscle ticked along his jaw as he drew his scimitar.

"We are ready to assist you, Mast... Josephine."

I let a wry grin play over my lips. "Put away the mini-Guillotine. I need your magic more than your muscles."

"You have but one wish left," he said. Good thing he said it, too, because I'd been so used to having free genies around, I forgot my promise. I felt like crap when his eyes showed he knew I forgot. His belief I'd welch out on him hurt. I had enough baggage without the added guilt.

Well. Only one way to deal with the problem.

"I wish you free."

The words left my mouth, and I wasn't sure who the shock hit harder: Omar or Mena. He never believed I'd free him. Mena should've known better. She probably expected, without his bonds, he would leave right when we needed him. I lifted a shoulder in her direction.

"If he leaves, we'll deal with Amun on our own."

My wish flowed into the djinn. Poor Omar's transformation from enslaved whacko to free genie turned out to be anti-climactic. He didn't get a sparkler's worth of fizzle. One second, I had an unwilling servant. The next he became his own man again. We'd party hard over his emancipation after the drama ended. If we all survived long enough to celebrate.

Of course, as a free man, he could kick my ass as easily as thank me. If I'd thought about the situation beforehand, I would've cringed. I might've prepared a defensive wish. I just had to hope if he vented his anger, the brunt would fall on me instead of Mena. She didn't look up to an ass kicking.

His hands lifted toward me. Power surged around him like ball lightning. With all that juice, Omar could take out half the building. Whatever happened now, I couldn't take the wish back. Even if I could, I wouldn't. A promise is a promise. Bracing myself, I waited for the impact. When it didn't come, I opened one eye to find him lowering his hands and sheathing his energy.

"Thank you. Josephine." He released a tiny wish, giving himself the lightshow he deserved. When the spectacle died down, his traditional Bedouin garb had been replaced. He resembled Omar Sharif before. Now? I let out a long whistle. Gone was the dashing leader of some nomadic band. This new look still oozed Sharif, but more like his part in *Funny Girl*—all silk suits and suave assurance. Sexy oozed out the man's pores.

"You have no idea how I longed to get out of that," he said.

"The situation or the outfit?"

"Both." He brushed an invisible piece of lint off his lapel and turned those devil-dark eyes on me. "You require my assistance?"

"If you will." He should be afforded the courtesy all free men should have. "Whether you offer your services or not is up to you."

He swallowed hard as his dark eyes glistened. "You offer the first choice I've had in more years than I care to remember."

Every inch of me longed to turn away. I've never been forward thinking enough to be comfortable around crying men. In the twenties, it simply wasn't done. Still, not facing him would be a slap in the face.

After several moments, he spoke again. "I accept."

I held up a hand. "Hang on a second. You haven't heard what we need."

"It does not matter. I trust your judgment. Except." His eyes hardened toward me.

Sensing his meaning I said, "A little paranoia never hurts. Don't worry. My sanctuary is locked up and guarded by a dozen carefully-worded wishes."

Power whispered over me, and Omar nodded. "You speak the truth. What is it you need of me?"

"You and Mena need to help me change Major… I mean, Trygvyr back into a genie."

I expected some argument, if not from the therapist then at least from the man who'd fought wars against the Efreet. I ended up being pleasantly disappointed. They merely walked toward the dog and joined hands, thrusting their fingers toward me to complete the triangle. Their support felt weird, but I wouldn't argue. Much.

"You both sure about this?"

"Aren't you?" Mena's question shot out as she arched one delicate eyebrow. I didn't know if she thought I was bluffing or if my shrink knew me better than I knew myself.

"You may ease your mind, Josephine," Omar said. "After only a few moments to evaluate Trygvyr's new incarnation, I sense no malevolence in him. His evil faded long ago."

And once again, I felt like a shit for not using my own magic to figure it out. Of course, I'd never done this before, but still. As soon as we finished kicking Amun's ass, I'd buy Major the biggest steak he'd ever seen. Or I'd buy Trygvyr whatever he wanted to eat.

I nodded. "Let's do this."

Gathering my power, I let it fill every pore to the bursting point. The other djinn did the same until we became a giant, magical transformer. We focused our energy around Major until his fur stood on end. Mounting magic crackled in the air. Its radiance blinded me.

When the glow subsided, we three genies slumped to the floor. Major was gone. In his place crouched a lean male, whose white hair and dark eyes would've proved his identity, even if a boatload of residual energy didn't still sizzle around him.

"Mistress," he said in a hushed voice. "I am yours to command."

TWENTY-SIX

~-~-~-~-~-~-~-~

His hair hung in a frozen waterfall, cascading over his naked shoulders and down his back. Those damn eyes I thought so wonderful in a dog unsettled me now. So deeply black I couldn't see his pupils. The shape, like a plump almond, made them too exotic for a man's face. If he'd been anyone else, I would've said he presented a perfect specimen of manhood. But thinking of him as attractive made me feel like I had the hots for my pooch.

Ew, ew, ew.

"Mistress?" he said.

His husky voice made me wonder how he'd sound after a night of—

"Is something wrong?"

"So many things are wrong with this I don't know where to begin." My gaze traveled the length of him before I could stop myself. I don't know how much of him was natural, and how much magic had enhanced him, but—*Yowza.* I tried to speak. Too bad everything I wanted to say got stuck behind a massive lump of lust and discomfort.

"You need to get..." I choked on the word, but finally managed to spit it out. "Clothed."

"Seems a shame." Mena whispered a quiet wish. All at once, she'd outfitted Major… no, *Trygvyr* in a tight, white t-shirt and painted-on jeans. "Time enough for eye candy later."

I shook my head. "I think you left enough candy to give your eyes diabetes." I waved my hand, loosening his clothing enough for comfort and circulation. He still looked better than your average supermodel, which didn't help my libido.

"Thank you, Mistress."

"Call me Jo. Please. We've spent enough time together for a little familiarity, don't you think?"

He blushed. I couldn't believe it. My dog, the centuries old djinn, actually blushed. "Yes, *Jo*. You may continue to call me Major if you wish."

"Major was my pet. You're? Sorry, but I can't think of you and him as the same person. Not yet. How about I stick with Trygvyr? Or Tryg, if you don't mind." I'd never think about dogs the same way again. "And since introductions are done, we have work to do. Mena? Round up the djinn guests and any of your patients you can safely move. Transport them to Zeke's place. He's expecting you. I'll have Renee gather up the… Fuck."

"What?"

"She can get the employees out, but she doesn't know about our guests. As far as she's concerned, there's nothing behind the warehouse but mountainside."

"Tell her the truth," Trygvyr said. "She's a level-headed woman. She can handle it."

"Says the guy who had a dog's brains until a few minutes ago," Mena said. "No offense." He might not have been offended but I was. As I opened my mouth to tell her off, she changed directions. "Besides, Duarte would have Jo's guts for garters. She's in enough hot water with the Council as it is."

"Someone has to get everyone out. Who else do we have?" I flicked a glance over at Omar. "The Bedouin can't go. Renee will have a conniption if he shows up and starts giving her orders. Either that or she'll drown in her own drool."

"I will charm the human. Concern yourself no more with this matter."

"She's only half the problem. What I really need is to split myself into pieces." I checked my powers. "Anyone got any juice to spare?"

"I believe I'm fully charged," Tryg said, flexing his muscles. If he looked this good in his original form, he must've been fending off the Viking girls with his horny helmet.

"I'll bet you are," Mena said on a whisper of breath.

"Down girl," I told her before turning back to Tryg. "I need you to make copies of me."

"Real or illusion?"

"What's the difference?"

"Real copies," he said, "are both form and substance. They interact with other beings around them as the original would. An illusory copy has no substance, and no ability to interact with the outside world unless the illusionist is nearby providing the motive power. In either case, though, any djinn who's paying attention will know they are not Jo."

Mena nodded. "Because neither would be imbued with power."

"Precisely." Tryg tapped one hand against the other. "May I present a different option?"

"Go for it."

"A wish to disguise a member of the brethren will perhaps fool the casual observer."

A strange frown creased Omar's face. "Oh, most certainly not. Such a thing is unacceptable. I refuse to carry the shape of a female."

Tryg let out a barking laugh. "Consider it a contribution to a larger cause. I swear the change will only be temporary."

"Says the Efreet. I do not trust you enough to allow you to muck about with my manhood."

Definitely not the time for humor. I tried to stifle the laugh bubbling in my cheşt. Really, I did. In the end, though, I couldn't help myself. I gave up trying and a bellyful of laughter burst out. Soon the room shook with the combined noise from Tryg and myself. I even heard Mena's lilting tone join in.

"I fail to see the humor," Omar said.

His words created whole new gales. For a moment, I tried sobering myself, but I couldn't. I don't know if my hysterics were due to the stress-bomb my life had become or to the sheer ridiculousness of the situation. After several minutes, with the Bedouin ready to draw his meat cleaver again, I finally sucked in a deep breath and halted the laughter.

"Thanks." I let out a little wheeze while I righted myself. "I needed that. I think." Mena wiped tears from her cheeks. Tryg still wore a grin wide enough to split most faces. "I think our freshly-djinned friend here suggested he make you look like me for a little while only. Once we clear the building, you'll be your good, old, testosterone-filled self again."

"What guarantees do I have? After this display of yours, I can imagine the great laugh you will all enjoy while I spend the next decade in skirts."

I almost lost it again, but this time I kept a tight rein on my hysteria. "How about Tryg words the wish with a time limit?" I glanced at Tryg. "That's doable, right?"

"I'll go first," he replied. Then he spoke the words to change himself. "I wish to look and sound exactly like Josephine Mayweather, but retain my own self, until the sun sets on this building." Before I had a chance to absorb the shock, I stood in front of myself.

"What do you think, Sheik?"

Omar didn't look convinced, but he gave his assent. Soon the room held three of me, plus Mena.

"Okay, one task down," I said. "Now, Omar needs to round up the guests. Mena takes care of her patients. Tryg? Do you remember what I said upstairs?"

He nodded and it was disconcerting to see me nodding at myself. "Tell the employees we have bugs and are fumigating the place. Right?"

"If they give you any crap, tell them it's a paid vacation. At least a week's worth. We'll let them know when to come back."

"And while we're off doing your bidding, what'll you be doing?" Mena asked. I didn't appreciate the extra snark, but after what she'd been through, I tolerated it. Sooner or later, though, she'd have to snap out of it. Or I'd slap her.

"I'll be closing the place down and checking for uninvited guests while I'm at it." I checked my watch. "We'll meet at Zeke's around sundown."

The other two of me nodded, but Mena just shook her head.

"What now?" My patience slipped a little. "You have a better idea?"

Regardless of her change in behavior, her next words were pure Mena. "You say we'll meet like it's a foregone conclusion. What if you aren't at Zeke's by then?"

"Call out the Marines," I said, "because it either means Amun's kicking my ass, or he got to my sanctuary somehow and he *owns* my ass. Either way, I'll need help."

TWENTY-SEVEN

~-~-~-~-~-~-~-~

I made one last pass through the building. If the silence was anything to go by, the others were long gone. Only one more hallway to check and I could follow them to Zeke's. I glanced out a window as I walked. The sun hadn't set. Yet. I should've finished an hour ago. I guess I never realized Mayweather Antiquities had gotten so frigging huge. Too many years with too many wishes left nooks and crannies everywhere, each capable of hiding an Efreet.

I had to check every damn one.

The first four rooms in the last hallway came up empty. In the fifth, however, I discovered an unwanted surprise.

"Michael! Why are you still here?"

"I'm studying," he said, without looking up. At least I didn't think he glanced my way. With his blond hair flopping over his eyes, I couldn't tell. Suddenly, he seemed more surfer-dude than future attorney. His tie-dyed T and flip-flops rounded out the look.

"No kidding," I said. "You need to—"

"Not now, Jo." His hand waved me toward the hall. "The bar exam's next week. I need to cram a lot into this human brain." He pointed to his notebook with his pen, but otherwise ignored me. I returned the favor by stepping across his room to slap my hand down on the open text.

"This is important."

"No. This is," he said, trying to push my hand away. I didn't move. His ballpoint tapped so hard on his pad I feared he'd jam it through to the desk. "Come *on*. It's not like I can wish the damn stuff into my head like I used to." He tried to nudge me away again. "I'm grateful for all you've done. Really, I am. But it's your damn rule about not leaving until I can fend for myself. Well, neither of us wants that more than I do. I've been sitting here filching off you for too damn long already. I need to *study*."

His words gave me more than a little to think about. I'd heard people talk about a stay at Mayweather as a necessary evil. I guess I hadn't thought to some genies it could be more evil than necessary. I had other evils to deal with before I worried about my guests not being happy.

"I haven't been here yet today?" Whichever one of my clones skipped Michael should be smacked upside the head.

"Uh, *no*? This is the first time I've seen you since, *you know*." His face reddened. Bruised pride is tough for a human, but it doesn't come close to a genie who's gotten his ass kicked.

Adding his mortification to the list of things to address after I got this massive shitstorm under control, I touched his shoulder. "Forget about it. We have to leave."

"I can't."

"Unless you want to face a much nastier and less sane dude than Omar, you can."

"Another one's loose? What the hell?" His skin paled beneath his ever-present tan. I didn't blame him. Omar was one scary guy.

Someone worse running around made *me* want to wet my pants, and I hadn't almost died.

"Something along those lines." What he didn't know wouldn't hurt him. I hoped. "No time for questions. You're lucky I did a bed check. Gather your stuff and let's go."

Michael inclined his head toward the bookshelf-lined walls. "Unless you grant me superhuman strength, I can't carry the stuff I need."

I waved a hand and emptied his shelves. Before he freaked, I handed over a brick-sized package. "I'll expand everything again once we arrive."

"And where are you taking this young man?" Amun's voice dropped my heart into my innards.

"Who the hell are you?" Michael said.

Before I could stop him, he positioned himself between me and the Efreet.

"I am your salvation." Amun stretched his hand toward the law student. "I believe you lamented your inability to absorb your educational materials?"

Power swelled around the Efreet as I pushed Michael out of the way. Not the most effective defense mechanism, since it bypassed me and wrapped around Michael's mortal form. Nothing I did would help. Once a wish is released, there's no stopping it. I waited for Michael, the newly human kid I promised to protect, to drop over dead. Instead, the energy flowed into him with no apparent effect.

Or so I assumed. I changed my mind when I caught a whiff of something I hadn't smelled in over a year: djinn Michael.

"What the—?" Michael's eyes widened.

"You are most welcome," said the Efreet.

Amun stretched out the other hand. Any power I could muster wouldn't be enough to stop him, but I had to try. The Efreet's fingers twisted and a metal flask appeared. He unscrewed the cap and sniffed inside. "No alcohol? Disappointing. Well, if I can't drink, maybe something else will keep me warm. I know! A wish will do the trick."

He winked at me. His fingertips tapped against his lips. "Hmm. What to wish for?"

I could've kicked him for acting like some cardboard villain. He would've been great at a half-assed comic book convention. Too bad this was real life.

The only positive aspect of Amun's games was they gave me time to plan. I didn't have much energy, but maybe I could wish Michael away, as long as I didn't care how far he traveled. The parking lot should be far enough. At least then he could try for a vehicular getaway.

"Umm, Jo?"

"Not now. I'm trying to get us out of here." I knew whispering was pointless. If my hearing had been improved becoming djinn, no telling what the Efreet could hear. Still, I couldn't help myself.

"Doesn't matter. I can't leave."

I spared a second to glance at Michael. His particular shade of green told me what I didn't want to accept. "Let me guess. Your sanctuary?'

I should've expected this wrinkle. If only the Rules didn't prevent me from grabbing the flask away from its Master. Maybe a little push of energy would knock the thing out of Amun's hand. Except the gods never made anything easy.

"I'm afraid I'm left with wants." Amun stared straight into Michael's deer-in-headlights expression. "What I want more than anything else is to hurt your pretty little friend here with another opportunity to witness death first hand. Yours should be a nice change from those anonymous djinn."

Shit. I released a hurried wish without knowing exactly what I'd wished for. Amun didn't bother to flinch. He just licked his lips and opened his mouth in the theatrical beginning of a sentence.

I braced myself for the spectacle of Michael's death with my heart clenched up against my ribs. The power surging around us coalesced. *Coalesced? What the hell?* was all I had time for before realizing Amun's wish had nothing to do with this new spectacle.

Michael took advantage of the distraction and dove for the bed. I couldn't muster the presence of mind to duck. I braced for whatever the gods decided to visit upon my head.

"You called, Babydoll?"

Seeing Zeke's semi-annoyed face was more than I could've hoped for. I didn't know sending an amorphous wish into the universe would summon my old lover, but my demoralized eyes loved the sight of him.

Amun was amused. *Well, screw him.* I couldn't let it bother me. I had to keep the Efreet's attention focused away from Michael and borrowing a lesson from late-night TV might work. With a little prayer sent up to the gods, I did the best imitation of Jackie Chan my untrained muscles could muster.

Thrusting my leg out in a roundhouse kick Chuck Norris would *not* have been proud of, I aimed for Amun's still outstretched hand. I guess after Atlantis, Amun never quite caught up on the latest kickboxing moves because before he could close his hand, my foot connected.

Way to go, Grasshopper! His hand jerked. The flask sailed across the room. It clanged against one wall, hitting the floor in front of Michael's trembling form.

"Grab it!" I shouted at the re-djinn. As Amun let out a hellacious scream, the would-be lawyer reached for his sanctuary. Zeke had pooled enough energy to light up Lambeau Field, but through the spots in my vision, I saw Michael's fingers close around his home.

"You cannot take my servant!" The Efreet's shriek shook the walls, jiggling several of Michael's tiny pewter figures onto the floor. "The Rules forbid it."

"Lookie who's paying attention to the Rules now." Rubbing it in probably wasn't the wisest thing to do, but I've never been famous for doing the wise thing. "Sorry, bud, but you've been away so long you forgot how things work topside. He can't take his sanctuary from you by force, but he sure as hell can claim it while it's laying on the ground." Amun began to power up again, even as Zeke's wish wrapped around him.

"Michael," I said through gritted teeth, "get your sanctuary out of here already."

His hesitation almost screwed us both as the Efreet's energy glowed like the Times Square ball going nuclear. I caught the lawyer's eye. "Don't worry about us. We'll catch up later."

Before the word 'later' got out of my mouth, he disappeared. If all the lawyerly stuff he shoved into his brain indicated his smarts, he'd stake out a quiet spot in the Himalayas. If he'd learned anything from me, he'd find help before he hid. As strong as Zeke was, the past few days had to have him drained. Holding off Amun now couldn't help matters.

"A little assistance, Josie?"

I didn't have the heart to tell him the last of my juice went to summoning him. Besides, the Efreet didn't need to know.

Except he already did.

"You should choose your battles more carefully, Ezekiel, lest you find yourself fighting for a damsel who can't aid in her own rescue." Amun's laugh grated along my last nerve. "Such a pathetic little thing you gave your heart to. You used to be a better judge of character and of power. She has no more energy left to give and no way to gain more. So sad."

A second later, Zeke had confirmed the truth. I never want to see that defeated expression on his face again.

"Got it," he said. Innocuous enough words, but they shouted his disappointment louder than any bullhorn. "I guess we'd better leave, eh, Babydoll?"

Amun's laughter made me regret every particle of energy I'd ever wasted. If I could've generated a piece of glitter's worth, I'd knock the smirk off his face. Hell, I would've broken every Rule to watch those pearly whites fly across the room. As it was, though, I could only manage a cold, hard stare.

Take that.

"Run away, little Miss Mayweather."

"He who fights and runs away, lives to fight another day," I quipped, borrowing a phrase from my long dead father. The words drew a crease down Amun's forehead but it disappeared so quickly, I might've imagined it.

And then Zeke teleported us through space at such a velocity I could be fairly certain I'd hurl up every lunch I'd had for the past decade. When we landed on some dusty, windswept plain seconds later, I lived up to my expectations and then some. Well, not ten years worth, but it felt like it.

Once my stomach stopped trying to kill me, I finally spoke. "Where are we?"

"Western China. If you're up to it, we have to leave again. Unless I miss my guess, Amun isn't far behind us." I barely finished nodding before we were hurdling into the wind again. Good thing I remembered to close my eyes, because the next stop had us up to our asses in alligators. Literally.

"Actually, they're crocodiles," Zeke said. I could've hit him for reading my mind, but he'd only deny it again. "Don't worry about them. We won't be here long enough for a spot on their menu."

For the next few hours, or maybe days, we skipped from one remote locale to the next. With all the course changes we'd made, I hoped we'd left Amun eating our dust somewhere outside Tulsa.

"He's always been a tricky bastard," my ex said as we took a breather on the side of some snowy mountain. Judging from the cold in what was mid-summer back home, we had to be south of the equator. The Andes, maybe. It didn't matter. As long as we kept Amun guessing, maybe we'd give the others some time to get settled.

"You're sure everyone is safe at your place?"

"For the dozenth time, yes." As much energy as he'd put out, I half-expected him to fall over, but the exertion barely winded him. Where he got all his power from stymied the hell out of me. "I called in some favors. They're safer than in their own mother's arms."

I didn't want to know what kind of favors he meant or what beings owed him favors. At least I didn't want to know while teleporting all over hell and creation. Time enough for an information download later.

"Ready?" he said, breaking into my thoughts.

"The only thing I'm ready for is a trip home." My teeth started to chatter as a strong wind blew ice down my tank top. Summer in the Rockies isn't balmy, but it sure as hell wasn't this cold. "Are we there yet?"

A wide smile finally broke the stern set his face had taken. "Amun's probably lost interest by now." He didn't bother saying what we were both trying not to think about. If the Efreet lost interest, he had dozens of other genies he could play with. The largest concentration of which sat in a mansion in Colorado.

"For all we know, he's there waiting for us." I didn't want to think about it, let alone say it, but it needed saying.

"No time like the present to pop in then, Babydoll." He looped my hand over his arm and whispered in my ear. "Now close your eyes for a big surprise."

I didn't think it would surprise anyone, but I closed my eyes anyway. I didn't want to risk tossing my cookies on his front lawn. Except we didn't land on his front lawn. When I opened my eyes, I stood in the same room he'd hijacked me to before. The fire licked along several newly placed logs.

"Your Fortress of Solitude?"

"Indeed," he said, with a wink. "Nice to know you think I'm Superman."

I stifled the heat rising to my cheeks. "I didn't mean..." *Change the subject. Change the subject.* "Why here? Shouldn't we be where the action is?"

"We could both use a breather before we approach the masses downstairs."

He deftly ignored my stammering. It was a kindness I would've appreciated if he wasn't stalling. To prove my point, he strolled over to the liquor cart and poured two snifters of the brandy.

"There's no battle going on, is there?"

He shook his head. "Amun hasn't arrived from what I can tell."

I thought back to my last words to Mena. Surely by now they must have been mobilizing the fifth army. "How long were we gone?"

"Less than a day, but long enough to be nearly dusk again. Don't worry. I sent word you were perfectly fine."

"When?"

"By a little pond in Malaysia."

"Did you also request a stoked fire and brandy?"

"I have very devoted employees." He held the snifter of golden liquid out to me.

This time around, I accepted the offering. I longed to gulp it down it, but made myself sip at its smoothness. Thank Evangeline for hammering the rules of polite society into me. At least my mother had been good for something. Not that societal rules are often handy in my line of work. Socializing was Basil's bag.

Basil. With everything happening, I hadn't given his disappearance a third thought. He was out there somewhere under the control of a sadistic freak. While I stood in a hoity-toity library sipping Napoleon brandy.

"Guilt never does anyone any good, you know," Zeke said.

"How did you—?"

"It's all over your face, Josie. You feel guilt because you're taking a moment for yourself while your friends are in danger, missing, or generally demoralized. Am I right?"

"Not even close." Maybe the fib would put distance between us.

"Liar. Let me guess. You were thinking about Baz. If not him, then Michael or Mena or Omar and the damnable dog." He put a finger under my chin, tipping my face until we were eye to eye. "I asked after them, too. The latter three are resting comfortably. Mena said they were treating themselves to my private stash of Godivas. She indicated the Sheik had never been introduced to the pleasure of good chocolate. Major is abstaining until he knows whether they're as poisonous to former dogs as to current ones."

"Wait'll Omar finds your hidden cache of Belgian seashells." Zeke gasped. I wasn't quite sure if he was joking or truly concerned. Gotta love a man who loves his chocolate—even if it meant sometimes fighting over the last piece.

"The others you were concerned about?" he said. "We can't help them at the moment. I have my best men tracking Michael's movements, but like us, he decided not to stick to one place too long. They lost him somewhere between Moscow and Minsk. When he turns up again, we'll send him our coordinates. Until then, he's on his own."

"And Basil?"

"Until the Efreet decides to utilize him, he's off the radar. Don't worry, Josie. We'll find him."

I narrowed my eyes. "It's entirely possible he's gone over to the dark side, you know. Hell, Baz must've been the one who ratted me out to the Moor."

Zeke lifted one shoulder. "Entirely possible. However, I don't think he's your enemy. I'd say the only fault poor old Baz rightfully owns in this mess is wishing for someone else to shoulder the burden of thinking for him. Well, and not hiding his sanctuary well enough. As for the rest, I say hold judgment until you talk to him. You might find out the real blame falls on Amun and—"

"And whoever might actually be helping Amun?"

"I think he may have attained more slaves than Basil, don't you?"

"I don't know what to think." I ran a hand through my ratty locks. Hours of whipping around the world left me feeling like a Rastafarian. When this was all over, I would treat myself to a spa day. And a short haircut. "I know I locked the company down personally. I changed all the codes Baz could've known. How did Amun still manage to get to Michael?"

"Could Basil have guessed the new codes?"

I shook my head. Leaning against the mantel, I look a long draught of Zeke's booze. *Screw Miss Manners.* As I relished the burn, I considered the possibilities. "There has to be someone else on the inside. Someone who isn't a slave. Basil tried to warn me. Michael would've done the same if I hadn't interrupted Amun. I think the Efreet's helper is doing it willingly."

Zeke snapped his fingers. Both his snifter and mine disappeared. "Well, what are you doing standing around drinking, Babydoll?" he said like this interlude had been my idea. "I think you might've dropped a traitor into my home."

TWENTY-EIGHT

~-~-~-~-~-~-~

Zeke strode out the door and disappeared into his maze-like
home before I could shout for him to slow down. With nothing else
left to go on, I followed the heavenly odor of his Clive Christian
cologne. Either his magic or his security business kept him in a style I
couldn't quite merge with my memories. This new Ezekiel couldn't be
the same guy I walked barefoot down the Champs Elyse with. Sure,
the old Zeke liked the finer things. In the old days, he hadn't quite
reached this degree of opulence. He sure as hell never owned a Rodin
like the one I passed as I headed down the stairs.

Led by the odor of decadence, I pushed through a pair of
mahogany doors near the back of the property. I fought to keep my
jaw from dropping to my toes. The place seemed spacious before.
This room could fit my entire operation inside with space for a pack
of pachyderms.

Being djinn means never having to deal with claustrophobia.

"Jo!" cried Mena from off to one side. "What happened to you?"

"You don't want to know," I said. "How's life on the 'refugee
from evil' front?"

"Controlled chaos. Zeke's staff have been excellent at making
everyone comfortable. Until they shuttled us into this room and
locked it down. No one's been allowed out for hours."

I raised an eyebrow. "Hours? I thought you only just—"

"What can I say, Josie? I'm a paranoid clairvoyant. I can sense ahead of time when people are thinking about screwing me over."

"Still. Hours?" Free genies don't necessarily appreciate boundaries, no matter the whys. I turned back to Mena. "How are they taking it?"

"A few of them are irritated, but they were waiting to speak to you anyway." She inclined her head toward a clique glaring daggers in our direction. "And others until they could shout at you."

"Let me guess. No one was thrilled when the wish wore off Tryg and Omar."

"Could be. Or maybe they're upset about Zeke." She shot him a glance. "He laid some kind of wish down. No one can use their power."

"Security measures," Zeke said in clipped syllables.

"And several of our guests don't appreciate being trapped in *his* home." The way her words dripped, their venom would've killed any other man.

"With you being among the unappreciative?" He stepped toward my best friend as his power began to build.

I grabbed his arm. "She's not the one you're looking for. Leave her be."

He gently laid his hand on mine. One finger brushed a delicate line along my ring finger. "For you. But only for now."

"What in the name of Tammuz?" she asked. "And why is he touching you that way?"

"A traitor has been allowed into my home." He stopped petting my hand. Power crackled in the space between his skin and mine.

"For now, you'll have to live with being 'trapped', as you called it, until I uncover the turncoat. In fact—"

He closed his eyes as his power became a tangible thing. After all the tricks he'd accomplished in the past day, I expected his head to explode. Instead, a shimmering veil fell over the room. "Everyone will remain exactly where they are until I release them."

Mena scoffed and stormed away. Before she went more than a yard, she blinked out, reappearing right where she'd been when the wish went into effect.

"What in the seven hells do you think you're doing?" She shook one shiny fingernail inches from Zeke's nose.

"You are in my home by my invitation. With the liberty such an invitation allows you'll understand if I protect what's mine. The wish guarantees everyone plays nice until I can verify their intent. As such, each of you stays where you can do the least damage." He ditched his relaxed demeanor in favor of 'severely pissed-off genie'. "The nicer you all play, the sooner you'll be free to partake of my hospitality."

He nodded to those within hearing distance. "Pass it along to your friends. I won't bother to explain myself again."

A murmur went through the crowd, then most of them quieted down. A few became indignant. Some of the djinn tried to storm from the room. Like Mena, they ended up right where they started. Their efforts to counteract Zeke's wish would've been funny if this hadn't taken on a surreal quality.

"If you're all finished playing, we can proceed."

A petite djinn of Japanese origin tapped her cane on the floor to draw Zeke's attention. "I did not agree to Ms. Mayweather's idea of freedom only to be held like some common criminal."

"Lady Mei." Thinking back to our previous encounters, I wouldn't put it past the diminutive bitch to be the traitor. "If you feel slighted, I suggest you go first."

"I'll do no such thing." She shook a jewelry-bedecked fist. "And don't think the Council won't hear of this."

"They probably already have. If not, I'm sure you'll be the first to tell them. In fact, maybe you could explain the absolute necessity of our actions tonight." I amplified my voice so the rest of the djinn could hear me. "Yesterday evening, after I reset all the security at Mayweather, an Efreet ambushed me in Michael's room. Inside guest quarters for those of you who haven't been paying attention." Dozens of lungs inhaled at once. "Not only that, but he used Michael's sanctuary to turn him djinn again." On some of the gathered faces, I could see the implications dawning. Several of the brethren got the point. I hammered it home anyway. "Which means someone who lives there invited the Efreet past security."

"Are you accusing someone of treason?" blurted a younger genie.

"She's not accusing anyone of anything." Zeke's voice came out a little above a growl but amplified so all could hear. "I am. If no conspirator is found among you, I'll admit I'm wrong. In fact, you'll all receive my most profound apologies. However, I'm not wrong. For the person hiding inside my walls, no amount of power will save you."

Mena shrank back. Grabbing her hand, I pulled her to my side. "He's harmless," I whispered. Let Zeke have his suspicions. He wouldn't find any evidence among my friends.

Methinks you protest too much, said a little voice at the back of my head. I stuffed it farther back and told it to shut the hell up.

Slowly, we walked through the refugee camp. I had Mena's hand through my arm for a few steps. When she disappeared and showed up in her original spot, I smacked Zeke's arm. "Let her loose," I hissed. He didn't look happy, but he complied. The next time we moved forward, she kept pace.

Zeke shook his head at the both of us and went strolling through the crowd. From all appearances, he could've been browsing the inventory before a big sale. Every once in a while, he'd stop to gaze into the eyes of one individual or another, only to nod and move on. I knew what he was looking for. I didn't have the foggiest notion how he'd spot it from something in their eyes.

In front of a teenage girl, he did something I never saw him do before. He flinched. "How long have you been with Jo?"

The girl remained silent. Her head lowered so far, her chin pressed into her neck. In all the time Raye had been with us, she never said much of anything to anyone. "I found her a little over—"

"Let her answer, Josie."

The girl's big, green eyes raised toward him and grew larger beneath his steady gaze. She couldn't be the one Amun recruited.

"Thirteen months, three weeks…" She swallowed hard. He eyes veered upward as if she counted specks on the ceiling. "…and five days. I think."

He nodded. "And do you like the guest quarters?"

"I guess I do. Why?"

"Because you're too powerful to sit around letting Miss Mayweather pamper you."

"Knock it off." This kid didn't deserve harsh words. "Anyone can stay at Mayweather as long as they want." A curt shake of his head stalled me. I almost smacked him, until I realized he needed to do this his way. Up to a point.

"Well?" he said to Raye.

"I like being at Mayweather." The poor girl couldn't keep the tremble from her voice. "No one makes me *do* anything I don't want to do."

Zeke reached out one hand and laid it on her shoulder, as if he could pull the truth out by osmosis. Within seconds, he simply nodded and walked away.

Sunuvabitch. T*he asshole really can read minds.* "How long have you been able to do that?" I muttered.

"A few hundred years." His focus was intent on getting to the next djinn in line, but I wouldn't let him off so easy.

"And how many times have you used it on me?"

His head did a slow half-turn. "Never." The word came out under his breath. "When we're through with this," he said, "Raye needs time with a *real* therapist. Her last Master did so much damage a team of psychologists might take decades to undo it."

"I've been working hard with her," Mena said. "And I resent your insinuation."

He didn't bother to acknowledge her words or her presence. Frankly, his attitude pissed me off to no end. I grabbed his arm and pulled him to face me. "Is any of this necessary?"

"All of it is, Babydoll."

I bristled, but I couldn't let him know he riled me. "Seriously, Zeke, you are a major asshat."

"It's my job."

"Then you're doing swimmingly. Tell me. Have you learned anything other than we have a few damaged genies in our midst?"

"I'm seeking out the damaged because they're the most susceptible among us. If Amun whispers the right words in one fragile ear, he creates a new ally. In no time, he has a wealth to choose from amongst the very people you're supposed to help." He shot Mena a look. In his glance, I could see the wheels turning. "One would think someone wasn't trying her level best."

"I'm sure I don't know what you mean."

"Well, with all your degrees, these damaged djinn, especially Raye, could be on the road to mental health by now. Or do your fancy pieces of paper mean nothing?"

"Results from therapy take time. For anyone." She lifted one shoulder. "Djinn take longer than humans. Raye spent decades becoming the way she is. You can't fix her overnight."

"You knew?" As Zeke's anger acquired a physical presence in the room, I got the sudden urge to wrap my arms around myself and chart an escape route. Several nearby djinn ran only to have the wish zap them right back. Others simply stared.

To her credit, Mena didn't flinch. "She suffered severe abuse, but she refuses to talk specifics. What happened to her is not something women, *especially brethren women*, will freely admit to."

"And yet I didn't have to push her to gain access to those memories." He clicked his tongue. "Tell me something, Doctor. Are you really so incompetent or have you been recruiting genies for your Efreet friend?"

His accusation dropped. My jaw went with it. "Stop it, Zeke. You're not funny."

"I never intended to be." The air twisted around us and suddenly Mena became statuesque. For real. He only left her face mobile. "I'd tell you to feel free to loose a wish, but you don't have the guts for an old-fashioned genie battle. Do you have the guts to tell Josie the truth? No matter how twisted you've become, *she's* still your friend. She deserves better."

"Zeke?" I did *not* want to look at Mena. "You can't be serious."

When he did nothing but stare holes through my best friend's head, I risked a glance her way. Her eyes were glued to some speck of dust at her feet.

"Mena?"

Her eyes clenched tight and a single tear slipped free. "It's over, Jo."

"Damn straight it is." Anger swelled, burning like bile in my throat. I turned all my rage on my old lover. "I know you two haven't seen eye to eye over the years, but this is fucking—"

"I had hoped you would come to the right conclusion on your own, so I wouldn't have to force the issue. I've certainly laid enough bread crumbs, but still you refuse to see what is in front of your eyes," he said as he shook his head. "Look at her, Josie. Really look at her."

When I did as he asked, my blinders dropped away. All at once, I couldn't stop staring. This person I'd known for what seemed like forever didn't appear any different. Her eyes still held a wicked blaze. Too bad for us both, I finally saw her inner fire wasn't lit with the same fuel as mine, no matter how much I wanted it to be.

"Why?" My own voice sounded foreign in my ears.

"It's not like I'm any use to Amun after this anyway." It was so much like the Mena I thought I knew, misunderstand my question on purpose, I wanted to barf. When she rolled her eyes her characteristic fashion, I almost did. "The minute Zeke locked this place down, the Master probably suspected my part had ended."

How can she still be the same when everything's changed?

"I expect Amun will kill me the next time we meet. Maybe letting Zeke do the job first would be kinder."

"Don't count on kindness from me, Sweetpea."

I put my hand on his arm. "Zeke." I poured more hurt into his name than one syllable should hold. He had to back off, at least until I could figure things out. "Please. She's my... She *was* my... I need to deal with this."

He cracked his knuckles as he moved forward. I expected her to shrink away. Instead, her chin lifted in some kind of twisted pride. All at once, I wanted to kill her myself. Squelching those violent urges, I put a steady hand on Zeke's chest.

"Why not continue with the crowd? See if they recruited anyone else."

He didn't like my suggestion, but he accepted it with as much grace as he could manage. With one hooked finger, he motioned to two bulky men I hadn't noticed before. They moved toward us as one.

"You'll get your way for now, Josie, but until she's nullified, these guys will have your back." I gave the man-mountains a quick once over. They were like opposite sides of the moon, one light, the other dark. Both pulsed with a power nearly as strong as Zeke himself. "I've changed the security so the four of you can leave the room, but do *not* attempt to leave the house.

"And, gentlemen? Nothing happens to her. Understand?" Zeke pointed at Mena. "If this one so much as breathes funny, she sees forever on four legs."

My mind flashed briefly on what kind of dog she'd be. If true personality had anything to do with transformations, she'd wind up as the ugliest dog ever.

Shaking off thoughts of Mena as a walking flea circus, I let Zeke resume his task before addressing my new bodyguards. "Got somewhere we can do this in private?"

The dark one inclined his head toward the front of the room while the blond indicated I should lead the way. Grasping Mena's wrist, I tugged her along. I didn't need to glance back to know the men followed close behind. The energy pulsing behind me proved those guys were locked and loaded.

Once outside the impromptu auditorium, my light-haired guard took point, while his counterpart slid in behind us. Sure, Zeke's paranoia went over the top, but I couldn't blame him. As my best BFF, the odds of Mena getting past my defenses were high.

"What did I do to deserve this?" I muttered as we walked along the hallway. I don't know if I expected an answer, but I didn't expect abject silence. The bitch wouldn't look at me. Her eyes stayed glued to the carpet in front of her. Her long hair even kept me from judging her expression. She walked like a condemned man being led to the gallows. *What a martyr.* I only wanted to talk. Whether she got pooched was up to her.

Before too long, Blondie stopped to one side of a thick door. Brownie moved forward to open it. "We will wait out here," he said, a Germanic accent turning all his Ws into Vs.

"*Danka shoen,*" I said as I dragged Mena past their stony gazes. If her fate had been left to them, she'd already be barking. I could only hope she would avoid a canine future. With my life turning shitty in so many ways, though, hope ran pretty thin.

The door shut with an ominous click as I checked out the space they'd picked. Except for the lack of dust, it didn't appear anyone had been in the little sitting room for decades. Hell, I couldn't be sure whether Zeke knew the room existed.

The fragile, slim furnishings definitely didn't suit his taste. But they suited me fine, especially since the décor was about to get truly messed-up. Whoever he had paid to decorate, I hoped the person could work miracles.

As I saw it, this show could only go a couple ways: We'd go at it genie-style, possibly destroying half the house, or we'd go old-school.

From everything I knew about Mena, our powers were pretty evenly matched. Too bad I had reason to doubt everything about her.

Old style it is then.

As I dropped into a wing-backed chair, one simple wish padded the room with energy. Until I revoked the wish, neither of us could use any power with negative intent.

"Have a seat." I did my best at faking casual. With narrowed eyes, she shook her head and remained standing.

"Seriously. Sit. We'll be here a while." She still didn't move. With a flick of the wrist, I sat her ass down for her. She didn't even cringe a little. Damn it. "You're the one working with the bad guy. If you think the martyr act will get you anywhere, you're out of your mind."

Her head raised until her eyes met mine. Where I expected to see rage, I saw despair. Too bad for her my anger wouldn't give her an inch of emotional real estate. "Funny position for a head shrinker to be in, eh? You enjoyed playing around in everyone else's neuroses, and now you're the crazy one. I bet you got off on tiptoeing through my subconscious. Hell, my childhood alone would keep any human doc in Bentleys and t-bills for the rest of his life."

Mena's dark eyes opened wide. "It wasn't like that. I helped you because I'm your friend. That didn't change."

I tried to ignore the plea in her tone. She'd played me long enough. Of course, this 'righteous anger' thing would've been a lot easier if she acted like a bitch. I needed to see the evil inside the person who was my best friend. Her reticence only made the experience more painful.

"I thought I knew you," came out of my mouth before I could stop it.

"You do know me, Jo." Her hand reached out. When I didn't reach back, she let it fall into her lap where it twisted like a tortured beast. "I'm the same person. I still have the same feelings and beliefs I always did."

If I hadn't heard it, I wouldn't have believed she'd say it. "The same person? The Mena I knew would never condone this. You killed innocents."

Her head shook hard enough to send hair whipping into her face. "I never."

"Don't play with semantics. You helped a killer." I pressed the point as much for my own benefit as for hers. "In my eyes, you're just as guilty."

"I didn't know he—"

"Oh please. Grant me the courtesy of pretending you don't think I'm an idiot. You helped him, and you kept helping after you knew what he'd done. He killed Greta, and you still helped him. You had his back after he murdered one of your own patients, for petesakes." The Princess' dead face swam before my eyes. "He *murdered* her. If you had tried to stop him, I might believe you. For godsakes, Mena! He tried to kill Michael."

Her gasp didn't go unheard but I tried to leave it unnoticed.

"If not for a shitload of luck, one of our friends would be gone. For all I know, while we were leading Amun on a merry chase around the world, he knocked off a dozen Michaels. Where were you? Hiding here, in Zeke's own home." My voice shook so bad I had to scream to get the last few words out.

Silence greeted my volume. And a sudden thought occurred to me. "You handed the Princess over to him, didn't you?" I didn't need her admission. Her head dropping slightly told me what I didn't want to know. Instantly, the map of her deception laid out before me.

If I could've unleashed my anger, I would've redecorated the whole room in extra-crispy turncoat. In fact, I felt more juiced than I had in years. I let the sparks of pent-up energy arc from one hand to the other, watching as her eyes got bigger. Her skin went pale. Her reaction felt great.

"I didn't know." Whatever else she had so say, I didn't want to hear.

In a rage I didn't know I had in me, I swept my hand toward her, intending to hurt her as bad as she hurt me. Imagine my surprise when, instead of her sliding into the wall, chair and all, not a damn thing happened.

Recovering first, I lifted one nonchalant shoulder.

"Lucky for you, I planned this while I could still be rational. Otherwise, you'd be wearing that wainscoting." I stepped toward her. "On the other hand, I'm so sick of your games I don't care if I kick the crap out of your sorry ass. It's the least I can do."

Her lips moved in a silent wish. While I laughed, she sputtered. "What did you do to me?"

"Not a damn thing. This room, on the other hand? It's a pacifist genie's dream." I cracked my knuckles in front of her nose. "No fighting wishes allowed, but I don't need magic to mess you up. Tell me where to find Amun."

"I don't..."

Physical violence isn't usually the most effective tool for extracting information, especially not with djinn healing in the mix, but in a few moments, I learned how very cathartic it can be. At least for the one doing the ass kicking. In the back of my head, I hated myself and my thoughts. I'd deal with the guilt of throttling my best friend over the next few decades. Right then, I needed answers.

Answers Mena would give to me, even if she had to do it from traction.

TWENTY-NINE

"Enough," Mena said from where she'd crumpled to the floor. Blood trickled from the corner of her mouth. Crimson shot through her left eye as the area around it darkened to a nasty purple. I didn't want to think about my own appearance, but I hoped I'd fared better. Personally, I wasn't feeling too sparky myself, but the injuries incurred during our catfight still pained me less than her betrayal.

As I eased my sore ass onto a lovely brocaded chair Zeke must've spent a fortune on, I spared a brief thought for the mess. Blood is a bitch to get out. The chair could be replaced, though. I couldn't easily find a new best friend.

"One more time. Where the hell is Amun?"

"If I don't give you the answer you want, are you going to attack me again? Because I'm sure I don't have the faintest idea where the Master is right now." She held up a hand as if to push a wish in my direction. I sat back against the chair's wings. The moratorium on magic still held. Unless I released it, the wish would last until I died or she did.

For her part, she kept tapping at her power every chance she got. For my part, the temptation to drop the barrier just to zap her skinny ass hummed in my veins.

"Whatever it takes." I cracked my knuckles again, noticing my middle finger's odd angle. As I pulled it straight, I said, "I'm ready for another round." Evangeline would've been mortified to see me acting like a thug, but I bet my father would've been pleased. Especially since he was fond of saying: *It's never right to start a fight, but if you're in a fight, make sure you finish it.*

"And you wonder why I side with the Efreet." Mena's grin showed a tooth dangling like a warped circus act.

Damn, I really must be slipping. I was sure I knocked that one out. She tugged the incisor free. With a flick of the wrist, she tossed it into the fireplace.

"Fine. Since you won't tell me where your boss is, tell me what the fuck you were thinking falling in with him."

She tugged her hair into some semblance of a ponytail, letting out a sigh. "If you really must know, Amun said you needed to be taught a lesson." Her words came out with a newfound lisp. "And I agreed. We are proved right with every action you take." With the back of her hand, she wiped the blood from her skin. Her split lip had already healed. In seconds, the slight scar would be gone.

The cut where her signet ring caught me still oozed blood down my cheek. So much for *my* awesome healing prowess. "Why would a djinn I've never met feel the need to teach me anything?"

The woman raised her eyes. The bruise had disappeared along with any vestige of our friendship. "You're a child playing with toys you can't begin to comprehend. All djinn are, but you are the worst."

"So Zeke was right. You really feel this way? Amun isn't manipulating you?"

She let out a humorless bark. "I never thought I'd see the day when you'd believe Ezekiel could be right about anything," she said, "but I suppose, yes, he was correct."

"You went willingly? I thought you were supposed to be the smart one in this friendship." I shook my head, ignoring the soft snick of a well-abused vertebra. "I never would've pegged you for naïve. Amun doesn't give a tinker's dam about teaching me a lesson. He's just killing. And you know what? He likes it. Whatever other reasoning he foisted off on you was pure bullshit."

Mena tried to rise and slumped to the floor instead. Judging from her grimace and the way she clutched her side, I'd broken several of her ribs. *Goodie.*

In short breaths, she managed a warped chuckle. "You think you're so damn noble. No djinn left behind, right?" She pressed a hand to her side. Several sharp pops echoed as she put things into their proper place. "God save all the good little genies. *Please.* You're the one who doesn't care about those dead brethren. You're only pissed because Amun got to them first. This has nothing to do with the loss of life and everything to do with the damage to your super-sized ego."

I had to admit she had part of her theory right. Sure, the Efreet killing people before I could save them made me mad as hell. But his getting away with it pissed me off more. I should've been able to stop him before he killed Arthur. I should've saved Greta. We all should've put an end to his bloody lesson before he stole the Princess's life in front of a hundred humans. The whole damn scenario ticked me off to no end. Still, my reasons for kicking the shit out of Mena went deeper.

"I'd be lying if I told you I didn't get any satisfaction from watching you bleed," I said, "but it never had to come to this. You lied to me. You helped a killer. You betrayed your own people."

"My people?" A hiss of breath carried her words. "You have no idea who I am. I watched my people die a thousand years ago. I alone survived." Her eyes grew dark. "I refuse to acknowledge the Many as anything other than an endless stream of the broken and the demented." She pointed one slightly less manicured hand at me. "The insanity will never end until there's an end to the Rules."

Her admission of a long life set me back a bit. Then again, I never asked. We were friends. I didn't need to know anything else. As her bruises turned yellowish before my eyes, I saw how wrong my assumptions were. I healed fast. Her healing rate went beyond ridiculous. Of all the djinn I'd ever met, only Zeke healed faster.

Good thing I didn't opt for genie brawl. She would've pulverized me.

"I see you never renounced those Rules you supposedly hate." I was fishing and I knew it, but I needed time for my brain to reset. "I'm guessing they still stand for something."

"The Rules mean nothing to me." Mena tossed her hair back and inspected her fingernails. Her bored act pissed me off, but who was I to call her on it? I was playing out a script of my own. And it didn't include letting old feelings cloud my new reality.

"The world would be better off without such limitations." She could've been addressing a lecture hall full of students. Her attitude had been carefully designed to put me in my place, which put me, of course, beneath her notice. "Only then will the brethren know freedom." She smiled and her missing tooth had already grown back. "All the time you spent liberating the *enslaved*, you never once understood. Our kind can never be free as long as we live according to the Rules. God, Jo, how stupid are you?"

She flexed her fingers causing several joints to snick into place. "I hoped, given enough time, you could be taught. I had been so certain if I crawled around your head for a while, I'd bring you over to our side. I see now Amun and the others were right. You're too pig-headed to recognize the truth."

I don't know when she began gathering power around her, but suddenly she glowed like she'd put her finger in a light socket.

"Mena? Don't even think it." Before the words escaped my mouth, I could tell she had no plans to zap me. She was stepping onto a path she'd chosen long ago.

"I renounce the Rules of the brethren." Her chin thrust out like the proudest moment of her life had arrived. Power coursed through the room, knocking both of us to opposite walls.

My head throbbed and my vision fogged over, but my voice still worked. Before either of us moved an inch, I dropped the wish against offensive magic. I didn't know if I could take Efreet-Mena by myself, but the situation definitely called for more violence. The Energizer genies were the men to bring it.

"Guys! A little help here?"

Mena staggered to her feet as the door burst open. Her juice ramped up a fraction, but whatever power she held wasn't enough. Blondie loosed a wish, dropping her sorry ass to the carpet, while Brownie helped me to my feet.

"She's no longer of the Many, Miss Mayweather," he said, apparently taking a page from his boss and trying on the Captain Obvious costume. "You know what we must do."

He didn't have to mention our only option. I held out my hand to Blondie as he grasped his fellow guard's hand on the other side. We formed a triangle, pulling power from deep within ourselves until we became a magical bonfire. As one, we pushed the swirling mass toward Mena's prone form.

"I'm sorry." The whisper ripped itself out of our shared past as the light enveloped her. Now I understood Mary Killigrew's reluctance to talk, and why Zeke abstained from the last war. Self-appointed judge and jury or not, I had to neutralize the threat Mena posed. Still, turning your friends into dogs wasn't as easy as it sounded.

The wish itself felt like the re-transformation of Major in reverse. But this time, the power shredded my heart. *No wonder shit like this takes three genies.* When the light faded, a skinny sighthound lay where my friend had been. My heart lurched against my ribs.

Blondie's immobility wish disappeared with Mena's human form. When she raised her muzzle to growl, the last of my misgivings disappeared, too. My best friend hadn't been a friend at all. The transformation gave her the form her heart had taken long before. In reality, Mena was nothing more than a bad dog.

A growl rumbled in her chest and translated in my head as, "I won't be like this for long."

I suddenly regretted the wish I created for Major. Probably for the best. Hard to interrogate a prisoner I can't understand.

The prisoner. Mena. My best friend. Amun's accomplice. Only one designation mattered anymore.

"I need to talk to Zeke. Hold her until I get back." I couldn't bear to look at what she'd become. I needed a face I recognized. Someone who was exactly what he said he was. Besides, I had to see what other recruits we needed to poochify. Might as well transform as many as we could while we had the time.

And if I was honest with myself, I needed to get a grip on what I'd just done.

Finding the auditorium would've been easier if I'd paid more attention on the way out. As I wandered, following the scent trail we'd left, I poked at the sore spot in my self-assurance. I freed Mena almost a decade ago. Everything about her made her the perfect friend. She was funny and gritty and more than a little irreverent. She thumbed her nose at her djinn gifts by going to human college. When she got her doctorate on her own merits, it didn't surprise me any more than when she used her degree to help other genies.

What an idiot. The whole act had been designed to worm her into my confidence. Hell, I bet freeing her been part of the game, too. Was any part of her real?

I still didn't have the answer when I returned to the crowd.

Zeke stood at the front of the room with a clipboard, calling names and slapping obedience wishes on anyone who didn't step lively. "Alright," he said, addressing the two groups he'd formed. "Anyone whose name I didn't call? Follow my assistant through the door to your right. She'll direct you to your assigned lodgings."

People?" He called to the mass of retreating backs. "As long as you refrain from wishing while you're here, we'll get along fine."

I raised an eyebrow. I'd seen a lot of his sides but never the administrative one. It fit him well. Not that I'd tell him. Instead, I opened my mouth to question his motives. His upheld hand stopped me short.

"If I called your name," he said, ignoring me, "you'll be in special accommodations until I determine whether your, let's call it an error in judgment, warrants further investigation." He waved his hand as if brushing away a gnat. Once the room cleared, he turned his attention to me.

"Well?" he said.

"Mena's an Efreet now." The sentence came out so easily for the hardest thing I've ever had to say. *Last week I didn't know the Efreet existed. Now my best friend turned into one. Somehow I should've known. I should've seen. I should've stopped her.*

"Sorry, Josie, but her heart belonged to the Efreet long before you met her." His words echoed the path my thoughts wandered, but that didn't make them any easier to hear. "She simply hadn't planned on changing until she finished Amun's work."

"They can wait?" I brushed aside his attempt to make me feel better. It wouldn't work anyway. "Isn't being so twisted inside that you throw away all your beliefs enough?" To me, wanting something so bad it seeps into your heart should make the change automatic. Needing to speak the words seemed asinine.

"I'm guessing, if she knew how to change, she could wait. I'm betting Amun taught her his little trick right off." A couple couches appeared in the center of the room. Between sat a table laden with food and beverages. Oddly enough, the thought of eating wasn't what made me want to barf.

"I don't know if I can ever look at another couch again." I wanted him to take it as a joke, but the words came out raw. "You know? Psychologists? Couches?"

"I got it," he said as he moved closer. Before he came close enough to touch me, the tears started. Zeke, bless his heart, simply opened his arms. No other encouragement needed. As I fell against his chest, the floodgates opened. Not bothering to ask permission, he swept me into his arms. "Close your eyes, Josie."

He didn't need to say anything. My eyes were already clamped tight against a waterfall to rival Niagara. Before I could nod, he settled me onto the most comfortable cushions my ass ever had the pleasure to meet.

I cracked one eye open, expecting his sitting room. Instead, I sat smack in the middle of a king-sized bed. "Damn it, Zeke. This isn't the time for—"

"Rest?" He shook his head. "You're in no shape for fun, Babydoll. Despite what you think, I'm not a bad guy. In fact, I'm a little hurt you'd suggest otherwise." His hand pressed against his chest in mock injury. "Besides, when I make love to you again, I want it to be in my own bed." Lifting one corner of the frilly comforter, he said, "Does this look like my bed?"

For the first time in what felt like forever, a smile tugged at my lips. "Not unless you started playing for the other team."

"Perish the thought, darling Josie. Thousands of women would tear their hair and rend their garments." He tapped his chin as though the mysteries of the universe needed to be considered. "Then again, I'd have a whole new gender to amaze."

That did it. The thought of Zeke turning away from womankind merely to gain a new audience unraveled my poor brain. I started giggling. Before I knew it, the giggle turned into full-on, belly aching, unladylike snorts.

Which nosedived into a bout of heart-shredding wails.

Once more, he wrapped me in his arms. I don't know how long crying myself out took, or how long afterwards I lay cradled in his brand of safety. When my inner-strength finally showed its pathetic face, I realized any time in his arms was too long. I sure didn't want that dynamic back. Hell, I wasn't sure he did either.

"Thank you," I pushed gently against his chest.

"My pleasure."

He eased me off his lap and onto the feather mattress. I tried not to think about how comforting his embrace felt. Or how being settled against the angle of his thighs and hips made me feel safe. My brain had scattered too far to want to probe any feeling too deeply. I loved Mena like a sister, but she betrayed me. I loved Zeke once, too, and I'd almost betrayed myself. At this point, none of my emotions were dependable. I doubted I'd ever be able to depend on my own judgment again.

"Pity party's over," I wriggled toward the bed's edge. Zeke didn't buy it, but he gave me the distance I needed. "Mena's not going to bark up the information to Brownie and Blondie."

"Who?"

"The goons you assigned to guard me. You never bothered with introductions."

"Hans and Frank," he said. "And don't call them goons. They're the best men I have."

"Sorry. You have to admit they're walking mountains, though. If you ever fire them, they'll fit right in with any mafia family." The thought of them working for some mob boss almost brought on another fit of giggles. "Which one's which, by the way?"

"Hans is light. Frank is dark."

"Got it. Well, they're certainly intimidating. But Mena won't talk to them, even if they speak dog."

He lowered his face until his forehead pressed against mine. For once, I welcomed the familiarity. Hell, I didn't merely welcome it; I needed it. He kissed the top of my head and whispered, "I'm sorry, Josie," into my bangs.

"She renounced the Rules. I had to either pooch her or let her go." I tried to sound cavalier. From his expression, I missed the mark, landing at pathetic.

"What happened to the benefit of the doubt?" he said. I almost slapped him. Lucky the twinkle in his eyes let me know he was playing devil's advocate.

"Any doubts I had, she wiped away. Hell, until I kicked her ass, she played the injured party." My voice dropped. "I wish it hadn't come to that."

"But I bet it felt good." He cracked his knuckles. "Sometimes I miss fisticuffs. Magic makes them moot, though. Why'd you choose that route?"

"I could take her in a human fight, but not in a genie battle. In retrospect, I wanted to slap the stupid out of her, whether she talked or not. After I started, it felt so good I couldn't stop." I shook my head. "It's so damn frustrating. She hates me so much. Maybe she always has. And I don't understand why."

He brushed a strand of hair behind my ear. "You may never understand. The point is you stopped her. You stopped her, and she'll help you stop Amun, whether she likes it or not."

With Mena as a dog, another round of brawling seemed problematic. As for magic, I didn't know what else how else to make her talk. "I wonder if Tryg can get her to talk. After all, he's experienced with this Efreet thing."

"It's worth a try. Where is he?"

"You went through the crowd. Wasn't he in here?" When Zeke shook his head, I ticked through all the genies I'd seen since we arrived. In fact, I hadn't seen him since he became my clone. Stretching my senses, I checked the large home. Not a whisper he'd ever been inside. Next to me, Zeke's senses surged.

"Nothing," he said. "You?"

"Not a gods damned thing."

"What about the Sheik?" In all the drama, I hadn't thought of him. I couldn't find Omar's signature anywhere in the building either.

"Oh shit." I didn't want to give words to my new disturbing hunch.

"What now?"

"Mena. She was the last one to see those guys. I even gave her the job of transporting Omar's sanctuary to a safe place." The guilt hit me like a sack of dirt. He trusted me, and I gave him to someone no one should've trusted. "Amun has his favorite toy back."

"Which means he has at least two djinn, possibly three, working for him when they should be working with us." Zeke's words felt like a well-deserved slap. "Where does that leave us?"

"Hanging in the wind, with whatever employees are hidden around this cathedral, plus a boatload of former slaves. No way I want to sweep them into this shitstorm." Besides, I wanted the bastard all to myself. Too bad, I couldn't take him alone. We needed power. Lots of it. Which meant warm, fully charged brethren.

"And Mena?" Like I really needed a reminder from him.

"I left her in your boys' tender care, so she's not going anywhere any time soon. Unless Amun decides he wants her back."

Zeke held my hand. "Hans and Frank can take care of whatever comes their way. Trust me."

After feeling the power those two beefy boys put out, I didn't doubt their abilities. But I also didn't think they were impervious. "How about if an army of dissatisfied genies led by one seriously unhinged Efreet comes at them?"

"I have no doubt they'll figure out a way to deal with it." He tapped a rhythm out on the bed's footboard. "Let's concentrate on our main objective: kicking Amun's waterlogged ass back to Atlantis."

Speaking of which. "Maybe I can make the score a little more equitable. I think I know how to make one skinny bitch tell us where our friends are."

THIRTY

~-~-~-~-~-~-~-~

Hans opened the door to Mena's impromptu cell before we got within a couple yards. One look at the hound curled up by a now-blazing fire knocked all my intentions into the dirt. My half-formed plan had been to charm her before hitting her with the big guns. Good cop, bad cop all in one genie. So much for plans. I strode straight to the bitch and knocked the four-legged turncoat across the floor. Her big hazel eyes gazed at me with more puppy hurt than Major ever tried to conjure forth. It almost broke my heart.

Which only pissed me off more.

"Cut the crap, Mena."

"How could you?" Her tiny whimper drove the ice pick deeper. I already felt like shit for so many reasons the guilt gave me a migraine. It didn't help my 'friend' knew it. To think, I *paid* for the therapy sessions where she gleaned the knowledge to fuck with me.

"When I said 'cut the crap', I meant it." I raised one steel-toed foot for punctuation. "Tell me what you did with them."

One corner of her mouth twitched in a canine smile. "With who?"

"You know perfectly well."

The grin pulled her face into a comic mask, but the loathing in her eyes turned it into a grotesque parody. "Oh. Them? They're quite safe, I'm sure." I didn't need Zeke's psychic powers to determine her words were only half true. All the psych degrees in the world couldn't teach Mena to lie effectively.

"One of them must've gotten away," Zeke said, giving voice to my next thought. "I'm guessing the Viking, since this little pain in the ass already had the Bedouin's sanctuary."

An unearthly giggle slipped through the dog to human translation. "Gone, but not forgotten. Such a beautiful specimen, both as a man and as a pet," she said. "If he's a good boy, I'll make him mine when this is over. Maybe even as a human." Her voice held way too much satisfaction, but I couldn't do much about it. "Unless, of course, Amun requires him for another purpose. His luxurious white fur would make an excellent rug."

Any lingering qualms I had about hurting an innocent dog disappeared. I launched a swift kick at her ribs. She scooted away, catching no more than a glancing blow. Her cry would've been more satisfying if it hadn't reached me as a yelp. When I ended this thing, we genies needed to find a different way to punish Efreet. It's hard enough to fight your best friend without feeling like an animal abuser, too.

"Enough," I shouted, squelching my trepidation. Once I got rid of Amun, I'd need a new therapist to work through all my newly acquired neuroses. "Tell us what you did."

"Or what?" She licked one paw and rubbed her snout like a damned cat. "Josephine Mayweather, the great dog kicker. You can't really hurt me, so give it your best shot. You know you want to." A low growl rumbled from her slim throat as she bared her teeth. "Look at me, I'm such a mean puptart."

Relaxing into a casual stance, I dropped my arms to my sides. This hadn't gone at all like I planned. We both knew violence wouldn't do it this time. Except I had a hole card she never considered. I hoped it would be good enough to win me this bizarre poker hand.

"You got me," I said. "I can't possibly beat the truth out of you. But see? The problem you have, Mena, is one you created for yourself. You pretended to be my best friend for too long."

I lowered myself into a nearby chair. Placing my forearms on my thighs, I leaned forward until my nose almost touched hers. "Sure, you know all my anxieties and fears. But then again, I know all yours." My face stretched into a wicked grin as the words fell away. Silence filled the room, broken only by the crackle of flame on wood.

The guys looked at each other. None of them knew what the game would be, which played into it perfectly. They couldn't let on what they didn't know. I could only hope my gambit worked. When her eyes brightened with understanding, I had her.

"You wouldn't dare."

"As a matter of fact, I would." I crossed my legs at the ankles and leaned back. Probably pushing the relaxed attitude a little, but from the looks of it, Mena had become too freaked to notice. "Tell me what happened to Tryg and Omar, or these lovely gentlemen will transform you again. How does life as a python sound?"

I still hadn't been quite sure the little quirks she shared over the years weren't part of the act. Her one little movement told me she was less of an actress than she wanted to be.

"And *then* we'll drop you into a nest of the creepiest crawlies we can find. I'm sure you'll have a new, slithery boyfriend in no time." A whine pierced the air. "Huh. I guess you didn't lie about everything. Hard to fake your way through scary movie night?"

"Wouldn't you like to know?" She sounded like a third grade, prissy chick. But she shook in her mangy hide.

I grinned at the men. "*Anaconda* totally freaks her out, but any film with a few snakes has her screaming like a banshee. One time, she almost had a conniption right on my couch."

"Might I recommend the Tula Exotarium in Russia? I have heard they house the world's largest reptile collection," Hans said.

"Don't forget the client who breeds cobras," Frank added. "He always seeks new females. Apparently, the others keep expiring. From overzealous mating."

Zeke's face split into a wide smile. "I'm sure we'll come up with something to make those ideas pale by comparison."

"You can't be serious," Mena said, scooting her furry body into a corner of the room. "I know you. You don't have it in you to be so cruel."

I rose to stand over her while she cringed. "One would think you, of all people, would understand exactly how cruel I would become when my friends were endangered."

A little illusion turned her skinny tail into a rattle. Before then, I didn't know dogs could shriek. "Really, Mena. I'm surprised at you. What was it you said once? 'Because of Evangeline, your maternal instinct overcompensates'." I sussed out the strength of the men. All three rippled with power. "Your choice. You can talk. Or these fine specimens of male djinn-hood can turn you into a scaly, slithering, slimy, legless wonder. It's up to you."

The djinn-Efreet-dog gasped and then tried screwing her courage back together. "It doesn't matter what you do. Amun will find me. He'll change me back."

"He could." I let the pause draw out a heartbeat longer than necessary. "But not before those writhing bodies rub all over yours." A wicked smile stretched my face. "I wonder if it's mating season."

"Probably somewhere in the world, Babydoll. I saw something on the Discovery Channel about a spot in Arizona where thousands of snakes gather to breed. One big pile of black worms on steroids."

I didn't know if such a place really existed, but Zeke played the card well. Hell, he could always wish one up, if he wanted.

"What do you think, Mena? Wanna get lucky? Trust Amun to find you before you get all filled up with snake eggs."

"I hear some snakes have live births," Frank added.

"Snake babies then. Take your chances as something cold-blooded instead of merely cold-hearted. We've got enough power to transform you."

I laid the bluff on pretty thick, but I didn't care. She was about ready for a coronary. Whether she would pony up with the information before her heart exploded was anyone's guess. As her silence stretched, the guys' collective will rose around us, surging as the wish began to coalesce into a single potent orb.

"No! Wait. Stop." The dog quivered next to a puddle of her own making. "I'll talk."

"You'll tell us everything." She looked about as sullen as a dog could get. If she'd been a child, she would've stuck her tongue out. I nodded toward the men, and their power pulsed. "Okay. If that's the way you want to play it—"

"Fine," she barked. "*Everything*."

The three men reabsorbed their power and resumed their sentry-like stance. I wouldn't lower my own guard any time soon. For one thing, as acquiescent as Mena seemed, she might still turn rabid. For another, despite the security at Zeke's place the chance of Amun finding a way inside hovered over us.

Amun. Mena. Basil. Omar. Duarte.

With the stress throttling me from so many different angles, I needed to sit—and fast. I was lucky Hans and Frank repaired all the damage I'd caused. My brawl with Mena hadn't left much to sit on. Flopping into the wing-backed chair, I kicked my feet over arm like none of this was affecting me.

"All right. Start talking."

"What shall I tell you first, my most perfect Mistress? Shall I start with whatever knowledge I might possess in my tiny dog's brain about Amun's location? Or shall I begin with where your friends might be? Good for the many or good for yourself?" Both her tone and her words told me she would needle me all through this. I could handle it, but I still longed to smack the smug right off her.

Maybe I would later.

"Tell me about Tryg and Omar for now. We'll have time to kick the crap out of your boss later."

Her mouth lifted in doggy distain. "As you wish." She lowered herself to the floor. With her head on her paws, she continued, "Omar's with Amun anyway." She closed her eyes like any contented dog. "As for the scrumptious Viking, he's gone."

My teeth clenched so hard I thought they'd disintegrate. She drew this out to punish me. I couldn't let her guess it had worked. "Spit it out, Mena. Now. Or it's hiss and slither time."

She didn't open her eyes, but the fur on her back shivered. "You want the sordid details? Fine by me. As much as I hate to admit it, I needed your boys. After you left, we all played obedient, little soldiers, running around doing your job for you. Those two would've been excellent in our army. I almost hated what I had to do." Her eyelids flickered open, and she winked at me. "Are you sure you want to know?"

"Quit stalling and get it over with."

"Patience is a virtue, you know. Maybe Reggie should've taught you that one along with all his other irritating maxims. No wonder you turned into what you did. Your father was an ass."

I closed my eyes and counted to ten. Then twenty. When I reached fifty still wanting to kick her teeth in, I reminded myself the insults were a game to her. No luck there either. My only option had me wishing my feet attached to the floor and my ass stuck to the chair.

"Anyway," she said, "your clones really helped gather everyone up. If I'd had my way, I would've turned the whole herd over to Amun and been done with their whiny asses. But he wanted to proceed with the plan. Your boys were perfect. They kept enough wits about them to stay away from each other so no one wondered about two of you running around the place. Brilliant plan, by the way." She winked at me again.

"Once Omar and Trygvyr finished their jobs, I advised them to remain separate from the group until they looked like themselves again." She adopted a parody of my voice. "Wouldn't want the slaves to find out they'd been tricked, now would we?"

Since I'd glued my mobility to someplace immovable, I smacked my hand on the arm of the chair. The cracking wood shut her up. "I get it, Mena. You hate me. You hate everything I stand for. Blah blah blah. From now on leave the bitchy out of your story."

"As you wish, my most gentle Mistress," she said. "Although to be honest, I wasn't going for bitchy. I owe you one. Your plan made getting them alone so much easier. Once we rendezvoused in Basil's office, they waited for you, chatting about nothing. I already had Omar's lamp, so he never had a chance. Before either of them knew what hit them, I reclaimed him as a slave and then re-activated Trygvyr's punishment." She flexed her paw. "You never said the cur was a biter."

Good for him. I hope it hurt.

"The next I knew, he scurried down the hall, tail between his legs. From what I gathered eavesdropping on your guests, he tried to warn them. But really a barking dog is more of an annoyance than anything. I guess none of them ever watched Lassie." She opened her eyes and stared into mine. "Of course, you never bothered to tell anyone his real identity anyway. In hindsight, their ignorance became one of the great favors you did me. Thank you."

Shifting my head from one side to the other rewarded me with the resounding crack of my vertebrae settling. With the tension eased somewhat, I could handle this bitch with a little calm. Oh, I still wanted to bash her head repeatedly against the floor until she shut the hell up.

"I didn't see Tryg on my last trip through the building." I spoke as calmly as I could.

"You're welcome."

And the calm shattered, leaving me with the urge to beat her unconscious. In the end, I gritted my teeth and forged ahead. "What am I thanking you for?"

"I put him outside so he wouldn't do his business on your rug." Her mouth curved into a fanged grin. "Messy beasts we dogs are, don't you know?"

Something in her tone told me I wouldn't find Major on the front lawn. "You left him outside where?"

The inhuman giggle returned. I cringed. "Outside a dog pound. In Arizona somewhere, I think. But with my new sub-par brain, I can't really be sure. If you find the time, though, you might want to track him down soon." She licked her front paw for a moment, waiting for the obvious question.

"Why?"

"Those facilities euthanize after a few days." She spoke like I asked about the weather. In her world, the forecast looked suddenly sunny.

"You better hope we find him before they try," I said. "Think about what'll happen when they discover they can't kill one particular dog. You'll be the first Efreet the Council gets to test new torments on. And sweetheart?" She stopped mid-lick, leaving the tip of her pink tongue sticking out from her furry lips. "Remember, no one in the world cares enough to speak for you."

For all the bluster, I wasn't too worried about Major. Frank already had his cell phone out, giving someone a lame story about his champion Kuvasz being stolen. I didn't know if Zeke authorized the reward being offered, but if he didn't, I could foot the bill. If big money didn't bring Tryg home, nothing would.

"Now, where's Amun?"

"I don't think you need to worry about where he is right now." I picked her up by the scruff of her neck. When her thin legs dangled a foot off the floor, she got the point. "I mean... I don't... I don't know."

I dropped her. Her yelp didn't give me a damn bit of pleasure.

"Besides," she said once she'd recovered her voice, "if I had any idea *now*, he wouldn't still be there by the time you arrived. If I had to guess, he's either on his way here, or he's already outside finding chinks in Zeke's security."

I nudged her with the toe of my boot. "You're holding something back."

She shrugged. "I'm merely retaining some sense of loyalty. Something you wouldn't understand."

"Hans? Do me a favor. Wish up a diamondback. A big one."

Mena shuddered. "Fine. By now, Amun should've already completed his tasks and there's not a damn thing you can do about it."

"His tasks?"

"While I keep you occupied, he's at Mayweather, searching. I wouldn't be surprised if he claimed half the sanctuaries hidden in your ugly ass building. With any luck, he has yours, too."

I tried not to let my jaw drop. From the satisfaction on her face, I failed.

"And once he gets here?"

"I don't know the details. I expect he'll find Zeke's sanctuary and enslave him, too. After that, I couldn't begin to guess. Amun's not big on sharing his ultimate plans. You know, in case something like this happens."

Zeke snared the dog with a look. "Ultimate plans? You mean other than punishing Jo?"

"Could be his end game, but I suspect not." She licked the end of one paw and then the other. "For some reason, his fun with your Babydoll is more personal, I think."

Grabbing her by the scruff again, I shook her hard. "What's he got against me?"

"You're ruining the djinn race." Her tone implied I should've known the answer already.

"Ruining it? What the hell?"

"Genies aren't meant to be free. If they were, the gods would never have created Rules and sanctuaries. By setting the djinn free, you're upsetting the natural balance. Amun has to correct it."

Now I knew Mena and her boss really had slipped off the carousel. "And the Efreet don't upset anything?"

"Of course not. We are the superior beings after all. Efreet are meant to be free. No Rules. No Masters. We represent everything natural and right." She studied her claws. How close her dog actions mirrored the real Mena creeped me out. "Genies have been slaves since time dawned, as the gods ordained. Free djinn are not only unnatural, but they prevent the natural order from occurring. We cannot allow another war like the last one. By keeping the djinn enslaved, we won't have one."

"So you're gung-ho about making us into either captives or corpses." The more she talked, the more I should've understood, but the whole mess made less sense by the syllable. "How is that natural?"

"Oh, each genie will receive a choice other than death or slavery. Usually." She gave a doggy grin. "We welcome more Efreet. Once all the djinn are sorted into one of us or one of our possessions, or one of the necessarily deceased, everything will become balanced again. Efreet will rule djinn and human alike. Just as the Universe intended." She shook her head at me like I was the one who turned into a nutburger.

"You have to admit, the world will be a better place once we force peace."

"Force peace?" I said before the stupidity of it all struck me mute. When I could speak again, I couldn't help but ask, "Do you hear yourself? You can't force people to be peaceful."

The zeal in her eyes indicated she believed she could do exactly that. Talk about 'physician heal thyself.' She needed more therapy than your average schizophrenic.

"You spend far too much time amongst humans, Jo. Or it's possible you're too young to forget what humanity tastes like." She shifted one leg to scratch her shoulder. "Humans can't force peace *on each other*. A simple wish will make the world a peaceful place. Like the gods meant it to be."

I couldn't decide if these were her own ramblings, or if the insanity falling from her mouth had been planted by a charismatic Efreet. All I knew was the boatload of money I spent on her degrees would've been less wasted buying a padded cell.

"Amun is coming, Jo. Can't you feel him?" In her doggish glee, she warbled like a horny bird. "Are you ready to make your choice? If you ask forgiveness, if you admit how wrong you've been, you can join us in the new future. We can be friends like before. I'll even bring the popcorn this time."

I waved my hand. Her head dropped to her paws. Within seconds, her breathing became deep and even. Another instant had her snoring. She lucked out I only sent her to dreamland. If I had to listen to ten more seconds of 'zealot gone wild', I would've gone postal. Maybe that's what she planned, irritate me until I lost control. I would've loved the opportunity to open a whole barrel of whoop-ass on her, but remembering how Tryg became an Efreet stopped me. Judge, jury, executioner meant renouncing the Rules—something I could never do.

"So," Zeke said into the stillness. "Amun thinks he can waltz through my security? I'd like to see him try."

I shook my head. "Don't get me wrong. I believe in your ability to do your job, but I have a feeling he's already found a way to bypass you somewhere along the way. Now he's waiting for the right moment to strike."

Suddenly, a metaphorical light went off over Zeke's head. What triggered it escaped me. "This whole business with Amun has been a set up from the beginning. He's been one step ahead of everything you've done. He's got everyone thinking he's after you and he's not done yet."

"Yeah, I assumed that was his point to this little exercise."

"Oh, he's after you, all right. But you're the icing on his cake. He wants to hurt you, but he wants something else, too."

All at once, things fell into place. "He's not after me. Not only me, anyway," I whispered to no one in particular. "He's after the network."

THIRTY-ONE

~-~-~-~-~-~-~-~

When I started out saving my brethren, I could only help a genie when I stumbled across him. The process was tedious as hell. Finding enslaved genies used up all my time and mental power every day. I mean, Masters didn't exactly wear sandwich boards advertising they owned a wish machine.

After the first dozen or so rescues, I began to hear back from the genies I'd saved. They brought me the locations of others. They called with hints where a sanctuary might be. As technology advanced, they began emailing GPS coordinates. The more I rescued, the larger my contact base became.

I thank the gods every day for computers. The machines made everything so much more accessible. Thus, so much easier to steal. If Amun got hold of our database, hundreds of brethren would be endangered. With the conspiracy of silence, most would be totally ignorant of what was coming.

"If he's got Basil, doesn't he already have access to the network?" said Zeke, tapping directly into my fears. Damn him.

I nodded. I didn't want to give words to those thoughts. The deeper this got, though, the more my certainty grew about one thing: Knowledge can hurt, but ignorance is deadly. "Names. Locations. Every piece of information on any genie I've ever encountered is saved in an interconnected database. Hell, with Basil's access, Amun could email all those djinn from my account. Some made-up crap about my needing help would have them flocking to Colorado."

"And with the time you wasted fucking with this bitch, Amun has free rein to tiptoe around your system." Like I needed Zeke to rub lemon juice in those raw spots.

"*Schist*, boss," Hans said, "we were too late the moment Ms. Mayweather's business was vacated. If this Efreet has any savvy with the computers, he needs only ten minutes and a flash drive." Herr Bodyguard may have thought his words were helpful, but they swirled in my stomach like an eyes-wide teleport around the world.

"But," I said, trying to salvage some shred of hope, "Amun can't possibly know too much about technology. Not after spending centuries underwater."

"He's been on land through most of the computer age," Frank chimed in.

I reminded myself to thank him with a brick. Later. I'd had enough negativity for one day.

"I wouldn't worry too much, though," my ex said, saving me from more immolation. "Amun's too focused on his master plan to learn the finer points of the information age. And without losing a wish, he can't force Basil to get him up to speed. Unless I miss my guess, he can't afford to tap his ace in the hole so soon. Not with losing Mena. Basil's his last tie with the network."

Salvation. Well, almost. Whether the maniac Egyptian got the information out of the building was moot. Hell, a luddite could cart reams of printed data away. I envisioned the Efreet with a list and a big highlighter, traveling the world to kill or enslave the brethren I helped. *Abdul Azimana. Check. Bartholomew Boone. Check.*

My own personal devil-pup still snoozed. I longed to kick her bony ass again. Instead, I woke her with a bolt of power. She yipped a little. *Too bad, so sad.*

"Wakey, wakey. Eggs and bakey." I took some sick pleasure in throwing her own obnoxious greeting at her. Mena growled her lack of appreciation as she leveled herself upright.

"What do you want now?"

"Time for you to get to work." I'll be damned if she didn't sneer at me.

"If you think I'll help you with anything else, you are crazier than someone with my substantial background could've conceived." She feigned boredom. "Turn me into a snake already. I don't care anymore." She lifted her snout into the air like a pampered Fifth Avenue pup.

"Bad dog." Conjuring a newspaper, I rolled it into a loose cylinder and whapped her on the snout. "You're going to help me and you're going to like it, whether you like it or not." Her thin body cringed. Fear works wonders on people who use it as their own favorite tool. I couldn't wait to strike some terror into her boss.

Her tongue slipped out to lick at the stinging spot. "As you wish."

"You're going to tell me where Amun is. Now."

"How would I know where he is? Ishtar's tits, you didn't even make me a scent hound. If you'd given me a better nose, I might've been able to track him for you. I definitely know what he smells like. It's not milk and honey, thank you very much."

Zeke arched an eyebrow at me. He didn't know where I was headed with this. Quite frankly, neither did I.

The idea of that bastard strolling through my home, touching my things, staring at my artworks, thumbing through my books, looking for my sanctuary slapped me in the face. This whackjob badly wanted to hurt me, and he could do irreparable damage if he got inside my library. Talk about hitting me where I lived. All those irreplaceable manuscripts would become dust in his greedy claws. Journals written by djinn who decided they couldn't bear to live with the world anymore, djinn just like Amun.

My heart stopped for a moment. The library didn't merely contain journals from genies *like* Amun. Unless I'd gone completely insane, I read words written in the Egyptian's own hand the day Arthur died.

"*And so I realize I must divorce myself from this world of walls I cannot see and Rules I can neither live by nor break.*"

"What the hell is she going on about now?" Mena said, glaring at Zeke.

"It's from some writings I stumbled across while looking for information about the killer." I winked at the dog. "You had your narrow ass right next to it when you sat on my desk." With a nod to Zeke, I continued, "If I remember correctly, a member of the network discovered it in Istanbul. It dates back to—"

"About the time Amun disappeared to Atlantis," he finished.

The pooch in residence snorted. "I fail to see how anything he wrote back then will help you now."

I lifted one shoulder. "It can't hurt. Right now, the best shot we have is in those old journals."

"Then I'm betting he'll be along to free me sooner rather than later." Mena turned three times and settled herself onto the rug. If she wasn't such a vicious creature, it would've been cute.

"Stay." I threw out the barb not really caring if it hit its mark. Still, Mena's growl played music in my tired ears. "Boys?" I met their eyes. "Keep close watch on the fuzzy fiend for a while longer, please. Zeke? Shall we?"

He didn't bother commenting. He simply opened the door. I strode through. He followed.

"What was that all about?"

"A hunch." He looked at me sideways. "If it works, you'll see. If it doesn't, I'll look like less of an ass if you never know it failed." *Which works for me.*

"First things first," I continued. "You need to send all the genies hidden around this place somewhere else. They don't need to be in the crossfire if Amun brings the battle here." A slow smile tightened my face. "And I have the perfect harbor for a few dozen wayward djinn."

He raised his eyebrow at me again. My grin stretched wider than a human face could take. Judging by the look on his face, my expression creeped him out. *Good.* "Duarte's place. He doesn't have enough to do. A few of the brethren's flotsam on his porch should keep him out of my hair for a while."

"What about the not-so innocent?"

"The vault? No. If Amun's there then—"

Zeke snapped his fingers. "Consider it taken care of. They're confined to their sanctuaries until I say otherwise. What now?"

"Back to my place for a little gin and light reading. If we're lucky, we might catch a thief while we're there."

I raised my hands toward the door we passed through. Pushing a little power, I whispered a wish.

"What did you do to my home?"

"Early warning system for your employees along with a gift for Amun if he tries to reclaim his girlfriend." My ex wrinkled his brow at me. "Don't worry. It won't damage your beautiful home. Well, not much."

With Zeke in command, clearing any potential collateral damage out of his place lasted little more than a minute. My guests would all be confused about the transition, especially since we didn't bother warning them, but them's the breaks. I wished I could've seen Duarte's face. I needed a good laugh.

"Shall we?" I held a hand out for Zeke.

"You driving?"

"If I had enough power left to run a moped, yeah. But I need you to do the honors." With a smirk I didn't quite feel, I closed my eyes. "Put us in the shed, Jeeves. I need to collect the car."

Seconds later, we stood in the dim gloom and the slightly mousy funk outside my car. As he slipped into the passenger's seat, Zeke reached over to squeeze my thigh. For a moment, I wanted us to be a human couple prepping for a day trip, instead of two genies getting ready to stop a war. Having Zeke beside me felt good. Too bad I couldn't let good feelings distract me. Once we dealt with Amun, I'd spend some time poking around the old wound, if only to see if these yearnings were real or purely stress-related. The last time we tried to make a go of our relationship turned out bad enough to hesitate over a repeat performance.

"Everything okay?" he said. I realized my hand hovered over the gearshift. Nodding, I put it in drive and pulled toward Mayweather Antiquities.

As I parked in the closest space, the moon rose full in the sky above us. My building sat dark on the inside, but the exterior was lit up as usual. The footlights glinting off the bronze lettering gave the M and the A an ethereal glow. Looking at it hitched my heart up against my ribs. If this plan didn't work, I might never see this place again.

Of course, if it did work, chances were my life would never be the same. Basil was missing. My best friend was a traitor. My dog was a djinn who may or may not be a dog again. I didn't want to think about what else could go wrong. The gods do like to leave a djinn wondering about future calamity. It gives them the perfect opportunity to be malicious.

"Shall we?" The words passed through my throat like a sandpaper shooter. I didn't want to do this. But it was too late to turn back now.

As soon as we exited the vehicle, Zeke grabbed my hand and threaded it through his elbow as if we were still lovers. He leaned over to whisper nonsense in my ear. I laughed at his non-existent joke and snuggled closer. To anyone watching from inside, we were as carefree as birds. I hoped someone bought the act. It was too bittersweet to be for nothing.

I punched my code into the door's lock and reached toward the magical security I'd left in place. Nothing reached back. The whole place should be humming with magic and tougher to get into than a defective pistachio. Except it wasn't.

"Feels like you have visitors," Zeke said on a breath in my ear. I didn't bother answering. From any human's perspective, everything appeared perfectly normal. From a djinn's, not a damn thing felt right. "Basil, maybe?"

I shook my head. "I've been around him too long to miss his signature. This is..." Rubbing the goose bumps off my arms, I suppressed a shudder. "Cold. Slimy. Hell, it doesn't feel like Amun anymore. It's just evil." I inhaled a large whiff of air. "And wrong."

"They already know we're here." His tongue clicked against the roof of his mouth. "I hate when the trap for them ends up as the trap for us." He tucked my hand tighter into the crook of his arm. I shot him a look, unable to keep the surprise out of it. "You didn't really think I bought your crap about coming here to read old journals, did you?" He tugged me toward the door like he owned the place. "I say we find a way to turn this predicament to our advantage."

"If we're going to make a positive out of this steaming pile, then let's really do it." I dug in my feet, halting our progress. "They expect us to come in the front door, right?"

"Do you have a better suggestion?" His power rippled and dispersed. "We still can't teleport ourselves in, so at least a bit of your security still works."

I let a grin play over my lips. "They're also expecting us to think like genies." I pulled him the rest of the way out of the building and reset the alarm. "Like Reggie always said, *Why use a door when you can slide in a window?* So that's what we're going to do."

"You want us to start thinking like thieves instead of djinn? Good plan." I ignored Zeke's sarcasm as I pulled him around the side of the building. "Although, I don't see how going in a window will bypass the security you just rearmed."

"You're thinking too literally." I headed for a massive rock outcropping near the back of the building. "Which reminds me, Reggie's addendum."

"Which is?"

"If you can't find a window, make one." I smirked. Good thing genies can see in low light, or my expression would've been lost on him.

Zeke caught it and let out a soft chuckle. "That's my Babydoll."

For once, his pet name didn't bother me.

Reaching out for my power, I found myself with more to spare than I assumed. I wasn't sure where it came from, but I wouldn't question it. Instead, I allowed myself to be happy with the windfall. Using a sizeable chunk of stored energy, I sent a wish zooming into the rock face ahead of us. The air crackled a little, but I'd shaped the wish to be as undetectable as possible. We couldn't afford a light show, no matter how much fun those can be.

The rock held steady one second. The next, a cave appeared in front of us. If I'd shaped the wish right, we'd find stairs leading down into the mountain. If I didn't, we'd probably plummet thirty feet and break some bones.

Thank the gods my foot found solid rock. I shuffled forward to find the first step down. Zeke stayed right behind me, pressed so close his breath ruffled my hair. As soon as the last bit of him passed the threshold, the opening disappeared behind him.

"What the hell?"

"Covering our asses." I called a flashlight into existence. "We can get in and get out, but just us. It'll be there again when we need it. Trust me."

"Always, Josie. If I didn't, you wouldn't catch me buried in here for long."

I would rather he hadn't said 'buried'. *No help for it now.* Taking a deep breath, I forged downward. After what felt like hours, but was probably only minutes, the air grew stale. The blackness beyond my beam felt smothering.

"You sure this is leading somewhere?"

"To my living room. The opening should be a few steps ahead."

The words no sooner escaped when, a few feet in front of me, the mountain melted away. Beyond, a fire flickered cheerily in the hearth. The smell of home wafted toward me on a slight push of new air.

"O ye of little faith." I strode the last few steps of the tunnel. Zeke's deep chuckle followed me. Too bad it was the last thing I heard before Amun's slimy energy encircled me so tight I could hardly breathe. Let alone scream.

THIRTY-TWO

~_~_~_~_~_~_~_~

Not breathing and not moving don't necessarily equal not feeling. Immobility wish or no, falling face first onto chiseled granite really hurts. Especially when the first part to reach the floor is your nose. I heard a crack right before my eyes exploded in excruciating pain. My upper lip itched as blood oozed from my nostrils. The urge to sneeze hit me, but the wish trapping me wouldn't allow it.

Whoever did this to me would pay. Right after I sneezed.

"Josie!" Zeke's voice echoed to me from within the tunnel. I hoped he was smart enough to stay put. Even smarter, he'd move back to let the doorway slap shut. No Efreet could get through the little tweaks I put on my cave wish, not without the supernatural equivalent of a tunnel boring machine.

I probably should've known better. Lord knows Zeke could often be smart enough, except when he chose not to. Behind me, I heard him shuffling along one wall, attempting to reach me. His power built around him as he readied himself to take on whatever took me out.

Shut the damn door, I longed to shout. Since I couldn't, I directed every molecule of my being toward projecting my thoughts. I never tried it before, but I didn't have a sack full of options. I had to hope Zeke's little ESP trick worked at a distance. *If you can hear me, you big dork, don't take him on alone. Free me.*

My ex didn't cease working up a wish, but its target shifted. To my shock, when Zeke's focus moved, I could feel the other power in the room. Except the juice had several sources.

I thought hard at Zeke, trying to relay the information. He rewarded me with a voice in my head.

"One step ahead of you, Babydoll." His deep tones echoed in my skull. "You'll be free in a jiffy, but once you can move again, play possum. I need someone doing recon while I kick Efreet ass."

I didn't need to worry about them attacking me. They never bothered to look my way. Amun and his posse attacking Zeke while he was otherwise occupied? Now *that* was a worry worth having. Oh, I couldn't do a damn thing about it, but impotence never stopped my worries before. As the distinctive strains of my ex-lover's energy snaked forth, I readied myself. The second he freed me, I'd need to provide as much backup as possible.

My heart chugged like a freight train, throwing so much blood into my skull cavity I feared I'd black out before Zeke did the 'saving Jo' thing. My head swam, and my vision darkened around the edges. On the verge of fainting, shiny ribbons of light twirled across my peripheral vision. Dark bands with razor sharp edges snaked deeper into my home. Lighter bands flowed from the hole I'd created. Something deep inside me longed to gather those glowing streamers, to let them twine through my fingers like a lover's hair.

While the urge nearly drove me insane, Zeke's wish wrapped those gorgeous strands around me. All at once, I was free. And they were gone. The energy they represented hadn't dissipated, though. My hands tingled to grab all the power and drag it toward me. If it wouldn't totally mess up Zeke's plan, I would've rolled naked in the damn things.

"Come out, come out, Ezekiel. No one else has to lose their life over this." Amun's voice rang thick through my cozy little abode. The Maxfield Parrish print over my fireplace tilted and almost fell. Without thinking, I pushed a little wish to keep it from dropping into the flames. Good thing, the 'frozen' genie on the floor didn't warrant the attention.

"No one had to lose their life in the first place, Asshole." Good ol' Zeke and his lack of diplomacy. Bless his heart. "And you can drop the best buds act. You forfeited the right to my friendship when you became an Efreet."

Amun clicked his tongue, launching into an explanation for Zeke of all the reasons he still considered them friends. Something about a shared history and a future goal they could both get behind. Yadda yadda, blah blah. Typical 'evil dude justification of his actions' crap. I gave him the attention he so richly deserved. Which was to say none. Zeke wasn't buying it either, but he did a damn fine job of keeping the maniac distracted.

Still refraining from moving, I extended my senses. Both the blood and the power around me confused my trusty genie-sniffer, but I needed to pick out the major players.

And there they all were, as easy to pick out as a Trekkie at a sci-fi convention.

The Efreet stood near the back wall, right off the kitchen. Since Zeke hadn't clobbered him yet, I guessed he stood just out of sight from the tunnel entry. To the Efreet's right, Basil's fear and anger rolled across the floor in waves. If I could get my partner away from his Master, he'd happily help on either offense or defense. On the other side of Amun, Omar's signature pulsed with rage. The Bedouin had notched back up to the crazy-dude levels. I'd like nothing better than to unleash him on his sadistic Master. After all, the Efreet earned whatever payback the Sheik unleashed.

Too bad for us all, both genies still stank of slavery. Their actions weren't their own and I couldn't help them.

I relayed all the information to Zeke via our mental connection then continued my pretend paralysis. The Efreet was still going strong with his villain's speech—right out of some campy-ass movie, if you ask me. I blocked it out. I had to pretend his wish still paralyzed me, but I didn't have to subject myself to his shtick. I guess no one told him protracted explanations of one's villainy were passé.

And hey, if he didn't know, I wouldn't tell him. Long-winded and boring he might be, but his diarrhea of the mouth bought time for my side. Although, I couldn't help but feel for the guys who couldn't play for my side. As it stood, the playbook showed three working for the Visitors against two for the Home team, and the other team had the ball. I needed a way to even the playing field a little.

Or a way needed to find me.

"Jo?" I barely heard the voice through Amun's evil dissertation. "It's Michael. Can you hear me?"

Where are you? Shooting the thought in his general direction, I hoped he was tuned into my frequency.

"About ten feet up the stairwell," he said. "I shadowed Amun after he followed you out of my room. Too bad I never got the chance to jump him. Once he got down here, I didn't like the odds. I may not be a lawyer yet, but that's a case I can't win." I didn't have the heart to point out that him versus Amun wouldn't be good odds, no matter the location. "Anyway, are you okay? It looked like he killed you there for a second. So how are we going to take this guy out? He's got Basil and the Arab dude who attacked me. I thought he was on our side, but he's hanging out with the asshole. We need to get those guys away somehow. You have a plan right?"

My future attorney needed to find a way to control his nervous chatter if he ever hoped to convince a judge of anything. He did do a bang up job of convincing me Amun hadn't claimed him. Which is what mattered at the moment.

Of course, I could be wrong. In which case, what I intended could screw up Zeke's plans. I simply had to believe in my re-djinned friend. And hey, if I couldn't trust my own lawyer.

I'm peachy. Zeke's the man with the plan.

I expanded my mental connection, turning my brain into one big-ass switchboard. Michael talking in one side with Zeke in the other gave me one hell of a headache. In the scheme of things, though, having evenly matched teams was worth every excruciating brain cell.

"Are we ready?" Zeke said in my head. "This Mexican standoff isn't going to last much longer."

"Ready," Michael replied.

I echoed the sentiment, even though I'd been too lost in my own head to know what I was supposedly ready for. I really wished I'd paid attention because the agreement no sooner slipped into my thoughts than all hell broke loose.

A wish flew from the edge of my homemade tunnel, hammering Amun back a few steps. I gave up the pretense of immobility, leaping to my feet like some damn superhero. The Efreet was still recovering, but his slaves were powering up quicker than I could think.

Before I knew it, words flew out of my mouth that had nothing to do with wishing.

"Oh, puhleeze. You have got to be freaking kidding me," I said. "Come on, guys. You don't have to protect this asshat."

"Though I would desire otherwise, he is my Master," Omar said through gritted teeth. "I am deeply sorry."

I shook my head and turned to my partner. "Baz? You don't have to do this."

"No 'elp for it, love," he said as a tear slid down his cheek. He raised his hands toward me. The way I saw it, I had seconds to defend myself before they smashed me like a bug on the windshield of a bullet train. Except I couldn't bring myself to move an ion of power against them.

Zeke didn't feel the same compunction. As their combined power released, a wall of solid energy fell between us. From the looks of it, his shield absorbed the majority of destructive force. My home faced the rest. Before I could think, my couch exploded in a cloud of blue smoke. The wall hangings melted and dripped into puddles around the moldings. My precious Parrish print ended up as nothing more than colorful goo.

"For the love of Pete," I shouted. As if possessed by Reggie's ghost, rage roiled inside me over the loss of so many priceless objects. *My* priceless objects to boot. "Is *nothing* sacred?"

"Now you've gone and done it." Zeke's voice drifted from the tunnel. As pissed as I was, his dry wit still made me smile. Apparently his warning went over like a lead balloon. Neither Amun nor Omar seemed fazed by it. Basil, bless his Limey heart, took one look at my formerly cozy home and turned a wicked shade of green. If anyone knew how much I loved my things, it was the Brit who'd helped acquire them.

I didn't have a mirror handy, but I guessed my face turned a shade opposite Basil's. Fury filled my brain as I stood in the middle of the mess, gazing at a puddle Waterhouse once used to create beauty. Out of the corner of my eye, I caught Amun recovering from Zeke's blast. He swaggered like he owned the place.

You sunuvabitch. My place! My belongings! Well, I'd be damned if he'd take anything else from me.

"Back off, asshole." I gathered my remaining power. The internal spark I found throbbed, but it was nowhere near enough to take on three wish generators by myself. Hell, I couldn't be sure I had enough juice to take out one of them. Between the Efreet trashing my home and stealing my friends, and the short-powered circumstances I found myself in *again,* I was mad as hell.

What good is being fucking super-powerful if my batteries keep running low, goddamn it!? I directed my anger toward whatever deities happened to be watching the show. *I bet they have popcorn. Assholes.*

All at once, the ribbons reappeared. Multiple changing colors flowed around each genie. Those bands called to me, urging me to simply absorb their glorious energy. The only difference between now and then lay in their proximity.

I lifted one hand to touch the closest—a shimmering band of olive green. Its power seemed to wind around my fingers and meld with my flesh. The energy tasted delicious. But so wrong. Wave after wave of the most wicked thoughts flowed through me. I wanted to rip off someone's head and piss down the hole, to bathe in the blood of my enemies, to drink their energy as they exploded. Pretty soon, I had a hard time distinguishing friend from enemy.

Before the taint enveloped me entirely, I snatched the ribbon entwining my hand. Ripping it away felt like filleting my own hand. But hanging onto the damn thing would hurt worse in the long run.

Another band snaked closer. I sure as hell didn't want that experience again. Still, I needed more power and the cornflower strand sang to me. *What the hell. No guts, no glory.* Before I could over think it, I snatched the writhing strand of blue from the air. As this power sunk into my flesh, I filled with contentment like I'd only ever had in one place—Zeke arms.

Time seemed to stand still while I pulled at the power. Every molecule flowed into me like drinking from a clear stream in the deepest part of the Rockies. I'd never been so thirsty.

"Babydoll?" Zeke said in my head. "Not so much, eh? I still have work to do."

I jerked away like I'd kissed a cobra. Then, I realized each strand emanated from one living being or another. The gross green strand originated with Amun. Another glowing gold band belonged to Omar. Mauve came from my partner. The last one, blacker than sable and just as warm, Michael generated. No matter which one I drank from, I'd be tapping into someone else's energy.

All well and good if I could stomach another grab for the Efreet's. Depleting him might make the damage to my soul worthwhile.

Since my only other options would drain a friend, the power I had accidentally siphoned from Zeke would have to suffice.

Unless...

Near the floor, little wisps of unattached energy clustered like spun sugar. If a cotton-candy machine had been handy, I could've wound them onto a cone for a supernatural snack. I reached toward the nearest puff, but Amun turned toward the movement like a cobra tracking a rabbit.

Keeping my eyes steady on the Efreet's, I pushed a toe toward the nearest clump of power. With any luck, my boots wouldn't hamper their passage. Amun began talking at me and slowly powering up, as if he could somehow scare me with his profound ideas. Meanwhile, the little pastel puff seeped through the leather. It sort of tickled my toes as it spread into me.

Hmm. No nasty aftertaste.

I began absorbing every puff within kicking distance. The others had to think what little sanity I had went south for the winter. I know it distracted the hell out of Amun. My friends looked at my whirling Dervish routine with growing astonishment. Before any of them could recover their wits, I pulsed with more energy than a wish ever generated. Swirling my new energy into a large ball, I prepared to blast the Egyptian back to whatever hell he called home. The idea my friends could be injured had to be secondary.

And then I saw Basil's wet cheeks. He prepared himself to be torn apart. His eyes begged me to end his torment, even if meant his particles got rearranged. No matter how pissed Amun made me with his destructive rampage, I couldn't allow myself do more of the same.

"Kill her already," Amun said.

Omar did a slow turn toward his unwanted Master. "We can but stop her. Your control over the djinn you own does not include wishing for what the Rules forbid. Perhaps you've been so long away you've forgotten djinn limitations."

"Rules be damned." The Efreet's shriek echoed through the room, rattling three porcelain kittens, which had miraculously survived the onslaught so far. If the bastard wrecked one more of my things, I would go postal. "If you won't kill her, turn her into a mayfly. She may not die, but such a pathetic existence will be like death."

Basil raised his hands toward me. He wavered so badly he looked like he'd contracted some kind of palsy. Poor guy didn't want to hurt me. Somehow he thought he had to.

"Baz?" I poured all my fear out as disdain. "What in the sam hill do you think you're doing?"

"What my Master wishes." His voice broke halfway through. My heart broke along with it. This mess had bent poor Basil in ways I couldn't begin to understand.

Marshaling myself, I hoped like hell my gambit would work. "I didn't hear him make a wish. Did you?" I clicked my tongue. "If you're willing to let a Master order you around without wasting his wishes, you're not half the djinn I thought you were. What happened to my Artful Dodger?"

The reminder worked. His jaw dropped so hard I thought it'd break. For a minute, he did his big British bass imitation as his mouth opened and closed. It would've been funny, if the situation didn't suck so hard.

"And what about you, Omar? You been letting this Efreet push you around like a tin soldier, too?" Something about his sudden downcast eyes told me I'd hit my mark. I bet both of them had been so overwhelmed by their loss of freedom, to a dirty Efreet no less, they forgot the basic game of being a genie. Along with one majorly big Rule: Masters have to use the word 'wish' for it to count. Otherwise, it's a choice.

Glaring at Amun, I said, "Shame on you. Afraid to waste a wish, so you're mooching freebies." He blanched. "In fact, unless I miss my guess, you're almost out of wishes and you don't want to lose—"

"I wish for you to transform Josephine Mayweather into the pest she's been for so many years." The words were out of his mouth before I could blink.

I flinched. I didn't need to. Neither genie moved.

"So prosaic of you." Reason wandered lost through my overtaxed brain, but it finally arrived. "Two problems with your wish. First off, you didn't specify which of your slaves you wanted to—"

"You!" He thrust a finger toward Omar. "Fulfill my wish."

A laugh escaped my lips before I could stop it. *This is easier than I thought.* I couldn't believe my luck. After centuries sequestered beneath the sea, and years more without either Rules or Masters, the Egyptian forgot the basics. Ignorance is a bitch sometimes.

The air shimmered between the Bedouin and myself, but nothing happened. As I suspected. "Your wish was my command," Omar said as Amun's bonds fell away.

The Egyptian's face went slack. "You cannot be free!"

"I am not a free djinn, but I soon will be." Omar stepped over to my side of the room and turned to face Amun. On an outstretched hand lay the lamp he called home. With a snap of my fingers, it appeared in Michael's hands.

"I wish you free."

"Impossible! You never fulfilled my wish. You belong to me."

"In millennia of life, you learned nothing," Omar told his former Master. "Your thinking is as flawed as your wording." He let his own magic pulse over him until he was dressed in a suit and tie once more. "You wished for her to transform into exactly what she's always been. Therefore nothing changed." He winked at me. "Words mean everything."

Amun looked, to borrow a word from Basil's lexicon, gobsmacked. The little wheels turned in his head as he tried to follow the thread of logic. "Then you still owe me my original wish."

My desert friend shook his head slowly as if facing a naughty child. I guess in some ways, he was. Thinking about it, Amun didn't strike me as the most mature superpower in the world. "Your original wish dissipated once Josephine freed me. You would've had to make the wish again for it to be valid. Unfortunate for you, it would've been your last wish."

Amun's scream could've pierced eardrums in China. For a split second, I feared he'd have Basil zap me. Instead, the Egyptian rushed me in a classic rugby move. I didn't have time to sidestep, and any other movement would send Amun hurtling toward my friends.

Physical violence wasn't a bad plan on the Efreet's part, considering I'd used the same line of thinking on Mena. His main problem, though, he didn't think to block my own use of power beforehand. In the moments before we collided, I packed every stray speck into one big sphere of a wish.

When he hit, the blast rocketed between us, sending us both flying. As my head collided with the wall, the sad little kitten with its paws over its eyes dropped to the floor and shattered.

THIRTY-THREE

~-~-~-~-~-~-~-~

"Bay-bee-doll." The singsong word tickled my ear and irritated my brain. I swiped at the gnat with one hand. "Come on, Josie. Time to wake up."

"Leave me alone," I grumbled as various body parts started checking in. None of them were happy to be there, and they let me know it.

"Josephine Eugenia Mayweather. If you don't get up this instant."

For a second, I almost believed Evangeline had gotten a sex change while I was away. Except my mother rarely bothered to wake me up. Unless she felt ill and demanded my companionship.

I lifted one sore eyelid to send her a baleful glare. Only I wasn't in our Fifth Avenue penthouse. This also wasn't the canopy bed she insisted should hold any daughter of hers. Instead, I lay sprawled across a stone floor, gazing at a pair of artistic hands. I turned my eyes upward. The face grinning down at me couldn't be mistaken for the pasty-pale visage of my drunken mother. Hell, it wasn't even female. The next thing to hit my consciousness came when I realized my bleary sight had nothing to do with sleep and everything to do with the smoke filling my cozy cavern.

"What happened?" My voice did its best to out-croak a bullfrog. I inhaled to clear my throat and sucked down a lungful of my home's burning remnants. As I sank into one hell of a coughing fit, memories came flooding back.

I wrapped myself in my power and pushed Zeke away. "Where's Amun?"

"In here somewhere." He waved at the smoke. "At least I hope he's trapped with us, not masquerading around the world as the coming of the djinn messiah." I began crafting a wish to clear the air, but Zeke stopped me. "As soon as you can see him, he can see you."

I hissed into the gathering cloud. "Michael?"

"Here," said a voice a few feet to my left. "Ready when you are."

I expanded my senses to get a fix on the Efreet and his djinn slaves. *Slave*, I amended. *He only has one now.* Between the energy floating all around us and the smoke dulling my natural senses, finding anyone was futile. "We've got to—"

A ball of energy exploded to our right. If Zeke hadn't already been on the floor with me, he would've taken a direct hit. I cursed myself for providing a target, switching back to the mental connection we'd established.

We've got to think of a way to locate them without putting up a big 'aim destructive wish here' sign. As I stifled a cough, energy surged beside me.

"Fire's out," Zeke said in my head. I slapped his arm.

What about...?

"I know what I said, but it's no use hiding ourselves only to turn to cinders."

Thanks. I tried to keep out the sarcasm and failed. We were running out of options. Of course, we could always take the tunnel way out, but making a break for it would leave us exposed. Omar's power alone could take us out.

"Omar's free," Michael said, breaking into the thoughts I hadn't realized I had broadcast.

Right. I knew that. Maybe the explosion knocked more brain cells loose than I wanted to admit. I shook my head to clear the fog. If I couldn't keep the players straight in my head, I might end up zapping an ally. *Then where the hell is he?*

A light flared from my kitchen. Baked Alaska, it wasn't. Another power burst shot from behind me, coinciding with a loud pop. The smell of charred food and Freon swept over me. I almost cried as I pictured my SubZero refrigerator becoming a pool of molten steel and oozing plastic.

"There's your Bedouin." Zeke said, touching my elbow.

I found the source of the latter power burst. Through the fading smoke, I could tell Omar wasn't happy. He'd be less so when he found out he owed me a new fridge.

"Easy on the appliances. The warranty doesn't cover explosions." My words drew another energy pulse from Amun.

"Sunuvabitch." My allies' faces had become clearer. Across the dining room table, the Efreet lobbed another sphere toward Omar.

"Look out," I shouted, but my warning was unnecessary. Amun's wish went wide. "And there goes my recliner. Damn it all."

"On the bright side, Josie, you're going to enjoy one hell of a shopping trip when this is over."

"Very funny." If I hadn't needed every ounce of juice I had, I would've turned my ex-boyfriend into a potted palm. "I don't think you'd be laughing so hard if he was trashing your place."

"Then I suggest you stop cowering like a sissy before he decides to go for the big prize. I wonder what Amun would do with your library." Zeke nudged me and I shot him an elbow to the ribs. "Unless you want Omar to keep fighting your battles for you."

If he thought goading me would work, well, it would. Whatever else happened, I couldn't simply lay back and take it. I reached toward my newfound power source. Instead of colorful bands and tiny puffs, though, I only found thinning smoke. "What happened to them?"

"You're too calm," Zeke said, not bothering to question my meaning. "Get pissed or get used to working with double-A instead of NiCad."

Another sphere flew toward Omar. From the sound of it, at least a partial hit landed on my Bedouin friend. "Omar?" No answer. My rage built but still no power puffs. Well, I'd never had them before, I sure as hell could work without them now. Drawing my remaining power into a shield, I stepped into the smog. As if they were attached to my ass by a tether, the men followed.

"Basil?" I said into the haze. "If you can hear me, get the hell out of the way. If he uses his last wish, you know what to do."

As cryptic as those words sounded, I hoped Basil would remember to twist the wish however he could. He'd fucked up enough already. One wish from Baz could do some serious damage, and then Amun could step in. Sure, my partner would be free, but he couldn't whomp the Efreet on his own.

"I need no wish from this inferior being to defeat you."

"If you start with another stupid monologue about how much better the Efreet are, I'll kick you in the nuts just to shut you up. Then I'll turn you into a pooch, like I did with your girlfriend."

That zipped his lips, but only temporarily. "You discovered her quicker than I would've assumed. Don't worry. I'll claim her as soon as I'm finished here."

"The only thing you'll be claiming is a fire hydrant of your own." I wasn't sure the four of us could take him. Amun was more powerful than Mena. Sure, Zeke held him at a standstill, but my ex had to be chugging along on fumes this time around. My senses told me Michael had been drained, too. Omar probably had less than half his power. I flexed my magic muscles. They still had a good heft to them, but I didn't want to hope I had enough juice to fry Amun.

Now. I directed my thought at the two beside me. Omar wasn't in the connection, but he got the gist. As one, the four of us threw as much power as we could behind the wish I crafted.

And as we released the power, Amun pushed Basil in the way.

While my old friend twisted in the bright light, Amun laughed. By the time a big sheepdog appeared where Baz had been my blood hummed in my ears. How I could have been so damn stupid as to not put a specific target on the wish, I'll never know. Chalk it up to haste making waste. Or maybe a combination of frustration and potential brain damage. Knowing where to lay the blame didn't stem my anger, though. It just grew.

And out of nowhere, the bands appeared again. Everyone on my side pulsed with dim bands. Only the remaining member of the visiting team lit up. My fingers itched to draw all his dark energy into myself. It tugged at me as though I was dehydrated and those streamers could slake my thirst like nothing else.

"No," I cried aloud. I searched the area for those perfect dust bunnies of power. They littered the floor, drifted through the air, lay on the shelves next to my tchotchkes. How I never saw them before escaped me, but as long as they were there when I needed them, who cared where they went afterwards.

Amun drew his hands back. Between his palms grew a black sphere, sucking the light out of everything around it. I didn't know whether the super-charge I acquired gave me special sight or if everyone could see the dark hole he created.

Before I'd even considered the possibility this was no longer a sadistic game for him, his intent had shifted from making me suffer to making me dead. Hell, if this was any indication, he wanted everyone I ever knew dead right along with me.

And as the bits of my ruined home skidded toward him, I realized he wasn't playing with a ball of yarn. I'd never been great at science, but the words 'black hole' leapt to mind.

Suddenly, I understood. Changing him into a dog wouldn't stop him. It sure as hell wouldn't quench his thirst for destruction. He'd be a terror for centuries to come. Even as a Chihuahua, Amun would gnaw and nip and rend his way through eternity, whizzing on every single inch of space along the way until the world smelled of mutant puppy puddles. The only alternative I could find meant doing to him what he'd done to others. Except the Rules prevented me from ending his polluted existence.

But you know how to get around the Rules now, don't you? said a niggling voice I couldn't identify. I checked the connection, but neither Michael nor Zeke would ever suggest such a thing. Reggie, for all the bad things he'd done, would never condone what my thought suggested. Sure, renounce the Rules. I could kill Amun, save the day and walk away a hero. I could pay him back for every horrible thing he'd done to ruin my life. I could—

I could ruin my own life instead.

As much as some part of me wanted to believe I could go back to being the same person afterwards, becoming an Efreet meant more than whether I followed a set of rules. Capital R or otherwise.

"Wise people, even though all laws were abolished, would still lead the same life."

"Zeke?" His words struggled to fight against the lure of power.

"Close, but no. Aristophanes. Find another way, Babydoll."

The old Zeke would've taken over my decision, or at least told me what he wanted me to do. Which would've been fine by me. Someone needed to take over the reins and finish this. My bones were tired right down to my marrow. I didn't want to have to deal with any of this anymore.

Omar's story echoed in my head followed by Basil's wish. I almost laughed at the irony. I couldn't conceive of ever wanting to give up control over my existence, but when times were tough, there I stood, headed down the same filthy road.

"What are you thinking, darling Josephine?" Amun said, letting his power settle. "Would you, too, desire a Master? I can help you. I can take away all your need for decisions and the worry they bring."

Anything worth doing is worth doing yourself, Reggie always told me. He'd never know how true his words were. Dear old Dad had been fond of doing for himself, as long as he could do so with someone else's stuff. When he wasn't stealing or swindling, he stayed home reading. To him, books held their own power, breathing knowledge into him page by page.

I threw the power I'd been building before I understood the wish I'd formed. Whether Reggie's hand guided it, I couldn't tell. Maybe my subconscious figured out the problem my conscious mind couldn't. However it happened, Amun became engulfed in a blaze of purple light.

When the light dissipated, the Efreet had disappeared.

"What the hell did you do?" Michael said from behind me.

"Josie found another way."

"What?" Poor kid. I'd never seen the pre-lawyer look so confused.

Zeke didn't bother answering. He merely walked past us both. When he reached the spot where we'd last seen Amun, he stooped to retrieve a thick text.

I began to ask him what he found but the answer hit me like a stack of encyclopedias. He held the transformed Efreet.

"Heavy reading?" he said instead of stating the obvious.

"Superb, Josephine. A stroke of brilliance." Omar stood beside Zeke. Reaching over his shoulder, the Bedouin opened the book.

"I am not finished here," he read. "You have no concept of what you've started. Nor do you understand who will finish it."

"What's going on?" Michael said. If he couldn't find better ways to express himself in stressful situations, he'd make the worst attorney ever. And he was *my* attorney. , as long as the kid lived, hope remained.

I never envisioned myself turning a man into a book. I sure as hell never thought it would talk to me afterwards. Turning to Zeke, I asked, "Didn't you say no inorganic transformations?"

He sniffed the air. "He's as organic as they come, Josie."

Eww, yuck. I stared at the monstrosity I created. "Is that all he wrote?" As I asked the question, I admitted to myself I didn't really want to know.

"The rest is blank."

When Omar spoke, a smidgen of relief washed over me. I mean, Amun still had a lot to answer for, but the answers I wanted weren't the things he'd want to talk about. Not at first. Anything he said now would be vitriol and venom.

"Wait," the Bedouin said. "Now the page says 'you will pay for this'."

"Typical villain," said Zeke. Grabbing *The Book of Amun*, he flipped the damn cover closed. "I think you have the perfect place for this, Josie. Right between Louisa May Alcott and Piers Anthony." He winked. "They'll keep him company for the next couple, let's say, centuries? That should be enough time for him to think about what he's done."

"A cosmic time-out would be perfect, but we're going to need to talk to him before then, I think."

"Your choice." Zeke tossed the book to me and I laid it on the charred kitchen counter.

"But what did he *mean*?" Michael reached for the tome.

"Don't." I slapped his hand away. "I think Amun's had more than enough attention for one day. If we need to delve into Mr. Cryptic's meaning, we can always flip through him later."

"Next year maybe."

"Sounds like a plan, Zeke." I surveyed the contents of my home. With all the wards I had on the library, I could be pretty certain nothing had been harmed in there. The rest of my place? It was trashed. I snapped my fingers. The most I accomplished was setting one filthy chair upright. Fat lot of good that did. The damn thing still smoldered.

"I need a drink," Zeke said, claiming the burnt chair for his own weary butt. The charred wood promptly dropped his ass onto the floor. From his new seat, he stared at the fried liquor cabinet with its dozen bottles melted together. "Now I really need a drink."

"Then I suggest you either wish something up or we head to the main level," Michael said. "There's a fifth of Jack in my room. I was saving it for after the bar exam, but I think we need it more now." He narrowed his eyes at us. "Unless you broke it when you packed my stuff."

Reaching into my pocket, I withdrew the tiny box I'd held since shrinking Michael's room to moveable proportions. "I'm too tired to wish it right again. But if you think you can get a buzz off the whiskey in a tiny, tiny bottle, go for it." I tossed it toward him. He caught it one-handed, but the disappointment on his face damn near shattered any sense of sanity I still had left.

"There are liquor stores in town," Zeke said. "Who's driving?"

After the day I'd had, normal conversation seemed ludicrous. But I was trying to hold it together. I winked at Michael. "I don't care who's driving, but Zeke's buying."

Ignoring the argument I started, I hefted myself off the floor. Near my wrecked fridge huddled a sheepdog with a severe case of the shakes. "I don't care who buys the booze, but somebody turn Baz back into a person before he freaks out."

With unsteady steps, I began to walk up to what used to be my antiques warehouse slash underground railroad for socially-retarded djinn. I didn't want to think about whether I still had a business. I didn't want to think about whether I would still take on the mission of saving my fellow brethren. Time enough for those decisions after I found some whiskey. Or the gin I remembered was in my lower desk drawer.

Maybe after both.

THE END

About the Author

Former sales 'road warrior' and corporate 'Jack of all trades', B.E. Sanderson now lives the hermit's life in southwest Missouri, where she divides her time between doing writerly things, inhaling books, networking on the internet, and enjoying the 'retired' life with her husband and her crazy cats.

You can learn more and connect with B.E. at:

Outside the Box - http://besanderson.blogspot.com/
Facebook - https://www.facebook.com/be.sanderson.writer
Twitter - https://twitter.com/BE_Sanderson

Or email her at: be.sanderson.writer@gmail.com

If you enjoyed reading *Wish in One Hand*, please consider leaving a review at your favorite vendor or at Goodreads.

Other books by B.E. Sanderson:

Dying Embers

Dwelling on the past can be murder.

Emma Sweet looks more like a trophy wife than a killer, but as she watches her cheating husband burn alive in his Mercedes, she knows her trophy life is over. Every man she ever loved hurt her. Now it's time to hurt them back. As she travels from state to state, crossing a name off her list each time she ends a life, she's only one step ahead of Agent Douglas. She doesn't care if she gets caught really, as long as the last name on her list—the first man to break her heart—gets the justice he's earned before the law catches up with her.

With the memory of a fatal house fire looming over her, no one can blame Jace Douglas for being pyrophobic, but agents with the Serial Crimes Investigation Unit don't get to pick and choose assignments. When a series of murders all have the same killing signature, she can't let the flames of her past interfere with the job. Alongside one pushy—and altogether too attractive—detective, she embarks on a cross-country manhunt to catch a killer before another man dies.

Accidental Death

Murder doesn't happen here.

Serenity is the safest, little town in Colorado. But residents are dropping like flies. No big deal. Accidents happen.

Detective Dennis Haggarty is there to comfort his recently widowed sister, not investigate a homicide. However, finding a corpse means he can't avoid doing his job—especially since the local authorities are determined to disregard the facts. Delving deeper, he finds a string of deaths everyone wants to ignore even when all the evidence points to murder. Lucky for the detective, one person in town seems rational enough to help him.

Too bad she's his prime suspect.

Printed in Great Britain
by Amazon.co.uk, Ltd.,
Marston Gate.